The
ITALIAN
GIRL'S
SECRET

BOOKS BY NATALIE MEG EVANS

The Dress Thief
The Milliner's Secret
Gown of Thorns
The Wardrobe Mistress
The Secret Vow
The Paris Girl
Into the Burning Dawn

The
ITALIAN
GIRL'S
SECRET

Natalie Meg Evans

bookouture

Published by Bookouture in 2021

An imprint of Storyfire Ltd.
Carmelite House
50 Victoria Embankment
London EC4Y 0DZ

www.bookouture.com

ISBN: 978-1-83888-607-3
eBook ISBN: 978-1-83888-606-6

This novel is dedicated to my friend Kate Cheasman,
who has done so much to inspire writers

Prologue

Wednesday, 8 September 1943

Honey-gold, her back sheltered by pine-scented hills, Naples lay tense under a veil of motionless air. An invasion fleet was approaching the southern Italian shores, bringing fear and hope in equal measure. Battered by long months of bombing, lapped by the sapphire waters of the Mediterranean, she waited for death or liberation.

Up on the second floor of a crumbling apartment building in a poor district of the city, Sebastiano Alonso struggled to contain his impatience at his wireless operator's laborious technique. *Dah-dit-dah-dit…* the finger on the Morse key was almost hesitant. And hesitancy was dangerous.

'Speed it up, can you, Mio?' Sebastiano muttered. 'It's a long message.' Urgent too. The Allied troops that would swarm off the ships needed details of what they might encounter as they approached Naples: locations of hostile airfields and any German gun defences. The country was under Nazi control. 'I want it sent before we're intercepted.'

'Stop making me nervous.' Mio wiped away droplets of sweat with a handkerchief. '"Slow" is my signature. If I speed up, I'll confuse the operator at the other end.'

Curbing his impatience, Sebastiano went to a window that was open a few inches to allow a wireless aerial to be slung over the sill. From there, it was attached to a bracket on the side of a road bridge that ran level with the roof of the house. The bridge, and the domed church that loomed over it, cast deep shadows into the courtyard below. Mio deserved better lodgings than this. The powers that be at SOE – Special Operations Executive – had sent Sebastiano's team into Naples without first establishing a proper support network. They had people helping them from across the city's social classes, who acted as couriers and provided their safe houses, but their numbers were dwindling. Many of the younger men had left to join partisan bands. Those who remained were scared. It was hard to wage war on Nazi tyranny when you were starving, and your neighbour might betray you for the price of a meal. Six months in a city crawling with Fascists and German military was taking its toll on Sebastiano too. He was hearing footsteps in his sleep. Mio was starting to resemble a scared rabbit and the third member of their trio, Nico the expert saboteur, was growing slack. Almost as if he wanted to get caught, which would be insane as the consequences were so horrible.

Let the British and Americans come soon. Sebastiano was sick of holding his breath.

He turned back to Mio, still slowly tapping out the top-secret message, shoulders hunched and looking so young and vulnerable. Sebastiano bit his tongue, and pictured the cipher clerk at the other end in Algiers, transcribing the coded Morse into English. There must be no errors in this complex message. These days, everything they sent back to SOE had a single purpose – to save the lives of Allied soldiers. Today's transmission was extra-critical as it detailed German plans to site anti-aircraft guns at hilltop farms and machine gun nests on top of abandoned stone towers. A fine welcome for the Allies as they pushed across open terrain.

What was that sound? His ears picked up the hum of an engine. As he went to check, Mio stopped tapping and demanded, 'What's up?'

'Nothing. Keep going.'

Walking through to the adjoining room, Sebastiano pressed his ear to the glass in the balcony doors. The shutters were closed on the other side and he wasn't going to open them. The noise was still there. It sounded like a large car purring slowly past, heading towards the bridge. A well-maintained engine, in the heat of the day on a working-class street... not right. The hairs rose on his arms. The creak of the street door below injected urgency into his bloodstream.

'Mio, stop. Pack up your wireless. Now.'

Mio stared at him. 'You heard something?'

A soft tap at the door to the flat made the question redundant. Sebastiano touched his finger to his lips. As Mio hurriedly unclipped the wireless's battery connector and unplugged the crystals, Sebastiano crept to the door. He slid a light service pistol from a holster under his waistcoat, primed it, then unlocked and yanked open the door.

As he recognised their comrade Nico on the threshold, he lowered his gun. 'What the hell are you doing?'

It was directly against orders for all three SOE agents to be together in one place. The risks of being captured together were unthinkable.

'*Ciao*, Sebbe.' Nico sidled into the room. He was older than Sebastiano and Mio, with shocks of silver nestling in his black hair and untrimmed beard. A gleam of sweat shone on his upper lip. He darted a fearful look over his shoulder. 'We need to talk.'

'I don't care – you don't seek me out. Ever. It's why we have couriers.' Sebastiano went to shut the door and saw a white handkerchief on the threshold. It hadn't been there when he'd arrived. Picking it up, ice-cold doubt trickled into his gut. Nico's mouth was twitching, his gaze jumping from Sebastiano to Mio, who had packed the wireless in its leather suitcase and was now in front of the empty fireplace, trying to burn incriminating codes with a cigarette lighter.

Sebastiano locked the door again and asked Nico, 'Did you walk?'

'Course. How else would I get here?'

When Nico gave a rictus smile followed by a flush of perspiration, Sebastiano felt a flare of suspicion.

And when booted feet filled the downstairs lobby and guttural commands echoed up the stairwell, he knew for sure. They'd been betrayed. Letting none of his fear show, he gestured Nico away from the door then fitted a silencer onto the pistol, mouthing, 'I'll take the first one who bursts in. You stake out the window.' As Nico turned, Sebastiano got behind him, pressing the silencer muzzle into the back of his comrade's skull.

Two shots at point-blank range, both no louder than the cracking of a goose egg. As Nico crumpled, Sebastiano joined Mio in front of the fire. 'I know,' he muttered, though his colleague hadn't said a word. 'Brutal, but he's sold us out. Stay calm, try to stop shaking. I'm going to open the door and I want you to leave.'

'But they're on their way up. The Germans—'

'Walk past them innocently. They might fall for it.'

'And you?'

'I'll get out when this lot is ashes.' Mio's code books were smouldering, some of the pages still readable. 'Take your wireless and go. Go!'

But it was too late. The shouting and the boots on the stairs became a thunder as every door up to their level was kicked in. Gripping the brown leather case, Mio looked like a passenger who has just missed the last train out of hell. Sebastiano cradled his hands around the burning code-sheets to intensify the flame and, as it seared his flesh, he knew there were only two ways out of this situation. Fight or suicide.

Mio took one way, Sebastiano took the other.

Chapter One

Friday, 10 September 1943

Carmela del Bosco woke with a terrible start. Night filled the bedroom of the farmhouse in the hills outside Naples. After a day listening to the thunk of gunfire striking the town of Salerno fifty kilometres away, a lull had fallen. Her grandmother snored on the other side of the room. Nonna had taken a shot of grappa before bedtime, which always made her wheeze. That was what had woken her, Carmela decided. She turned her pillow over, determined to get few more hours' sleep.

It came again. A noise outside at ground level. A fox on its way to the chicken coops? Daring to come close to the house because the farm dog had been scared off by the boom of the invasion and the fighter planes screaming overhead?

Pushing back her bedcovers, Carmela went to the window and opened the shutters. She rested her elbows on the lintel and night air poured over her shoulders, warm as cream in contrast to the sweltering day. The sky told two stories. Far to the south, smoke and flame marked the theatre of violence but here, perched high above Naples Bay, the night was alive with stars. A silver three-quarter moon floated in velvet. Carmela could easily make out the farmyard below her window, and the donkey cart parked against the milking parlour wall. Her heart sank at the sight of the empty dog kennel. 'Renzo, Renzo, where are you?' she breathed into the darkness. 'The fox is about!'

'*Sssst!* Come down, open the door.'

That was not Renzo. Nor was it a fox.

She leaned out as far as she dared. With its tomato terraces, orchards, hen houses and dairy, this farm was literally ripe for plunder. The hills were full of deserters, Italian troops who had left their units on the news of Italy's recent surrender to the Allies. Hungry and determined not to be caught by the Germans and sent back to fight, they were creeping in droves towards Naples and living off the land. 'Who is it?' she demanded in a fierce whisper.

'Me.' A figure slipped out of the shadows directly under the window. 'Your *fratellastro*, Danielo.'

She couldn't be certain. The figure below was the correct height to be her half-brother, and the same lean build, but she couldn't make out the features. He was head to foot in black, his hair swathed in some kind of scarf. 'Danielo who?'

'Danielo Vincenzo of course. Come down and let me in, Meluccia.'

Meluccia was the pet form of Carmela. Only a few people called her that. Still, she needed to be sure. 'Show me your hair.'

With an impatient grunt, the figure tore off his scarf to reveal curls that shone copper in the moonlight. 'Still not convinced?' he rasped. 'You once had a white cat called Dante and he had a collar with a bell on it. Our papà told me how the cat would bring birds into the house, and you'd try to nurse them back to life. Now do you believe me?'

'All right.' She'd forgotten about Dante's bell and collar. 'But not another sound,' she warned. What on earth had brought Danielo from the city at this hour? She suspected he'd been trying to scale the wall. The pipe that took rainwater down to a sunken cistern ran past her window. Had he climbed into the bedroom and disturbed Nonna in her night clothes, he'd have remembered the moment for the rest of his life.

Creeping downstairs, Carmela reached for a deerskin coat that had been her grandfather's, thrust her bare feet into work boots and piled her loose hair under a hat. If Renzo, her Spinone, had been in his kennel he'd have barked a warning the moment Danielo set foot on the property. Worryingly, Carmela hadn't seen the big, wiry-coated hunting dog all day, though she'd searched for hours. Most likely, Renzo was hunkered somewhere on the hillside, his earth-coloured body camouflaged among the thorn bushes. After a long summer the hills were parched, the streams dry, and he wouldn't survive long. She would go out at dawn, she promised herself, and search again.

She found an oil lamp and matches. Her final action was to fetch a hand axe from a cupboard. It was a tool with a flat blade and a beaked tip, used for pruning fruit trees and hacking at scrub. It doubled as a kitchen implement, for cutting meat bones or slicing husks off sweetcorn. Though she had no doubt it truly was Danielo waiting for her, the weight in her hand was a comfort.

'Follow me to the milking parlour,' she whispered as she closed the kitchen door behind her. She couldn't invite him into the house. Danielo was her father's illegitimate son, born while Carmela's mother was still alive and, while she had long ago forgiven Danielo – it was hardly his fault, after all – Nonna would never pardon the insult done to *her* daughter, Carmela's mother. If she discovered Carmela giving the hated cuckoo bread and coffee, war would break out in the kitchen.

She led Danielo past the barn where gentle rustlings told her the cows and goats were restless. Like Renzo, they were terrified by incomprehensible human strife, and cowered close to each other, refusing to leave their shelters. In the milking parlour, she lit the lamp.

'*Cavolo!*' she exclaimed as the glow spread around them. 'You've shot up since I saw you in the summer.' Danielo had become handsome too, all in the space of a few weeks.

'Course I've grown. I'm eighteen next month,' he came back. 'Can't have my big sister being taller than me.' His grin was perfunctory. Unusually for him, he looked nervous. Something told her he'd rather be out in the open.

'So what's amiss?' she asked. 'You never come here.'

Danielo pushed unruly hair off his brow. As it flopped back he took a bandana from his neck and knotted it around his forehead. He'd inherited their father's colouring: dark-gold hair and green eyes. He'd won the other lottery too: the aristocratic Del Bosco features, though in his case they were marred by a broken front tooth. Carmela was all Cortazzi, her mother's side. Black eyes, black hair, olive skin. The one thing that hadn't filtered down from their father – to either Danielo or Carmela – was his privilege. Don Gonzago del Bosco, lawyer and minor nobleman, had been declared bankrupt in 1924 and his children had to make their own living. While Carmela kept the farm with Nonna, Danielo's bronzed forearms bore the scars of life in the backstreets of Naples.

'It's not a social call,' he said.

'Really?' She spoke sarcastically. Danielo's trousers were held up by a belt that went twice around his waist. His shirt must have been passed down by someone better fed as it hung off his shoulders and the cuffs had been hacked off, showing a recent injury along his arm. She asked how he'd got it.

'A bit of flying metal.'

'Oh?' Last time she'd called on their father, Don Gonzago had hinted that Danielo had fallen in with a group of rebels in the city. She'd asked her father what kind of rebels and he had replied gravely, 'The kind that likes to overthrow Nazis. *Resistenza.*'

Resistance. All over the country, partisan bands were fighting German occupation, living out in the wilds, acquiring guns, their numbers swelling with deserters and young men who wanted to avoid the newest form of oppression – forced labour for the Germans. If Danielo was involved, he was in danger. Partisans had three enemies: the terrain, the Germans and every loyal Italian Fascist. Her mind flew away to a town square not far from here where a wall was stained with the blood of partisans executed for firing at a German patrol. The youngest had been sixteen.

'You won't do anything stupid, Danielo?'

In reply, he glanced through the open door of the milking parlour. 'Where's the dog? Where's your friend Renzo?' Carmela had taken the Spinone to Naples the last time she'd called on her father, in the back of the donkey cart. Danielo had joined them briefly and made a big fuss of him.

'Missing.' Carmela gave the brief, sad story. 'I took him his breakfast at six this morning and he'd burst out of his kennel.' She'd found the mesh door on the ground, fur and blood on the kennel doorway. 'We had planes flying so low over the farmhouse, I thought we'd lose our chimneys.'

'We heard them too. Luftwaffe bombers,' Danielo said knowledgeably, 'cutting across the back of the Allied fleet. Picking off ships. Did you see the flames out to sea?'

'Yes.' It had appalled and distressed her. Nonna too.

'He'll be back, when he's hungry.' Renzo, Danielo meant.

'He'll already be famished, yet he's not back. Come on, Danielo, there's nothing wrong with Papà, is there? Tell me if there is.' Danielo saw their father far more than she did. Naples was a compact city, rich and poor quarters intermeshing.

'No, he's same as ever. I'm here because I need you to hide something.'

'Hide, here?' She instantly sensed a pitfall. 'Not guns, is it?'

'No. It's on the back of the van I came on.' Danielo jerked his head vaguely towards the road that ran past the farm. 'We were meant to unload somewhere else, but it was too dangerous so we had to drive on.'

Her heart skipped. Was he going to ask her to conceal black-market goods? She knew Danielo and his friends had little choice when it came to honest toil versus crime, but she couldn't afford to get drawn in.

'I won't hide illegal stuff. It's hard enough keeping this place together without—' Hearing Danielo's tut of impatience, her voice rose. 'People come down from Santa Maria every day to buy milk and eggs.' Santa Maria della Vedetta was Carmela's village, and the farm hugged its skirts. Twenty local women were coming to pick tomatoes at eight in the morning and it would only take one of them to stumble on an illicit food store... 'Can't you hide whatever it is on the barren side of the hills? There are caves in the rocks where nobody goes.'

'Not possible.' Danielo probed his broken tooth with his tongue. He'd chipped it as a child, diving for limpets. 'The "something" is a person. He needs help.'

'Rebel or criminal?'

'Neither.'

'From Naples?' At Danielo's nod she asked, 'Why not take him to Papà? There's no shortage of room at Palazzo del Bosco.'

Danielo held her gaze. 'It's not possible. Papà had a visit from some Germans earlier today. Officers, *Heil Hitler*, creaking boots and shiny medals. They were still there when we arrived, but fortunately Tomaso intercepted us.' Tomaso was their father's live-in helpmate and assistant.

Her breath had caught at the mention of Germans. 'What did they want?'

'The Palazzo. They're expecting reinforcements against the Allies, and need extra billets.'

'*Gesù-Maria*, will they seize Papà's house?'

Danielo shrugged. 'He's hardly in a position to refuse, if they want it.'

She knew what her brother meant. Their father had lost his legal career in 1924 after he had defended an Italian intellectual who happened also to be a Jew and a strident opponent of Fascism. The defence had failed and the intellectual had been imprisoned, later dying in suspicious circumstances. Don Gonzago had escaped a similar fate by paying the massive fine that bankrupted him.

'The house isn't the point,' Danielo said. 'A man needs help and we've brought him to you because nobody will look for him here. They're searching in Naples.'

'So he is a criminal!'

'He's a soldier.'

'A deserter?'

'Not in the way you think.'

She wasn't in the mood for guessing games.

'I can't tell you. *Please*, Meluccia.' Danielo reached for her hand. 'Turn your back, look the other way. Just until someone comes to fetch him away. You will be paid.'

'Keep your money! Don't you understand? This is not Naples. I can't scuttle down an unlit *vicoletto* and hide in a different quarter if I'm in trouble.' Two faces manifested in her mind; those of male second cousins in the village who kept framed portraits of Italy's deposed dictator, Mussolini, over their fireplaces and raised a glass to 'Il Duce' at every opportunity.

'If I was caught harbouring a wanted man, members of my family would see it as a God-sent opportunity to get me under their thumb.' She had to make Danielo understand that it wasn't cowardice or selfishness holding her back. 'Until I came to live with her, my grandmother worked this place single-handed since the day my grandfather was laid to rest. And since that day, his Cortazzi relations have searched for a way to prise the farm from her.' Carmela put on a gruff voice: '"Admit it, Zia Rosaria, la Casale is too much for you. Let us men have the place, we'll see you right."' Long-standing anger took her over. 'Her nephews love her so much, they want her to retire. Or die. They're staunch Fascists, so breaking the law even for a day could be their chance to tear this place from us. After all, you can't defend a property if you're tied up in a police cell. Danielo?'

Had he heard? She suspected not when he said, 'I want the Germans out of Italy.'

'As do I.'

'But I'm prepared to die for it. As are my friends.'

'Don't you dare!' Unwittingly, Danielo had prodded a tender spot. She had once almost given up on existence. The farm, her love for her nonna and her animals had pulled her out of that pit and nobody, not even a beloved half-brother, had the right to push her back. 'I am prepared to *live*, Danielo. Despise me if you like.'

'I don't despise you, but please… By helping this soldier, you help Italy to freedom.'

'I am helping,' she said stubbornly. 'I'm getting in a harvest, so people can eat. What you are doing is brave, but does it fill hungry mouths? What if *you* get caught? Ha?'

Danielo shrugged. 'Better to be shot than end up as factory fodder. The minute I turn eighteen, the Germans will have me digging coal or making munitions. I tell you, I'd rather die.'

He sounded as if he'd actually weighed the possibility. But he couldn't have. 'Wait till you're facing death. I know what I'm talking about, Danielo.'

As she said it the terrible memory, over four years old now, entered her mind. The bedroom she had just left. The pains of childbirth. The blood – so much blood. In agony, she'd felt the dark waters closing over her and had fought back. 'Life's sweet when it's slipping away from you.'

In reply, Danielo raised his arm, displaying the fresh injury. 'Yesterday morning, I and my friends lobbed bricks at a German armoured car and the soldiers fired back. Because we wouldn't disperse, they sent tanks across Piazza Plebiscito to swivel their guns, to frighten us.'

That would have certainly frightened *her*.

'Next time, it won't be bricks. We're armed now, and training ourselves.'

Dio. The jeopardy for boys like Danielo was they thought themselves invincible. His bravery only exasperated her.

'I climbed the *vedetta* this morning,' she told him, referring to a crumbling lookout tower that dominated the ridge behind the farm. 'I was hoping to catch sight of Renzo.' She'd looked out across the bay. On the horizon, Allied warships had glinted like iron filings beneath a southern sky streaked with smoke and flame. Pinprick infernos in the hills behind Salerno had hinted at destruction and slaughter. 'Soldiers and ordinary people dying with each salvo.'

'It's war. People die.'

'Yes, and enough will do so without you and your friends goading the Germans. Imagine those guns in the alleys of Naples. There'd be nothing left of you.' Her words were bouncing off him, so she appealed to his imagination. 'When I collected the eggs this morning, their shells were misshapen as though the guns' echo had got inside the hens.'

Danielo's eyes widened. 'Can I see one? And take some home with me? In Naples, eggs are like gold.'

She sighed. Of course she would send him home with eggs. Danielo had six younger half-siblings as well as a mother and a stepfather. Whatever income came into the family, it was never enough. 'I'll see what I can rustle up, and then you'll go, yes? And don't squander your life, Danielo Vincenzo. I care about you.'

'Then help me, *sorella mia.*' Danielo put his hand to his heart. 'Take in a desperate man.'

For the first time, she hesitated. Only for a breath. 'No. It might be different if I lived alone, but my grandmother hates trouble and she's afraid, though she tries to hide it. It's not fair to drag an old lady through that. Come on, I'll put some eggs in a basket, and maybe I can sneak in a provolone. Nonna will notice a cheese is missing but...' She didn't finish as Danielo was peering into the pitch of the roof.

He said, 'What about up there, in the loft?'

He was still trying to palm a fugitive off on her! Her exasperation spilled out. 'Hide him in the hay pile and hope nobody thrusts in a pitchfork? The women bring their children to work with them. The little ones love to explore.' She could imagine the scene, a child tearing along the tomato terraces shrieking, 'Mamma, Mamma, there's a man in the hayloft!'

'What about the *vedetta?*'

'I wouldn't hide a rat in there. It's damp and windowless. It stinks of bird droppings.'

'He won't care, we gave him some morphine. A good big dose. I know a doctor who gets it from the Germans, if you're prepared to pay.'

'So, this man is injured and in pain?'

'He fought off a pack of SS troops before jumping from a balcony. He landed badly. But listen, by this time tomorrow he will be gone, I swear.'

Just as she was about to insist again that it was impossible, a low whistle from the farmyard made Danielo peel away. She followed. Two figures stood in a pool of moonlight, a man in a dark jacket, the other a shoeless boy. Between them they carried a stretcher. Heavy, judging by the way the boy all but dropped his end on the yard.

'You were to stay in the van,' Danielo said in a harsh whisper.

'And you said you'd be five minutes, 'Nielo. How long does it take to get a woman to do you a favour?'

'Longer than it takes you, Gio,' Danielo said, giving Carmela's arm an apologetic pinch. 'We've dragged my sister out of bed.'

'But she's agreed, yes?' Without waiting for an answer, the speaker came up close and thrust out his hand. 'Giovanni Troisi, but everyone calls me Gio.' Carmela cautiously extended her hand, expecting it to be shaken, but Gio raised it and kissed it. 'I expect Danielo's told you about me.'

'Not that I remember.'

'No? He's told me about you, Signorina, and I've looked forward to meeting you.' Gio slung an arm around Danielo. 'I only let a boy become my best friend if he has a beautiful sister.'

In her oversized hat, deerskin coat and work boots, Carmela wondered how Gio could possibly ascertain her level of beauty. But then, flirting was as natural as breathing to the average Neapolitan male – apparently even in the middle of the night, in the middle of a war. Gio couldn't be more than twenty but his lusty confidence made her feel gauche. Like an old maid who had never been kissed.

Though of course she had, and rather well too.

'I haven't agreed to anything,' she said curtly.

'You didn't say no to us using the tower,' Danielo reminded her.

'He can't go in the house?' Gio's surprise made Carmela feel suddenly ashamed.

Danielo explained about Carmela's grandmother. 'The tower will do for a night. It's on the ridge behind the farm, an old *vedetta*, nobody ever goes there.'

'I go there, and I haven't agreed!' Carmela marched to the stretcher and looked down at a prone figure, swathed in blankets. Objections died on her lips. Last time she'd seen a man on a stretcher, it had been on an airfield in the east of England with the wind hurling the stink of burned fuel into her face. A memory visited only when she was strong or, like now, caught unawares.

'What happened to him?' Only his face was exposed and, in the moonlight, it looked like a bloated mess.

Danielo answered, 'He and two comrades were ambushed inside a house by the Germans, and he battled his way out.'

Ambushed. What could that mean? What had he been doing to set the Germans after him? 'And the two other comrades?' she asked.

'Captured or dead,' said Gio. 'We don't know the whole story, but it had to have been a planned assault. This man came to me for help, covered in blood. Danielo and I know him because he's been stationed in Naples and, well, I can't tell you any more, Signorina, but he's a brave man.'

Her brother gripped her wrist. 'Twenty-four hours, then we'll come for him. He risked his life for our freedom and he won't survive if we abandon him. Meluccia? He's called—'

'I don't want to know.' She shook off Danielo's grip.

More memories. On an English airstrip, she had held a man's hand that was a clawed stump of burned skin and leather glove. She'd run alongside a stretcher as they raced to an ambulance but she'd known before they reached it that there was no hope.

'If it was me, would you help? Probably not. But if it was your brother?' It was Gio asking. 'One day, it might be.'

That cut through. Carmela dragged in a breath. 'All right. What's his name?'

Danielo answered, 'Sebastiano. Sebbe for short.'

The die was cast. A name gave the man a personality, a soul. And, by extension, a claim on her goodwill. 'He's a soldier, you say?'

'A fighter, yes.'

'And a friend of yours?'

'A comrade. Also a friend.'

Gio told Danielo to grab one end of the stretcher. Dawn wasn't far off, and they needed to drive home under cover of dark. Aware that they'd lost precious time, they lifted their burden and a moment later were walking through the open farmyard gate, aiming for the rising land behind the farm. The little barefoot boy, who had spent the last minutes peering over the barn door at the cows inside, picked up a kitbag Carmela hadn't seen until that moment. It was almost as tall as he was, but he slung it over his shoulder and, without a glance for her, ran after Danielo and Gio.

Chapter Two

Retrieving her lantern, which she extinguished because light at this elevation could be seen from the city or even out at sea, Carmela followed. While she'd been arguing with her half-brother, the guns had restarted on the distant horizon.

Sebastiano. Sebbe for short.

When Gio and Danielo paused in a farm gateway, unsure where to go next, she walked ahead of them, saying, 'This way.'

A simple choice. She was now complicit in hiding a fugitive who had evaded the Germans. If there was anything more perilous, she didn't know what it was. Her heart pounding, she led the way through a peach orchard, inhaling the scent of fruit on the verge of full ripeness. If someone tipped off the authorities about strange goings-on at la Casale in the dead of night, she might not see this harvest's end. Nonna would be left to struggle on alone. Or arrested alongside her.

White-winged moths, lured out by the moon, danced around their strange procession. She led the way across a cow pasture where every tussock was alight with glow-worms. If you could ignore the carnage down the coast, it was a magical, southern Italian night.

If.

One day only, Danielo had said, and then the stranger would be gone. Sebastiano. Sebbe for short.

Glancing back at the stretcher, she saw one of the injured man's arms had fallen free, the hand dragging on the grass. She waited until the stretcher was alongside, and picked up the trailing hand. It was broad and weighty but ice cold, and she curled her fingers round it to impart some warmth.

'Straight on,' she instructed Danielo, who was at the foot end of the stretcher. 'It gets steep when we're among the tomato vines.' The *vedetta* reared up ahead of them, like a ruined chess piece on its ridge. It had been built centuries ago as a lookout against Turkish and Saracen pirates that had raided along this coast, and it gave her village its name: Santa Maria della Vedetta, 'Our Lady of the watchtower'. She whispered a prayer. 'Watch over this man and protect me and my nonna.' She called to the barefoot boy, 'Here's a lantern and matches, but don't light it until you're inside the tower.' To the others, she said, 'Get Sebastiano settled while I go back for water and some food. He'll wake at some point, I suppose?'

Gio answered, 'I would, if I had you as my nurse.'

'I'm not a nurse.' She detected a contraction of the hand in hers. 'So you can hear, can you, Sebastiano?' she murmured. The hand fell limp and, to her dismay, she discovered her eyes were full of tears.

La Casale meant 'fortified farm' and her home lived up to its name. No running water, no electricity and no glass in the windows.

Back in the farmhouse kitchen, Carmela put some cold courgette frittata into a basket, along with a spoon, fork and a tin cup, and decanted water from a pitcher into a screw-top can. She moved quickly but softly, trying her best to make as little noise as possible as she went about her work.

Stopping by the farmyard, she crammed fresh straw into a sack. Dawn was edging out the moonlight and she was able to move about easily without any kind of lantern. The straw smelled sweet and would insulate Sebastiano: she couldn't bear the idea of an injured man being laid on an unsanitary floor. Before she left, she glanced into the kennel, in hope. But hope was dashed.

As she trudged back to the tower, she scanned the ridge for signs of intruders but saw nothing to cause any alarm. The *vedetta* lay within la Casale's boundaries and as far as she knew, she was the only person to have climbed it in a decade. It was little more than a stone tube, fifteen metres high, with arrow-slit windows on the sea-facing side. The doorway faced into the hill. Carmela's grandfather had told her it was like this to make the tower easier to defend. Her sack caught on the thorn bushes crowding the entrance, and as she shouldered her way inside she made a face. Ugh. That loamy, fetid stink.

They had laid Sebastiano at the foot of stone steps that led, minus any kind of handrail, to the *vedetta*'s summit. Three steps up, the barefoot boy held her flickering lantern, which cast octopus arms on the mossy stone. The child had hollow cheeks, uncombed hair and huge, silent eyes.

'How is he?' Carmela asked, glancing at the injured stranger.

'Exactly the same, Signorina.' Gio gave her a curious glance. Perhaps she hadn't wiped her tears away well enough.

It wasn't a stretcher her guest was lying on, she realised as Danielo and Gio hefted Sebastiano a couple of feet clear of the earth so she could spread her straw beneath him, but a canvas camp bed. In fact, wasn't it familiar? She was certain she'd used it in the stifling summer of 1926 when her mother was dying with typhus fever. She was ten years old, and had been sent up to the attic to sleep alongside the maids, out of harm's way. 'What's in that?' She indicated the green kitbag, which had been dumped next to the steps.

'Spare clothes and boots, things we think will fit him, and these...' Danielo opened the drawstring top and removed a number of bent steel rods. They were the camp bed's legs, which slotted into the frame.

'Shouldn't you put them in, to raise him off the floor?'

'We forgot,' Gio said. 'No time now and no point disturbing him again. When he's able to get off the bed by himself, you do it.'

Wait a minute... 'I thought he was only staying one night.'

Danielo put the metal legs down by the camp bed. 'That's right. One night. We need to go.'

'What happens if – when – he wakes up?'

Danielo patted her arm. 'He'll need some help, obviously.'

'What kind of help?'

'Water and food. Reassurance.'

Did 'reassurance' include telling him where he was? she asked.

'For sure.' Danielo rolled his eyes. 'Because if he's caught and tortured, you really want him giving your name and address to the Nazis.'

Carmela returned a stunned look. 'Caught and tortured... What kind of soldier is he, Danielo?'

Her half-brother returned a slow shrug, the kind that ran in his blood and which meant nothing at all. Or nothing of use. Gio, whom the lamplight revealed to be a young, roughly chiselled Apollo, asked her to please hide the kitbag somewhere. 'Unless it's too heavy for you, ha?'

'I'll manage.'

'*Va bene, a dopo.*' Till next time. Gio gave her a brisk salute then jerked his head at the barefoot boy, who sprang off the steps. And then they were gone and it was just her and the stranger.

Kneeling down in the straw, Carmela pushed damp strands of hair off Sebastiano's forehead. It was thick, dark hair like hers. His blankets had been folded down and she saw his upper body was dressed in a soft shirt and a darned blue jersey. Something about it suggested 'mariner' or 'fisherman'. Danielo had said he was a sort of soldier, 'a fighter'. She couldn't quite figure his age from a face that was a patchwork of bruises and bloody lesions, but he looked fit with a wide jaw and muscular neck. His lower lip was split but his upper lip was wide and spare, stubble outlining it below a high-bridged nose. A Roman nose – or it might be broken.

His eyes were so swollen they resembled ripe figs. His hands, clasped over the top of his blanket, were criss-crossed with raw cuts and what looked like identical burns in the centre of his palms. An inexpensive watch hung around his left wrist, stainless steel with a half-broken strap. She cringed, imagining the pain that went with his injuries and, though the risk terrified her, she knew she'd done the right thing in helping this man.

She dipped her hanky into the water and dabbed the closed eyelids. He muttered something unintelligible. 'I'm Carmela,' she said. No point making up false names for herself. It was possible he'd heard Danielo calling her 'Meluccia' and *sorella mia*. 'I'm going to take care of you until you go to your next safe place. First, I'll give you some water.' Bunching the handkerchief under his chin, she raised his head and dripped water through his lips and he swallowed. 'Could you eat something?'

He didn't respond. Probably too soon. 'I'm going to have to leave you,' she whispered, 'because the birds are starting to sing.' If her grandmother discovered Carmela's bed was cold, lies would be necessary and she hated those. 'I won't abandon you but it may feel like that. Don't be scared.'

She wondered if she dared leave the lamp burning. She wouldn't relish lying here in the gloom, listening to distant detonations and the ravens roosting on top of the tower. On the other hand, the saffron glow had been filling the arrow slit too long. So she doused the lantern, and offered a final reassurance.

'The darker it is the safer you are, Sebastiano. Or do you prefer Sebbe? I'll come back in daylight and see if you're ready to eat.' There was the kitbag. *Unless it's too heavy for you.* Maybe once, but not after many seasons spent farming. Why had she cast such a frost over Gio with her cold responses? He was attractive, good-natured. Brave. Too young for her, of course, and if he knew her secrets he would no doubt consider her to be tainted. A gentle flirtation wouldn't have hurt, but unlike him, she hadn't a talent for it.

The sensual Italian side of her had been stifled, then roused, then crushed. Dispatched aged ten to school in England, still crying for her recently dead mother, she had been plunged into an unfamiliar culture. In a Cambridge girls' academy, she'd been educated by clever spinsters. Later, as a teacher in the same town, she had worked alongside liberated women who had looked men in the eye as equals. From them, Carmela had learned the creed of independence: get a profession, pay your bills on time, button down the passions. Good advice, but *Dio santo*, her buttons had flown off like hailstones the day a man had finally awoken the red-blooded Neapolitan inside her.

Basta, basta. Enough. She lugged the kitbag up the steps to where a niche had been dug into the wall. Once used to store firewood, or weapons, it was invisible from below, and it hid secrets of her own.

Placing her feet carefully, as there was nothing to break her fall if she slipped, she extracted a satchel, heavy with mementoes brought back from Cambridge. Books and letters, a marriage proposal. Precious things. Opening the straps, she inhaled the smell of leather and paper.

As an unwelcome tear worked its way down her cheek, she mentally shook herself. Now was not the time to indulge in memories. She pushed the satchel back into its hiding place, shoved the kitbag in lengthways then clambered back down. She straightened a blanket across the sleeping man and picked up his food tray. It wouldn't do to leave it, with the birds roosting above and the ground home to insects of all descriptions. She was preparing to leave when muttered words stopped her in her tracks.

'Thank you so much.'

English. She held up the lantern, her hand unsteady. 'What did you say?' She too spoke in English.

He repeated, 'Thank you.'

A kind of soldier, Danielo had said. One who spoke English in the middle of Fascist Italy. How about, 'a spy'?

Chapter Three

The thorn shrubs coating the slopes above la Casale had a proper name: pyracantha. To Carmela, they were firethorn. As summer faded, their blazing berries fed the birds. In the clear ground between, scarlet poppies grew and her homeward walk in the strengthening light was like wading through embers.

She was harbouring an Englishman. One who had been ambushed by Germans and escaped while his comrades had fled, or died, or been captured. He wasn't in uniform, which meant he could be arrested as a spy, not protected by the Geneva Convention.

As for her... she almost laughed. She wasn't covered by any convention other than the one that ended in interrogation and execution. She was twenty-seven and she wanted to live. To love. To be a mother someday and hold a child in her arms. But this moment of weakness, her taking him in, could end every hope of that.

Carrying the food she'd intended for Sebastiano, she paused in the farmyard and whistled again for Renzo. No gruff bark in response. Where was he? She hated the thought of him being hungry. She'd already knocked on doors in the village, asking her neighbours to keep a lookout. If he'd run away from the planes as they headed out over the sea, then he'd likely have passed through Santa Maria. It was still a lot of ground to search and now, thanks to Sebastiano's arrival, she'd have little opportunity to get away from the farm before evening.

'You picked up bad habits abroad, Meluccia,' her grandmother had chided when Carmela asked if Renzo could live with them after she'd found him straying in the hills, in a pitiable state. 'The English like animals better than their children.'

Not true, Carmela had protested. The English she'd known viewed their dogs as companions rather than living chattels like the Italians, but not as children. Her grandmother had been unimpressed.

'Climbing up to the table and getting into bed with them. And when they die, they make graves in their gardens. I know it.'

'How? The closest you've been to an English person is bumping into a sightseer in the village.' Though she wouldn't admit it to her grandmother, Carmela had once walked through an English shrubbery and seen headstones dedicated to various Mollies, Bessies and Rovers. 'How do you know about the graves?'

'Your mother told me, and *she* got it from that *inglesi*-worshipper, Gonzago del Bosco.'

Carmela had asked her grandmother to please not speak of her father that way. 'Just saying he likes the English could get him into trouble.'

'I live in hope,' had been her nonna's response. Lucifer would be readmitted to heaven before Rosaria Cortazzi would forgive the man who had married, then betrayed, her only surviving child. That particular day, however, their argument had ended in a truce. Carmela could take in the stray dog, but not bring him over the threshold.

'The hairy fool stays in his kennel.'

Except he hadn't. Carmela went into the house where she took off her coat, grimacing at the state of her nightdress hem. Returning the hand axe to its cupboard, she went upstairs and found both beds empty. The farmhouse had just one bedroom, and it was normal for Carmela to wake first, creep downstairs to begin the day's work and brew coffee. Nonna must be up already and in the dairy, scalding out jugs in preparation for the morning's milk. Because casual workers would be on the farm today, Carmela cast aside the trousers she preferred and put on a dress with a crossover front over a dark blouse. In Santa Maria della Vedetta, a woman in trousers could expect a visit from stern Padre Pasquale. The addition of beige cotton stockings, a triangular scarf over her hair and clumpy boots finished off her transformation to 'spinster dowd'.

As a young teacher, she'd loved taking the train from Cambridge to London for the museums, art galleries and shopping. She had discovered a second-hand dress shop in fashionable Belgravia and, as a result, had earned a reputation for being rather chic. She'd given away some lovely outfits before she left England.

Ah well. Fitting in made life easier in the countryside. And as she set to work on the milking – fourteen cows and four goats to get through – she reflected that her elegant clothes wouldn't have lasted long on the farm.

When the nanny goats were done and she'd taken a brimming can to her grandmother, Carmela moved on to the gentle-eyed cattle. Their milk was flowing slowly this morning, and when an aircraft roared overhead the veteran cow she was seated beside almost did a somersault, knocking her off her stool. Carmela picked herself up and sat back down, resting her forehead against the warm, brown flank. 'The world has gone mad, Berta.'

'Name them, you weep when they die.' Nonna's advice, wise yet ignored. After the milking was done, Carmela filled a bucket with cornmeal and persuaded Berta to follow her to the meadow. The rest of the herd plodded in the senior cow's wake, but even in their field, they clumped together anxiously, ears twitching.

Next, it was the donkey's turn. Carmela pinned back his stable door so he could amble at his leisure. Nearco seemed unbothered by war. Perhaps he was growing deaf. She'd bought him at a knock-down price from a neighbour who had no more use for him and had named him after Italy's greatest thoroughbred racing stallion, earning another roll of the eyes from her grandmother.

As she carried the pails of warm cows' milk to the dairy, a stone lean-to that was her grandmother's province, Carmela pondered her habit of assuming guardianship for waifs and strays. It had started in childhood, as Danielo had reminded her, trying to mend the birds her cat brought in. Returning from England emotionally numb, it had been easier to pour love into the animals around her. Animals were simpler than people, and safer. Yet last night, clasping a stranger's hand had torn something open inside Carmela. It had ripped the bandage off unhealed grief.

Her grandmother was at work making curds in the dairy. Carmela put the pails down on a stone bench and watched. After a moment, she began to feel she was eavesdropping on an older version of herself. Carmela had inherited Rosaria Cortazzi's above-average height and she took after her in other ways. They shared a stubborn temperament and a reserved demeanour that some people read as coldness. On the plus side, she'd inherited Rosaria's curves – or perhaps she had stolen them, as these days her grandmother's black dress hung loose. At seventy-two, Rosaria's shoulders were round from years of stooping over vats, cutting curds, pressing and shaping la Casale's sought-after cheeses. Her porcelain-white hair, pinned in a bun, was as transparent as thistledown.

She looked up from her work then and saw Carmela. 'Salerno's getting it. Those damn guns haven't stopped for breath. What's happening to the people who find themselves in the way?'

'They escape, I hope,' Carmela said.

'You can't pack up farm animals, so the country folk will stay put and hide under their beds. Will it come here, to Naples and into our hills?'

'The battle?' Carmela had wondered the same thing. 'There's bound to be a fight over Naples. After all, it's the biggest port on the coast. I can't see anybody's army coming into these hills, though. There's nothing here.'

'Mm. Did you sleep? I didn't get a moment's rest all night.'

Carmela raised an eyebrow. 'Who was snoring, then?'

Rosaria chuckled. 'The house. It sleeps too, you know.'

'I like that idea, Nonna.'

They got on well these days, though it hadn't always been so. Arriving without warning in January 1939 with a suitcase, a broken heart and a pregnant belly, Carmela had thrown herself on her grandmother's goodwill. At the sight of Carmela's four-month bump, Nonna had let out a cry of pain. Since her husband's death, her reputation as a proud and respectable widow was her only defence against the predatory eyes coveting her property. Taking in an unmarried, pregnant granddaughter would engulf her in scandal. The predators – those second cousins of Carmela's who were sons of her late husband's brother – would strike. Still, she had not turned Carmela away and had instead put it around that her granddaughter had come to Santa Maria to recover from a nervous disorder.

Keeping Carmela out of sight had contained the secret. Nonna hadn't let the village doctor visit. Not even when Carmela went into an early labour.

'I'll go fetch the eggs, then I'll be ready for breakfast,' Carmela said abruptly and turned away.

'I hope they look better than yesterday's,' Nonna called after her. 'A misshapen egg is an ill omen.'

'It's shockwaves from the gunfire, Nonna, getting into the hens before the eggshells have hardened.'

'All the way from Salerno? No, trust me, the devil is in the hen-house.'

Their Siciliana fowl produced eggs with creamy white shells, and the birds were usually prolific. This morning, Carmela found just five eggs, all oddly elongated as before. As she headed back to the house, she looked towards the ridge, and the *vedetta*, and murmured, 'Sebastiano, Sebbe for short, pray someone collects you today. The omens are bad.'

When Carmela got back to the kitchen, her grandmother was already there, grinding grey-white powder in a stone bowl. They were mussel and oyster shells that Carmela collected from the rocks at Santa Lucia, the pretty port on the edge of Naples.

'Calcium for the hens, Nonna?'

Sighing as she counted the eggs Carmela put down, Rosaria said, 'It'll strengthen the shells, and we'll sprinkle some in the doorway to keep the devil out.'

That was Nonna, an unpredictable fusion of wisdom and superstition. A devout Catholic who loved a glass of grappa and a risqué joke. Full of love, but struggled to show it. She'd borne four children, with Carmela's mother, Nina, the only one to survive. And then Nina had died too.

Suddenly, lies felt unbearable. Nonna deserved to know that a fugitive was hiding on her property. It was only a matter of time before she found him anyway, and Carmela couldn't risk that. 'Nonna, I need to say something.'

'I'm listening.' Rosaria waited for her to go on.

But as quickly as her courage had come, it left her again. Sebastiano would be gone by tonight, so why burden Nonna with pointless knowledge? 'The hens don't need calcium,' she said. 'They need the guns to stop.'

'Whatever is the problem, we cannot sell shell-shocked eggs. Sit down, I'll make you your coffee.' When Carmela ignored the instruction and spooned ground coffee-substitute into a battered old percolator known as a *cuccumella*, Rosaria clicked her tongue. 'Rest. You have done a man's work already this morning.'

'That's because she needs a man, Zia Rosaria.'

Neither of them had noticed the kitchen door open or heard Tino Cortazzi, the elder of the predatory nephews, stepping inside.

Carmela's heart skidded through several beats as she speculated how long her cousin had been listening. Tino was no mere supporter of Mussolini: he was a captain of the Blackshirts, the volunteer militia also known as *squadristi*.

Their self-appointed job in these parts was to root out and beat up anybody who opposed Fascism, or who spoke against the Germans. Even at this early hour, Tino looked ready for parade, shirt ironed, his hair sleek with oil. Tino strongly resembled Carmela's late grandfather Mario with his short neck and round head. He had the dark Cortazzi complexion, though his hair was ashy grey. His age, forty-four, had kept him out of the army and allowed him to seize his advantageous job.

His gaze tracked around the rustic kitchen, measuring it. Coveting it.

Carmela's grandfather had bequeathed the farm to Rosaria and Carmela, leaving his late brother's sons, Tino and Santo, some outlying fields as their share of the inheritance. Tino had no legal claim on la Casale, but when his eyes came to rest on Carmela his expression was speculative. Sly.

'You are looking fine today, cousin. A peach ready for harvest. Speaking of which, how are the orchards? I wasn't happy when I last inspected them.' Tino's paid job was as overseer of all the farms in the commune. With his younger brother Santo, he weighed and checked yields and controlled the distribution of crops. It added to his power.

She answered him coldly. 'I'm surprised you were dissatisfied, because I predict a good harvest.' She wouldn't give Tino an excuse to nose around and she willed her grandmother to stand firm and freeze him out too. It went against the grain not to offer hospitality, but this man was dangerous. To her dismay, her nonna fell back on old habits.

Wiping her hands on her apron, Rosaria asked, 'What brings you from the village? Tell us while you have coffee. You will take some? Get your cousin a cup, Meluccia.' Encountering Carmela's stony gaze, Rosaria nodded hard. *Do it, please.*

'Coffee, yes I think I will.' Tino went to kiss his aunt's cheek. He wasn't overly tall but he was powerful, with bull shoulders.

Carmela added water to the *cuccumella* and, withdrawing to the stove, put it on to heat. She knew Tino was watching her. Determined not to show fear, she practised a smile while her back was to him, then turned and said pleasantly, 'I'm surprised to see you here so early.'

'Nothing to keep me in bed.' Tino winked. 'Being a bachelor gets a man up early, you get my meaning? If you had a husband, Meluccia, you could stay at your stove all day while he did the hard work. Your grandmother knows how things go.'

'I worked hard every day I was married to my Mario,' Rosaria said sharply.

Tino kept smiling. 'Meluccia would soon have sons to keep her busy.' He came to stand behind Carmela. 'Don't you ever think about that?'

'Never.' Carmela kept her eyes on the percolator, which was coming to the boil.

'You should think it. A good man won't wait forever.'

'I'm not asking him to.' Today wasn't the first time Tino had hinted to her about his sexual needs. His liking for her... it made her queasy. She took the pot to the table, turning it over so the boiling water could percolate through the grounds, then put out cups. Real coffee was impossible to buy and they had learned to do with a substitute made from roasted barley. By the time she was pouring the bitter, black brew, her grandmother was asking after Tino's brother Santo's family.

'His wife is whining, as ever. Their house is too small, the children too big. But my brother is well. Full of fight, Zia Rosaria. His latest hobby is trapping deserters and giving the filthy cowards the beating they deserve. Let me explain why I am here.' Tino sat down at the table. 'This is what brings me.' He placed a red dog collar in front of him and asked, 'Missing something, Meluccia?'

'Oh!' For a moment, she didn't know whether to cry or laugh. 'You have Renzo?'

'No. I found this collar on the ground, near the church, and hung it on a bench, then I heard you lost your Spinone. I thought maybe he'd slipped his collar. Is he back?'

'Not yet.' Carmela picked up the collar. It was one she'd found in the harness room. She'd punched extra holes in it to make it fit Renzo's hungry neck. She'd moved the buckle a hole at a time as he'd gained weight. 'Did you catch sight of him?'

Tino opened his fingers, implying sympathy. 'I didn't, I'm sorry. Was it the gunfire that made him run away?'

Carmela said it was the aircraft noise. 'You can almost see the pilots, they dive so low!'

He nodded. 'We thought the attack would come further south, in Calabria. The Americans and British stole the advantage but the Germans are giving a good account of themselves. The beaches run red with blood, so I hear.'

Resting his thick forearms on the table, he clenched his fists, as if he was spoiling for a fight. Well, he wouldn't get one here. Carmela and Nonna knew better than to express an opinion in front of him. A silver ring on his middle finger bore the fasces symbol above the letter 'M' for his hero.

They drank their coffee, Nonna doing most of the talking, jumping from subject to subject in her anxiety. Carmela lifted the red collar to her nose. She desperately wanted to go out and search for Renzo, to call and whistle till her lips were dry. But she couldn't leave Nonna alone with Tino. The women would arrive any moment to start tomato picking and she had to work alongside them for at least the first hour... no... she had to work with them all day!

Madre Maria, how was she going to look after Sebastiano? The tomato terraces were directly below the *vedetta* and she'd have to stay there, in case any of the women or their children took it into their heads to take a peek inside. She drained her coffee. She should go and check on him now.

Tino put paid to that. Putting his cup down – he always banged cups and glasses, either because he didn't know his strength or was testing it – he said, 'Give me the guided tour, Meluccia. I want to see everything. Your tomato weights have been holding up, but only just.'

'We've had a fantastic season so far.'

'Mm, but others are better. And it's a while since I looked over the apple orchards.'

'They're fine.' She hated seeing his boots stamping their land. Nonna looked helpless. Ready to cry. 'Sorry, Tino, I can't spare a moment. I have to take a feed supplement to the hens.' She seized the pulverised seashells her grandmother had abandoned.

'All I want is to help. To advise, cousin. No need to be defensive.'

Nonna cautiously advised Tino that Carmela knew her work. 'She came here often, as a little child with her mother. My Mario had her with him all day long so she learned how to farm from the best.' It was a subtle reminder to Tino of the deference due to Mario Cortazzi's widow. To the owners of la Casale.

Subtlety gained no traction with Tino. 'Shall we see the peaches first, then the apples?' He walked out, giving Carmela little choice but to go with him. In the orchard, he commented favourably on the laden trees, though he observed that some of the fruits were small.

'It was the cold spring,' Carmela explained. 'Everything was slow.'

'Aha?' He reached up, picked a velvety orb and bit into it. 'Good flavour.' He nodded, agreeing with himself. 'Not bad. Let's see what they're like at the northern end. Not so much sun there.'

By the time he had satisfied his curiosity over the peaches, Carmela was grinding her teeth. He hadn't forgotten about the apples, either, and she followed him, mouthing her dislike to his broad back. La Casale had four hectares of annurca trees producing a small, red fruit. The species dated from Roman times, and their trees were over a hundred years old. All knees and elbows and thick bark. Tino twisted an apple between his powerful fingers, breaking it in two. He put one half to his nose and inhaled. Then he removed a pip and examined it. Carmela wasn't sure why.

'The orchard suffered from the freak weather,' she said. The winter of '41, two years back, had been the coldest southern Italy had known in living memory. It had rung the death knell for many olive groves, vines and orchards.

'Maybe,' he said.

No 'maybe' about it. She'd walked out in the snow, frozen up to her knees.

'You'll bring in a hundred and seventy tons of apples this year. Less, perhaps,' Tino informed her, finishing his visual calculation of the laden branches.

'We picked two hundred tons last year,' she answered brusquely.

'Last year, exactly my point. These trees are ageing. There's a peak decade for an apple tree, after which its fertility declines. Same as with women.' In a gesture that was blatantly suggestive, he pushed the half-apple into his mouth and chewed on it, never taking his eyes from her. 'By thirty, a woman should be ten years married.'

She could have told him that she had three years to go before that landmark, and unlike him, had not a shred of grey to her hair. She resisted, because all she wanted was to watch him walk out of the farm gate.

He wiped juice from his chin, his eyes on her bosom. 'I like you in a dress. I don't understand a woman in trousers. It's not natural.' Before she could retort, he changed the subject. 'Did you hear anything odd last night?' He was examining apple leaves, raking a thumbnail along their underside. Not looking at her.

She hastily adjusted her expression. 'I heard the guns from the south. At first, I thought it was thunder.'

'I'm talking about an engine, a large van or a truck. I heard it stop near here, then start up again an hour later.'

She shook her head, hoping the gesture hid her cold fear. 'The only vehicle I ever hear is the doctor's car, when he's going out to a patient.'

'It wasn't Dr Baccolini's Lancia, it was a bigger engine. Anyway, Baccolini lives opposite me so I know when he takes his car out. I was on duty until after midnight, and I couldn't sleep. Too much in my head. I went out into the street and walked down to the viewpoint to watch the horizon. That's when I heard the engine and saw headlights stop close to this farm.'

She didn't know what to say. Just counted the bumps of her heart.

Throwing down the leaves he'd been inspecting for scab, or grubs, or just to annoy her, Tino grinned. 'Let's have a squint at the tomato vines, ha?'

God preserve her. What if Sebastiano had woken and was stumbling about, looking for her? 'I'll be seeing quite enough tomatoes today,' she said firmly. 'I need another cup of coffee, and I daresay you could find room.'

She strode towards the house, and knew Tino was following because he was a noisy breather. He wasn't fat. Nobody was fat in this part of Italy other than privileged officials and German top brass, but Tino carried a lot of bone and muscle. It must press on his lungs. When they were out of the trees, he hooked his hand under her elbow.

'I'll check the tomatoes before I go. There's been reports of blight in the Marzano crop. You go get the pot on the stove, I'll see you in a moment.'

Carmela willed words to her tongue. Anything to stop him going near the *vedetta*. No words came.

'What is it?' Tino said, his voice silky. 'You had something delivered last night, perhaps, and are hiding it among the tomato vines? Tell me, cousin. You can trust me.'

'I… don't know what you mean. Nothing came here.'

'I understand. There *is* blight on the plants, and you hope I won't see it?'

'No. They're healthy. Superb, in fact.'

'Then what's making you so nervous? You are aware, tomato blight is a notifiable disease and failure to report is a serious matter. A prosecution would call into question your fitness to run la Casale.'

'There's no blight.' With every instinct on edge, she picked up a low, grinding sound travelling through the cirrus clouds above the hills. Her ears were learning to cancel out the crump of shellfire, but this noise cut through. 'Planes!' she shouted. It came out almost as a cheer.

They both stared up into the sky.

'FW 190s,' Tino pronounced, straining his voice over the throb.

'German?'

He gave her a withering glance. 'Fighter-bombers. Yes, of course they're German. The Luftwaffe still commands the skies.' The planes overhead made a cruciform shape against the blue, their nose cones dark through a blur of propellers. They were heading towards the sea. 'Go strafe the beaches, my boys, don't leave a single barbarian standing!' Tino kissed his silver signet ring then pumped his fists, shouting, 'Musso! Musso! Musso!' He believed the Italian surrender was an aberration and that his hero would soon return to seize back power.

Carmela muttered, 'Mussolini won't hear you. He's in prison.'

Tino's hearing was sharper than she'd suspected, or he could lip-read. 'Il Duce will return.' He gave a final punch of the air, shielding his eyes for a last sight of the planes. 'Those boys are from the airbase at Avellino. They're patrolling the bay, and any Allied ships getting close to Naples will get a pasting. Their guns can fire nine hundred rounds a minute.'

'Thanks to those brave boys' – she kept the sarcasm from her voice – 'my poor cows will be stampeding across their meadow. Will you help me round them up?'

He fell for the bait, and after they'd herded the panicky cows into their barn, asked if the offer of coffee still stood. He'd made himself hoarse with shouting into the sky. After he'd finally gone, Rosaria emerged from her dairy. Taking in Carmela's expression, she sighed, 'When I became engaged to your grandfather… *Dio*, was it really fifty-two years ago… my family was aghast. "Never marry a Cortazzi, even one with a farm. The men are criminals, the boys are violent and the girls are sluts." I went ahead, because I knew my Mario was different. I wish Tino was more like him.'

'But he isn't, Nonna.'

'He has his eyes on you. A peach ripe for the plucking, *per Dio!*'

'He'd soon discover the stone inside.' Carmela looked for Renzo's collar but it was gone.

'I didn't touch it,' Rosaria assured her. 'Tino must have. Perhaps he means to search.'

'Another excuse to come back uninvited.'

Tino had heard Danielo's arrival last night, even if he was unaware of its significance. Silently, Carmela offered a prayer that was wearing thin from repetition. *Please, let Sebastiano be collected tonight.*

Rosaria took their used coffee cups to the sink whose sandstone rim was worn to satin from years of use. She stroked the stone before pouring water from a ewer into the cups. 'There are many days when I wish you had married that man in England.'

Carmela put her arms around her nonna's bent shoulders. 'If I had, I wouldn't be here with you. It would just be you and the house, snoring away at night.'

'Oh, go on with you.'

The tinkle of the dairy bell announced that somebody wanted milk. Moments later, the pickers arrived carrying their lunch baskets. Carmela put on a straw sun hat and filled a can with water, enough for herself and for Sebastiano, for when she got the chance to slip into the tower. Pray God, he was still asleep and not dying from neglect.

Chapter Four

On the tomato terraces there was no shade and the heat was blistering. Carmela worked alongside her team, filling basket after basket with Marzano plum tomatoes while guarding the route up to the tower. There were little boys among the pickers, and she needed eyes in the back of her head. At last, the church clock struck one and, on cue, the women and children retired to the orchards to eat their lunch. Saying she was going to look for her dog, Carmela picked up the water can and began to climb towards the tower. She'd only gone forty paces when one of the women came running out from the trees.

'Signorina del Bosco, your donkey is among the apples, filling his cheeks. He refuses to move.'

She had no choice but to save Nearco from a bout of colic. By which time, lunch was over. The afternoon was agony, as she had to leave the tower unguarded while she brought in the cows and did the evening milking. Her nerves must have transferred into the udders because even docile Frederica kicked out at her and Berta swung her tail.

Sebastiano must be desperate for water, but she didn't dare go to him. The longest day ended with ginger sunlight spilling over the terraces, giving the *vedetta* an exaggerated shadow. Carmela gave the laden tomato crates a cursory inspection and scrawled her initials on the workers' time sheets. Tired women trooped towards her, knotting light shawls over their shoulders. Go, go, she urged them.

'One more session here, I'd say, then on to the orchards, no?' The question was put by Cristina Gennaro, one of the village matrons. Round as a pumpkin and nosy with it, she was a relation and contemporary of Nonna's.

Carmela smiled tensely. 'I'm almost too tired to think. *Buonasera*, Zia Cristina.'

The hint missed its mark. 'I heard you were searching for your dog. No luck?'

'He's still missing, sadly.'

Zia Cristina tutted in sympathy. 'We'll keep our eyes open. You had a visitor too last night, people are saying.'

'They're saying that?' Carmela heard the click of anxiety in her voice. You couldn't sneeze in la Casale without someone in Santa Maria hurrying down with a handkerchief. Had Tino blabbed? 'Who says I did?'

'My neighbour, Signor Esposito, he has to get out of bed three times a night to use the latrine… his belly hasn't been right since he came back from the last war… well, he heard a motor. He told me so, as I fed my chickens this morning. "Signora Gennaro, we had a visitor in the early hours," he said. A vehicle. Its lights were dimmed but he heard it stop close by here. That's what he told me.'

'I didn't hear a thing,' Carmela said stoutly. 'Perhaps it was a military truck, lost on its way to Salerno.'

'Very lost, in that case.' Dimples formed each side of Cristina's mouth. 'So not a lover of yours, ha?'

'Definitely not.'

'Good.' Cristina's humour faded. 'It took years for your poor mother's mistake to get forgotten, and there are those who never will let it go.'

'So I perceive, Zia Cristina.'

'And take care, ha? Santa Maria men are red-blooded to the day they die. When one of them decides what he wants, he usually gets it. You know who I speak of.'

Carmela wished with all her might that Zia Cristina would go home.

'Are you taking these tomatoes up to the village, Meluccia?'

'Not yet. I have to check on my animals.' And Sebastiano, who was becoming a raging priority.

'No, you need to get the crops away,' Cristina told her. 'They'll be bringing in cartloads from the villa farm, and you'll be waiting an hour if that lot gets ahead of you. I'll accept a lift up the hill while you're at it. You harness the donkey, and I'll help you put the crates up.'

Cornered, Carmela fetched Nearco. With Cristina's help, she loaded the tomatoes onto the back, then gave the older woman a heave up onto the box seat. She sprang up herself and shook the reins. '*Arri!* Nearco, I said *go*, not stop. Come on, you've had a day of rest, not to mention apples. *Arri!*'

Santa Maria della Vedetta lay at the end of a steep, spiralling road. One main street was really all there was, culminating in the white villa, which, since the outbreak of war, had sat empty. Its formerly magnificent gardens now grew tomatoes and tobacco. A church, dedicated to the Virgin, overlooked a piazza with an ancient olive tree and a spring-fed fountain. The houses along the street had once been brightly painted but their colours were weathered now to pastel. Even so, it was a postcard scene in the mellow evening sunshine. Carmela helped Zia Cristina down when they reached a house with sage-green shutters.

'*Mille grazie.*' Cristina patted Carmela's cheek. '*A domani, tesoro.*' See you tomorrow, precious.

In the church square, a commune employee weighed and tallied the tomatoes as Carmela unloaded them. To her relief, Tino was nowhere to be seen. Her day's effort tumbled into a huge wooden hopper to join the ruby-red torrent, which would go by cart to Naples tonight. They'd end up in the one canning factory that had survived the Allied bombing of the industrial zone. Many kilos would disappear on the journey, and the factory owners would have to grease numerous palms, Tino's included. By the time she and Nonna were paid for their crop, an entire layer cake of officials, inspectors, middlemen and racketeers would have taken their cut.

As she waited for a signed chit acknowledging her delivery, she asked the man if he'd seen a dog, and described Renzo. 'Very friendly, with bushy brows. Someone thought he might have been up here, near the church.'

'A Spinone? Maybe… we get stray mutts nosing around the crates all the time.' The man pulled a thoughtful face. 'I'll keep my eyes peeled.'

She was thanking him when her name was called.

'How you doing, cousin Meluccia?'

It was Tino's brother, Tomaso-Antonino, known without intentional irony as Santo. Like Tino, he had a bit of a swagger, having won medals as a *squadrista*. The first into a fight and the last out was what they said of Santo, who also had links to the Camorra, the criminal clan that ruled much of life in these parts.

He came to stand too close to her. 'How's Zia Rosaria?'

She told him her grandmother was well.

'It's time she retired. You tell her, Santo lives with five children in a two-bedroom house. He could use that pile down the hill.'

Pocketing her paperwork, Carmela got away. After stabling the donkey, she at last made her way to the tower. One pocket was full of tomatoes and there was a blond provolone cheese wrapped in waxed paper in the other. She hadn't had the chance to give Danielo the cheese and eggs she'd promised him. Sebastiano would get them instead.

It was now almost dark. Sebastiano had been alone nearly twenty hours. As she fought her way through the undergrowth, her skin crawled at what she might find. He could be dying. He could be dead.

Outside the entrance, she lit her lantern, the match flame exaggerating the trembling of her fingers. Steeling herself, she pushed inside and followed the lantern beam.

The camp bed was empty, blankets discarded on the straw. Muttering something between a plea and a prayer, she lifted the lamp. 'Sebastiano – Sebbe?' Let him not have found his way out and got lost. Or worse, blundered into the village. '*Dove stai?*' Where are you?

'Up here.' The answer came from the top of the tower, which acted like a loudhailer. Once again, he was speaking English.

The lantern beam reached no further than halfway. Carmela felt she was staring up through a rabbit hole to a circle of violet night. 'You're at the top?'

'I… suppose. Yes.'

Did he have a death wish? When she'd seen him last, his eyes had been swollen shut. 'Don't move. And speak Italian.'

Taking off the deerskin coat, which hampered her, she climbed. Shining the lantern ahead of her, she finally made out a head and shoulders outlined against the sky. He'd reached the topmost step and was sitting just below the *vedetta*'s summit. If he stood, his head would poke out over the top. 'You thought this was a good idea, climbing while unable to see?'

'I don't remember—'

'Italian! Speak Italian!'

He swallowed. '*Mi dispiace*.' Sorry. 'I don't remember how I got up here, but I can open my eyes wider today.'

'*Dio*, if you'd lost your balance!' Had he considered the consequences to her if he'd fallen? Probably not. His Italian was well articulated, but his voice sounded weak. Still drugged, perhaps. 'I really hope you didn't put your head over the parapet.'

'I wanted to. It's why I'm here, isn't it? Intelligence gathering? How high is this tower?'

She told him that it was just under sixteen metres. 'High enough to kill you if you fell.'

'Mio. Have you seen Mio?'

He was rambling, she decided. 'I don't know who you mean.'

'Mio. My wireless operator… did I come here alone?'

She confirmed it. 'You were brought by my—' She caught her mistake in time. 'By friends. Just you and your kitbag. You're lying low and they're coming back for you tonight.'

'I can't hide here!' He sounded wild all of a sudden. 'Mio's dead and I have to resend the message. We were too slow. They have to know about the gun positions.'

Who were 'they'? she wondered. His next words confirmed her worst fear. This man was no simple soldier.

He buried his head in his hands, groaning as though a harsh memory had sliced through the fog in his head. 'Nico turned. He led the Germans straight to us. I have to find another wireless operator. Do you understand?'

She didn't want to understand, and said sharply, 'You won't find an operator here.' She was desperate to shut him up. Dreading what he might do next, she reached out and laid a hand on his knee. 'Please be calm.'

'Where am I? Where is this godawful place?'

'Your substitute safe house,' she said, a little resentfully. The *vedetta* was hardly the Ritz but he might show some appreciation of the risk she was taking. 'The first choice was unsuitable and I wasn't given much option but to take you in.'

'I see.' He seemed to consider what she'd said and repeated, 'I'm sorry.'

'Oh, and the van that brought you was heard in the village. People are talking about it, so you need to go, pronto.'

He swore and the tower amplified his disgust.

'Yes, I agree,' she responded. 'This situation is less than wonderful. For both of us.' Remembering he was injured and in pain, she softened her tone. 'Was it the Germans who beat you so badly?'

He blinked dark-brown eyes, as if remembering took effort. 'It happened very fast. A car going past was the first… then Nico… then boots up the stairs. Abwehr officers, Nazi intelligence with military backup. I knew they'd want to take me alive, so I played dead.'

'How did Mio die and what about Nico who you say betrayed you?'

He shook his head and Carmela guessed he wasn't ready to share details.

'You jumped from a balcony,' she finished for him.

'I didn't jump. I rolled over the edge and dropped. I landed badly. I heard ligaments tear, the sound you get when you rip a canvas sheet.'

She winced.

'The fox will rip off its own leg to escape the trap. I knew where to go but I don't remember…' He stopped and looked at his hands, burned and lacerated, and she pictured him biting down on pain, staggering like a blood-spattered drunkard through alleyways on his way to find sanctuary. His teeth were chattering as he mumbled, 'My wireless operator, dear God. Mio, dear God. We didn't finish sending the message. SOE won't know.'

'Let's get you onto solid ground and give you some water.' That might put a stop to his rambling. 'I'm going to guide you down, so take my hand.' Their fingers met and she almost pulled back. His willingness to trust her launched a memory so piercing her eyes pricked. This wouldn't do. The last thing she could cope with was a needy stranger prising open a Pandora's box of sorrows. 'I'll reverse, and we'll go slowly,' she said curtly. 'If you feel dizzy, just sit down.'

They made it to the ground and she got her first impression of her guest standing on his feet. He was well made and tall, though not so much so that he'd stand out in Naples. There, any man over six foot was generally assumed to be German. Yes, she thought, he would pass in a crowd. So long as he remembered to speak Italian, of course.

'This bit of me really hurts.' He touched a lurid swelling above his cheekbone.

'It's very colourful,' she agreed, 'but it's gone down since yesterday.'

'Someone bathed my face with cold water. It was you?'

'Yes.'

'Did I thank you?'

'As best you could.' She discovered that his irises were actually deep black, as were his lashes. Was she harbouring an Italian who spoke English perfectly, or an Englishman who was fluent in Italian? He'd mentioned 'SOE'. Whatever that was, it was clearly vitally important to him. So important, messages were sent by a wireless operator. Who was now dead. The fact that he'd survived a Nazi assault proved he was part of something dangerous and clandestine. A wanted man, and she his only protector until Danielo returned, heaven help her.

As if he read her thoughts, Sebastiano suddenly sat down on the steps, shivering visibly. 'Sorry,' he muttered. 'I overdid it.'

'That's an understatement. How about some food?'

'Not sure.' He wrapped his arms around his body to quell the shaking.

'All right. Some water first?'

That he accepted, and after he had drunk the contents of the can, he wiped his mouth and said, 'That feels better. I could be dehydrated. It affects the mind.' Falling silent again, he took several slow, deep breaths and it seemed to Carmela that he was battling with himself. Driving weakness back inside. A visible change came over him, his shoulders opening out and squaring. When he looked at her again, it was with a mixture of ruefulness and steely purpose. 'What did I tell you a moment ago?'

'You described your escape, and someone called Mio dying. That really happened?'

'Yes. Mio's dead. We burned the codes in time, but the bastards have the wireless.'

The bastards were the Nazis, she presumed. 'You told me you hadn't finished sending a message… about gun positions to SOE. Who is that?'

'I shouldn't have said any of it. Forget everything you heard.'

'Are you a spy?' She'd blurted out the question before she'd considered if she really wanted to know.

'What I am,' he said after a pause, 'is desperate for coffee.'

'I can fetch coffee,' she said, glad to be able to offer something so simple. She took out the tomatoes. 'Just picked,' she said. 'And this cheese is our own. Shall I screw the legs in?'

He looked completely baffled.

'The boys forgot to put the legs on your camp bed. Shall I fix them in?'

'Don't worry. With the straw underneath, this pallet is quite comfortable. Real coffee or ersatz?'

'It's roast barley, but it's all right. Hot and bitter, at any rate. I'll go and make it now.'

'Wait.' He kept her back with a staying gesture. 'Pass me a blanket. I'm cold to my bones.'

She did so, but as she went to the tower door, she was conscious of the chill underfoot. Sebastiano would suffer if there were clear skies tonight and the temperature dropped, as it could at this time of year. He'd recovered his faculties, thank goodness, but he was far from well. Probably still in shock from his injuries and needing compassion as well as shelter. With no idea what time Danielo would arrive, Carmela made a dangerous decision.

'Sebastiano, take my hand and start thinking up a good story. I'm going to introduce you to my grandmother.'

Chapter Five

Rosaria was at the stove, stirring a pan of bubbling tomato sauce. Grated pecorino campano cheese was ready on the table. Steamy basil and garlic scents filled the kitchen.

'Go and change,' she ordered Carmela without looking round. 'Get into a skirt, put on stockings.'

'I'm already wearing a dress.' Carmela cleared her throat. 'Nonna, I want to introduce you to somebody.'

Rosaria put down her spoon and turned. Her jaw fell. 'Who have we here?'

'His name is Mario.' Carmela had chosen to bestow her grandfather's name on Sebastiano in the hope it would soften Nonna's reaction. She had worked out a story as she helped Sebastiano limp to the farmhouse. A story inspired by the darned mariner's sweater he wore. 'He's a deserter from the Regia Marina,' she said. Placing him in the Italian navy ought to give him status in Nonna's eyes. 'He jumped ship at Naples and is trying to get home to Battipaglia, but that would take him into the battle zone. I found him wandering among the thorns.' Ascribing Sebastiano's multiple injuries to a tangle with a shrub was pushing things, but Carmela had a second story lined up. 'Mario' had run into a police roadblock on the road out of Naples and had taken a bad beating before escaping.

'He can't stay.' There was panic in Rosaria's voice.

'Just one night, Nonna. I thought he might sleep in the parlour. We could light the fire.'

'He has to go.' Rosaria shot a harrowed glance towards the door. 'Your cousin Tino is coming.'

'Tonight? You invited *him*?'

'Of course not. He sent a boy with a message, saying he'd been given a whole smoked sausage and wanted to share it with us.'

Carmela made a sound of disgust. 'He stole it, or his brother did. I won't eat it.'

'Then don't eat it, but he's coming. And you mustn't provoke him, Meluccia.'

'Smile and simper?'

'I'm not asking you to dance the seven veils, just be polite. Remember, he came out of his way to bring back your dog collar.'

But he hadn't brought the dog. 'I don't like the way he looks at me.'

'And I don't like the way he stares around my kitchen, measuring my shelves for his pots and pans. But unless you have a better idea?'

'What time's he coming?'

'When he's done working.'

'Around seven, then. What time is it now?'

Sebastiano, who was leaning against the table and listening, tilted his wrist and presented his watch for Carmela to read. Its scuffed steel rim and scratched face bore witness to his fight for survival. She'd fix the strap if there was time; she had strong thread and a leather needle she used for repairing harnesses.

Sebastiano had turned his injured ankle during the walk from the tower, and his cheeks once again had the pallor of pain. She had to hold his wrist steady to read the time. 'It's a minute to the hour.' Carmela went still. 'Was that a gate closing?'

Sebastiano's gaze flicked around the kitchen. Searching for exits, presumably. 'Who is Tino?'

'My second cousin and my favourite *squadrista*.' She laid the irony on thick, and pointed towards a door on the other side of the kitchen. 'Get upstairs.'

'Our bedroom? It's not decent,' Rosaria protested but Sebastiano was already moving. A moment later, his boots were clumping up the uncarpeted stairs.

'Will he have the sense to stay quiet?' Rosaria hissed furiously. 'Because I doubt Tino loves deserters any more than his pig of a brother.'

Carmela hadn't time to answer. She had brought the cheese and tomatoes back from the tower and raced around, piling food on a tray as her grandmother looked on.

The old lady tutted. 'That bread is yesterday's, stale as a brick.'

'It'll give Mario something to do, getting his teeth through it.'

'Mario really is his name?'

'Half the men in Campania are called Mario, aren't they?'

'Battipaglia is in the mountains. Are you telling me that town sends sailors to the navy?'

'Perhaps that's why he deserted. A mountain lad, he got seasick.' No time to make the promised coffee, Carmela poured red wine from a carafe into an earthenware mug. She was halfway up the stairs when she heard Tino's confident knock.

She found Sebastiano sitting on the end of her bed. 'You don't have to perch,' she whispered. 'Get in but don't snore.' Putting the tray down, she offered to take off his boots. 'In case you sleepwalk. We hear every footfall downstairs.'

'He's a Blackshirt, this cousin Tino?'

'Oh, it's worse than that. He leads the pack. "Capo Cortazzi". So, stay quiet. Just a few hours, and my bro— *the boys…* will come to take you to safety.' She pulled back the bedcovers, blushing as it revealed a neatly folded nightdress. Nonna had made the beds during the day. 'Eat and rest. I'll come when it's safe.'

As she passed a mirror, it occurred to her that she was still in her work clothes. They needed to keep Tino happy and entertained. Her grandmother was right: she should change. Discarding her headscarf, she gave her hair twenty or so crackling brush strokes and swapped her boots for shoes with a heel. Her reflection showed large eyes and a tense mouth. Finding a stub of lipstick in a drawer of the dresser, she gave her lips a lick of coral.

'Don't make yourself too lovely, Signorina. You want to get rid of Tino, not fix him here for the night.'

She cast the man on her bed a sour glance. 'You're in no condition to make sarcastic remarks on other people's looks.' She left, firmly closing the bedroom door behind her.

The smoked sausage lay on a board – a fat, wrinkled obscenity. Tino presented her with sunflowers. 'From my neighbour's garden, to cheer you up as I believe you've still not found your dog.'

'I get no chance to search for him,' she said, filling a flower vase with water. 'It's heartbreaking.'

'I can look for him if you're too busy. Ask me.'

She looked askance, then nodded. 'Very well, but you're busy too.'

'I will get up an hour earlier.'

She thanked him gruffly, and her grandmother, who was giving the tomato sauce a last stir, sent her an undetectable nod.

Tino sniffed the air. 'Your own pasta tonight? Mm, I miss my mamma's cooking since I lost her. There never was a Cortazzi wife who could not cook, ah, Zia Rosaria?'

Don't look at me, Carmela wanted to say. Her cookery skills encompassed shepherd's pie, rice pudding and cheese flan. She had learned domestic arts in a different world to this. French, German and of course fluent English and Italian were her principal accomplishments, to which she could now add orchard and herd management.

When the meal was ready, she observed the etiquette. Only when Tino's plate was loaded did she serve her grandmother and, finally, herself. It was a simple meal: fresh egg pasta slathered in piquant sauce, mopped up with bread. Nobody starved here in the countryside as they did in Naples. Nonna had sliced some of the sausage and they ate it with *sottaceti*, garden vegetables pickled in vinegar. There was red wine from a local vineyard, which was strong on the palate. When not fetching salad, slicing more bread, dishing up seconds, Carmela listened to Tino talking. He firmly believed the Americans and British would be run back into the sea.

'The guns in the hills are burning red-hot. If the enemy get past those, they will meet the tanks. Show them a disciplined panzer division, they fall apart. Course they do! German Tiger tanks are monsters.' He threw out his arms to illustrate. 'Imagine, you cross the sea expecting an easy victory only to have guns flaying you as you come ashore. You push up mountain roads, and they are still firing on you. You file into a mountain pass, and tanks scream towards you and there is no escape.' Tino waved a loaded fork and tomato ragu flew onto the cloth. 'They should throw down their arms.'

'As our troops did?' Carmela suggested.

'We would never have surrendered had Il Duce not been betrayed.'

'I don't blame men for turning tail.' Ever since the invasion had begun, Carmela had wondered how she would acquit herself if faced with fire and carnage. Grit her teeth and plough on, or drop onto her face and scream? 'Why should any man, or woman, go to certain death because they're told to?'

Rosaria banged the end of her fork on the table. '*Basta, basta.*' That's enough. Because she'd broken her promise to guard her tongue, Carmela apologised. She managed an ingratiating smile for her cousin. 'You know a great deal about war, Tino. Where do you get your information?'

He looked pleased. 'From German high command in Naples. The Germans see me as their enforcer in these hinterlands, their eyes and ears.' Tino held out his glass for a refill of wine. 'From the Spinosa estate?' He rolled the liquid around his mouth, swallowed and gave a contented sigh. 'Not a bad year, last year. Not the best but drinkable.' He picked up his thread. 'The Germans appreciate my local knowledge. They look to us to root out partisans, and any fugitives hiding in these hills.'

With impeccable timing, a floorboard creaked loudly above their heads. Abruptly, Rosaria said, 'Do you remember the song your grandfather used to sing, Meluccia, the one that he used to make you go to sleep? How did it go? "There's a girl in a valley, in a valley…"' Rosaria sang in a quavering voice as Carmela gathered up their plates, clashing cutlery. Tino seemed not to have heard the creak but his next question threw her.

'Your *fratellastro* never calls on you here, I believe?'

'Danielo?' She stared at Tino, suspecting a trap, then at her grandmother who was rolling her napkin between her fingers. Clearing her throat, she said, 'I don't have to explain why my half-brother keeps his distance.'

Tino supplied the answer. 'Because his mother was the whore that stepped between *your* mother and her husband.'

She couldn't hold back a gasp of shock at his language and might have hurled the dirty plate in her hand at him had Nonna not shaken her head warningly, and said, 'Why do you ask such questions, Tino?'

'Curiosity. He never comes, yet in the early hours of yesterday, Danielo Vincenzo was stopped at a police checkpoint not five kilometres from here. He was a passenger in a van travelling back towards Naples, transporting illegal goods.'

Carmela took a sip of wine to alleviate the sudden dryness of her mouth. 'Every truck stopped at night probably has something questionable on board, if only illegally bought fuel.'

'Ha, that's for sure. There is such a shortage, the Germans get their supplies through Switzerland, which is supposed to be a neutral country. Nobody can get enough. But Carmela, we are cousins and good friends, no?'

'We are cousins,' she agreed, knowing a trap still lay in front of her. 'Was it the carabinieri who stopped the van?'

'Yes, and I have friends among them who keep me informed. I should warn you, your half-brother was found to be in possession of…' Tino paused, tantalisingly. Her heart had apparently stopped beating, the moment stretching on and on.

Not guns, please not guns. Not another fugitive either.

'Tins of pork and beans.'

It was all she could do to hide her relief. 'That's all?'

'With German labels. The driver tried to gun the engine and burst through the checkpoint, but a shot into the cab brought him to a halt. He and your half-brother jumped out, with some little *scugnizzo* who was with them. The driver and the lad got away but your brother was caught. He spent the night in a cell, and will probably be sent to the youth jail. Lucky he's only seventeen, or he'd be charged as an adult.'

She nodded. Danielo was seventeen for another month, thankfully.

'He's lucky I didn't catch him,' Tino said. 'Food smuggling is a serious crime.'

It took a lot for Carmela not to look at the sausage sitting on the board. Rosaria flung her napkin down. 'Time for the cheese and coffee, something to warm you on your way home, Tino.'

'I'll do it.' Carmela sprang to her feet, glad to be away from Tino's gaze.

She felt sick. She had slowed Danielo down last night, forcing him and Gio to travel as dawn rose. She'd never forgive herself if harm came to either of them. God help her – what if her brother talked? An armed squad might be on its way. What if her brother's arrest meant Sebastiano could not be collected tonight, as promised?

Turning to the window, she guessed the time by the moonlight seeping through the slatted shutters. It must be gone nine. She had to alert Sebastiano to this turn of events. If only Tino would disappear. Carmela arranged cow's and goat's cheese on a board with a few of their own apples, which kept rolling off the end. She had to cut them in half to make them stay still. Stepping from foot to foot, she began the long-winded business of brewing coffee. When she finally returned to her seat with a pot of *caffè d'orzo*, roast barley coffee, Tino met her with a grin that made her want to scream.

'I wouldn't say no to a nip of grappa.'

'Really? It's quite late.'

'It'll warm my stomach on the way home.'

Tino knocked back two glasses of the colourless brandy in fast order, then sipped at a third. Drunk neat, it was potent. When Carmela briefly opened the door to glance out at the night sky, the moon was high over the horizon. The floor joists above the table gave a series of cracks. 'Brr. It's getting cold out there,' she said as she shut the door hard. She could hear her voice splitting hysterically. 'When the temperature drops, all the beams in the house shrink. *Crick-crack*. It used to scare me when I was little.'

Her grandmother glanced around in apprehension. Tino, following the turn of her head, asked, 'Is that Mario's?'

'Mario?' Rosaria shot a petrified look at Carmela. 'You know about Mario?'

Carmela felt the blood seep from her cheeks. Borrowing her grandfather's name now felt utterly insane.

Tino shook his head. 'Zia Rosaria, your mind is slipping. Of course I remember my uncle Mario. That's his mandolin on top of the cupboard.' He pointed to where the old instrument lay wrapped in a strip of blanket. 'He and my father used to strum together. I loved to listen to them; their voices were like velvet.' He pulled a face. 'Why is the mandolin not in its case?'

Rosaria stared at Carmela for an answer. Another crack sounded above their heads.

'It got damp and we found weevils inside, so we burned it.' Carmela fetched the mandolin down. She and her nonna knew perfectly well where the case really was, but they hadn't spoken of it since the day they'd last seen it more than four years ago.

Handing the instrument to Tino, she invited him to give them a song. 'Before you go. Sing "Santa Lucia" for Nonna while I start the dishes.' If Tino got it into his head to investigate the source of the creaking, Sebastiano was done for. The upstairs windows were shuttered to keep out flies and the late summer heat. There was no glass to break, but they were narrow, designed to be defendable in the days when the farm had been fortified against raiders. Sebastiano would have a job squeezing through, even if he could survive a second jump.

Fortunately, Tino needed no coaxing to perform. He sang the famous Neapolitan ballad lustily, and then began a succession of love songs. In between, he tipped the grappa bottle. As Carmela moved between the table and the sink, the crockery cupboard and the larder, Tino's gaze followed her. Alcohol acted differently on different men, she reminded herself. Some became dreamy-eyed, others revealed darker emotions. Tino's stare felt like that of a tomcat who knows there's one last mouse in the barn. When he chucked a question at her between songs, she jumped.

'I said – why do you care so much about your skinny half-brother? He replaced you in your father's affections.'

She gave a shrug, intending to brush off the comment before deciding that the truth would give Tino something else to think about. 'I didn't always love Danielo. As a child, I was bitterly jealous of this new baby because I could see that my father was entranced by him. He was angelic, as well as being a boy. After Mamma became ill, I was lonely in that great palazzo. Danielo's mother—'

'Your father's whore.'

She ignored the blatant obscenity. 'His mother would bring Danielo to visit and while she and Papà talked, I was allowed to hold him. He would stare up at me with green, unblinking eyes. I too was entranced and you know what? His first ever smile was for me. From that moment, I loved him.'

'Your father wishes he was legitimate. He'd prefer a male heir.'

Probably. Almost certainly. Carmela waited for her grandmother to angrily change the subject, or bang the table with a spoon. But Nonna looked shattered, as if she hadn't slept for a week.

'Your mother died from neglect,' Tino said confidently. 'That's what people say.'

'Well, they should shut up!' Carmela had finally had as much as she could take. Her mother had died in the typhus epidemic which had swept through Naples in the summer of 1926, but what Tino said carried some truth. Betrayed by her husband, Nina del Bosco had sunk into melancholy. Her spirits so oppressed, she had all but opened her arms to the fever. Carmela remembered lying beside her mamma on her bed and hearing Nina whisper, '*Santo Dio*, let this be it.'

Tino hadn't finished with her. 'Why does he have green eyes?'

'My father, or Danielo?' Tino must be jealous, she realised, asking so many questions and gnawing away at the subject.

'Both.'

Sighing, Carmela chose to humour him. If it kept his mind on her, and not on the noises upstairs, it was worth a little effort on her part. 'We have to go back a thousand years when a Norman knight called Hugh de Boscoët came to this part of Italy with a mercenary army. He liked Naples and stayed. Papà traces his line back to Hugh, and claims his colouring comes from Norman blood.'

'So he is foreign, then?'

'He is as Italian as you are, cousin.'

'But he likes the English, no? He sent you there, after all.'

'He sent me away to get the kind of education girls cannot get in Italy.' Following her mother's death, an English friend had recommended a complete change of scene: an excellent girls' school in Cambridge. The friend had paid her fees, assuring her father that while it might be an ordeal for a young girl to travel so far alone, once she was settled it would prove a remarkable opportunity. And so it had. In Italy, girls rarely had the chance to study the so-called masculine subjects like mathematics or science. It was all sewing, cooking and child-rearing. In her new school overlooking the River Cam, no intellectual pursuits had been off limits, and in time she had found her stride and learned to be happy again.

'He sent you there to make you one of them,' Tino slurred. 'Where, like all English women, you learned to be cold as the tits on a marble Madonna.'

'That is enough.' Rosaria too had reached her limit. 'Tino, go home.'

'You're right,' he said. 'Thank you for a fine dinner, Zia Rosaria.' He got to his feet, bowing unsteadily. He leered at Carmela. 'I cannot help thinking of the time I won't have to walk home, cousin. Oh, and watch out for desperate fugitives, ha?'

She saw him to the door, wondering if he meant to frighten her and Nonna, or if he had somebody particular in mind.

Chapter Six

Once she was certain Tino was truly gone, Carmela hurried upstairs. Sebastiano was soundly asleep, her bedspread pulled up over him. She picked up the empty crocks from the floor by the bed and went back down.

'Nonna, why don't I bring a mattress and blankets down for you and put them in the parlour?' Her grandmother would never consent to share a bedroom with a stranger, even a comatose one.

'You're not going to bed down beside him, I hope?'

'Certainly not.' Carmela intended to stay up and keep watch. She was still hoping Gio would relieve her of the responsibility of Sebastiano since it seemed that her brother was locked up. Though how would Gio get here? She doubted the police would have returned his van.

She wrapped the mandolin in its blanket and put it back on top of the cupboard. Her grandmother watched, kneading her temples.

'Are we being punished for a sin?' Rosaria asked.

'We aren't sinners, Nonna, unless love is a sin.'

'I have such regrets, about what I made you do. Your baby—'

'Don't. Please. There are some things I can't let back in, not if I'm to stay strong. I'll get your mattress down.'

Once her grandmother was settled, Carmela drank the last of the coffee and went outside to make a final check on her animals. She lit a lantern, though the moon, which was four days away from full brightness, made it unnecessary. Far to the south, the air throbbed like a broken tooth. How long would the battle last? The shelling, the bombing. The war. At times it felt like an eternal bad dream. The farmyard was quiet, thankfully. Swinging the lantern, she walked the short distance to the chicken coops and found the hens huddled in their nesting boxes rather than on their perches. There'd be few eggs again in the morning, she judged. Heading back to the farmhouse, a figure blocked her path. Oh please, not Tino. The relief when her light picked out Sebastiano's taller shape was enough to make her raise her face to the sky. *Dio*, her heart would give out if this went on.

He spoke first. 'Take me back to my hideout. I should never have come to the house. I put you in danger.'

'Because you got out of bed and made the boards creak,' she hissed, furious because her nerves were shredded and life was drifting out of control.

'I didn't – I leaned down to hear what that fellow was saying about the Germans making him their "eyes and ears". Who's he kidding? No self-respecting German trusts an Italian further than he can chuck him, since the surrender.'

'You got out of bed. So I don't trust you.'

'Unfair. My leaning over pressed a squeak out of the floor. I didn't move a muscle after that, but that didn't stop your house groaning like an old battleship in a storm. Any news about my transport out of here?'

'Come into the farmyard. Nobody can see us there.' She put the lantern down and tugged his arm. When they were standing in a shadowy corner, she passed on the news Tino had so gloatingly reported. 'Stopped at a checkpoint, one of them arrested but the driver got away, along with the little boy.'

Sebastiano absorbed this information. 'I'm guessing the driver's the older one, Gio. He's a good lad.'

'So is my brother Danielo!' Anxiety and resentment made her incautious.

'Danielo is your brother?'

'Half-brother. You weren't supposed to know.'

'No. What else do you want to tell me?'

Nothing, except Danielo had been accused of food theft, which everyone was guilty of, one way or another. 'He should be let off with a fine.'

'Let's hope so. You say the police shot out the van's window? Sounds like my taxi ride out of here is cancelled. I'll leave on foot at first light. I'd go now but I'd probably end up walking round in circles.'

'Back to Naples? Is it safe for you?'

'With your brother in police custody, the safest place for me – and you – is anywhere that isn't here.'

'What about your ankle? You could hardly walk earlier.'

He gave a sigh. 'Fear of capture is the best painkiller. Signorina, why are you trying to hold on to me?'

She realised only then that she was still gripping his arm. She let go abruptly. 'Make no mistake, I want you gone.'

'Glad to hear it. You need to clear everything out of that tower. Burn all the straw and get rid of that camp bed. And while you're doing it, forget everything I told you. I'll go back to the tower and sit out the night. If anybody comes, I'll say I found my own way in. Go to bed and dream like the innocent woman you are.'

It was a gallant offer, but an impractical one as he needed her to guide him up to the ridge. He was limping badly again by the time they reached the *vedetta*. She had wrapped the lamp in a scrap of sacking to smother its beam; once inside, she used its light to climb the steps and fetch down his kitbag.

When she set the bag down at his feet, Sebastiano pushed a hand inside, checking the contents. 'No gun,' he muttered. 'I must have dropped it in the room. Damn. It was a German Luger that Gio purloined for me – I hope to God the bastards can't trace it back to him.'

'Trace it back – how?' Her fears were all too ready to latch on to a comment like that. 'You're saying the Germans could identify Gio and Danielo, from a gun?'

'Possibly, if they discover who owned it last.' Sebastiano groaned. 'I wish I could piece together what happened after I hit the ground. It would help me plan where to go next.'

She said, 'Perhaps it's a mercy that day is lost in the fog. Some memories are too painful to recall.' The fate of Mio, for instance and whether or not the treacherous Nico was still at large. 'I'll pack some food for you.'

'Mm. Tell me again – Danielo was arrested but Gio got away. In the van?'

'Gio escaped into the darkness with the little lad, so my cousin Tino told me.'

'So the vehicle has almost certainly been seized.' The burst of energy that had got Sebastiano to the *vedetta* vanished, and he sank down on the steps exactly as he'd done a few hours ago. He wouldn't make it to Naples, she realised. Though it was less than ten kilometres, the roads were rough and steep.

'I'm going to take you,' she said, deciding in that instant. 'I'll harness the donkey, and you can ride in the cart.'

He looked up at her, his eyes welling with surprise, then shook his head. 'It's asking too much. Let me rest, and I'll leave at dawn.'

'I'm not offering out of charity, but because otherwise you'll be found collapsed somewhere between here and the city.' By cart, it would be a five-hour round trip and she had the cows to milk at first light. They needed to get on their way.

'I still can't accept,' he said. 'I'd like to but it's not fair.'

She could see he was weakening. 'How about I make you that coffee you were desperate for earlier, and then we'll decide?'

He nodded. It wasn't an agreement, but it was a concession.

She returned to the house and cobbled together a meal of sausage, bread and sweet apples that he could take on his journey, whatever form that took, and brewed fresh coffee, which she poured into a can. Winding her way back to the *vedetta* some forty minutes later, she had a sense that the thorn branches, usually so intent to scratch her, had been bent back. One was snapped right off. Perhaps Sebastiano had taken it into his head to scout out the path up to the ridge. Clearly he hadn't gone anywhere, as she heard a cough from within the tower.

She risked a greeting in English. 'Here you are, sir, as ordered. The best coffee in the house. I even mixed in some cream— *O, santo Dio!*'

Sebastiano was sprawled across the camp bed, his hand clutching his face. Blood streamed through his fingers. Had he climbed again, and fallen? She glanced upwards and everything ground to a halt. A few stairs up, illuminated by her flickering lantern, sat a bulky figure, a Blackshirt-issue cosh across his knee. Her cousin Tino.

Chapter Seven

Tino cast the lantern beam at her. 'I knew somebody was upstairs while we ate. Was Zia Rosaria in on it? Did my sainted old aunt lie to me?'

'She knew nothing.'

Sebastiano got himself to a sitting position. Carmela suspected the cosh had been swung across the bridge of his nose, and the thought of fresh pain inflicted on him sent a violent rage through her. 'This man is a navy deserter,' she improvised, 'a distant relation of mine. Mine, not Nonna's. On my father's side,' she emphasised. Her brain was churning. 'His mother was a Del Bosco. It's why I'm hiding him, why I couldn't tell you.'

Tino constructed a smile from blatant contempt. 'Regia Marina? Let him prove it. Show me your identity card, deserter.'

To Carmela's surprise, Sebastiano fumbled in a pocket and tossed a folded card to Tino, who caught it and shone his torch on it. 'Alonso, Sebastiano,' Tino read laboriously. 'Born 8 May 1913, in…' He peered closer. 'It's blurred, I can't read it.'

'North Africa,' Sebastiano filled in. 'In Cyrenaica.'

'You're a colonial?' Tino grunted. 'This isn't a military identity card.'

'No. We all threw those ones away,' Sebastiano muttered.

'"Distinguishing marks, mermaid tattoo left forearm". Show me.'

Sebastiano hesitated. Carmela waited for his story to collapse.

'Show me.' Tino leaned forward, his tongue making an eager point between his lips.

'I'll need help.' Sebastiano held out his arm and Carmela rolled up the jumper sleeve and the shirtsleeve beneath. It gave Sebastiano the chance to tell her, in the softest whisper, 'Whatever happens next, keep back or run.' He extended his bare arm and Tino's torch picked out the image of a voluptuous blonde mermaid with a sea-green tail.

'I had it done in Benghazi, in a kiosk by the port.'

'In a brothel, more like.' Tino laughed scornfully. 'Well, sailor, there'll be a reward when I hand you in.'

'No there won't,' Sebastiano contradicted. 'The Germans are disarming Italian servicemen. Leaving a ship that docked for reprovisioning isn't a crime. We surrendered, remember? The Italian navy is now a neutral force.'

Tino's expression turned nasty at the word 'surrender'. 'Then why are you hiding?'

'He isn't,' Carmela put in. 'He got hurt and he's recovering. Look at his face – and you haven't helped.'

The light in Tino's hand played over Sebastiano's battered features. 'If he's your relation, what's he doing in this pigsty?'

'Nonna won't let any kin of my father's over the threshold. You know that.'

'But he was in the house. In your bedroom.'

'Because I spirited him up the stairs, without Nonna seeing. I felt sorry for him.'

Tino regarded her, his expression flat. 'There's only one bedroom in the farmhouse. How were you going to hide him from Zia Rosaria all night?'

'I – I don't know. I suppose I hoped Nonna's heart would soften, when she saw him, and let him sleep downstairs.'

Tino snorted. 'Let's see if my heart softens.' He treated Sebastiano to an intense stare. 'No. My heart appears to be as hard as…' He gave it a moment's thought. 'As a mandolin case.'

The fight seemed go out of Sebastiano. Carmela wasn't surprised. Even to herself, her story had sounded like the next best thing to drivel. How long would it take Tino to make a link between a vehicle outside the village at dead of night, Danielo's subsequent arrest and this man?

It looked to be all over when Tino said, 'This is no Del Bosco kinsman. He's too dark.' He sounded like a man bashing a hammer long after the nail was driven home. 'Tell me why you are protecting him, Meluccia.'

'He is my cousin,' Carmela replied doggedly.

'Not your lover?'

'Certainly not.'

Tino sneered. 'He can start being friendly to me then, can't he? And begin by handing over his watch.'

'You wouldn't get it round your wrist. Anyway, the strap's broken.'

'I don't need to wear it; I can sell it *like that*.' Tino clicked his fingers, then came down from the steps, ordering Sebastiano to hold out his left hand.

Carmela got between them. 'Have you no shame? You're a bully, Tino Cortazzi. You're disgusting.'

'You find me disgusting?' Tino's gaze fastened on her breasts, searching for their outline under her dress. He gripped his crotch and made a suggestive jerk of the hips. When she looked away, he chuckled. 'You know what you need?'

She refused to answer, though she knew well enough what he was implying. Tino grunted.

'Get out. Leave.'

'I'm not leaving you alone with my kinsman.'

In reply, Tino flicked her face with his thumb and first finger. The gesture was almost playful, except it landed beneath her eye like a wasp sting. 'Go back to the house like a good girl and wait for me there.' When she still didn't move, he hustled her outside, shoving her into the thorn thicket. At her cry of pain, he laughed and pulled a hunting knife from his belt, holding the blade up to the moonlight. 'You need to learn to do as you're told.' A moment later, he was back inside the tower and she heard him badgering Sebastiano to give up his watch.

Carmela caught Sebastiano's reply. '*Va' a puttane!* Go to the whores.

A cry like that of an animal with its leg caught in a trap made her run back inside. The lantern lay in the straw, in danger of setting it alight. She put it in a safe place. Tino was kneeling on Sebastiano's chest, and Sebastiano held Tino's wrist in a fierce clamp. Carmela heard the crack of joints and sinews.

'Both of you, stop!'

Sebastiano's grip seemed to wobble. He was losing strength. The knife was against his throat.

Carmela looked around. What could she use against Tino? The lantern might spew burning oil on both men. The can full of coffee, hot liquid in Tino's face? Would it just antagonise him? In the end, she grabbed his sleeve, unbalancing him. At the same moment Sebastiano struck an upward thrust with a weapon Carmela had not seen him pick up. Screaming in agony, Tino toppled sideways, clutching at his cheek.

Sebastiano flopped back, exhausted. Carmela took the weapon from his limp grasp, then dropped it in disgust. It was one of the camp bed legs Danielo had left behind.

'I thought you'd given up,' she said breathlessly. 'You've really hurt him.'

'Thanks to you, I only got his cheek. I missed his eye socket.'

'That would have killed him.'

'That is rather the point. Get his knife, let me finish him off.'

She picked up the knife Tino had dropped and flung it out through the doorway, then retrieved the lantern. Nobody would be finishing anybody off. Tino lay on his side, still clutching his face. She had to stem the blood before he lost consciousness. Heaven knew what infection the rusty spike would put in his system. And she had to persuade him to stay quiet about this, though that was a vain hope. Nothing for it, she took off her stockings to sop up the blood. 'I'll help you home,' she told Tino. The path along the ridge was a shortcut to the village. Getting Tino away would give Sebastiano a chance to escape. Though whether he could get more than a few steps in his condition… *Caro Dio*, how had a simple choice, to take a stranger in for a night, become this hell-ride on a bolting horse?

She managed to get Tino first to his knees, then to his feet. The walk to his home was slow and exhausting, Tino stumbling and whimpering when he wasn't snarling threats of vengeance. They made it unseen into the village's main street and to his house, which was unlocked, as she'd known it would be. The most feared man in the village had no need to bolt his door.

After helping him to a kitchen chair, she set about bathing the wound to his face. It was a deep, messy puncture.

'Pour me a grappa.' He told her where to find it, and took the glass from her ungraciously. 'If you hadn't pulled my sleeve, I'd have got the bastard. I need the doctor. Fetch Baccolini.'

She hesitated. Rousing Dr Baccolini at this hour risked exposing her to gossip. Not from him as he was a friend of hers, but from neighbours. She and Emilio Baccolini had played together as children on her visits to la Casale, but now they were both grown up and single, they had to behave cautiously around each other. Indeed, his mother had always regarded her with suspicion. To Signora Baccolini, Carmela was the daughter of a woman who had been with child on her wedding day, and therefore a danger to her son. But on reflection, she had no choice, she decided. People died from lesser wounds than Tino's.

'While you're there,' Tino muttered, 'have him telephone the carabinieri, to come here with handcuffs and a hood to blindfold that scum. If the man in your *vedetta* is more than a common deserter, interrogation will get at the truth.'

'He *is* a deserter, from the navy. Why do you insist on disbelieving me?'

'Then why did you come into the tower talking English? Don't deny it. I know the language. When I was young, I worked at the Villa Bianca.' Tino was referring to Santa Maria della Vedetta's former hotel, which, before the war, had been popular with foreign tourists.

'Tino, please,' she begged, 'if you make this a police matter, it won't just be Sebastiano Alonso you destroy, but me and Nonna too.'

He regarded her through pain-burned eyes and bit his lip, considering. 'What's my silence worth, Meluccia?'

She shook her head. 'I don't know.'

'You know.'

Yes, she knew. Even in extreme pain and humiliated, his thoughts were sinking to his belt buckle. His pupils dilated as he stroked his thigh and his voice thickened.

'Tell me what I want, Meluccia.'

'Me. My body.'

'You wrong me. I want more than that.'

He was saying that he wanted to marry her? He'd hinted at it time enough.

Tino touched his wounded cheek and gazed at the blood on his fingers. 'My brother says I can do better. Santo says your time in England makes you suspect, and it's true. Your father's shameful conduct, defending a Jew, makes you doubly suspect. And your mother's history does you no favours.'

'Don't speak of my mamma.'

'She was your father's mistress and he only agreed to marry her when she was having his child because your grandfather went to Naples and pleaded with him. You know what they say – like mother, like daughter.'

'So how can you want to marry me?'

'I need a woman in my bed, and underneath that cold shell you have a beating heart. What's more, if I get you, I get the farm in the end. That's my price.' He touched his wounded cheek again. 'I'll say I was carving wood and the chisel slipped. Your deserter can walk free.'

'It won't happen, Tino. Marriage between us, I mean.'

'You'll throw that man in the tower to the wolves? You're saying you won't marry me?'

'No – I'm saying *you* won't marry *me*. Not when you know.'

'Know what?'

She gathered herself. This felt like dancing on the edge of a crumbling cliff, but she couldn't think of any other way out. Allowing Tino to move into the farm, ousting Nonna, was unthinkable. The thought of his thickset body writhing on hers made her breath stick in her lungs.

'The man who did that to you' – she pointed at Tino's wound – 'isn't my lover, but I am not a virgin. There was a man in England. We grew close and I gave myself to him. Many times, willingly. I enjoyed it. There's a lot of my mother in me, you see.' She felt sick at this betrayal of a beloved mother, but she forced herself to go on. 'When the spirit takes me, there's no stopping me. Now you know that, do you still want to marry me?'

Tino tilted his head back and spat in her face. 'You are disgusting.'

She snatched up a cloth and wiped the spittle from her cheek. 'I'm going to fetch you some medical help, then I'll go.'

'Yes, go. And you know what? You just signed a death warrant.'

With those words ringing in her head, she didn't bother with the doctor, all her energy directed towards getting Sebastiano out of Tino's reach. She'd promised to take him to Naples, and she'd do it. Damn his objections.

She stopped briefly on the ridgeway path to catch her breath. Tino could already be using the doctor's telephone, summoning the police or the Germans. Or both, knowing him. Painting herself as a promiscuous woman had been a high price to pay. In a place like this, virtue was a woman's only claim to respect and status. She'd bargained hers away and used precious, private memories like gambling chips. Sebastiano had better appreciate what she'd done for him.

The moon was an hour from setting, the darkness intense on the sheltered side of the ridge. As she approached the tower, she saw a light on the track that wound towards Naples. Easily a kilometre away, it moved at speed, periodically disappearing only to reappear moments later. A single light. It had to be a motorcycle.

She found the tower deserted. The coffee she'd made was drunk, the can empty. The food was gone. The kitbag too. Sebastiano Alonso had dissolved into the night.

Chapter Eight

Nobody came to arrest her the following day. No police swoop, no Blackshirts searching for a fugitive. But then, it was Sunday. Tino might be unwell, or resting. Or simply biding his time in order to torment her. He liked having power over people. Her grandfather used to say of Tino that he would watch a trapped rabbit until it died rather than put it out of its misery.

Carmela climbed the *vedetta* after she'd finished the morning's milking, in the fading hope of spotting Renzo. Peering over the summit towards the smudgy horizon, she located Salerno by the pall of grey smog over its hills. Pockets of flame suggested the battle was flowing against gravity into the mountain passes. From where, she realised, it might well take a course along the highway to Naples.

Rather than scare herself, she shortened her gaze to take in the vaporous cone of Mount Vesuvius and the glittering sweep of the bay. Inching around the tower, she was able to look out over the volcanic landscape towards Posillipo and the island of Ischia. She imagined her distant ancestors standing where she was, hair ruffled by the breeze, watching the same horizon for pirate ships. She now knew what it was like to live with constant threat.

A familiar sound cut through the sky. Planes on a straight course for the *vedetta*. Within five heartbeats, they were overhead, sending the ravens into the air in cawing panic. One plane swooped so low, the force of its downdraught almost took Carmela off her feet. Gripping the tower's rim, she pressed her cheeks against the stone and gabbled a hysterical prayer. Only when the aircraft were faint dots and the noise was a scar on her eardrums did she dare clamber down. She had a strong idea they'd been German planes. Why had that one pilot tried to terrorise her? She was still shaking an hour later as she accompanied Rosaria to Mass in the village church. Her grandmother knew that Sebastiano – 'Mario' – had gone and had accepted the information with obvious relief. As far as Nonna was concerned, the disturbing episode was over. Carmela let her believe it.

She scanned every face in the congregation. Santo Cortazzi was present with his wife and children, but Tino was absent. People were friendly and polite, so clearly her name was not yet sullied.

The bell rang, incense burned and Padre Pasquale intoned.

Afterwards, Carmela declined an invitation to join her grandmother in taking refreshment at Zia Cristina's. Telling Nonna she meant to ask around the village if there'd been any sightings of Renzo, she knocked on Tino's door. Waiting for the axe to fall was intolerable. She had to know whether her cousin intended to report Sebastiano.

When Tino opened his door, which was only a dozen paces down from Zia Cristina's, a sour expression dropped over his face. He was in uniform, everything jet-black from his boots to his shirt and his greased hair. Even the stubby little tie he was knotting continued the theme. A white, criss-cross sticking plaster covering his facial wound added an almost comical note.

Carmela wasn't in the mood to laugh, however. 'I'd like a quick word.' She didn't ask to come in. Churchgoers were on their way home and even though Tino was family, he was nevertheless male and single and it wouldn't do to be seen going into his house unchaperoned.

He curtly informed her that he was due on parade in ten minutes. 'This won't take long. Tino. You have to tell me what you intend.'

'About what?'

She gritted her teeth. He couldn't be in any doubt of her meaning. 'You said I'd signed a death warrant. Whose? My own or Sebastiano Alonso's?'

Tino stepped back. 'Come in.'

'I'd rather not.'

'Come in if you want to talk because I have to leave soon.'

Choosing a moment when no eyes were on her, Carmela stepped inside and quickly shut the door. Tino's kitchen opened off the street, and the massive table that dominated the room was a chaos of fishing tackle, bait jars and hunting kit. A bottle of surgical spirit with its cap off gave off a medical smell. The one domestic touch was a dirty plate, knife and spoon suggesting he'd recently eaten breakfast. It amazed her that Tino, so precise and military in his appearance, should live in squalor. Il Duce's portrait glowered down at her from the mantelpiece. 'Just tell me what you mean to do, so I can prepare.'

'I have my plans, Meluccia.' Tino drew an air circle around the sticking plaster on his cheek. 'There's a price for what that man did to me. I suppose he's run off and left you, but he'll be picked up soon enough. The Germans need labour, and he'll do for that. It was kind of you to offer me your body last night—'

'I did not offer it!'

'… but a man has to be careful of the pond he wades into. If the waters are dirty, he might catch more than a fish, no?'

Her palms pricked from wanting to slap his face. He was playing with her, taking charge of the conversation, as was his habit. 'I told you the truth about my time in England but it wasn't an invitation,' she said as calmly as she could. 'Now I need to know what is going to happen to me. Tell me whose name is on this so-called death warrant.'

'The women are all harlots in England, and in America. Your father would have done better to put you in a convent.' Tino picked a black leather jacket off the back of a chair and shrugged it on. It was very tight on him, and when he put on a tasselled fez he looked like a skittle. To hide a sudden, crazy desire to laugh, Carmela cast her eyes down.

'You are a fool, Meluccia. Proud and uppity. I offered you my hand in marriage and you spat at me.'

'*You* spat at *me*!'

He made a 'tsk' sound. 'They said you were a bit mad when you came here, hiding in your bed, only walking around at night. I saw your little lantern, wobbling about la Casale's orchards in the dark. Even so, I was prepared to marry you and give you respectability and status, but you threw it back.'

'Just tell me what you mean to do. Please.'

Tino gave a soundless laugh that shook the fez's tassel against his cheekbone. 'The name on the death warrant is one you love most.'

'Not Nonna. You wouldn't.'

'I will take from you the things you most cherish and you will weep. Now get out, because I have important duties to perform.'

By the end of Sunday, la Casale's first tomato harvest was complete. The picking women would be back on the terraces in October when the vines produced a second flush. Early the following day, they flooded into the peach orchard. Carmela worked alongside them, always scanning the horizon. How would Tino carry out his threat? The roll call of those she cherished wasn't long, but it formed the fabric of her life. Nonna, her father, Danielo. Her animals. Where would his malevolence fall first?

For the first time ever, she felt insecure on the land she loved. Shaken by her narrow miss from fighter planes, she feared the *vedetta* was no longer a benign curiosity, but a target. Even the ridge, which she had always viewed as a sheltering backdrop, now had a less friendly aspect. Something would come over it sooner or later. Military vehicles, Tino's Blackshirts, or the Germans would spill over the top.

Chapter Nine

It was the morning of Friday, 17 September, six days on from Sebastiano's disappearance. War was creeping nearer. Bombers had hit towns on the Sorrento Peninsula, on the other side of the Bay of Naples but close enough for Carmela to map burning streets from the chains of red-hot smoke. Everyone said the planes were American Liberators, and last night they had struck at towns clustered around Vesuvius – even striking ancient Pompeii, destroying archaeological excavations. Though as Zia Cristina pointed out, 'How would they know? Those Roman ruins must look exactly the same from the air as Naples or Salerno do now.'

For Carmela, waiting edgily for Tino to take some form of revenge, the smell of charred stone on the wind touched a primitive nerve. Fire filled her dreams and she would wake, sweating, convinced the farmhouse was being engulfed. Each night before she went to bed, she prayed for Danielo and Sebastiano, invoking San Gennaro, the patron saint of Naples, to protect them. Not knowing either of their fates was a torment. She didn't dare make contact with her father to ask about Danielo, and as for Sebastiano, she might never know.

Renzo padded in and out of her dreams, always out of reach. And that morning before dawn her grandmother had shaken her awake, telling her she'd been muttering, 'Death warrant, no, please,' in her sleep.

Worry piled on worry. The cows were refusing to lie down in their pasture and chew the cud, and as a result, their udders were drying. She filled only three milk pails that morning, of which one got kicked over. She had little more success with the goats' milk, and Rosaria told her to take what she had up to the village where they had a regular customer in Signora Baccolini. The doctor's mother had a delicate stomach. Cow's milk did not agree with her. She opened her front door to Carmela's knock but instead of her usual guarded nod, she looked quickly up and down the street. 'Is it true what I hear, that Santo Cortazzi is to move his family into la Casale? Will I still get my goat's milk?'

Carmela stared at the woman, appalled. 'Of course Santo isn't moving into our home. Why would he?'

Signora Baccolini looked chastened. 'It's only what I heard. Gossip, I suppose, and I shouldn't have listened.'

Despite the reassurance, a blank fear struck Carmela. Neither of her cousins had a legal claim on the farm, but when had legalities bothered Tino or Santo?

Signora Baccolini was speaking still, telling Carmela how much she disliked and distrusted the Cortazzi brothers. 'My son, as the doctor, is legitimately entitled to get fuel for his car. Yet Tino notes down when Emilio is away, and for how long. Recently my son was out for five hours, attending a difficult birth, and your cousin came over and questioned him. "Who was the patient, give me the mother's family name—"' Abruptly, Signora Baccolini broke off. A woman had come out of Tino's house across the way, carrying a bulging cotton bag. She was a young widow, Annella de Rosa, who did Tino's laundry. Carmela nodded in greeting but Annella, who was generally friendly, pretended not to see.

Signora Baccolini took the pitcher from Carmela. 'If you'd like to wait, I'll pour the milk into my own vessel.'

When the doctor's mother returned a short while later, Carmela asked, 'Did your son recently tend to an injury of Tino's? He had a slip with a chisel.'

'That's what caused it, was it?' Signora Baccolini replied. 'He muttered something about an accident but he wasn't forthcoming. In fact, he seemed rather embarrassed. Actually, I tended to him as my son was on a call. I cleansed the wound with surgical spirit, which – I must be growing old – I forgot to dilute.'

Ouch. The thought of neat spirit on Tino's injury gave Carmela a perverse pleasure. 'He's alive, so it obviously worked.'

'So far. Signorina del Bosco, would you be good enough to take a fresh roll of lint to your cousin, since you're here? I advised him to clean the wound twice a day, but you know what men are like.'

A face-to-face encounter with Tino was the last thing Carmela wanted. She murmured something about being needed urgently on the farm.

'But it's only a couple of paces.' Signora Baccolini looked quite put out. 'I'd take it myself but a moment before you knocked, I put some oil on to heat. My son will be home soon, and hungry.' Without giving Carmela time to conjure up a new excuse, she took a roll of white lint bandage from her apron pocket. Having all but thrust it into Carmela's hand, she shut her door.

Feeling she had no choice, Carmela slowly crossed the street. At this time of day, there was a fair chance Tino would be away from home, so she could leave the bandage and get out without him knowing.

*

Her hunch was correct: there was no sign of Tino as she stepped into his kitchen, but as she dropped the lint on the table, she noticed Renzo's red collar among the mess. Tino had promised to search for the dog, but she doubted he'd done so. As she turned to go, her sleeve swept a tin mug off the table onto the stone floor.

'Who's down there?'

She froze at the question hurled from a room above. It took her back to the moment in the *vedetta*, when she'd swanned in with coffee and found Tino waiting.

A creak of a floorboard suggested Tino had been in bed and was getting up. His voice was louder as he called, 'That you, Annella? I told you not to come this week.'

Was that why Annella had been so furtive a moment ago, because she'd collected a bag of washing in defiance of Tino's instructions? It crossed Carmela's mind that her cousin might be hiding at home to avoid comments about the wound to his cheek. Whatever the reason, she needed to go. Should she take Renzo's collar? Yes, because leaving it would be to admit her fear that her dog would never return. Not waiting to find out if Tino was on his way down, she seized the collar and left.

'Signorina!' A young boy came running from the direction of the church. 'Please stop! Mamma saw you and sent me to say she can't work today. She says I can come in her place and my brother too.'

Carmela recognised the child as one of the sprawling De Rosa clan. His mother was Annella's sister, and one of her sturdiest pickers. Casting a nervous glance at Tino's door, she muttered, 'All right, Peppino, as long as you boys work and don't run off to play. Is your mamma unwell?'

'Headache, she can't sleep. The guns frighten her.' The boy wiped his nose with a grimy sleeve and looked at the red collar looped over Carmela's forearm. 'Is it true, you lost your dog, Signorina?'

She was anxious to hurry away, but the question stopped her. 'Yes. My Spinone, Renzo. You haven't—?' Carmela's voice stuck. She couldn't bear any more false hope. 'I don't suppose you've seen him?'

'No, but I heard a dog yelping. I've been foraging this morning.' Carefully turning out the lining of his shorts pocket, Peppino showed her a hoard of porcini mushrooms. It explained his filthy state, if he'd been grubbing among tree roots.

'You were in the woods?' she asked.

'Yes.' He pointed towards a russet-yellow chestnut plantation behind the church.

'That's where you heard the dog yelping?' Carmela was on the verge of pounding away to search.

'No, behind Signor Cortazzi's house.'

Her heart bucked. 'Tino Cortazzi's house?'

'*Sì.*' There was no guile in the child's eyes. 'In the courtyard, where the wash house is.'

'When did you hear it?'

'Last Saturday morning. My aunt Annella asked me to take back some sheets she had ironed.'

That was almost a week ago! With Renzo's collar seeming to burn through the sleeve of her jacket, Carmela strode back to Tino's and straight through the house, not caring if he confronted her. He did not; he must be upstairs still, dressing perhaps. The wash house was a squat, stone building that took up most of the yard, its door closed with a hasp and a metal rod. Her pulse lurching, she unfastened the door and reared back at a terrible stench. She saw a rusty pan of water, a scrap of canvas and Renzo lying on his side, his neck stretched forward. He wasn't moving. She fell to her knees beside him with a desperate cry. 'My poor boy!'

Now she understood the meaning of 'death warrant'. Every rib in the dog's body was visible and his eyes were closed. But the flesh around his teeth, under his rough-coated muzzle, was pink, suggesting Tino had not yet carried out his threat. Gently pressing Renzo's ribs, she detected the faint push of short, spaced-out breaths.

'*Bambino mio.*' She stroked his red-brown head, feeling the bones of his skull, massaging hope into him.

The dog opened his eyes, with a message of bewildered misery. Carmela lifted his head onto her lap, shielding his eyes from the daylight. His neck felt limp. How long had he been shut in, unfed? The smell, the ordure in the shed, suggested many days. She knew instinctively that Tino had lied about finding the collar outside the church. He had taken it off Renzo's neck and brought it to la Casale... Why?

The man had to be sick in his mind. She needed to pull herself together and act. Renzo had lost so much body weight she was confident she could lift him. As a child, she'd seen her nonna carry an injured goat down from the hills on her shoulders. She'd get Renzo home in the same style. But what if she stumbled and dropped him? If only she'd come in the donkey cart... She needed a safe house. The doctor's? Would stiff Signora Baccolini consent to keep Renzo for half an hour?

It was the best – the only – option. A layer of straw in the back of the cart would protect Renzo's poor body from the bumps. She fetched a stone water jug from the kitchen and in the malodorous yard, she palmed liquid into Renzo's mouth and told him to be good, to wait. She'd be back soon.

She ran from Tino's house, leaving the door open, not giving a damn if he saw her. Signora Baccolini answered her frantic knock, exclaiming, '*Caro Dio!* You look as though you've seen a column of tanks!'

'It's my dog.' Carmela blurted out the story.

'Tell me again… Tino Cortazzi stole your dog and shut him up, to starve?'

'Renzo ran away but Tino must have found him and wanted to torment me.'

'Or for you to be grateful to him, as the creature's saviour. He likes to play God.' Signora Baccolini shot a glance towards Tino's house. 'Be very careful of Signor Cortazzi. Cousin or not—'

'I understand, Signora. I really, really understand.' Carmela clasped her hands, to ask her favour. 'May I bring Renzo here while I get the donkey cart? I'll be as quick as I can.'

'No.'

Carmela stared in dismay. Was she never to be trusted? Never forgiven for being wayward Nina's child?

'No, stay here. My son is back now. He will fetch your dog and take you both home in his car. Don't go into that house alone, ever.'

'But your son might—'

'Get reported to the authorities?' Signora Baccolini snorted. 'My Emilio may not be a big, strong man but he is loved here, and not even Tino Cortazzi would dare do actual harm to the doctor.'

'I just want my dog safe home.'

'Then wait while I fetch my son.'

Emilio Baccolini was Carmela's age, but round shoulders and thinning hair added ten years to him. He viewed life through thick spectacles, when he wasn't rubbing eyes reddened by lack of sleep. He had been a valuable playmate to Carmela in former days, whenever her mother had brought her to la Casale while she went to the island of Capri for one of her prolonged and never-quite-explained rest cures. Emilio and Carmela had shared a love of make-believe games until the inevitable day he realised that playing with a girl made the other boys snigger. Their friendship had broken abruptly.

Visits to la Casale had stopped when Carmela went to England. Emilio had studied in Naples, only returning to Santa Maria della Vedetta a couple of years ago. Taking such a remote practice was a death knell to ambition, but in his own words, 'Somebody has to, and as I haven't a wife or children to support, I can survive on less profit.' 'Less profit' was heavily gilding the situation. Everyone knew he paid for children's milk, and medicines for the poorest patients, from his own pocket. Just as everyone knew he had funded himself through medical school by playing the violin at night in Neapolitan restaurants. The only criticism ever levelled at the doctor was that he let his mother rule him, and his voice was so soft, people had to ask him to repeat his diagnoses.

Carmela wasn't going to let her old friend face Tino alone. Her cousin was waiting for them even before they reached his door. *Spying*, thought Carmela, *as Signora Baccolini knows you do.*

'We're here to retrieve property belonging to Signorina del Bosco,' the doctor announced politely. Tino's brows contracted.

'What property?'

Carmela pushed past him, into the house. She heard Tino's objection:

'What do you mean by property? Come back, Meluccia. Now!'

Carmela kept going, slamming the back door behind her. Renzo lay where she'd left him, his eyes closed, and he didn't respond to his name. He was all spine and limp legs and he whimpered as she braced her knees and picked him off the ground. His fur smelled musty – he'd need a bath when he was stronger. Keeping him alive over the next few days would be challenge enough.

To her surprise, as she staggered in carrying Renzo, she found Tino squirming on a kitchen chair. Dr Baccolini stood over him, holding white sticking plaster between finger and thumb. He must have ripped it off fast. The doctor looked up, took note of the burden she carried, and said, 'I was obliged to explain to Signor Cortazzi that there is devitalised tissue building up around his wound. Hiding it from the air won't do at all.'

'Devitalised?' Carmela just wanted to keep going, but the front door was shut. 'You mean "dead"?'

'Where it is black – see?' Dr Baccolini made a circular gesture in front of Tino's face. 'The tissue has become…' He whispered the next word.

'Neurotic?' Carmela had once attended a lecture by a Cambridge don on disorders of the mind.

'Not neurotic, *necrotic*.'

Tino asked anxiously, 'What does that mean?'

'Dead, as the Signorina says. A chisel, deep in the flesh, will spread infection that develops over the passage of days. Gangrene is the next stage.'

'It wasn't a chisel— Wait a minute, gangrene?' Tino looked appalled. He could see perfectly well what Carmela carried in her arms, but his emotion was directed towards the doctor. 'I could die?'

'Let's make sure you don't, ha?'

'Doctor, could you open the door for me?' Carmela's arms were aching.

'Of course. Poor fellow.' The doctor gave Renzo a pitying shake of the head. 'Signorina, when you've deposited your friend somewhere comfortable, would you have my mother bring my medical bag? Tell her to put in a scalpel. The sharpest.'

The open door beckoned like a draught of freedom, but before she left, Carmela said in the clearest voice she could manage, 'There's a place in hell for you, Tino Cortazzi, and I will see you there before I speak to you or look at you again. Did you ever imagine I'd marry you? Not if I live to be a hundred.'

Tino half rose in his seat. 'Take care, cousin. Remember what I know.'

'What do you know? You can't prove a damn thing.' There wasn't a trace left of Sebastiano at la Casale. The story of the chisel would by now be rife in the village, and was Tino really going to admit that he'd been stabbed with a bed leg, by an injured deserter he hadn't even reported? She had one last message for her cousin. 'I hope your face rots.' To her lasting shock, words she'd never uttered before in her life spewed from her lips. '*Figlio di troia!*'

Dr Baccolini shook his head, shocked too and also sending her a warning. 'My bag, Signorina, please?'

Their eyes briefly met and a look was exchanged, acknowledging that they were friends still – but this was no game of make-believe.

Chapter Ten

The remainder of her day was dedicated to Renzo – and to her grandmother, who was deeply unsettled when she heard that Carmela had publicly, and in ringing tones, called Tino Cortazzi a 'son of a whore'.

'Let us hope he lets the insult pass.'

'Let us hope he wakes up to the miserable reality of his own soul, Nonna.'

Another difficult conversation took place as Carmela revealed that Tino had proposed marriage and then withdrawn the offer. And yet worse, that he had discovered the stranger, the so-called Mario, in the tower.

Rosaria flinched. 'That sailor fellow – Tino knows about him?'

'Ye-es.' Carmela wavered. The lies she'd told were unravelling.

Her grandmother folded her arms and a deep pucker formed between her eyebrows. 'Don't you dare pull a rabbit out of a bag and tell me it's a duck. Yes or no?'

Carmela felt five years old again, being scolded for evasive answers. 'Yes.'

'So – tell your nonna.'

This reminder that her fierce grandmother could also be kind and wise made it easier for Carmela to confess. 'It's even worse than I told you. Sebastiano isn't a deserter. I think he's some kind of foreign agent. British. He's on the run.'

'I thought he was called Mario.' Rosaria looked faint suddenly. Carmela helped her to a seat.

'I gave him a false name to protect you, Nonna.'

'How does any of this protect me?' Rosaria grasped handfuls of air. 'How, tell me?'

It didn't, Carmela acknowledged. 'I acted stupidly and now I've started a war with Tino, and I don't know what he'll do next.'

'Try to win, that's what. No Cortazzi man allows himself to be beaten by a woman. What else? There's something more, I can see it in your eyes.'

With a heavy sigh, Carmela described Tino's crude offer of marriage, and how she had changed his mind by revealing details of her past. Her English past.

Rosaria twisted her hands. 'You didn't need to do that, Meluccia. I know Tino has been hinting forever about marriage, but remember, he's your second cousin. The church doesn't allow cousins of such close degree to marry.'

'Except by special dispensation, if you're prepared to pay for it. Tino would have bullied Padre Pasquale to get his way.'

'And what if Tino blabs about your English lover with his friends, over glasses of grappa?' An awful idea struck Rosaria. 'People will guess that you came home pregnant!'

'They won't. Nobody saw me until it was all over. That isn't what we have to worry about, Nonna. The worst part is that Tino saw Sebastiano. They fought.'

'Fought a foreign spy, *ohimè*! Tino could arrest us.'

'I know. I know.'

'I thought the worst times of my life were over. Losing my babies, losing my own Mario. And then Nina, and finally your trouble… all that pain. Are we cursed, Meluccia?'

'No we are not. We are living through hard times and we battle on, Nonna. Tino doesn't want me any longer, but he wants la Casale. We can't let him win.'

Renzo's desperate condition provided a distraction from their bigger worries. Unsentimental as Nonna was about animals, locking one up in the dark and depriving it of food was, in her simple view, a perversion. From a Cortazzi, it was a slur on the beloved memory of her Mario. When Carmela had brought Renzo home in the doctor's Lancia, Rosaria had warmed a pan of goat's curd which she then fed to the dog in teaspoons. She'd astonished her granddaughter further by suggesting Renzo might be allowed to sleep in front of the kitchen stove. 'Until he's recovered.'

Never had Carmela loved her nonna more, or more regretted her choices this last week. She hadn't caused Renzo's disappearance, but everything else – Danielo's fate, Sebastiano's near-capture and now her grandmother's terrible distress – could all be laid at her door. Curled stiffly on a mattress in front of the stove that night, beside the dog, fear descended. Tino wouldn't forgive her for finding Renzo and exposing him as a brute. With Sebastiano out of his reach, his vengeance would fall on her.

The question was, how and when?

The following morning, Saturday, Carmela rose with the dawn. The stove had gone out and a chill rose through the terracotta tiles. Renzo seemed a shade more alert, and his skin, pinched between finger and thumb, felt less flaccid. After tending to him, she went out for her chores, saving the worst until last: stamping down the muck pile, needing to keep it in good shape because she'd hidden Sebastiano's camp bed beneath it. She hadn't dared burn it in case the smoke attracted attention. Of course, the camp bed would be uncovered when the muck came to be spread around the fruit trees at the end of winter, but by then she'd have an excuse for building a bonfire. Late winter was the time for cutting back the firethorn and making a roaring blaze of the branches. But what would their lives be in six months?

Shaking off her thoughts, she went in for her breakfast, washed and changed into a skirt, put her hair up and got ready to greet the pickers. They didn't come.

By nine, only Cristina Gennaro and one of her sisters-in-law had turned up. 'I won't be made to lose a day's work,' Zia Cristina announced as Carmela looked forlornly for latecomers.

'You were told to stay home by Tino Cortazzi?'

'No, by nobody at all. Word went out at evening Mass yesterday. "We are not to pick at la Casale today, by order." Whose order, I asked. Nobody could say.' Cristina snorted. 'Nobody tells *me* to stay home. Only my priest. Or the police. The real police. And my husband, I suppose,' she added grudgingly.

'Same with me,' echoed her sister-in-law.

As they set to work, Carmela forgave all the intrusive questions she'd endured from Zia Cristina over the years. The women threw themselves at the work but three pairs of hands weren't enough to strip the peaches, and though Nonna came to help, the consignment Carmela took to the village that evening was a tenth of what it should be. She hadn't supposed her heart could plunge any lower, until she saw Santo Cortazzi lolling beside the weighing machine.

Tino's younger brother said nothing while he dealt with her load, handing her a ticket without a flicker of friendly recognition. She frowned at the figure written on it. 'That can't be right, Santo. I know we're short today but even so.'

'Actually, I was being generous.' Santo waited while a labourer transferred the crates of peaches into the back of a high-sided cart. 'You'll lose half your crop on the tree at this rate.'

'Because the women didn't come! And we all know why.'

'No. Why?' The smile kicking the sneer off Santo's lips showed her that this conversation was for pleasure. His pleasure. 'Tino will have to check things over. We can't have a farm wasting good harvest because it's run by an old woman and a girl with a filthy mouth.'

Ah. *Figlio di troia* had done the rounds, then. Her impulsive tongue had handed Tino another grudge. 'Tell him not to trouble himself to visit,' she said coldly. 'The fruit will be picked.'

'Tino will do whatever he sees fit. You need hands for the apple orchard next, and your scabby hazelnuts, though they should be grubbed up and the land used for something better.'

'That will never happen. Those trees were my grandfather's pride.'

Santo gave a shrug of the mouth. 'The commune can take over any farm not contributing to the war effort. We have the Cortazzi name to protect too.'

Breathless from impotent fury, Carmela got up on the cart and shook the reins to wake Nearco. Would her women come to work tomorrow if she asked them personally? It would mean knocking on a lot of doors, and Santo would see her doing it. In the end, she stopped at the house with the sage-green shutters and asked Zia Cristina to spread a message. Double wages for all who turned up.

God speed the Allies, she said to herself as the donkey plodded home. Diehard Fascists like Tino would then get a taste of what they had meted out. What would Tino do if the British and Americans got this far? Wrap himself in the Stars and Stripes or the Union flag, or both? He probably had a German flag tucked away in his blanket box too, just in case.

A new Sunday dawned with a mist that hinted at an imminent shift of season. Carmela's grandfather Mario had always said, 'September flies in like a songbird and leaves like a wet squid.'

Zia Cristina and her sister-in-law dutifully arrived after church and stayed until lunch time, when they returned home to prepare family meals. Not even the prospect of double wages had enticed the others. Carmela and Rosaria worked on. As the bell of Santa Maria struck for afternoon Mass, Rosaria groaned. 'My elbows ache, I cannot do more.'

'Go inside, Nonna. I'm good for a few more hours. Will you feed Renzo?'

'*Sì, sì.* He can have a little stewed apple with honey.'

Smiling at her grandmother's absurd change of heart, Carmela moved her stepladder to the next tree. She was balanced on the top rung, reaching her picking tool for a single, stranded fruit, when she heard engines. At first she thought 'planes' and tensed, ready to jump and drop. Then it became obvious the noise was close by. Through the trees flashed the glint of khaki-green metal. Not the vegetable wagons, which had canvas backs, and they weren't passing by either. Carmela scrambled down, turning her ankle in her haste. She hopped along until the pain subsided, and then she ran.

Three armoured cars had stopped in front of the farm. Two carried German soldiers in field-grey uniforms and flanged steel helmets. The third was stuffed with men in black uniforms. The oldest of them sat beside the driver, his lips set in a grimly satisfied smile. Winded with terror, Carmela could only stare. Tino had put on his best uniform. Silver shoulder flashes winked in the sunlight. When he got out of the vehicle, she saw a service pistol and a cosh in his belt.

She managed to ask, 'Soldiers here, why?'

'Follow me.' Tino knocked at the farmhouse door with his cosh and when Rosaria opened up, he walked straight in. Carmela followed, too numb for further questions.

'Sit down.' When they gaped in confusion, Tino repeated, '*Sit down.*'

Rosaria collapsed onto a seat. From his rug in front of the stove, Renzo gave a faint bark. Carmela went to reassure him. 'Tino, what are Germans doing on our land?'

'Inspecting the *vedetta*.'

Her blood ran cold. She had picked up the last wisps of straw with her bare fingers but the mementos she'd brought back from England – her letters, *love* letters – were in the tower wall. Along with a wisp of fine, brown hair wrapped in muslin. 'They can't just storm in! This is our land.'

Rosaria frowned in deep concern. 'Nephew, what do they want with that old *vedetta*?'

'To see if it's suitable to mount an anti-aircraft gun on the top. American bombers cannot be allowed to have free run at our ports and towns and this is the perfect position.'

'Perfect for what?'

'For shooting them down if they try for Naples, Posillipo or Bagnoli. It's high, it has long and clear views.'

It's high… Something suddenly made sense to Carmela.

It's why I'm here, intelligence gathering. Sebastiano's words, when she'd found him delirious at the top of the *vedetta*. She'd thought he was talking through a morphine muddle but now she realised he knew, somehow, of these German plans.

It was as though an axe had appeared above her head, threatening to slice her in half. If Tino's words became reality, la Casale would be a nest for German gunners, shooting down the Allied planes who were destroying Italy while also trying her to liberate her. 'You shan't use our tower,' she gasped. 'Italy's surrendered.'

Tino's look smeared her with contempt. 'Germany hasn't surrendered. We're still at war, girl.'

'No Germans on this land. You agree, don't you, Nonna?'

Rosaria nodded. 'No soldiers, no guns. You hear me, nephew?'

Tino's shrug made clear that he didn't care what they wanted. 'The guns will be manned by my own Blackshirts and I'm here to tell you ladies to move out.'

Rosaria froze as if iced water had been poured down her back. 'Leave the house I came to fifty years ago, as a bride, and the orchards my Mario tended all his life? No, Tino. No. No.'

'Auntie, you have no choice. I'm moving Santo in, with Brigitta and the children. This place needs a man – and a wife and family to bring life back to it. I hadn't realised how run down it had become.'

Movements outside took Carmela to the window. Blackshirts and German soldiers were setting off in the direction of the *vedetta*, the field-grey and the black mixing like oyster and mussel shells. She faced Tino. 'Your father would be ashamed of you if he were alive to see this. So would my grandfather. What a blessing they died before this day.'

Tino raised a hand. 'Hold your tongue. You have no right to speak of my father – you are used goods.'

'I am not!'

'No? A deserter in your bedroom, an *inglese* lover in your dreams? You are either a whore, a collaborator or both. You should leave.'

She choked back her fury. Any answer would incriminate her.

'I don't need you, Carmela del Bosco. Your nonna belongs in this village but you don't. Hankering after you nearly sapped my manhood and I thank God I learned in time what you are.'

Rosaria struggled to her feet and grasped her nephew's hands. 'Stop this. You can't send her away. When did you become so cruel? This is my home and I need Meluccia and she needs me.'

'You're better off without her, *zia mia*.' Tino tried to unlatch Rosaria's grip but her fingers had fused on his arms. 'Calm down, I won't hurt her. Blood is blood, after all. For my uncle Mario's sake, Carmela can go free. I give my word, but you must both quit this house. You have kinsfolk in the village, Zia Rosaria, unless you too wish to go to Naples. Your son-in-law could find a corner for you in his palazzo.' He looked past Rosaria to Carmela and his eyes were flinty. 'I want you out. Go to Naples, to your English-loving father.'

Tears rolled down Rosaria's cheeks. 'I don't belong in Naples. I belong here.'

'Haven't I just explained?' Tino was growing impatient. 'This is a failing farm, and people are starving. The commune has tolerated your slack management long enough.'

That was too much! Carmela hurled at him, 'If the commune wasn't hand in glove with profiteers and the Camorra, there'd be food for everyone.'

A flush rose in Tino's cheeks, creating a halo around the gouge in his cheek which the doctor had recently scraped clean with a scalpel blade. 'You have an hour to pack what you need, and to get out.'

*

As the sun climbed to its noon height, Carmela drove the donkey cart away from the village. Handing Nonna into Zia Cristina's care had left her feeling like a criminal. Her grandmother had cried all the way there, clutching a carpet bag like a little child being sent off to strangers.

La Casale was lost. The moment she'd said 'yes' to Danielo, agreed to hide Sebastiano, the house of cards had started to wobble. She couldn't blame anyone else. Apart from Tino, of course.

In the rear of her cart was a trunk full of clothes, supplies and utensils, along with photographs and other precious items she'd seized so nobody could get their hands on them. And Renzo, wrapped in sheets, his head poking out. Her identity card was in the pocket of her grandfather's coat, spread over her knee.

A terrible dread pressed on her, and as she passed la Casale, it became too much to bear. Pulling Nearco to a stop, she got down from the cart. Tethering the donkey to the branch of a free-growing apple tree, she leapt a dry ditch into the hazel grove and wove her way through the trees in short, darting movements. She could hear men's voices in the peach orchards. Laughter, conviviality. Italian Fascists and Germans together. It seemed that the reconnaissance party had retreated to the shade to pass the noonday hour.

She found the *vedetta* deserted, as she'd hoped. From the niche in the wall she retrieved the satchel whose seams were grey with accumulated dust. Carrying it away with her tested every nerve in her body. If her heart pounded any harder, she'd pass out.

Luck was with her. Nobody challenged her and she wound her way down the tomato terraces. As she crossed the pasture, the cows followed her to the gate. There she made another decision, leaving the gate wide open. In the farmyard, where she collected a spade, she opened up the goat pen. Passing the chicken coops, she did the same so the hens could escape if they wished.

Taking the spade to the hazel grove, she walked straight to the oldest of the trees, which lay on its side. It had blown down in a winter storm years ago, its roots tearing up the soft soil as it fell, leaving a deep depression. Carefully aiming her spade, Carmela dug a deep hole into which she emptied the satchel. Working fast, she shovelled the soil back over the incriminating hoard of books and letters. It broke her heart, but it was too dangerous to leave them or travel with them.

Not everything went into the pit. Inside her bodice was Sebastiano Alonso's wristwatch. She'd found it, smeared with dry blood, when she'd cleared away the straw in the tower. She had fulfilled her unspoken promise to mend its strap, though she doubted she'd ever find a way of returning it to him. Simply keeping it out of Tino's grasp felt like a small triumph. Beside it was a little muslin bag containing a snippet of hair the colour of a ripe nut. It weighed no more than a sneeze but it carried the weight of everything beloved that she was leaving behind.

Only when she was back on the cart and Nearco was stumbling on the bumpy, downhill road to Naples, did she take a proper breath again. She was going to her father's house, to seek refuge and to find Danielo, hopefully. To a bombed city crammed with Germans, where the shops were empty and life balanced on a razor's edge. She didn't know if her father's house was safe, of if her papà was even there. The uniformed Nazi who had inspected it as a possible military billet might already be in residence.

What a welcome that would be.

Chapter Eleven

For over an hour, Castel Sant'Elmo had been Carmela's landmark. The ancient armoury glowed apricot in the late afternoon sunshine, marking her journey's end. By the time she reached the outskirts of Vomero, the hilltop district where her father lived, the castle shone deep amber and her cart wheels were crying out for grease. Pulling over, Carmela gave Nearco water. She'd filled a bucket at a rock-face spring they'd passed a distance back. Pouring some into a tin mug for herself and into a bowl for Renzo, she gazed down at Naples: a shimmering mosaic of ochre stone and terracotta roof tiles, of bell towers and domes, squares and gardens, narrow roads and cross-hatched alleys. A breeze off the sea brought the smell of burned oil.

Since the start of the war, British and then American bombers had reduced entire sections of the city to rubble. They had clearly been busy in the weeks before Italy's surrender as the docks curving around the bay were junkyards of blackened steel and wood. The sea that lapped around stranded hulls of sunken ships had an iridescence that explained the oily stink. Like the city, the water itself was bruised and burned, but amidst the carnage of the docks, ant-sized trucks moved in and out. Naples had been conquered and occupied many times over the centuries and had always fought back. If Danielo was to be believed, now was no different.

'The place is a snakes' nest of informants.' That had been Emilio Baccolini's parting warning to her. The doctor had passed her on the road in his dusty Lancia, returning home from a call. Reversing, he'd got out to talk to her. When she revealed what had happened to la Casale, he'd looked appalled. 'Guns on the *vedetta* will make the farm a target for Allied bombers. It makes the whole village a target.'

It wasn't a comforting send-off. She brooded over thoughts of Santo and his wife Brigitta using her and Nonna's beds, their linen and blankets. And Tino strutting about, overseeing the arming of the *vedetta*. And wondering if they had called the women back to work. But of course they had! There were thousands of lires' worth of fruit still on the trees.

She was crossing Piazza Vanvitelli, the hub of Vomero, as a church clock struck five. Grit in her mouth, lips dry, she spared a glance for the piazza's grand facades, and in particular the building where her father had once had an office. It looked closed up, its grand, baroque front covered in billboards. 'Take note' one of the posters shouted at her. 'Acts of insurrection or attacks on German personnel will incur the harshest penalties. For every German harmed, 100 Italians will be—' Someone had torn off the rest.

Imprisoned, fined, or worse? An image of Mussolini in his iron helmet had also been ripped away, but Carmela's eye was drawn to a different face. An artist's sketch of a solemn-eyed man with shadowy cheeks, handsome in an inscrutable way.

Just about recognisable to Carmela, too. It could only be Sebastiano, but was it a recent picture or an old one? A legend above his head stated, 'Sought for subversion and spying'. A reward was offered for information leading to his capture.

An old man who was tickling the pavement with a broom stopped and asked, 'Know him?'

'No,' Carmela said quickly. 'When was this poster put up?'

'A week ago, give or take. If you're hoping for a share of the reward, you're out of luck. Somebody will have turned him in by now for the price of a loaf of bread.'

'And?' Her throat tightened.

The old man put an imaginary gun to his head. 'A quick job, in a prison courtyard. That's how it's done.' His eyes were half concealed behind wrinkled folds. He was so cadaverously thin, this was the only spare flesh on his face. 'You seem upset.'

Carmela denied it, scenting danger in the speculative glint that accompanied the comment. 'Who likes a spy?' She bid him good evening. '*Arri*, Nearco!'

The street cleaner laughed. 'Nearco, after the racehorse? Good luck with that, pretty lady!'

From Piazza Vanvitelli, she drove Nearco along Via Aniello Falcone and turned off into a tree-lined avenue, stopping outside an imposing building of yellow-grey stone. Palazzo del Bosco's front door was carved from cedar wood, and the varnish was flaking. There were no vehicles parked outside, which encouraged her to hope that the Nazis had not moved in. Lifting the iron knocker, she pictured Sebastiano dying in a grim courtyard, alone and without ceremony. Had he fought back, defying death?

Her glance fell onto the Palazzo's steps where dry leaves had gathered in the corners. The place looked as sad and defeated as she felt, and the wondrous view from the avenue gave her, for the first time, no pleasure. Viale Bellavista was named so for a good reason. If Naples resembled an auditorium, with steeply raked hills rising up from the sea, then her father occupied one of the best opera boxes. Only one side of the avenue had ever been built on and, through the prick of tears, she absorbed an angel's eye view of the bay. Vesuvius, grey in the lowering light, exhaled a foxtail of vapour. At the furthest reach of the bay, the Sorrento Peninsula stretched out into the sea. Beyond that raged the war that Sebastiano had hoped to bring to a swifter end. She had wanted to help him do it, in her own small way, by giving him shelter.

'May I help you, Signorina?'

Carmela gave a start. She hadn't heard the bolts being drawn back. She managed a wan smile for her father's old servant who gazed politely at her from the doorway. 'Tomaso, it's me, Carmela. How are you? I was terrified the place might swarming with Nazis! Is my father home?'

'Signorina Carmela, a thousand pardons, I didn't recognise you. Yes, Don Gonzago is at home, and no, we have not yet been ousted. I had no idea you were to drop in. Business in Naples?'

Carmela opened her mouth to explain, then decided details could wait. She had no idea what kind of welcome her father would give her once he heard her story. 'Can I bring the donkey in? He needs to drink again, and rest.'

'I'll open the side gate.'

Tomaso Manetti had lived at the Palazzo for as long as Carmela could remember but his step as he went to open a wooden gate in the Palazzo's boundary wall was that of a much younger man. He had not yet begun to stoop. His age was instead concentrated in deep facial lines and cotton-fine hair. He told her he could rustle up a pail of water, 'Though you'll be surprised to learn, perhaps, fresh water is one of the most valuable commodities in Naples right now. The Americans scored a direct hit on the main aqueduct. We're praying we get a nice downpour soon.'

She tethered Nearco under a pine tree. The Palazzo's garden was walled around, making escape impossible, but given a chance he'd make for a vegetable patch that was colourful with squashes, tomatoes and zucchini.

'Ah, I thought it was a dog,' Tomaso murmured as he glanced into the back of the cart.

'You met Renzo last time I was here, remember?'

'I met a hairy Spinone who bounced around and tugged my trouser legs. What's the matter with him – poison?'

'Not poison. Long story, Tomaso. Can he come in the kitchen, will anyone mind?'

'There is nobody *to* mind. Your papà always used to keep a dog, and I am the full complement of the Palazzo's staff these days. Shall I carry one end of him?'

It took her an instant to realise he meant the dog. 'Best I do it. Renzo's used to me lugging him around. You lead on.'

Tomaso had come into Don Gonzago's service a quarter of a century earlier as a legal assistant, though he was many years his employer's senior. He'd been unable to complete his legal training. Carmela's father always said that in Tomaso Manetti, poverty had stripped Naples of its best lawyer. In the 1920s, as Fascism began to concrete over every aspect of life, Don Gonzago's work had dwindled and in 1924, bankruptcy and disbarment had finally nailed the lid on his career. Tomaso's role had mutated to that of household assistant and butler. Carmela doubted he was paid much at all these days.

It hadn't dented his amiable nature. Tomaso scuttled ahead of Carmela, and in a vast kitchen dominated by blank-eyed ovens and massive crockery cupboards, he laid newspapers on the tiled floor. A rose velvet curtain laid on top created a dog bed. 'The curtains are down to be washed,' he explained, 'but we can't spare the water and don't even mention soap. I'll bring in your things and then inform Don Gonzago of your arrival.'

'You don't have to announce me, Tomaso. I'll feed Renzo then wander up.'

'Allow me to announce you. We don't like surprises here.'

Carmela set about warming goat's milk on a portable gas burner she presumed was used for everyday cooking. The Palazzo had boasted electricity since the early twenties, but flicking a light switch produced nothing. Perhaps American bombers had got the power stations too. Last time she'd been here, the ovens had been in use. Three families, forced out of their homes, had rented the ground floor. She wondered why they'd left.

Into warm milk she crumbled goat's cheese and mixed in a capful of olive oil, then spooned in some maize porridge she'd made the day before. She'd been feeding Renzo this nutritious soup every couple of hours, day and night. A few mouthfuls at a time. Today, for the first time since she'd rescued him, she didn't have to support his head. His eyes were brighter. In a few days, he might stand unaided.

When he'd eaten, she went to the sink to wash the bowl only to recall the dire water shortage. Outside, she wiped it with handfuls of dry grass. It would be hard to justify nursing a dog when the city teetered on the edge of survival. Tales of Neapolitans boiling soup from chicken's feet and bird feathers had reached Santa Maria, and on her journey she'd seen children scavenging among the refuse. Carmela resolved to share her own food with Renzo and take nobody else's. Feeding the donkey would be a challenge, though, once he'd eaten down the overgrown lawn.

Weariness caught up with her and because Tomaso had not yet summoned her upstairs, she curled up next to Renzo. The pink velvet had a sweet scent that was achingly familiar. Smoothing out a fold, she discovered that the colour inside was ruby. She was lying on her mother's bedroom curtains. As a child, she'd wrapped herself in them, pretending to be a queen. She'd hidden behind them as her mother lay dying. Had they been fading at the same window all these years?

She drifted into a light sleep only to be woken by the jingling of a bell. Had she heard it or dreamed it?

'Signorina Carmela?' Tomaso was back. 'Don Gonzago invites you to go up. Will you dine with him? We take dinner early these days. I'm about to throw a repast together.'

'Yes please. I'm ravenous. Is there enough water for me to wash my hands?'

'Of course.' Tomaso picked up a jug and trickled water into a bowl, handing her a flannel and a sliver of soap the size of a communion wafer. He held the bowl as she delicately manoeuvred the slippery disc around her fingers. Carmela mentioned the ringing bell.

'Yes,' Tomaso said. 'I will answer it, but you go upstairs. You know your father doesn't like to be kept waiting.'

The family rooms were one floor up. It was the same in every grand home: functional quarters on the ground floor, the *piano nobile* above, removed from the noise and odours of the street. She crossed the echoing lobby towards the stairs, feeling more like a poor supplicant than a homecoming daughter.

Don Gonzago del Bosco was always referred to in Santa Maria della Vedetta as the city aristocrat who had seduced Rosaria and Mario

Cortazzi's daughter Nina and defied expectation by marrying her. They had met when she worked in the millinery department of Rinascente, Naples' finest department store. Deprived of a salacious tale of ruin, village gossips had set about predicting misery for them both.

The truth, as far as Carmela had ever managed to deduce, was that while her mother had passionately loved Gonzago, he had married her to spite the well-bred Englishwoman who had jilted him. He had spent his bachelor years in the drawing rooms of London where, as Tino had sneeringly reminded her, he had developed an appreciation of English manners. Nina had grown up on a farm, coming to the city to earn a living. By the time Carmela was born, the differences between Gonzago and Nina were a yawning gulf. Other women had come into the marriage. The longest-lasting infidelity had been with one of the housemaids, a girl called Violetta. Nina del Bosco had lived long enough to know that Violetta had borne a son: Danielo.

Her father's conduct was so hard to forgive. Carmela's fragile relationship with Don Gonzago had met its sternest test when she had arrived home from England just before Christmas 1938, emotionally shattered and secretly pregnant. He had welcomed her, listened to her carefully censored account of the previous months, and sympathised. But he had not looked into her eyes, or asked why she was so drawn. She had not told him about the baby because how could she trust him? Instead, she'd packed her bags and slipped away to her grandmother at la Casale.

Walking up the curving travertine staircase of the Palazzo, she fitted these memories into a sigh. Being sent to school in England within weeks of her mother's death had left her relationship with Papà in a half-formed state. It was probably too late to change anything now.

She poked her head around the drawing room door, and blinked. The furniture was gone, the floorboards exposed. A Turkish carpet was rolled into a fat cigar against the wall. Where were the pictures? The piano was missing too, a baby grand on which her mother had taught herself, and taught Carmela her first chords.

Had Tomaso understated things when he'd said they hadn't yet been ousted? A full-scale removal seemed to be in progress. Anxiously, she knocked at the door of her father's reading room. Getting no answer, she tried the dining room. There, at the head of a table that could seat twenty-four, sat her father. And there was the Bechstein in all its polished glory, pushed up against the double doors that linked the dining and drawing rooms. She wondered if they'd tried to get it downstairs and given up.

'Papà? I'm here.'

Don Gonzago was engrossed in his newspaper, wire spectacles balanced on the end of his nose. Burning candles were set about him, casting a sepulchral glow around the room. 'My dear Carmela.' He folded his paper and stood to greet her. 'I feared Tomaso was hallucinating when he said you were downstairs with a scrawny dog and a donkey. He is eighty-two next birthday, you know.'

'I didn't realise he was quite that old.'

'He lied for years about his age, but I found his birth certificate. Vanity takes many forms. You have come alone?'

'Apart from the animals you mentioned.'

'Mm. You look...'

She held her breath. She wouldn't have chosen to arrive wearing clothes she'd had on all day.

Don Gonzago gave his verdict. 'Given all, you look healthy. The Scots have a word for it. "Bonny". Yes, that word fits you perfectly.'

'Thank you. I think. You look well too, Papà.'

They exchanged a brief handshake before she sat down at his invitation. It was her turn to examine him. Like Danielo, fat never made a home on her father's frame. His hair, as white as Tomaso's, remained thick, its waves kept in check with a comb-through of scented oil. His features were aquiline. Perfect for a lawyer, he'd once told her, adding, 'Such a waste I never get to practise my arrogant stare.'

Now, as he took off his glasses, she received a glancing flash of green eyes. He said, 'When I looked up, for a moment I thought I was seeing your mother.'

Not an avenue she wanted to stroll down. She asked about Danielo. 'Tomaso didn't mention my brother and I didn't like to ask… in case.' In case the news was bad. 'Have you heard from him?'

'*From* him, not a chance. He's locked up. His mother keeps me informed. She sends one of her numerous offspring here with snippets of news.'

'Danielo's in actual prison?'

'In the boys' jail at Sant'Efremo. Nothing like "actual prison", fortunately.'

'But in Naples?'

Her father nodded. 'In Materdei, off Via Salvator Rosa. Does that mean nothing? You are probably more familiar with the geography of Cambridge than with the city of your birth.'

And whose choice was that?

Swallowing her retort, she asked instead, 'What was the charge against him?'

'Smuggling. Tinned goods were found in the back of the van, without documents to explain them. Yet worse, the truck was hired from a black-market operator. Fortunately, they were stopped two days before the new curfew came into force – you do know about that, don't you?' Seeing her shake her head, he explained that the new German commander of Naples had decreed that all citizens must stay inside between the hours of nine at night and six thirty the following morning. 'If they'd broken curfew as well, they might have been shot on sight. The consequence was that Danielo and the van were seized, though not the driver.'

'By "driver" you mean Gio?' She thought of her brother's friend, and felt again the sweep of a flirtatious glance, the careless grin that had flouted the danger of their situation.

'Perhaps.' Her father gave her a cautious look. 'Let's continue calling him "the driver". He is having to pay the proverbial pound of flesh to the criminal who owned the van, and since he has no money, he asked my help. Tomaso took funds to him, which left me nothing with which to purchase Danielo's liberty. To the great inconvenience of everyone, the police were obliged to drag your half-brother to a magistrate's hearing and into jail. Danielo's case is reviewed later today.'

'Will he get out?'

'One rather hopes not.' Don Gonzago's expression was as inscrutable as the prey bird he resembled.

Tomaso came in just then with a tray. Don Gonzago picked up his napkin, shook it and said, 'My daughter asks if I am optimistic about Danielo's chances of freedom. What say you, Avvocato?'

Tomaso put the tray down. Carmela's eyes went to the silver coffee pot with its aromatic wisp of steam. 'Coffee… have you run out of wine?'

'Not at all, but one has to be careful with alcohol on a permanently empty stomach. You will see what I mean when we lift the lid on *that*.' Her father gestured to the domed chafing dish on Tomaso's tray.

So ravenous and thirsty, she was tempted to pick up the coffee pot and drink from the spout. Her stomach cramped. Her last food had been a peach munched as she drove away from Santa Maria della Vedetta.

Tomaso was still considering Don Gonzago's earlier question. 'The solution to Danielo's predicament is that the prison governor is a Fascist.'

The maestro was losing his edge, Carmela thought. That was surely the worst case for Danielo. In the part-shuttered light of the dining room, Tomaso looked as wizened as a hazelnut that had rolled under the sideboard several Christmases ago. Her father, however, was nodding agreement.

Don Gonzago explained. 'The governor is unsurprisingly a Fascist, but intelligent enough to sense the tide is turning against his kind. Danielo's theft of a few cans of Germanic pork and beans may be strictly illegal, but such actions will be construed differently in the weeks to come if the Allies have their way. Less "stealing" as "liberating". Danielo has chosen his side, and it is my intention to invite the governor to choose which side of history *he* prefers to stand on.'

'You're going to see the governor?'

'Tomorrow, and looking forward to it.' Don Gonzago lifted his newspaper off the table so Tomaso could put down his cup and saucer. Carmela saw then that her father had a black armband stitched to his jacket sleeve and felt a vague premonition.

'Papà, who's died?'

Don Gonzago glanced at the black silk and answered, 'Civilisation. Since our brave generals all ran away and the very German Colonel Scholl took control of our city, we have mourned the loss of all that makes life sacred. We cannot bathe or eat or nurse our sick. Our

Jewish friends are being rounded up, as are our young men. It's why I'm relieved to have Danielo behind bars, by the way. Prison has kept him safe for a week.'

'Even by German standards, Scholl's a maniac,' Tomaso agreed grimly. 'He doesn't even pretend to understand Italian.'

'He doesn't understand Italians, full stop,' Don Gonzago agreed. 'Carmela ought to know, there was a stand-off in Piazza Plebiscito when some youths barricaded in a group of German soldiers. Shots were fired, the tanks were brought in—'

'Danielo told me about it, when we met at la Casale,' she cut in.

Her father sighed. 'I don't doubt he was present. Colonel Scholl was informed that street boys, *scugnizzi*, had incited the trouble and he thought that meant "students".'

'Has there ever been a less apt translation?' Tomaso murmured.

'Scholl found some students and had them shot along with a few sailors, home on leave, who were in the wrong place. Arbitrary violence to assuage a Bavarian bureaucrat's wounded feelings. His henchmen later fired on the crowd being forced to watch. And so I wear a black armband. Welcome to Naples, Carmela.'

It was worse even than she'd feared. She had expected danger in Naples, but in Colonel Scholl her father was describing another Tino, only this time, an irrational bully with an army behind him. Danielo had escaped, thank heavens, but Sebastiano had not, it seemed.

'Signorina del Bosco has brought us apples,' Tomaso said, changing the mood. He was laying out another place setting. Was he joining them? Carmela had no objection, except she'd rather be alone with her father while she explained her sudden arrival. It had struck her that her father had accepted her recent meeting with Danielo without question.

He wasn't usually one to let an inconsistency glide past him. He had met with Gio too, so he must also know something of Sebastiano.

'And she's brought caciotta di capra,' Tomaso added.

'Goat's cheese, very thoughtful.' Don Gonzago beamed at Carmela.

'Baskets of peaches too. Thank heavens for the countryside. Shall I serve, Signore?'

'Please do, Tomaso.'

Tomaso's movements were so mannered, Carmela feared the chafing dish lid would never be raised and dinner would never land on her plate. She couldn't hold back.

'Papà, I'm not here on a social visit.' It all flooded out, Danielo bringing Sebastiano and her secreting him in the *vedetta*. Then weakening and bringing him into the house, but without first enlightening her grandmother. A mistake, because Tino Cortazzi had invited himself to dinner. 'Tino is my cousin.'

'Yes, yes, your mother occasionally mentioned him.'

'And his father was—'

Don Gonzago lifted a hand. 'Enough to know he's a Cortazzi. What happened after Tino came to tea?'

She described the dinner, Sebastiano hidden upstairs, painting Tino as the vulture who had been circling la Casale for months. 'Wanting to own it, and me. He wanted to marry me, though no longer.'

'He never sought my permission. What extraordinary impudence.'

'Nonna is scared of him. I hate him. Anyway, he finally went and Sebastiano returned to the *vedetta*.' She waited, hoping her father would interrupt to tell her that he knew all this, that he knew who Sebastiano was. Knew *where* Sebastiano was, because Gio had already explained. To her frustration, Don Gonzago merely invited her to go on.

She described the heart-stopping moment when she'd taken coffee to the tower and found Tino waiting. Her father's expression seemed suddenly guarded.

'And?'

'There was a fight. Tino was hurt. While I was helping him home, Sebastiano disappeared. I have no idea who came for him, but I think it was someone on a motorbike. Could it have been Gio?'

'I couldn't venture to say. You are here to escape the vulture, I suppose?'

'Not exactly. The vulture drove me out.' She described the criminal seizure of la Casale, then skipped to Renzo's part in the story. 'Tino had locked him in a shed, without food or water, for days. I don't know what he intended, but it must have been designed to punish me in some way.'

That roused Don Gonzago, who, like Carmela, was inordinately fond of animals. 'The filthy sadist. Let me guess. Cousin Tino threatened to inform the authorities about Sebastiano?'

'Yes.'

'I do wish you had let him kill your loathsome cousin efficiently. What possessed you to leap between them?'

'How do you know I did?'

'It's what women do. Interfere at crucial moments.'

Carmela put her hands over her face. 'I've lost everything and so has Nonna. I'll never forget her tears. Tino's brother Santo will live in the farm, Tino will cream off the profits and the Americans will almost certainly bomb the *vedetta*.'

'Cain and Abel,' Don Gonzago said. 'Warring brothers. Perhaps they will kill each other.'

'It hardly matters if they do. Now Sebastiano is dead, he will never get to complete his mission. Allied soldiers will be killed who might have lived. My fault. All mine.'

Her father cut through the litany of self-blame. 'Sebastiano is dead? Where did this news come from?'

She related her conversation with the street cleaner on Piazza Vanvitelli. 'He was sure someone would have turned Sebastiano in. Fugitives like him are shot without trial, he said. Sebastiano would have come back to Naples, don't you think? The motorcycle was heading this way. He might have tried to come back here, no?'

Her father's expression offered no confirmation. She continued rather lamely, 'He was supposed to come here after he escaped, I know because Danielo told me. But you'd had a visit from a German officer so it wasn't safe. That is right, isn't it, Papà?'

Don Gonzago's reply was to ask Tomaso to pour the coffee. 'What of your grandmother?' he asked, in a slick change of subject. 'Where is my dear mother-in-law? The brothers haven't shut *her* up in the *vedetta* by any chance?'

'Oh, don't, Papà. I know you hate Nonna, but she is broken by this.'

'I do not hate Rosaria Cortazzi. She has a scowl that could wilt the blossom on wallpaper but I pity her. Age is hard under siege conditions. So?'

'She's at her cousin Cristina's.'

'In Santa Maria della Vedetta? She'd better keep her head down.'

'You think she won't be safe?'

'Who is safe with martial law on the streets? What of you, Carmela, should your gallant Tino track you here? What if he arrives at four in the morning, flanked by his Blackshirt kin?'

'He won't come after me. I doused his desires. The desire to marry me, at any rate.'

Don Gonzago studied her again. 'Yes… thick stockings and matronly boots are powerful weapons against lust.' The way he nodded confirmed her worst anxieties. Her hair had come down messily and was dusty from the road. She'd just realised her sleeve was covered in donkey hair. Of course he thought her scruffy. Superfluous to requirements. He would never love her as he did his son Danielo.

'I'll finish my meal, then go,' she muttered. 'I'll think of somewhere else to stay.'

'Oh, do stop,' her father said gruffly. 'We already have one potential martyr in the family with Danielo. Of course you can stay and share the few comforts we have left. Try and enjoy your food since you won't get anything else until tomorrow's breakfast. Tomaso, is our coffee fact or rumour? *Please* will you pour?'

Through a scribble of tears she saw Don Gonzago hold out his cup for Tomaso to fill from the pot. She wished she could read her father. With his mix of capricious humour and evasion, he always eluded her. 'I suppose you're appalled by what I've done.'

'Saving Sebastiano? I admire impulsiveness, when it's for the greater good.' He added a few grains of sugar to his cup. In the old days, he'd have stirred a spoonful in. 'Don't look so tortured, child. We know what passed off at la Casale.'

'Then why didn't you say? Why didn't you, Tomaso?'

Tomaso filled her cup next, with stately precision. When he placed it before her, she was physically shaking. Tomaso offered her the sugar bowl, and she copied her father, scooping up a few grains.

Tomaso finally whipped the lid off the chafing dish and stepped back. 'Dinner is served, Signore. I will come up later to clear.'

Carmela stared at the repast: a meagre arrangement of appetisers, then at the third place at the table. If that wasn't for Tomaso, then who?

Her curiosity was answered as a man in workman's overalls stepped into the room. He wore a cap pulled low, and her first impression was of a chin and jaw in dire need of a shave. He wished Don Gonzago and Tomaso a brusque good evening, and seeing Carmela, he nodded and said, 'You too, Signorina del Bosco.'

'Sebastiano... Sebbe?'

Disbelief and fearful joy swelled inside her until she realised there was no answering delight in the solemn eyes. Quite the opposite. He seemed to be asking, 'What the hell are you doing here?'

Chapter Twelve

'Sebastiano. I thought…' … *you were dead.* 'You vanished.'

He leapt forward in time to stop Carmela dropping her coffee cup. Prising it from her fingers, he put it back on its saucer.

'I had to go,' he said. 'It was neater that way.'

She stammered, 'A street sweeper said you'd probably been executed in a prison courtyard.'

'This is Naples. Everyone has an opinion.'

Sebastiano wasn't the messed-up man whose head she'd lifted to help him drink as he lay on a heap of straw. His bruises were fading, though he didn't quite resemble the handsome artist's sketch on the 'wanted' poster either. It was a complicated face: deep, black eyes above a Roman nose. She'd been right about the nose, glad to find it hadn't been broken.

'I told Papà that you must have returned to Naples. Is the Palazzo your safe house now?' She frowned, his silence unnerving her. He looked so grave and tired, like a man who has walked across a ravine on a tightrope and knows he has to do the same journey back, later. Seeing Sebastiano take the empty place at the table without any formality answered her question, however. This was his home. 'How do you know my father?'

Instead of replying, he picked up the sugar bowl. 'You look pale,' he said, and tipped the contents into Carmela's coffee.

Don Gonzago murmured in consternation, 'Leave some for later, *amico mio*!'

My friend. Nothing could shake her joy at seeing Sebastiano alive, but she was burning to know how he had become acquainted with her father. Neither man looked eager to explain and, once again, she was aware of being left on the sidelines.

Sebastiano unbent and gave her a slight smile. 'Sorry I glared at you a moment ago. It was a surprise, seeing you here. We have to be very, very careful. We're all friends, we protect each other. But beyond these walls things are very different.'

'I know. People in Naples will betray secrets for the price of a loaf of bread.'

'What is the price of a loaf of bread?' Don Gonzago asked Tomaso.

'A good pair of shoes, an hour of rumpy-pumpy or a small Rembrandt, Signore. Our currency's gone to pot.'

Carmela's glance kept sliding back to Sebastiano. Among the healing cuts on his hands were some more recent nicks. Red-brown dirt was ingrained around his nails. What had he been doing since leaving la Casale?

'I was so shocked to find you gone. Did Gio collect you?' she asked. 'Was it him on the motorbike, with you behind?'

Sebastiano replied, 'No chatter. No identities unless it's strictly necessary. Drink up.'

The sweet imitation coffee coursed into her stomach like hot lava and she put her head in her hands, dizzy from the inrush of sugar. She heard her father commenting on Tomaso's dinner offerings. 'Mm.

Sardine. All hail our brave fishermen, putting to sea on cupboard doors and coffin lids. The Germans have confiscated all the boats that survived the bombing. Baked tomatoes too. We'll keep Carmela's until she's ready. Allow me to serve you, Sebbe. How was your night's work?'

Sebastiano answered laconically. 'Laugh a minute. What was in today's paper? Is the propaganda machine still insisting the Germans are winning the battle for Italy?'

There was a rustle of newsprint, her father saying, 'The men who come down from the hills tell us that German divisions are retreating, beaten back by relentless naval firepower. Strangely, the front page of *Roma* describes the glorious victory the Germans are poised to secure as they push the Allies back into the sea. Take your pick.'

'If *Roma*'s editor still thinks it's about the beaches, he needs his head examined,' Sebastiano commented. 'The Germans are in full retreat in the mountain passes. Their Fuehrer has ordered them to stand and die. Anything to stop the Allies pushing on to Rome.'

'So certain they would win,' said Don Gonzago. 'Even without us on their side.'

Sebastiano shook out his napkin, and seeing his own hands against the white linen, he visibly flinched. 'The Germans have too few men, insufficient air cover and are running out of fuel.'

'How do you know this?' Carmela asked. Sebastiano's words were an injection of hope. If the Germans were literally being outgunned, the war might soon end.

'How does he know? It's his job, *figlia mia*.' Don Gonzago gestured at Sebastiano's hands. 'Don't be deceived by the marks of honest toil.'

'I know what his job is, Papà. Intelligence gathering. He told me more than he remembers.'

Sebastiano gave a slight head shake, then said, 'The enemy's in retreat, but they won't go quietly from Naples. They'll pummel the place, and leave a smoking mess for the Allies to enjoy, but by then I'll have moved on. And on, until the war is over. Carmela?'

Sebastiano was putting food on her plate. A medallion of toasted bread spread with flakes of seared sardine, a drizzle of oil and tomato halves, their edges pleasingly caramelised. Chopped basil added a piquant twist. In normal times, it would have been a morsel to enjoy with an aperitif. There was no sign of a second course, and if this was to sustain her until tomorrow's breakfast, she'd better do what her companions were doing: cut it into doll-size bits and consume it slowly. She wanted to ask Sebastiano if he'd found a wireless operator yet. He'd sounded so desperate at the top of the tower as he'd asked – *Mio, have you seen Mio?*

'Were you aware my daughter received an offer of marriage, Sebbe?' Don Gonzago spoke as if Carmela were not in the room. Sebastiano glanced her way.

'I know she has an admirer who visits la Casale. I tried to kill him.'

'Cortazzi.' Don Gonzago rolled his eyes. 'Thieves, whoremongers and pimps the lot of them.'

'My mother was a Cortazzi,' Carmela reminded her father, 'and my grandfather too. He was a good man.'

Don Gonzago allowed her last point. 'Your grandfather *was* a decent man. Had he been less so, he would have allowed me to compensate his pregnant daughter instead of insisting we marry.'

Sebastiano broke a thick silence, asking Carmela, 'I take it Tino survived his wound?'

'It was healing when I last saw him.'

'Does he still believe me to be a deserter?'

'He's no fool,' she said. 'But his attentions are elsewhere now.' She told him about the military takeover of the *vedetta* and quoted Tino: it was the perfect position for shooting down Allied bombers heading for Naples, Posillipo or Bagnoli. 'And you think so too, Sebbe.'

'I do?'

'It's why you climbed the steps, and asked me its height.'

'I don't remember that but I'm not surprised the Germans want to position a gun there. They'll be able to aim at anything coming in from the coast.' For a moment, Sebastiano drummed his fingers. Something was disturbing him. Tino, it turned out. 'Will he assume you've come here?'

'He knows.' Carmela explained how Tino had ordered her to leave, saying, 'Go to your father.' 'He gave me and Nonna an hour to get out. I don't think he means to harm me, because he has other priorities now.'

Don Gonzago agreed. 'Throwing in his lot with the Germans. The time may come when he has nowhere to hide.'

'Tino doesn't want to hide. You should have seen how his eyes gleamed when he described shooting down planes from our *vedetta*.'

'At least he let you go unharmed,' Don Gonzago said. 'Blood ties still mean something.'

Carmela took another morsel of food. 'You're right, Papà, I'm one of *them*. I used to wish for golden hair like Danielo, but perhaps being "all Cortazzi" has finally worked in my favour.'

'I do wish, *figlia mia*, you had succeeded in marrying in England.' Don Gonzago turned to Sebastiano, who seemed confused by the undercurrents, and as if he didn't understand where Carmela's self-criticism sprang from. 'Carmela was engaged to a very respectable young man there. Landed gentry. Had she pulled it off, she would have been safe. A naturalised Englishwoman.'

'They weren't landed gentry,' Carmela said, her voice clipped. She didn't want to talk about this, now or at any time. 'They were farmers.'

'Landed gentry, gentleman farmers,' Don Gonzago insisted.

'No, just farmers.'

'The poor boy was killed,' Don Gonzago sighed. 'Their only son.'

'I'm very sorry.' Sebastiano shared out the last of the coffee. He looked as though he too would like a change of subject.

'The boy was a flying ace,' Don Gonzago said.

Knowing her father would plough on, with all the inaccuracies he had woven into the story since she had first disclosed the news to him, Carmela gave Sebastiano a brisk account. 'His name was Cedric Folgate and he wasn't a flying ace. He died before the war even started. I met him when I was twenty-two at a Cambridge summer ball, if you must know. I was teaching in the city at the time, and he was working on his family farm.'

'What was the village?' Sebastiano seemed to ask the question for politeness' sake, though he added, 'I know Cambridgeshire.'

'Willow Farm, on the River Cam. The village was Camford Dauncey. We'd both tagged along to the ball with other people.' They'd found themselves sneaking away at the same moment from an argument about which Cambridge college had the best views. In spite of herself, she smiled. 'Cedric told me his farmhouse bedroom could knock spots off any of them.' She broke off in a flush of memory. A nightingale singing, an unexpected kiss. 'He turned out to be a good dancer, and the night just seemed… to disappear. There isn't any drama to impart. Our romance wouldn't make a novel. We loved each other, we both wanted the same things and his parents liked me. He wrote to

Papà, who gave consent and we announced our engagement. Shortly after that, Cedric applied to join the RAF.'

'There's a base at Duxford, isn't there?' Sebastiano was suddenly more interested in her very ordinary story. Perhaps it was the mention of the Royal Air Force, bringing the conversation back to something he could appreciate.

'Duxford is a few miles from Camford,' she said. 'Planes would race over, doing loops and barrel rolls. He was desperate to join.' Carmela steeled herself because that part of the story was not simple and she would not countenance any criticism of Cedric. 'The RAF turned him down.'

'A mere farmer,' Sebastiano murmured. 'They became less socially picky when the might of the Luftwaffe began to be realised. You don't mind me saying that?'

'It's true. He finally got into the Air Transport Auxiliary and he was jubilant, though he didn't need to join up at all.'

'Farming being a reserved profession.'

'He could have sat out the war, bringing in the crops. We set our wedding date for November '38. A quieter time on the farm. But a month short… a month before—' She couldn't go on.

Her father took over. 'I never understood why he didn't bail out.' Don Gonzago said the same thing whenever he made Carmela go through the story of Cedric's fatal flight, delivering one of the newly built Spitfires to Duxford airfield. 'He should have parachuted when his engine failed, then he'd have survived and my daughter would have been Mrs Cedric Folgate, safe from starvation, safe from the brutish lusts of Tino Cortazzi.'

She closed her eyes, her thoughts taking root on a blustery airstrip. She and Cedric's parents had been invited to watch him complete his twenty-first flight. A perfect October day, a guileless blue sky disclaiming all responsibility for the crash. *Take his hand, Carmela, and let's see a brave smile. Trust me, dear, he'll pull through.* He hadn't pulled through. Cedric had been trapped in a burning cockpit, still alive as they pulled him out but dead by the time they'd put him in the ambulance.

'Home she came,' Don Gonzago went on, 'and hardly had she unpacked her suitcase when she went off to the farm with her nonna. Giving up all this' – he indicated the watered-silk walls, the high, moulded ceiling – 'for the life of a medieval drudge. I find it inexplicable.'

'She's kind-hearted, Don Gonzago. But kind or not, she needs to know why I'm here, and all it implies.' Sebastiano looked straight at Carmela, who sat rigid, conscious of having disclosed too much about her past. 'Thanks to me jabbering while I was on morphine, you know what I am.'

Carmela grasped at the change of subject. 'A British spy.'

A silence fell across the little group until Sebastiano broke it with a sharp clearing of the throat. 'Agent. Gathering intelligence to help my side in this war. Hunted by Fascists of all stripes, dangerous to everyone I meet.'

'You don't have to tell me you're a danger,' she said fiercely.

Sebastiano did not blink. 'And that's why you should go.'

She flinched because it was a blow. She'd just gone through another desperate disaster of a day and he was trying to hound her out of the house she grew up in.

'Is there anywhere you *can* go?' he asked.

She turned to her father, who made a hopeless gesture with his hands. 'We are all on borrowed time here if the Germans decide the

Palazzo suits their needs. But I cannot think where else she might go,' Don Gonzago sighed. 'I was an only child, as was her mother, so there is no warren of cousins for her to burrow among other than the Cortazzi lot, and she can't go to them. Why are you so determined to evict her, Sebbe? My daughter is intelligent and trustworthy.'

She was surprised at her father's defence of her right to stay, lukewarm as it was. For most of her life, he had treated her as an afterthought. A daughter, so of limited use. Too shy to be entertaining and not beautiful enough to be an ornament.

Sebastiano gave Carmela a quick, hard glance. 'Intelligent, I will grant you that. But nobody is entirely trustworthy. I don't want to be responsible for anything happening to her. I don't have to tell you, Don Gonzago, what happens in police cells to anyone suspected of links to someone like me. She doesn't know how to move around the city, how to evade surveillance. If she was challenged, she'd give herself away in three breaths.'

'Hey,' she protested. 'If you want to insult me, do it to my face. I'm not an idiot, and I'm not planning to swan around the city attracting attention. I just need somewhere to sleep, and to take care of Renzo.'

Thinking of the dog made her recall the bell that had woken her as she dozed in the kitchen. Tomaso had ignored it, sent her upstairs, and minutes later, Sebastiano had appeared. Secrets woven into more secrets. Carmela sought her father's eye. 'Papà, this is your house. You're sheltering Sebastiano but you can't shelter me?'

Her father seemed to accept her point. 'We can find a corner for her, surely, Sebbe? She is my daughter, after all.'

Sebastiano shook his head, implacable.

Fury punched her between the ribs. 'This is the thanks I get for taking you in?' She got to her feet and was within a hair's breadth of hurling her cup at him. 'When you had nowhere else, I was your haven. I knew it might cost everything but I accepted you. Now it's my turn. I can't go back to la Casale, thanks to you. Throw me out, I'll be alone in Naples and we know what happens to lone women on the streets—'

Her father cut her off. 'Nobody has said you must go, Carmela.'

'He said it.' She jabbed her finger at Sebastiano. 'You look to *him* for approval.'

'I'm trying to make you understand what could happen if you associate with me,' Sebastiano said heavily. 'Whatever you've been through lately, bad as it seems, is nothing to what could befall you.'

'I'll take my chance.'

'I won't take that chance for you. I wish I could show you a cine film of the moment the Germans burst in on me and Mio, the day before I came to la Casale. You don't know what it's like, after months of dreading it, when your worst nightmare suddenly takes shape in front of your eyes. It happened to me, and to my comrade, and I'm damned if it will happen to you.'

There was a silence. Carmela didn't know what question to ask first and her father looked rather helpless. It was impossible not to conclude that Sebastiano was the one in charge here. He looked from Don Gonzago back to her and finally shrugged. 'If you've no other option, then I suppose neither do we. Stay until you find somewhere else.'

'Thank you,' she came back, clasping her hands in mock gratitude. 'How very generous.'

'Staying means you live by the rules. Walk the same line. All the rituals, all the caution. Trust nobody.'

'I can assure you, I have no difficulty obeying that last instruction.' She swallowed her resentment, accepting that she couldn't expect to be admitted into the hallowed circle within her first hour here. 'I will learn your rules.'

Sebastiano nodded, and got to his feet. 'I'm going to snatch an hour's sleep before the night shift.'

'What?' She stared into his exhausted face. 'A night shift?'

He rolled his eyes. As though he would answer that. 'Good night, Don Gonzago. Good night, Signorina del Bosco.'

Tomaso asked if she would like to sleep in her mother's old room. 'The bed's made up, and the other rooms are under dust covers. I hung blackout fabric at the window, so you should get a peaceful night's sleep.'

She was so tired she could have slept on the kitchen floor next to Renzo. She went to bed, carrying a small jug of warm water to wash in and a candle. She hung her few clothes in the wardrobe, alongside an azure silk robe she recognised as her mother's. It carried the same sweetly floral smell as the curtains. Her mother had disliked expensive perfume, saying it gave her headaches, but had splashed rose and violet water on everything. Sitting down at the dressing table, Carmela massaged her temples and examined her reflection in the glass. Mamma's headaches had been an extra member of the household as Carmela grew up. They came suddenly and lasted days, and Nina would lie in this room with the shutters and curtains closed. When Carmela tried to wriggle next to her for a cuddle she'd be greeted with, 'Not now, *tesoro*. Mamma's head hurts. Mamma's sick.'

Migraines. Emilio Baccolini had retrospectively diagnosed her mother's complaint during a conversation with Carmela a year or so back. Pregnancy could bring them on, which struck a chord because she had endured some thumping, flashing-light episodes during her own pregnancy. Not that she'd told the doctor that. He remained as ignorant of her own secret as the rest of the village.

As she undressed to wash, the snippet of hair in its muslin bag fell to the floor, along with Sebastiano's watch. She placed the hair under a pillow and, after some dithering, strapped the watch around the top of the bedside lamp, where it was hidden by the shade. She would give it to him… when she had forgiven his ingratitude and high-handedness. Putting on a nightdress she found in a chest of drawers, she blew out her candle, got into bed and closed her eyes.

Her eyes defied her and sprang open. She should have asked for a different room. There was such an aura of sadness here. According to her grandmother, Nina's unhappiness had intensified after she'd given birth to Carmela. 'There you were, a perfect and healthy child, but she looked at you as though you were a changeling. She couldn't explain why, nobody could.'

To Nonna, who had lost three children before their first birthdays, her own daughter's behaviour had been inexplicable. It had saddened her but frustrated her too. Staring up into the darkness, Carmela compared her own loneliness, her feelings of isolation, with her mother's. Perhaps they came from the same source. After all, the common denominator in their lives was Don Gonzago del Bosco. A man of great ability who sat alone in a vast house, doling out affection to chosen favourites, in teaspoonfuls.

She felt a scratch under her shoulder and discovered a hair slide, smooth like tortoiseshell. It was too dark to see it properly but it could hardly have remained from her mother's time. After Nina's death, her bed had been swapped with one from a different room. Assuming neither Tomaso nor her father had taken to wearing hair ornaments, there was but one explanation. Don Gonzago was still the ardent lover.

'Damn you, why this room? Why not one of the other nine bedrooms?'

Finally, she slept, and woke some time later hearing feet pass the door. The tread was cautious, and heading towards the stairs. Sebastiano, off for his mysterious night shift, she assumed. Her nerves on high alert, she woke again later, convinced she had heard a bell jangling. And then, distinctly, a bark from Renzo.

At this, she was out of bed instantly. Pulling the blue silk robe from the wardrobe, she belted it around herself as she hurried down two flights of stairs.

She paused in the corridor leading to the kitchen. Behind a closed door were men speaking Italian, gruffly and very fast, with a strong peppering of Neapolitan dialect. One was Sebastiano, telling the other man that he was leaving for work any moment. 'We're going back inside the perimeter at Capodimonte tonight, under armed guard, so there has to be something there they want to hide.'

'Course there is, but you said you needed a wireless operator. I found you one and we should go now and make contact. What's changed, Sebbe?'

'Nothing, but you were to come tomorrow night, Gio.'

Gio!

Carmela inched forward and, hearing the reply, knew that Danielo's friend was present and in a state of stress. He was telling Sebastiano that he had to leave Naples immediately because his home was under surveillance. 'This evening, there was a street vendor outside our house, a man none of us ever saw before, selling rubbishy shoelaces. It was obvious he was watching who came and went. Mamma chased him away, then told me to go.' Gio was on his way now to his grandparents' house, he said. Out in the countryside. He'd wait there for Sebastiano.

'But I can't stay there long either. If you want my help, Sebbe, and to meet this wireless operator, come tomorrow, no later. Tomaso knows how to reach me.'

The voices faded and Carmela heard a door shutting. The men must have left the building. At the sound, Renzo whined and she walked into the kitchen where she jumped in surprise. Tomaso was at the long table, his chin resting on his hands and a candle guttering by his elbow.

He sat up. 'Eavesdropping is a dangerous pursuit, Signorina Carmela.'

She apologised. 'I was woken by a bell, and I was worried about Renzo.' The dog looked peaceful though he whined again when Carmela crouched down and stroked his head. He was almost certainly hungry. She fed him a little of his maize soup. 'What work does Sebastiano do?'

'He's been part of a road gang since he first arrived in Naples. It's brutish work because the Germans use them as cheap labour, but it's also a good way to gather intelligence on defences and installations. The soldiers who guard them assume the men can't understand them, so they chatter freely.'

'Sebastiano speaks German?'

'I will leave you to ponder.' Tomaso got up, arching his back as if it ached.

'Just one thing. Why is Gio's house under surveillance?'

'I suppose there's no harm you knowing, since it's already a fait accompli. Take a seat.' Tomaso sat down again and waved at the chair on the opposite side of the table. 'When it was obvious that Sebastiano must be brought here to the Palazzo, Gio borrowed a van. The only people apart from the Germans and the police who have vans and fuel to put in them are generally bad men.'

'I know Gio borrowed one from a criminal and on the way home, he and Danielo were stopped.'

'The van was confiscated. Gio escaped but he had to tell the owner, who made him sign a *cambiale*.'

A promissory note to pay off the debt at a high rate of interest. The first repayment had fallen due and Gio had missed it, in part because he hadn't got the money and because by that time he was busy purloining a motorbike for another trip to la Casale.

'So it was him,' Carmela breathed. 'The bike was stolen?'

Tomaso shrugged. 'How else was he to get one? He's unemployed. Gio missed the next payment on his loan – they come every few days, you know – and he got a beating from one of the bad man's henchmen. It's the way of things, but Gio's hot-headed.'

'Like Danielo.'

'Yes, they're a pair, they have petrol vapour for brains. Gio pulled a knife, deeply offending the bad man. As a result, his name was passed across at the *questura*.' The police station. 'He's been named as a friend of the resistance and the net is closing, so Gio's getting out.'

'To his grandparents'. I heard. And Sebastiano is following him because Gio can lead him to a wireless operator. Am I right?'

'Signorina, you said, "just one thing" and I have answered you. Good night. I'll leave you the candle.'

This is down to me, she reminded herself. If she'd taken Sebastiano in quickly, without argument, Danielo and Gio might have got home unscathed and the van returned to its owner. Now Gio was on the run. She didn't think she could feel any worse, but before he left the kitchen, Tomaso dropped a brick.

'You must say goodbye to your four-legged friend, Signorina.'

Her eyes swung to Renzo. 'Never. I'd rather live with him in the gutter or a *basso*.' A street-level room, she meant, slum accommodation little better than a hole in the ground.

'Goodbye to your donkey,' Tomaso said quietly. 'Renzo we can deal with but there's no hay or straw for your donkey. He'll soon eat and trample our little patch of grass. Nor can we spare the water. I'm sorry.'

Turn Nearco loose in a starving city? It would be kinder to murder him where he stood. After Tomaso left her, she stared into the sputtering candle flame, holding back her tears. Instead, she conjured rebellious thoughts. Life had taken almost everything from her that mattered, and she was not going to surrender anything further.

Rebellious thoughts formed into a plan.

Chapter Thirteen

Don Gonzago supported Carmela's decision to take Nearco out of the city, but not her plan of looking after him from a distance. 'You cannot walk out each day, carrying vegetable scraps and water without drawing attention to yourself. You can't do it on a starveling's rations, either. Haven't you noticed how slowly Tomaso moves, and that I am almost always in my chair? We conserve energy in order to survive.'

They were in the dining room, eating a breakfast of tissue-thin slices of cheese, dark rye bread and olives. Ersatz coffee steamed in the pot.

'I'll drive Nearco up the Sentiero della Croce,' she explained. The Sentiero was the winding back road she had come down yesterday, which connected Naples to the unpopulated hills. 'If you take a path off it, you can reach the monastery of San Romualdo.' The slopes up to the monastery were steep and wild, which meant fewer people to seize Nearco and put him to work. Or worse. 'I can walk there every day and fetch water while I'm at it.' She described the spring spurting from the rocks, where she'd stopped on her journey here. 'Carrying water canteens would be the perfect excuse.'

Tomaso poured coffee for them. 'Why do you offer your heart up for torture, Signorina? When something is unavoidable, it's best to do it and walk on.'

'Abandon Nearco, because he's no longer of use?'

'Nearco. What a name for a donkey.'

'I know. Nonna always said, "Name them——"'

'And you weep when they die,' Don Gonzago finished for her. 'Your mother used to say the same thing, and like you, she ignored her own maxim. She would take in stray cats and name them and their kittens. Nearco must take his chances. Find a place with grass and shade and, with luck, he'll survive. Push your cart into a ravine or a thicket and come home. To be honest, I'm not comfortable with the idea of you going anywhere alone.'

A distant jangling made Tomaso leave the room abruptly. Carmela looked at her father, who looked back at her with a benign poker face. A minute later, Tomaso was back with Sebastiano, whose cheeks were grey with fatigue.

'Is the bell ringing down in the kitchen a signal to let you in?' Carmela asked Sebastiano.

Leaning heavily against the table edge, he returned a speculative look but didn't answer directly. 'Tomaso says you're leaving.'

'Only for a few hours. You're still lumbered with me here.' She wondered how he'd got on overnight, behind the perimeter fence at Capodimonte. It was one of Naples' hills, formerly a royal hunting ground and now in the grip of the Germans. What had Sebastiano seen? Hard labour while harvesting intelligence – under armed guard – must be exhausting. She explained her plan for Nearco, and the reason behind it.

'Makes sense. I'd travel with you but—'

'You've been working all night, Sebbe,' Tomaso interrupted. Gesturing him to sit down, he put coffee in front of Sebastiano. 'Signorina del Bosco wouldn't ask it of you.'

'I wasn't asking,' Carmela agreed crossly. She was tired of being manoeuvred onto the back foot.

Sebastiano looked at his hands, tallying the latest damage to them. 'I washed in a fountain that is still working. The Germans have a water supply still. It didn't seem to make me any cleaner.'

'We're not so fastidious these days.' Tomaso set a plate of breakfast down for him, with extra cheese on it as well as a hard-boiled egg, one of those Carmela had brought from the farm. He advised Sebastiano to eat, then sleep. 'We'll look after Signorina Carmela.'

Carmela repeated that she didn't need an escort. 'I used to drive my cart from la Casale to Naples and back in a day when I came here for the markets.'

'I know. You're an independent—' A movement caught Sebastiano's eye and he turned in his seat with a speed that belied his exhausted state. When he realised what he was seeing, he chuckled. 'I assume that is the famous missing dog?'

'Yes, it's Renzo.' Carmela and Tomaso had carried him upstairs on his pink-curtain bed, as he was showing distress at being left. 'He's not looking his best.'

'He's no thinner than many a Neapolitan stray.' Sebastiano broke off a piece of cheese and stretched out his hand. Renzo took it with delicate caution. 'Good boy.' Sebastiano looked at Carmela. 'Did he find his own way home?'

'Tino had him, locked up, and I was just in time.'

'Tino again. *Dio*, I really wish you'd let me—'

'Kill him?' she finished. 'Can you imagine the outcry if the most visible man in Santa Maria della Vedetta had ended up dead on my farm?'

'Mm.' It sounded like a concession. He followed it up with, 'I wish I had not come anywhere near you. *I* was the mistake, Carmela, not you.'

'The most dangerous enemy is the one you don't know,' Don Gonzago said lightly. 'Tino Cortazzi is a known quantity. I fear those who are waiting to strike, but haven't declared it.' He asked Tomaso if he had yet explained to Carmela the ritual for getting back into this building.

'Not yet, Signore, but I will be pleased to induct her into the mysteries.'

'Immediately after breakfast, if you would.' Her father turned to her and said, 'We never use the front entrance these days.'

'I'm sorry, I didn't know.'

'Indeed, how could you? We have a protocol for entering the Palazzo, and you need to follow it.'

'Of course.'

Once they'd finished eating, Don Gonzago asked Carmela if she would kindly make more coffee. Certain she was being dismissed so the men could talk, she got up reluctantly. Her father told her not to shut the dining room door behind her. 'We keep doors open, so we can always hear who is in the house, and where.'

When she returned with a fresh pot of *caffè d'orzo*, her father told her that he had reached a decision in her absence. 'You will stay safely here, Carmela. I will take Nearco into the countryside.'

'No, it's my job.' Carmela glared at Sebastiano. *This is your doing.*

Her father, noting the direction of her scowl, shook his head. 'I decided, not Sebbe. And while I shudder at playing the heavy-handed father, you are under my roof and owe me your obedience. No?'

She felt like shouting, *I'm not a child and but for a stalling Spitfire engine, I'd be a married woman with a couple of babies by now!* But she held her tongue. While she'd been down to the kitchen, her father had been busy drawing a map on a scrap of paper. It showed a lattice of roads and a large, upright cross with 'San Romualdo' written above it. That was the monastery where she'd suggested leaving Nearco, so clearly they approved her plan. The men all avoided her eye, however, and she deduced that she was still being kept out of something. Fine. Let her father harness Nearco and see how far he got.

Tomaso touched her arm. 'Shall we clear the table, and I'll show you our cunning escape route. We'll start in the cellars. Follow me, Signorina.'

'I know where the cellars are,' she said loudly as she followed him out. 'Don't forget, I was born here. Twenty-seven years ago.'

Palazzo del Bosco had been built in a luxurious age as an important nobleman's residence. Then, its grounds had covered several hectares of hillside with staff quarters, stables and coach houses. Such a household had required a great larder and its vaults ran beneath the house and stretched under the garden. Caves cut into the soft rock beneath the Palazzo had provided dry storage for wine, brandy, salted meats, cheese and grain. Lighting a candle he took from a sconce at the top of the steps, Tomaso led her down. She guessed he planned to show her the passage that connected to the caves, forgetting that he'd taken her along it when she was a child. It had been a source of great awe and excitement to scurry along a dark tunnel and emerge into a cave that faced a sheer drop into the ravine below.

To her surprise, the door to the passage was concealed behind an enormous wine rack.

'It exists still,' Tomaso said enigmatically in answer to her question, and walked to the far end of the cellar where he lifted his candle to show a metal grille. 'I'm going to tell you how to gain entry, should you need to leave the house and come back. Directly above this grating is Vicoletto del Bosco.' A narrow alley that had never merited a street sign. 'Whenever you return to the Palazzo,' Tomaso instructed, 'always take the backstreets. Never use Viale Bellavista at the front, as your father explained.'

'Because someone might be watching the house?'

'It is always a possibility. There's a bell pull hidden in the ivy on the wall to the side of this vent.' Tomaso rapped the wall to show her. 'Before entering the *vicoletto*, the alley, check you're not being followed. If you have even the faintest suspicion, keep walking. But if you think it's safe, give the bell a firm tug and walk on. As you have already guessed, it's a signal for me to go out and unlock the rear garden gate. Whatever you do, don't wait to be let in. There are German patrols around here all the time. Keep walking. Don't look back. Circuit the house before returning to the *vicoletto*. Repeat until you're admitted. Stay casual and *never* look back.'

'What if you don't hear the bell? What if you're too far from the kitchen?'

'Walk around Vomero at an easy pace, returning to Vicoletto del Bosco at intervals. Pull the bell each time you pass. Do not call down through this grate or try to get in through these cellars.'

'Is this how Sebastiano always gets in? And Gio too, in the night?' She asked with little expectation of being answered. And she was right. Tomaso behaved as though he hadn't heard a word.

When they returned to the kitchen, the door was open and she could hear the donkey's hooves on the courtyard flagstones. She went out to see her father struggling with the harness. He had the bridle upside down, and Nearco had put his head right up in the air and curled his lip.

Ha.

Wondering if Sebastiano had taken Tomaso's advice and retired to bed for the day, Carmela went back indoors. She quickly put her identity papers and a little money in an inside pocket of her dress. She shoved a cotton scarf in her pocket too and asked Tomaso where he kept the water canisters. 'Papà might as well fill one or two on his way back. His job, since he insisted on going.'

Giving her a wry look, Tomaso found two large, metal canteens with clip-top lids.

When she took them outside, her father was up on the cart. Nearco had been turned around to face the open gates, and was harnessed. *Neatly done*, Carmela reflected. In the back of the cart, something human-sized was covered with a canvas sheet. A bed of sorts for a stowaway? *Would he shout if I poked him hard?* she wondered. When she checked the straps and buckles of the harness, she found no fault with the way it had been put on. 'For a moment, I thought you must have forgotten how to do this,' she said to her father.

He looked sheepish. 'Just one of the things one never forgets.'

She patted the donkey's neck. 'Off you go, then. Have a good journey. Leave my faithful friend somewhere near water, you promise?'

'I promise.' Don Gonzago clicked his tongue. He told Nearco to 'Get on.'

'Say "*Arri*, Nearco".'

'*Arri*, Nearco.'

The donkey did not move. Carmela took the bridle and Nearco advanced a couple of steps. '*Tsh*, off you go. Walk nicely for Don Gonzago.'

Nearco planted himself. Ten minutes later, he was still in the same spot and Tomaso had closed the gates, for fear that someone might peer in and wonder what was going on.

'Would a carrot on a fishing rod make a difference?' he asked.

'Do we have a carrot?' Don Gonzago asked testily. 'Just a stick would do better.'

'If you show him a stick, he'll go backwards,' Carmela said. She went to the rear of the cart, lifted the canvas and asked Sebastiano if he was too hot yet.

'Boiling. Could you get that animal moving?' The part of his face she could see was beaded with sweat. 'I have somewhere to be and I don't need a bout of sunstroke.'

'I know. You're meeting your comrade Gio at San Romualdo, and he isn't going to wait long. Of course you need to get going, but did I mention? Nearco only goes for me. Papà, you can sit up there all day with carrots and sticks and he still won't budge.'

Don Gonzago batted a fly away from his face. He was pink from exasperation. 'What do you suggest, then?'

'What I suggested an hour ago.' Carmela took the headscarf from her pocket and knotted it over her hair.

Grumbling, her father got down. 'I don't like it,' he said. 'You come straight home, my girl.'

'I will. Look after Renzo for me.' Before climbing up onto the box, Carmela dumped the water canteens in the back of the cart, provoking a protest from under the canvas sheet. Don Gonzago said loudly, so Sebastiano would hear, 'If you even half suspect you're being followed, tell whoever stops you that my daughter had no idea you were hiding in the back.'

'I've a better idea.' Sebastiano got out and climbed up beside Carmela. 'If anyone stops us, we're lovers eloping at low speed.'

She appreciated his ability to joke, but there was tension in his voice. He wasn't riding alongside her for the pleasure of her company but to find Gio, who would help him deliver the intelligence he'd worked so hard, risked so much, to gain. When he had done that, he would start all over again until the day came when his luck ran out and he was caught.

The thought made her feel sick. '*Arri*, Nearco.'

Tomaso opened the gates again and they were on their way.

Chapter Fourteen

They reached the spring that poured from a fissure of rock in the heat of noon. A stone basin had been roughed out under the sparkling rivulet and a trough too, deep enough for a donkey to drink from. Carmela presumed that the monks of San Romualdo were the craftsmen. While the donkey slaked his thirst, she and Sebastiano swallowed as much as they could take. Afterwards, she half-filled one canteen to take on her journey up to the monastery. She'd fill it full again on the way back. She offered the other one to Sebastiano, but he declined.

'There'll be water in the village and I shan't stay there long.'

'Because you're travelling on with Gio. You need to find a wireless operator so you can send messages back home about the towers, and anti-aircraft guns and whatever you discovered last night on Capodimonte.'

Sebastiano seemed disturbed by her guesswork, but he didn't deny it.

'You told me some of it the night I first met you.'

'I was gibbering.'

Yes, gibbering about something that meant everything to him. Mio. Urgent intelligence that would save lives. She wished he would confide it all, but his expression had become deliberately blank. 'Could you give Gio a message from me?' she asked.

He stiffened, but didn't refuse. 'Go on.'

'Tell him I'm sorry for dithering when he came to la Casale, and that I wish him well. I wish he hadn't had to steal a motorbike and if I can ever make it up to him—'

He cut her off. 'I don't need to know the rest. Goodbye, and good luck.' Sebastiano pulled off the thick leather gloves he was wearing and held out a hand.

She clasped it briefly, resisting the urge to squeeze because of the raw wounds in his flesh. 'You too. I hope you meet your wireless man, and then find peace.'

'Peace, some hope.' He tilted his left hand as if to check his watch, and clicked his tongue in annoyance. 'I lost the damn thing. You probably burned it with the straw, without knowing.'

She hated herself then. What had made her hang on to the watch, when knowing the time might be life and death to him? An ugly thought struck her. *This is what my father does. Withholds the thing you want most.* A rush of regret made her catch her breath.

Sebastiano had dropped one of his gloves and she bent to pick it up at the same moment he did. Their lips met as they straightened up and, for a dumbfounded moment, they kissed.

The world melted like butter on a stove. The shriek of cicadas in the grass sank to a hum. Into the lapse of consciousness came Cedric's face. *Forgotten me, sweetheart?*

She pulled away. 'Don't. How dare you?'

'Woah, sorry.' Sebastiano stepped back. 'I apologise. That wasn't planned.'

She waited for him to blame the heat, or his state of mind, or hunger, or her. All he said was, 'I've lost my power of judgement. It's so long since I've been close to anyone.'

Her throat tightened painfully. To say, 'Same for me' would have been a release but she was done with self-indulgence. Instead, she nodded a cold goodbye and grabbed Nearco's lead-rope. She and Sebastiano had already pushed the cart into a stand of pine trees on the other side of the track, and she'd exchanged the donkey's harness for a head collar.

Matching Nearco's lethargic pace, she left Sebastiano still standing by the spring and restarted her journey along the Sentiero della Croce. Ahead of her, on a crag, a marble cross caught the shimmering light. The monastery commanded a plateau, its outlines melting in heat haze. She pictured Santa Maria della Vedetta, somewhere in the high distance, baking under the same merciless sun.

Should she go all the way up to the monastery? Yes, she decided, as a penance for her selfishness and bad decisions. The monks might find Nearco and have a use for him. And above the tree line, there was less likelihood of stray dogs or wild boar picking up his scent.

Sebastiano walked past her. Without looking back he said, 'Take care. Watch out for snakes.' He got well ahead of her and she saw him turn off onto a track between a double line of wind-scorched pines. Regret poured into her. All he'd done was kiss her impulsively, and it had felt good. She'd smacked him down like a spinster teacher and that, she smiled bitterly... that felt like her all over these days. And now he was gone.

It was too hot to plod on up the hill, she decided. Flies were clustering around the donkey's eyes. She led him into the trees and knotted his lead-rope into a loop so he could graze without stepping on it. Making a pillow of the cardigan she'd tied round her waist, she lay down. Hardly had she got comfortable when a sound disturbed her. Getting quickly to her feet, she saw a number of open-topped armoured cars approaching at speed. She didn't know what to do, but before they reached her, they each made a skidding turn onto the track Sebastiano had taken five minutes before. Sunlight jounced off steel helmets and machine guns held upright against field-grey chests.

There was no doubt, they'd come from Naples and they had to be after Sebastiano. Had Tino given him away, or had he slipped up somehow? Carmela hurtled towards the track, coughing as she entered the dust cloud thrown up by the wheels. Her only thought was to somehow reach Sebastiano and help him, though as she stumbled in a pothole and almost fell on her face, she suspected it was a pointlessly self-destructive mission. So why was she running as though her life depended on it?

A short way up the track, she called his name and a figure burst from a gorse thicket. He caught her before she had time to stop, spun her round and pulled her into the dense cover.

'What the devil are you doing?' Sebastiano hissed in her ear. 'They're Waffen SS and they're not on a picnic.'

Her thoughts exactly.

'I wanted to warn you.'

'How? If I was still walking, you'd have reached me in time to see me being shot.'

She felt his heart thumping against her back. The kiss she had flung back at him lingered on her mouth, mixed with dust. 'I'm sorry.'

'Why are you sorry? Did you send for them?'

'The Germans? No!' How could he ask that? 'I thought maybe Tino had.'

Sebastiano grunted and nodded up the track, where the Germans had gone. 'The village up there is San Romualdo Inferiore. Where Gio is waiting for me.'

'So – they could be after him—'

'Not necessarily. The road cuts through the village, so they might have somewhere else in mind. If he heard the vehicles in time, Gio will have run into the trees.'

That was a comfort. At this hour, the village women would be putting the lunch tables outdoors in the shade and could hardly be unaware what was heading their way. Carmela could still hear the grind of engines. And then they stopped. She looked at Sebastiano.

He said, 'We stay here for now.'

An instant later, she leapt at the rattle of automatic gunfire. They crouched stock-still and powerless in the shelter of their thicket as it went on and on. Carmela pictured German bullets raking sun-soaked walls, firing into windows while terrified villagers cowered or scattered in all directions. When the shooting finally paused, the breeze brought the sound of screaming.

The next minutes were measured in heartbeats. When they heard the approach of vehicles, Sebastiano pulled Carmela close inside their gorse shelter. They held their breath as the Germans passed on their return journey, not moving until they could once again hear the cries of birds in the pine trees. Stepping cautiously out onto the track, they saw a fierce halo of orange sparks above the trees surrounding the village. The air crackled fiercely.

Sebastiano told her to go back home. 'The Germans won't hang around. It'll be safe enough, though keep out of sight where you can.'

It was obvious he was going on. She said, 'I'm coming too. I need to know what we just heard.'

'God knows what we'll find. You have no idea.'

'If anything's happened to Gio, someone needs to tell Danielo. Believe me, I can face it.' To prove it, she began walking.

They were coughing before they'd reached the trees. As they emerged into San Romualdo Inferiore, into a blast of heat, and the truth was laid before them, Carmela crossed herself. 'Saints have mercy on us.'

Chapter Fifteen

In the deserted street, nothing moved but every outline flickered. An ancient church was ablaze, fire raging through its roof and windows. Over the ocean-roar of flames came the single-note clang of a bell. At first, Carmela thought it must be the monks in their distant hermitage, ringing the alarm. Until Sebastiano pointed to the open belfry, which was flanked with sheets of flame. The bell was swinging as if under the direction of ghostly hands. Again, Carmela crossed herself.

'It's the heat,' Sebastiano said, his voice gruff from smoke. 'Making the bronze expand—' He didn't bother to finish. What words could be added? All across the church piazza, lunch tables were overturned, platters and jugs smashed on the ground. And there were strewn bodies. Not human but animal. Dogs, mules, donkeys. A pig. Chickens, even cats whose tattered remains testified to a machine-gun spree. Her gorge rose. All this, because a young rebel had taken refuge with his grandparents? 'The people – you think they got away?'

'I don't know.' Sebastiano went towards the nearest house whose door gaped. Carmela followed, glad to withdraw from the furnace. Inside were signs of forced entry in the upended furniture, the pictures thrown down. A statuette of the Virgin, shattered. A hat, a shawl, a single shoe abandoned. Another house revealed much the same. Carmela repeated her desperate hope. 'They escaped, leaving their animals.'

Telling her to stay where she was, Sebastiano took off his jacket and cap and went to the stone well at the edge of the piazza. He hauled up a bucket and doused his garments before putting the cap back on and draping the jacket over his head.

'Don't go too close,' Carmela shouted as he went towards the church, hunched against flying sparks. That tower, that swinging bell, might fall any second. Her fears were justified when, with a dull cracking sound, a slab of mortar plummeted. She called, 'Take care!' but either he couldn't hear or he had blocked her out. He was reaching through the smoke towards the church doors, which were closed. Suddenly, he let out a terrible cry and she saw him reel back and tumble down the steps. Pulling off her headscarf and holding it to her mouth, she ran towards him. As she reached the church, smoke and flame parted briefly, revealing a body bound in chains that were secured around the iron handle of the door. It was man – young, his body blackened and blood-streaked, his mouth open in death agony.

As she backed away, spurting incoherent sounds, Sebastiano caught up with her. Together, they staggered back to the edge of the village. Moments later, the belfry collapsed, dropping a flaming barricade in front of the church door.

'Sebbe, what did you see?' She wanted him to tell her there had been nothing there. She'd experienced a hallucination. He stared at her, then managed one word. 'Gio.'

'They barred the door,' said a voice behind them.

They turned to see a monk holding the hands of two small children with blank faces. 'They forced the people inside, sprayed them with bullets then chained the door before setting the fire.'

Carmela felt the ground heave. She'd told Sebastiano she could face this, but she was wrong. 'Any… any survivors?'

'A few children, who were playing in the caves beneath the monastery. My brother monks have taken them in. These little ones are the last two.'

'What can we do, Brother?' Carmela could not bear to look at the infants, whose huge, unblinking eyes reflected the flames.

The monk moved his glance from her to Sebastiano, who was clutching his hands against his stomach. 'You're from Naples?'

Carmela confirmed it.

'Then tell them there of this day's work.'

'Why did they do it?' Carmela feared Sebastiano was about to collapse. His breathing was laboured. Beneath his workman's cap, his face was screwed up in pain.

The monk offered an opinion as they walked away from the burning village. It was known that the people of San Romualdo Inferiore sent support to resistance fighters and partisans, and sometimes hid fugitives. 'Rebel groups in Naples, young lads and former soldiers, have killed a few Germans and this is how the Germans answer. Reprisals. A warning to the others.' The monk turned for a last look at the devastation. 'As Colonel Scholl promised, it's one hundred Italians executed for every German killed or harmed.'

That was the detail that had been ripped off the poster Carmela had read on her way into Naples, but this was no random reprisal. Gio's name had been given to the authorities because he'd defaulted on a debt. A debt incurred because he'd lost a vehicle belonging to a vicious man. And all because he'd helped Sebastiano. A sob jerked from her throat as she remembered him coming into the farmyard to find out what was delaying Danielo, a hint of a strut in his walk.

'You said you'd be five minutes, 'Nielo. How long does it take to get a woman to do you a favour?' And Danielo's reply: 'Longer than it takes you, Gio.' Two friends, rogues in their way, living life to the full. Believing in something greater than themselves. She could say prayers for Gio for the rest of her life and it would never be enough.

'Your hands, *amico*.' The monk was glancing anxiously at Sebastiano. 'They look bad. You burned them? Come with me to the monastery and have them bandaged.'

Sebastiano refused. 'I have to get back to the city, I have to plan. Brother—' He stopped and Carmela and the monk did too. 'Are you in contact with the partisans?'

The answer was stern. 'We are not.'

'There's a group operating from the forests behind Nola. Do you know the name "Tarzia"? Gio was going to take me there. I have to reach them.'

'I don't know any place called Tarzia,' the monk said. 'Nor do I want to. We are a strict order and have no contact with partisans or rebels. If you want to do something, my son, return to Naples and tell all the young boys, so they know what their antics unleash on their families.'

When they reached the end of the track, they parted, the monk and the two children taking the road that scaled the hill. Carmela hunted with her eyes for Nearco, who was nowhere to be seen. She couldn't go off and search for him because Sebastiano needed help. His hands were badly burned; he was in shock. His teeth were chattering though the afternoon sun still beat down.

Gripping his arm, she encouraged him to walk and prayed that Nearco had ambled back to the cart and was waiting. But there was no donkey and no hoof prints either. The gunfire, the smell of burning would have driven him away. They had no choice but to walk.

Carmela picked up the water can she'd dropped when she'd run after Sebastiano, and the other one was where she'd left it, next to the cart.

She filled them at the spring, while Sebastiano held his hands under the icy flow. The smell of burning lingered in her nose, merging Gio's horrifying death with the final minutes of Cedric's life, which flowed back with shocking clarity. She hadn't been able to help that day either.

'Did you touch the red-hot chain?' She lifted one of Sebastiano's hands and what she read there spelled agony.

'I have to find Tarzia,' Sebastiano replied as though this was the only thing that meant anything. His voice was cut with hard breaths. 'I have to find the partisans.'

'Because they have a wireless operator. I understand.' With Gio dead, who would take him? Sebastiano wasn't in a fit state to do anything, let alone find a partisan hideout in the forested hills above Nola, the town he'd named to the monk. Nola was thirty kilometres off.

'Danielo knows where they are,' Sebastiano muttered. 'He and Gio had no secrets.'

'No.' The thought of Danielo sharing Gio's fate sent a violent shudder through her. She understood now what Sebastiano and her brother were fighting for, and what Gio had died for. The struggle for good against evil. But throwing another young life on the fire was unthinkable. However, she knew that Sebastiano wasn't in any state to reason. One foot in front of the other was about as much as he could manage for now.

As they began what was to be a slow trek home, she blanked out the horror of what she'd witnessed at San Romualdo Inferiore. The only thing that would drive away this nightmare was action, playing a part in ridding her land of Germans, and the most obvious way was to help Sebastiano fulfil his mission. If he would let her.

*

Two circuits of the Palazzo were required before the bell brought
Tomaso to the garden gate.

'Cutting it fine, Signorina. Forty minutes until curfew. Your father's
been fretting dreadfully.' When he saw Sebastiano a couple of paces
behind, Tomaso's expression fell. 'What went wrong?'

'Everything,' Carmela said. 'Sebastiano needs first aid.' She carried
the water cans into the kitchen and an empty corner caught her eye.
'Where's Renzo?' Emotion flared. She was ready to scream. 'You haven't
put him out, Tomaso?' It would be too much, just too much on top
of everything.

'He's upstairs,' Tomaso soothed. 'I fed him, then carried him up
because your father wanted company. Don Gonzago made a sortie
down town earlier and has spent the afternoon searching for documents. *Dio*, *Dio*, what's with you, my friend?'

Sebastiano had sunk onto a hard chair. He displayed his hands.
Tomaso, chirruping with distress, fetched salve and bandages.

'Use thin gauze,' Sebastiano directed. 'Don't turn my hands into
drumsticks. I can't be disabled.'

Carmela put water to boil and hovered while Tomaso bathed and
dressed Sebastiano's wounds. Leaving Sebastiano to relate what they'd
seen at San Romualdo, she took food upstairs for Renzo. She found her
father sitting at the dining table, poring over a set of papers with the
help of a hand-held magnifying glass. She told him about the village,
about Gio. To her distress, Don Gonzago put his hands over his face
and began to weep.

'Brutes. Animals. That sweet young man. Brutes.'

He didn't flinch away as she pulled up a chair, sat beside him and
wept too, with her arm around him. It was the closest she had been
to her father in all her adult life.

After a while he asked, 'How badly hurt is Sebbe?'

She dried her tears and sat up. 'His hands are damaged and he's in severe pain. He wants to travel to find the partisans, and a wireless operator to send his message, but he won't be up to it for a while.'

'Don't prejudge. He was trained in a hard school.' Don Gonzago took a handkerchief from his pocket and mopped his eyes. Tears had speckled the item he'd been reading and Carmela saw it was Danielo's birth certificate, naming 'Don Gonzago del Bosco' as the father. 'I was double-checking his age,' he said. 'Your brother turns eighteen on 2 October, which gives him under two weeks before he's eligible for forced labour.'

'Is Danielo out of prison? Is that where you went today?'

'Yes, to collect him but he'd already been let go. They can't accommodate all the young hooligans being brought in, apparently. The *scugnizzi* have gained a taste for fighting. Raiding arms dumps, making their own bombs, challenging the Germans and erecting barricades. Boys doing men's work, but they're safer in jail than on the street.'

'So, Danielo's home?'

'I hope so. His mother will want him under her eye, I can tell you.'

'I need to see him.'

'Not yet. Violetta will prefer him to herself for a while,' Don Gonzago said gently.

Carmela leaned away at the mention of Danielo's mother. Violetta Cicciano, now Violetta Vincenzo, had begun her affair with Don Gonzago when Carmela's mother was being treated in a sanatorium on Capri for nervous depression. She'd been well placed to slip into Don Gonzago's bed, being one of the live-in maids. The liaison had continued after Nina's return and for this fact alone, Carmela had no desire to meet the woman again. *But.* Danielo's safety and Sebastiano's needs were paramount. Sebastiano was now looking to Danielo to get him to the partisans, to Tarzia, wherever that was, and her brother needed no extra encouragement to risk his life. Saying none of this to her father, she explained that she wanted to be the one to tell Danielo about Gio. 'He'll have questions only I can answer. Where does the Vincenzo family live now?'

'Where they've always lived, in the Quartieri Spagnoli.' Her father disclosed the address, and because it was obvious she was memorising it, he sighed. 'You cannot go there alone, at this time of night.' The Quartieri Spagnoli, the Spanish Quarters, was a warren of unlit streets that accommodated Naples' poorest. 'Either I or Tomaso will do it. Let's go downstairs and discuss it.'

They found Sebastiano resting his head on the kitchen table and Tomaso preparing a dinner of vegetable soup and dense sourdough bread made from buckwheat flour. Rather than take crockery and cutlery upstairs, they stayed there to eat. They had to hold the bread in their soup for several seconds to make it edible, except Sebastiano couldn't hold his. Carmela did it for him, putting it piece by piece into his mouth. He wouldn't let her spoon-feed him and picked his bowl up between his bandaged hands.

He looked exhausted and it was clear someone would have to help him to his bed in one of the attics and out of his clothes. Don Gonzago offered and then suggested that Tomaso pay a visit to Danielo's household, to break the news of Gio's fate. 'Carmela's right, it has to be done now, and before the curfew.'

'I will, of course, but first—' Tomaso brought out a medicine chest and extracted a bottle of syrup. 'To help you sleep,' he told Sebastiano. 'It contains morphine.'

'Put it away,' Sebastiano objected, with a fury that spoke of pain and frustration. 'And if anyone's to go downtown it should be me. I need to see Danielo.'

Carmela held her breath as Tomaso insisted that he was capable of making the trip and wanted to do it. 'I would hate for the boy to hear the news from gossip.'

'You can't go,' Sebastiano snapped irritably. 'You took money to Gio so he could pay his debt on the van, yes? Well, Gio's family lives a few doors up from Danielo's, and you will have been seen by the neighbours, and who knows who else. If you're seen again, you could be followed back here.'

'I'm adept at avoiding trouble, Sebbe,' Tomaso said in his reasonable way.

'You're a good man but you can't run.' Sebastiano was implacable. 'And put that damn medicine away. Last time I was given morphine, I started babbling in English.' He turned his harrowed gaze on Carmela. 'Can you find my coat and hat?'

'No. I shall visit Danielo,' Carmela said.

'Don't you ever say yes to anything?' Sebastiano half-rose in his seat then dropped back again, disturbed by his own emotions. 'I'm sorry.' He closed his eyes briefly then spoke again. 'Losing Gio makes my mission even more important. A moral duty. Don't you understand?'

Don Gonzago answered, 'We do, *amico*, but while we've been arguing the time has ticked away. It's too late for visiting. The curfew began two minutes ago.'

There they left it, but later, on her way to bed, Carmela resolved to go to Danielo at dawn next morning, before anyone was sufficiently awake to stop her.

Chapter Sixteen

Bang on 6.30 a.m., Carmela left the Palazzo by the back gate. She'd not laid eyes on Sebastiano since he'd been helped upstairs after supper and he could not know that she'd been up since five, scouring a map of the countryside between Naples and Nola. Frustratingly, she'd been unable to locate anywhere called Tarzia, but she'd have another go later. Ahead was the painful task of persuading her brother to step back and let *her* become Sebastiano's guide. His new, trusted lieutenant.

Her brother lived on Vico del Vigneto, 'Vineyard Lane'. Threading her way into the Quartieri Spagnoli, she was very aware of being the only unaccompanied woman on the street, a magnet for staring eyes. Ragged men crowded in scruffy doorways, though whether they had slept there or were waiting for doors to open, it was hard to tell. A boy sidled up to her, asking if she 'wanted business'. He could find her a man who would pay for her services with a 'nice pig's trotter'. She dismissed him with bared teeth.

All the time, she was alert to the possibility of being followed and whenever a footfall landed behind her, she tightened her grip on the basket she carried. When a man crossing the street ahead shot her a sly look, she pretended to be interested in a wall poster blaring out Colonel Scholl's demand for civil obedience. She was still reading when a dozen ragged boys stampeded from a side alley.

'Wish us luck, Signora,' one of them shouted. 'We're on our way to Castel dell'Ovo!'

The Castle of the Egg was a medieval hulk between Naples docks and the little port of Santa Lucia. They surely weren't intending to lay siege to a military stronghold? One boy had a cartridge belt slung across his shoulders. Another had a chunky pistol in his hand.

She wanted to run after them, tell them in graphic detail what could happen, but they were gone. The encounter only strengthened her resolve. Danielo would not be dragged deeper into peril. It struck her then that her brother might be fast asleep and she would wake him with the devastating news of Gio. She stopped in her tracks. Did Gio's poor mother even know about her son?

Here was Vico del Vigneto. She was looking for number 77. Down this same street, light-starved from the laden washing lines strung between the houses, Sebastiano had run from capture, seeking out Gio. He'd said he couldn't remember a thing about it, so he must have been impelled by some kind of homing instinct. As she found number 77 and turned the street door handle, she heard a raspy squeak above her head. A girl had stepped out onto a balcony to draw in a washing line. Preparing to load it up with the new morning's laundry, no doubt. Carmela went inside the building.

The stink of yesterday's cooking and unwashed flesh was nobody's fault. The Germans might have water enough to keep fountains running in their enclaves, but the rest of the city was surviving on a trickle. A month more of this, and with intermittent electricity, there might well be a recurrence of the typhus that had taken her mother. As she trod up uncarpeted stairs, Carmela heard babies crying, children shouting, mothers scolding. The house was divided into flats and from the level of noise, it was probable that each flat was split into yet smaller units. She'd seen evidence on her progress through the quarter of dreadful over-crowding. On the fourth level, she knocked at a door covered in finger marks. There was no name plate, but she'd hardly have expected one.

The door was opened by a barrel-chested man with oily grey hair. He gawped at Carmela, scratching his belly through a string vest tucked into patched trousers. Because he carried a scrap of towel and his chin gleamed, Carmela guessed he'd been finishing a shave.

This, presumably, was Violetta's husband. Apologising for coming so early, she asked, 'Are you Danielo's stepfather?'

'For my sins.' He looked past her, checking she was alone. 'And you are?'

'Carmela del Bosco. You must be Signor Vincenzo.'

'Adriano Vincenzo, that's right.' The sluggish gaze sharpened. 'What do you want with Danielo?'

'A quick chat. I've brought him a "welcome home" gift for getting out of jail.' Carmela indicated her basket.

'Aha.' Adriano Vincenzo gazed at the cloth covering the basket's contents, and his tongue made an involuntary sweep of his lips. He didn't step back to let her in and that was fine. She wanted to avoid an encounter with his wife, Danielo's mother. 'Could you fetch my brother, Signor?'

'No, you'd better come in.' Adriano Vincenzo opened the door wider and beckoned. When she hesitated he said, 'It's not safe out there. Ears twitching everywhere.'

As soon as she was inside, he shut the door and asked what she was doing in Naples. 'Don't you have a farm to run or something?'

'Not right now.'

'You're living at your father's place?'

She nodded. 'So… Danielo?'

'Not here.'

'But—'

'You thought he'd be tucked up in bed? No. He got home from prison, ate a dinner, quarrelled with me, made his mother cry and left. He's been out all night, curfew-breaking. You'd think he'd given us enough trouble. Violetta!' Vincenzo called hoarsely over his shoulder, 'Don Gonzago's girl is here. She's after Danielo.'

'Bring her in, don't keep her standing,' a harassed voice came back.

'She is in. Loreto!' Adriano Vincenzo made a 'scoot' gesture to a boy of about fourteen whose nose was buried in a schoolbook. The boy appeared to be intently cramming the text while his free hand dipped methodically into a bowl of sunflower seeds. 'I said, Loreto! You need to get to school, so give the lady your seat.'

This time, Loreto rose without comment. He was a good-looking boy, Carmela thought, and better fed than Danielo. And with a freshly split lip, she noticed. Another fighter? Loreto was still in the grip of adolescence and wore grey shorts, a dark-green shirt and a neck bandana, the uniform of the Fascist youth movement. There was nothing odd in that. Most school-aged boys wore a version of the same outfit. Danielo had once told her that a younger brother of his had earned a scholarship to an important school. 'The brains of the family. He's going to be rich one day and save us all,' Danielo had laughed. Loreto must be the favoured one.

Carmela cast a covert glance around. Even though the sun had yet to make any impression on the street outside, the room was airless. Most of the floor was taken up by an oversized table and chairs, crockery cabinets and a stove where, to judge by the pans stacked beside it, all the cooking took place. A bed sheet hanging from a ceiling rail cut the room in two. Behind the sheet, Carmela guessed there were children's beds and perhaps more beds crammed into the adjoining room. *It must get noisy*, she thought, *and difficult for Loreto to study.*

Loreto's father gestured proudly at his boy. 'The teachers say he's clever enough to be an engineer one day. What d'you say to that?'

'That you and his mother must be very proud. Signor Vincenzo, where can I find Danielo?'

His answer was to call his wife again. Violetta came in, the sheet-curtain briefly draping her like a shroud. She must be preparing to go to work as she wore a white overall over a dark dress. Her hair, which Carmela remembered as being too black and abundant ever to be contained under a maid's cap, was now almost entirely grey and was scraped to the back of her head. Speaking once of Violetta, Carmela's father had informed her in his casually arrogant way that the Neapolitan slums bred uniquely beautiful women, from a fusion of Italian, Greek, Saracen and Frankish heritage. In Carmela's memory, Violetta had almond-shaped eyes, sensual lips and high cheekbones, and a figure that made men turn and stare. Although she was still striking, Violetta looked weary and downcast now. Whatever she had gained from her time with Don Gonzago, it wasn't wealth.

She was flustered by the unexpected visit and Carmela saw her cast a dismayed eye over the clutter. But her greeting was courteous. 'Signorina del Bosco, you are welcome. Adriano hasn't grumbled at you, I hope? He is never joyful first thing.'

'It's for me to apologise, Signora Vincenzo. I've brought a gift for Danielo. A cheese and some peaches.' She emptied the produce from her basket onto a table. Seeing Violetta's eyes flicker wistfully, she added, 'They're for you all.'

'From your farm?'

Carmela nodded and asked again where she might find Danielo. 'It's urgent I speak to him.'

Violetta's expression clouded. 'Sorry, but I have no idea. When he left last night, it was to pay his respects to Evelina Troisi. Her son – Danielo's best friend – was killed in terrible circumstances, and her parents too. She's beside herself, quite hysterical, poor woman.'

So the news was out and Danielo already knew. Carmela didn't want to sound tactless and pushy, but picturing a mother's grief made her even more anxious to track her brother down. 'Where would Danielo most likely be at this time of day?'

Violetta's husband answered. 'She doesn't know any more than I do. Zeffiro could tell you, but he's not here either.'

'Zeffiro?'

'Our youngest boy, Danielo's shadow.' Adriano Vincenzo dropped down onto the one armchair in the room, which had a tin of cigarette butts on its arm. 'Danielo's like a cat, comes for his meals, goes out as soon as it's dark. He'll be lurking with other *scugnizzi*, planning the great uprising.'

'Danielo is not a *scugnizzo*,' Violetta objected. 'He is cared for, with a home and family. He went to school.' She directed her next words at Carmela. 'He reads and writes as well as Loreto.'

'No he doesn't,' Loreto objected, clearly stung by the comparison. He fingered the split on his lip, offering a clue to Carmela as to how it had got there.

'Danielo has wits,' Adriano Vincenzo agreed. 'He's the lawyer's son after all, but you need to stop conning yourself, Violetta. Sure, Danielo went to school. He walked in through one door and out of another and spent his days on the waterfront, fleecing money off tourists.'

'Money that kept us going!'

Fearful a marital row was boiling, Carmela said, 'Please! If anyone has any idea…?'

Violetta said helplessly, 'I warned him, he'll end up like Gio and tear my heart in pieces. You could wait, see if he comes back but it might be a while. The news hit him hard.' Violetta seemed to sag. 'I knew him from a baby. Gio, I mean, Evelina's boy. For a little while we all hoped he and my girl Marcella… well. No point dwelling on that.'

On the verge of being engulfed by memories of the screams of San Romualdo, Carmela took a step towards the door. Then, thinking Violetta might yet reveal some latent knowledge of Danielo's whereabouts, she said, 'Signora, if you're leaving for work, perhaps we can go together.'

Violetta shook her head. 'Better not. I clean at a hotel, but it's not an ordinary hotel and I'm not allowed to discuss it. Security is very tight. Please, stay if you wish. My daughter will look after you.' Violetta called, 'Marcella, is Ettore dressed yet? Come on, Loreto needs to get to class.' She cast a glance at Loreto, whose nose was back inside his book. 'Did Danielo tell you about Loreto's scholarship? Everything paid, or it would not be possible.' Abruptly, Violetta shouted again, 'Marcella, I need Ettore now!' She explained to Carmela, 'Loreto and I walk together to Piazza Dante, where his school is, and we drop Ettore at the elementary school on the way. Marcella stays home and minds the little ones…'

Little ones? There were more children in this rabbit hutch? Carmela felt a brief but intense sympathy for the threadbare Violetta.

'… and Zeffiro just disappears,' Violetta finished with a heavy sigh.

Carmela saw no evidence of Adriano Vincenzo preparing for a day's toil.

Violetta interpreted her look. 'Adriano is a removals man, but nobody's moving house these days. Or not for the usual reasons. If they run away from the bombing, they leave their furniture behind. The job at the Palazzo was his only one in three months.'

At the mention of 'the Palazzo', Carmela's interest sharpened but no explanation was offered. It could be any palazzo of course. Naples boasted so many. Violetta went on, 'My husband parks his truck in a friend's yard, for safety.'

'Where the Germans can't find it, and ask me to donate it,' Adriano Vincenzo growled. He was puffing his cigarette with his eyes closed.

Violetta glanced covertly at him, then whispered to Carmela, 'Do you have a message from your father?'

'No. Nothing.'

'He wouldn't send you here without a word for me.' Seeing Carmela jerk back, Violetta said heatedly, 'He knows only I can do what I do for him.'

Carmela was spared the need to comment as the rest of the brood emerged from behind the bed-sheet curtain: a boy of around ten in uniform, who must be Ettore, and two small girls, the elder leading the younger by the hand. Both girls wore washed-out summer frocks. They stared at Carmela with eyes big as pansies. On any other occasion, she would have introduced herself, asked their names, but the need to get out was becoming urgent so she murmured her goodbyes and left.

Bursting out of the main door onto the street, she lowered her chin to steady her breathing. A family of nine, living in two poky rooms. How did they cope? No wonder Danielo preferred to be out on the streets. She thought of the Palazzo, the empty ground floor and the closed-up bedrooms, and how selfish her father was being, hoarding all that space. Not that she wanted him to offer it to Violetta, but some other hard-pressed family could benefit.

It did nothing to sooth her emotions that she'd failed in her goal, having neither comforted Danielo nor done anything to keep him out of Sebastiano's clutches. She now had to retrace her steps past the ogling doorways and, somehow, locate him in the labyrinth of Naples.

She'd gone only a short distance when she heard someone approaching fast behind. Swinging round, expecting to see Violetta Vincenzo, she instead discovered a girl of about seventeen. Very pretty in a dress that was too large for her slender figure.

The girl hurried up to Carmela, saying, 'I saw you come, Signorina, when I was on the balcony. I'm Marcella, Danielo's sister.'

The eldest girl, who took care of the children. The second born, no doubt. Judging by her age, she must have arrived less than a year after Danielo, and Carmela couldn't avoid another dig of sympathy for Violetta, forced by circumstance onto the trundle-wheel of childbirth. Marcella had inherited her mother's beauty. Was that a dash of lipstick on the girl's mouth? Definitely, a hint of carmine, applied then rubbed off. Violetta had hinted that her daughter and Gio had had an understanding. Carmela looked for the traces of tears on the girl's cheeks, and saw none. Marcella's eyes burned with emotion, however. Haunted. She'd brought the basket Carmela had forgotten in her rush to get out.

'Stupid me. Thank you.' Carmela held out her hand but Marcella kept it. From the way she was chewing off the vestiges of her lipstick, she had more to say.

It came out. 'Danielo and Papà had a fight last night.'

Carmela nodded. 'Your father said so.'

'It wasn't fair.' The girl's sloe-dark eyes flashed. 'Danielo got home from the jail and Loreto held his nose and said, "You stink!"'

'That's brothers.'

'Then in the next breath, he told Danielo that Gio was dead. I had heard already and was going to break the news. Danielo almost passed out. He wept and Loreto called him a little girl. Danielo threw Loreto to the ground and I'm glad he did, because it saved me the trouble.'

Carmela's feelings towards the studious Loreto darkened, though she doubted this graceful girl could floor a solid fourteen-year-old boy. There was more.

'Papà went for Danielo and asked if he wanted a punch from a real man. Danielo said, "If you want. I'll go out on to the street and find one." Mamma got between them but it's too late. We have lost Danielo.' Marcella looked wretched.

'What do you mean, "lost"?'

'To Danielo, Gio was a hero and now he swears he'll fight to the death, to honour him.'

'Please, not that.' This was the worst outcome.

Marcella leaned in close and whispered, 'He's vowed to kill one German soldier for every man, woman and child lost at San Romualdo. I begged him to leave Naples. I said he would be safer among the partisans, but Mamma screamed at me.' Tears spilled from the haunted eyes. 'She accused me of trying to send Danielo to certain death. I didn't mean to make it worse.'

Carmela felt desperately sorry for Marcella, but privately she knew that Danielo's mother had a point. Joining a resistance unit was to cross a line, and the Germans would show no mercy. 'Marcella, have you heard of a place called Tarzia, where the partisans hide out?'

Marcella shook her head. 'Danielo might know it. Gio joined a fighting band for a while, then his mamma was ill so he came back home, but he always said he would go back and take my brother with him. Someone informed on Gio and he had to get away. He went to his grandparents' at San Romualdo and that's where—'

'I know,' Carmela cut in quietly. 'I know how the people were killed, Marcella.'

Marcella made the sign of the cross. 'The church was burned but those devils chained Gio to the door, and let him die that way. They should burn in hell themselves for their evil.'

'Don't let the picture into your mind. I promise you, it won't help. Listen, Danielo mustn't go looking for the partisans because the police or a German patrol only have to spot him on the road and it'll be the end for him.' And for Sebastiano if they were travelling together. 'Your father said your little brother Zeffiro might know where Danielo is.'

Marcella glanced around, then spoke in an undertone. 'Danielo's gone to Santa Lucia, to dive off the rocks. He told me he would never sleep again.'

Santa Lucia was where those armed boys had been heading. Carmela asked what would be the fastest way to join them.

'Oh, no, they won't allow a girl along with them,' Marcella said urgently. 'You'd only draw attention to them. I'll tell Zeffiro when he comes home, and he will tell Danielo that you want to see him. Where can he find you?'

This girl's parents already knew Carmela was living at the Palazzo so there could be no harm in saying, 'At my father's house.' Briefly, she hesitated. Sebastiano had driven home the importance of keeping the Palazzo's secrets safe but it bore down on her that Danielo might one day be running for his life. He ought to have a bolthole, as Gio's home had been for Sebastiano. If he simply turned up at the Palazzo's front entrance, they would never let him in. Reaching a hasty decision, she said, 'I'm at Palazzo del Bosco in Vomero and there's a way—' Her attention was distracted by the sight of Marcella's baby sisters toddling towards them. 'Can they get down the stairs on their own?' she asked.

Marcella glanced behind her and sighed. 'Yes, whenever I turn my back. Mamma will be angry with me again.' She screwed up her face, but held her arms out and the little ones grasped her skirt. Carmela felt a keen pang of pity. All that grace and beauty was doomed. Give it five years…

Fearing she was squandering the moment, she said quickly, 'Tell Danielo not to knock on the Palazzo's front door, but to walk along a little alley at the back. It's called Vicoletto del Bosco, but there's no street sign.' Carmela explained the secret ritual for gaining entrance to the Palazzo. 'Tell him, but nobody else. It's very important we keep it secret.'

'Bell pull, hidden in ivy. One firm pull, keep walking, don't look back.' Marcella nodded. 'I'll remember.'

The little girls were impatient for their big sister's attention.

'Hansi!' The littlest of them stared up at Marcella. Getting no reply, she tried tugging at Carmela's skirt. 'Where is Hansi?'

Carmela frowned. 'You mean Renzo, my dog?' Danielo must have mentioned him. 'He's not with me. It was too far for him to walk, but I'll bring him some day.'

The little girl's mouth turned down. 'Pina not like dogs. Pina like Hansi.'

Marcella admonished the child for being rude. She seemed suddenly very agitated, which increased as her mother and the schoolboy brothers came out of the building. Thrusting the basket at Carmela, she ushered the two little girls back towards home.

Violetta, clearly running late, let out a string of reproaches at the sight of them. She snapped, 'Must I lose all my children? Don't let them out of your sight, Marcella – how many more times?'

As Carmela rode the funicular back up to Vomero, Marcella left the house again. Her father had gone out to make his daily check on his truck, the washing had been hung out and she was on her way to a clandestine meeting. Obeying her mother to the letter, she took the little girls with her and did not let go of their hands.

In a shadowy church doorway in the neighbouring quarter of Montecalvario, Marcella met her lover. They went into a secluded garden behind a church where he produced an unimaginable treat for them to share, a small bar of chocolate. He and Marcella fed each other squares, kissed and talked about the future while the little girls sucked blissfully on their chunks. As Marcella carefully wiped traces of chocolate from their mouths, Pina tugged the lover's field-grey breeches and said, 'Pina knows a secret. Shall I tell you, Hansi?'

Chapter Seventeen

Tomaso was waiting by the open back gate as Carmela made a second pass along Vicoletto del Bosco. The final part of her journey home had almost ended in her being trampled as people flooded out of their houses, drawn by the noise of a stricken plane. Grazing the rooftops, its shadow had run like a black shape along the avenue, which had filled with a grotesque, howling scream. Smoke had been pouring from one of its wings. It appeared to be heading out to sea, where presumably it had crashed to judge by the cry of horror from the people who had raced to the viewpoint to watch.

She mentioned it to Tomaso as he shut and locked the gate behind her.

Naturally, he'd heard it too. 'I was outside. I have no idea whose plane it was, but my blood ran cold. Signorina Carmela, in future, please don't leave the Palazzo without telling me first. I have spent the last two hours pretending to your father that you're in the garden, pruning the apple trees.'

'Nobody prunes fruit trees at this season,' she said distractedly. It was possible the plane had been shot at from her *vedetta*, if the Germans had installed their anti-aircraft gun on top by now. It had come from that direction.

'I told your father you were pining for the farm.' Tomaso began picking his way through the dry summer grass and Carmela followed. 'I take it you went to Danielo?'

'I wanted to save you a journey.' A forgivable lie, she assured herself. 'Danielo knows about Gio already.'

Tomaso gave her a sympathetic look. 'News travels through the innards of Naples at the speed of thought. I'm sorry you had a wasted journey, entering Violetta's den for no good purpose. A real test of character, I'd say.'

'I found myself feeling sorry for her.'

Tomaso nodded. 'The years have not been kind to Violetta Vincenzo, but perhaps that's fate at play. She wanted your father and used her beauty to win him, despite your mother's tears. Still, she's doing her best to make amends now.'

Making amends by offering services of a certain nature? 'He knows only I can do what I do for him,' Violetta had whispered. Carmela told Tomaso about the hair slide she'd found in her bed. It had turned out to be made of onyx with rhinestone studs, the kind of ornament that could be bought from a street stall. 'I understand desire, Tomaso, and Papà's weaknesses, but did he have to use my mother's room?'

Tomaso looked deeply uncomfortable. He said nothing, however.

'And another thing, isn't it selfish of Papà to keep the Palazzo empty when so many are homeless?'

'If we opened our doors, Sebastiano would not be safe here. Don't judge your father, Signorina.'

The reprimand reminded her of Tomaso's fierce loyalty to Don Gonzago. She changed the subject. 'Is Sebastiano still at home?'

'He was an hour ago, when I went to his room and found him trying to dress himself for work.'

'Work, is he crazy?'

'He is dogged. Bull- and pig-headed, a menagerie of stubborn virtues. I talked him out of it by reminding him that he now falls into the class that must surrender itself for obligatory labour. Just by walking down the street he could be seized and deported to Germany. It used to be men aged eighteen to thirty, but they've raised that to thirty-three. Sebbe's ID states he is thirty-one.'

'Is that his real age?'

Tomaso tutted. 'Ask him yourself.'

In the kitchen, weighing scales and an open bag of buckwheat flour promised that more heavy bread was on its way. They were lucky to have anything, of course. The public bread ration was down to one small slice per person per day, though ration coupons were so widely forged and black-marketed the system had fallen apart and bakeries were generally empty anyway. With wheat flour diverted to feed the German army, maize, chestnut and buckwheat were the new staple. 'Pity the toothless,' she said to herself. Hearing her voice, Renzo lifted his head and thumped his tail. Carmela stroked him under the chin the way he loved. A thought struck her.

'Where does the bell ring, Tomaso, when people want to come in?' The cellar grating he'd shown her was a long way off, down a flight of steps. She pictured Danielo, trying to reach sanctuary with the Germans in pursuit, and felt a panicky flutter.

'Well, I don't sit underneath the vent waiting for a ding-dong.' Tomaso pointed to a corner of the kitchen where a thin wire tracked along the wall and hooked onto a brass bell. 'The bell pull in the *vicoletto* connects to that wire.'

'How do you hear it when you're upstairs?' she asked.

'I don't, but I'm never upstairs for long. It's why I rarely sit down with you to eat, in case you wondered.'

She flushed, embarrassed because she hadn't wondered. 'What about at night?'

'If I suspect we might have a late visitor, I sleep down here. Generally, visitors don't come except by prior arrangement.'

'I did.'

'Indeed, and Danielo turns up unexpectedly if there is need.'

'He knows about the bell?'

'Of course.' Tomaso gave her a narrow look. 'Your father's son has always had access.'

She should have realised that.

Tomaso suggested that she go up to Sebastiano. 'Heat a little water – we have plenty, thanks to you – and bathe his wounds. I didn't like the way he was protecting his hands when I took him his breakfast. He wouldn't let me see them, said I was an old woman. Shame he won't let us administer morphine syrup, but we'll add a few drops of another tincture to the water.'

'Maybe you should go up to him.' Confiding in Marcella had been a lapse of judgement, Carmela knew now. She could blame it on the emotion of the moment, but it was unlikely Sebastiano would view it in the same way. 'He'd prefer you.'

'I doubt that. Anyway, I have bread to make. You know where his room is? It's where the maids used to sleep. I know for a fact that he had a nightmare about Gio, so go and give comfort. Find comfort for yourself.'

So, she carried the steaming bowl upstairs. As she passed the empty drawing room, her father stepped out and asked her how she'd got on. 'Tomaso fabricated some baloney about you pruning the apple trees, but I assume you defied me and went to the Vincenzos's?'

She admitted it. 'Danielo wasn't there, but he already knows about Gio. His sister told me he's gone to dive off the rocks at Santa Lucia. For limpets, I presume.'

Her father sighed. 'The Germans dumped an arsenal of confiscated weapons into the sea at Santa Lucia, to stop our rebel citizens getting their hands on them. Your brother will fish up more than limpets, I assure you. Did you see Violetta?'

'Briefly.'

'Any message for me?'

'No.' Did they think she was a letter carrier for star-crossed lovers? Carmela continued on to the nether end of the house, taking a flight of stairs up and then another that was so narrow her elbows grazed the walls. These stairs terminated in a closed door. Putting the bowl down on a tiny triangle of landing, she softly turned the door handle. The door didn't budge. Probably locked from the inside. Perhaps the kindest thing would be to leave.

'Who was Parthenope?' came a voice from the other side of the door.

'I'm sorry?'

'Who was Parthenope?' Tired and gravelly, more than a little impatient.

'She was the siren who drowned herself in the Bay of Naples after the hero Ulysses rejected her,' Carmela replied, surprised at the classics quiz. 'She believed her voice to be the loveliest in the world, but he wasn't impressed. Typical man.'

'That's not the right answer.'

'Yes it is. I know my mythology.'

'It isn't the answer I want.'

Clearly, Sebastiano was in an irascible mood 'I'll come back later,' she told him.

'Don't go.'

She heard a key turn. He stepped back to let her enter.

'So this is where you roost.' She looked around. 'I haven't been up here for years.' She blushed, realising that Sebastiano must have got up from his bed to let her in – if you could call the roll of felt laid out on the floor a bed. Beside it was the kitbag with his work jacket and shirt folded next to it. His boots were alongside, and a pair of black leather gloves. He was stripped to the waist, a state of undress that revealed dark chest hair and a muscled torso. His trousers, minus their belt, hung on his hips. Hardly a surprise that he was fit and strong, if he'd been working as a Neapolitan road mender. A road mender with a curvaceous mermaid emblazoned on his forearm. Flustered, she looked for somewhere to put her bowl. Sebastiano was watching her, watching him.

The only place she could put it was on the floor. 'Tomaso sent me,' she said, in case he assumed she'd come up to feast her eyes.

'I won't talk to you until you give me the code answer. Who was Parthenope?'

'Nobody mentioned any code.' She was truly baffled now.

'Parthenope was Florence Nightingale's sister,' he told her, following her glance to his makeshift bed, narrowing his eyes as he read her concern. 'Their parents travelled throughout Italy on an everlasting honeymoon. Their eldest daughter was born here in Naples, so they gave her the Greek name for the city.'

'After the siren.'

'They named their second daughter after Firenze – Florence. Their third daughter, they called Madge. Don't you think that shows a massive collapse of imagination?'

'There wasn't a Madge, was there?'

'I don't know. Perhaps I dreamed her.'

He was teasing, or talking for the sake of it. Nonsense-chatter instead of silence. It made perfect sense to her. Silence was a deep well in which people drowned. He hadn't shaved since yesterday. Black stubble coated his jaw, and was that a feverish slick on his forehead?

'Tomaso said you hardly slept.'

'I've been drifting in and out. I can't seem to fall into a proper sleep. I won't take morphine, so don't ask.'

'I haven't brought any, though Tomaso is still harping on about his special syrup.' She pointed out that he'd sleep better on a decent bed.

'Sleeplessness comes with the job and being uncomfortable can save your life, if it means you're always on the edge of waking. Anyway, it would feel wrong to be tucked up warm and safe.'

She knew he meant guilt at surviving.

He stared down at the bowl. 'Is that refined-smelling concoction for me to wash in?'

'Tomaso's worried about your hands.'

'Ah. So basically, you are Florence Nightingale. Remember the code next time, yes?'

'I won't make a habit of coming up to your room.' She immediately apologised because it was silly, being prudish after what they'd been through together. 'I'm still reeling, and I don't quite know how to be with you.'

He nodded, as if he felt the same. 'I was secretly hoping I'd see you this morning, as you're my conduit to Danielo. Does he know I need his help?'

'Not yet.' She fudged an answer, saying, 'Where is he…? By the seafront. His sister knows I need to see him urgently.'

'"Urgently" often means "next week" in Naples. Will he come?'

'I'm sure he will.'

'How – how are you sure?' He drove one hand against the other and then rocked with pain. 'I should be on my way to Nola by now.

I can't afford to lose another day. The partisans' WTO might be captured or compromised. Or turned. Anything could happen. Do you understand?'

'I do.' 'WTO', she presumed, meant a wireless operator. She appreciated that Sebastiano needed to contact the organisation that had sent him here to get a warning out to Allied command about threats to their troops, and delay might cost lives. 'I have a suggestion about finding this operator… this WTO… but first, let's get your hands healing.'

When he displayed them, she couldn't hold back a gasp. The gauze bandages Tomaso had applied the previous night were blood-soaked. 'Did you imagine you could set out on a journey today?'

He inclined his head. 'I really did so let's get on with it, Florence. Shall I sit down?'

There wasn't a chair in the room and he lowered himself to the floor without using his hands. Sitting cross-legged, he inhaled deeply. 'What's in the water?'

'Drops of myrrh from Tomaso's medicine box.'

He sang in English. '"Myrrh is mine, its bitter perfume…"'

'Shh!' He had a good voice, though.

'Yes, it's a gloomy old carol. Best sung in a candlelit church on a crisp Christmas Eve before going home to drink ruby port by the fire. I'm rambling because I know you're going to hurt me.'

'I won't. Well, not too much. Shall we go for full immersion, and soak these bandages off?' She sat down in front of him and held the bowl. He lowered his hands into the water.

'Ouch.'

She knew that was an understatement. When the bandages had loosened, the water was carnelian red. No blistering remained on

Sebastiano's hands. The flesh on his palms and the undersides of his fingers was raw. He must have been climbing the walls in pain. 'What were you trying to do at the church? Rescue the lad?'

'Too late for that. I had to be certain who it was. I have to report his death to SOE as he was their recruit.'

'SOE . . . remind me.'

'Special Operations Executive.'

'They'll be upset?'

'They damn well should be.'

Sighing, she patted his hands dry and put on fresh bandage. 'Tomaso says you've finished as a labourer.'

'It was time. The gangmaster was getting suspicious. Where was I living, why hadn't I been in the army?' He mimicked rough, city twang; '"*Uè, guagliò?* You're young enough to carry a gun. Why aren't you in uniform? What are you, a chicken?" I offered to show him my certificate of exemption, due to epilepsy.'

'Really?'

'I *really* have a certificate, but none of it is true, Carmela. The epilepsy, the name Sebastiano, my history, my engaging personality... it's all a mirage.'

'Sebastiano's not your real name?' That disappointed her. 'What is it?'

'I'm not telling you.'

'Don't you trust me?'

'I can't afford to. I was betrayed before by someone I believed in. Besides, you are second cousin to a Fascist Blackshirt.'

'So is every woman within spitting distance. Every able-bodied man over military age joined the volunteer militia and they all have cousins.'

He gave a sharp smile. 'Point taken, and if it makes you happier, I trust you on a personal level. I let you lead me down the *vedetta* steps, didn't I?'

That was true. 'And you will learn to trust me on a… a professional level.' She asked him if he'd heard the doomed plane that had roared over a short while ago.

It had woken him, he said. He'd watched it briefly blot out the light at the window. 'British, a reconnaissance aircraft, engine on fire and the pilot hoping to ditch in the sea. They fly low, so they're vulnerable to ground fire.'

She knew they were thinking the same thing. The *vedetta* at la Casale, and a hundred other similar towers, manned with German gunners with their eyes on the horizon. She shut her mind to the possible consequences to la Casale and asked, 'Are there no wireless operators in Naples you could seek out?'

'Not on our side, no. Mio's wireless fell into German hands and London will suspect from our silence that something's wrong. They won't drop a new operator in if they think my mission is compromised, which it pretty much is. I'm hanging by a thread. I can't tell them anything until I contact them, and so we go round the mulberry bush. I have intelligence that means the difference between life and death for Allied pilots and troops – hundreds of husbands, brothers and sons – and I need a WTO. I need your brother, *now*.'

She knew better than to come straight out and volunteer her help. She had to go softly. 'I met Danielo's family today. I didn't much like his stepfather, and there is a particularly unamiable brother. The mother, Violetta, apart from being my father's former mistress, was pleasant. She's a cleaner and has to go through security checks each morning.'

'Not unusual, if the place she cleans has German personnel.'

'This business, helping you survive, is starting to feel like a family affair. So…'

'So?'

'Doesn't it make sense for me to be involved?'

He held her gaze. Assessing her. Walking himself through various outcomes if he agreed. 'I'm not sure what you could do, Carmela.'

'Help you save all those husbands, sons and brothers. You're injured, so why don't I go to Nola and take your message to the partisans? Find your WTO.'

'Why not? Because it's a two-day journey and you have no credentials. They wouldn't take you seriously and the wireless operator would assume you were a Fascist infiltrator.'

It was almost as though he'd rehearsed the rejection. Before yesterday, she might have been knocked back but Gio's sacrifice had put some steel in her spine. 'Not if you gave me some information that only you could know. Like the name of someone in SOE, perhaps? That would give me credentials.'

'Carmela, we aren't in this together. Yesterday should have proved that.'

'Surely yesterday showed that I can deal with anything.'

'Haring up the track towards San Romualdo in pursuit of German armoured cars? What did that prove?'

'That I react fast. I don't run away. I'm reliable.'

'What you did was as futile as it was dangerous.'

She flushed. It was one thing to judge oneself… 'I was afraid for you. I didn't stop to think.'

'My point exactly. Did you suppose I'd stand with my mouth open and let them catch me? Suppose I *had* been caught and given a false reason for being on my way to the village along with a false name. And then you run up yelling, "Sebastiano!"'

She hung her head. He was right, of course.

'You haven't the temperament for risk. Why should you? I went through a harsh training regime. I learned when to attack, when to retreat. How to keep a clear head under unbearable pressure, and I can tell you, nothing prepares you for the real thing. I appreciate that you helped me home afterwards, but it doesn't make you an asset. Gio was tough and resourceful. He stole a motorbike and got me away from your farm in the nick of time but he left a trail of mistakes that cost him his life. Danielo had better have more savvy because he's going to take me to Nola.'

'Right.'

'You're a good nurse, however.'

That was the sum of her accomplishment, soaking his bandages off and applying new ones? 'I can only apologise for being useless.'

'Don't look so crushed. I've seen burly men go to pieces under less horrible circumstances than at San Romualdo.'

The concession slid past her ribs, into her heart. As tears pricked, she looked away. The only light in the room came through a sealed, circular window and she focused on the dust motes dancing in front of it. 'Can you breathe at night?' she asked. The Palazzo's sixteenth-century architect had added every baroque flourish to the building, including round windows cut into the roof, but they had no way of being opened, or none that she had ever seen. She remembered itching with heat the nights she'd spent up here on the camp bed, sleeping alongside the housemaids. Her mother dying one floor below. Violetta creeping down the stairs, taking her beauty to Don Gonzago's bed.

Carmela picked up one of Sebastiano's hands, which felt over-warm inside the muslin bandage. 'I understand how trapped you feel. When I walked alongside Cedric on his stretcher, and heard his breath catch in his teeth, I wanted to scream.' Not from grief, that had come later, but from impotence. 'I hate sitting on the sidelines, as you do, but you're being unjust towards me. When you needed shelter, I risked my life. That should be enough.'

'My judgement was pickled otherwise I'd have asked to be taken elsewhere.' He sandwiched her hand between both of his, though exerting no pressure. 'My world probably seems complex to you but in reality, it's weeks of isolation without sleep followed by bursts of action and the realistic possibility of violent death. You have no concept what it's like to be under interrogation, from men who have all the time in the world to break you with torture if they need to.'

'I'm expendable. I don't mean I'd court death or torture,' she said hurriedly, 'but if it happened only Nonna would be truly sad. Oh, and Renzo.'

'And your father too,' he said firmly, 'and I don't want to have to answer to any of them.' He leaned forward and to her surprise kissed her lightly on the lips. 'You matter, Carmela. I want you to survive, meet a good man, have babies. You remind me—' He broke off.

'Of a woman you know?' She'd been sure he was going to name somebody. A girl back home, perhaps. Or one he'd met here. In contrast to yesterday's passionate kiss, the one he'd given her a minute ago seemed almost brotherly. 'Is she dark-haired like me?'

The flush on Sebastiano's brow deepened. 'How did you jump to girlfriends? I was saying, you remind me what I'm doing in Naples. I'm here because I pass for Italian, I speak the dialect and I fit in. What I'm not here to do is get tangled up in sentiment.'

'It's all right.' She freed her hand, got to her feet, picked up the bowl and the bloody bandages. 'Why shouldn't you have a sweetheart too?'

'That's not what I said.' Sebastiano sounded riled. 'And what d'you mean by "too"? Have you replaced your pilot fiancé?'

It was her turn to say nothing. Let him guess. She went down the stairs feeling she'd salvaged a little dignity. There had been nobody before or after Cedric. She was a one-man woman and Cedric was seared on her soul.

And she had her baby, lost too, but much closer to home.

Chapter Eighteen

The reading room had always been Papà's province, its walls lined with legal tomes and dense political histories. Books that, as a child, she'd found intimidating except for the hand-painted botanical studies and one full of pictures of English country houses. That volume was missing. Too dangerous to keep. She wasn't here for nostalgia, however, but for something more practical. To draw a map of the road to Nola. Carmela was not going to let Sebastiano win the argument.

She took down the map she'd looked at early that morning, a heavy thing in a binder, 'Campania' tooled on its spine. It was out of date but, as so little had changed in this landscape in the last century, that hardly mattered. She put the binder down on the floor and carefully extracted the map. There had once been an inlaid ebony table in the middle of the room, but along with its chairs it too had disappeared.

There was only one way to read a map spread out on the floor, and that was to go on hands and knees. It was detailed, showing mountains, ravines and river valleys as well as settlements. Almost too detailed, and without electric light, she couldn't make out the smaller names. What she needed…

She heard her father's footsteps go by and the drawing room door open and close. She quickly ran into the dining room. Good. He'd left his magnifying glass, a pencil and a blank notebook. She took them all.

Back in the library and with the help of the magnifying glass, she got her bearings on the map. The town of Nola guarded the Apennine foothills, in whose shadowy dells the partisans could easily secrete themselves. The road from Naples to Nola crossed the Vesuvius plain and would surely be studded with police and military checkpoints. Beyond Nola, the terrain became more challenging. Sebastiano would really struggle, the state he was in. Her tongue between her teeth, she sketched a route taking back ways and mule tracks. Slower than the main road, but far safer.

Her father walked past the open door. He raised an eyebrow, seeing her on her hands and knees, but continued on towards the dining room without comment. She finished her drawing, then returned the map book to the shelf. Don Gonzago wasn't in the dining room and she put his pencil and pad back where she'd found them, hoping he wouldn't have realised they'd gone.

'*Keine Bewegung!* Freeze!

She dropped the notepad with a screech. 'Papà!'

Don Gonzago stood in an open doorway, a concealed one that, in more prosperous days, had allowed waiting staff to retire discreetly down a set of back stairs. She'd forgotten it existed. 'You scared the daylights out of me.'

'I meant to.' Don Gonzago closed the lightweight door, which had been artfully painted to merge in with the silk wallpaper. 'Why did you swipe my notepad?'

'To scribble something. Why did *you* nearly give me a fit?'

'Tomaso reminded me that I must show you all the escape routes.' Don Gonzago indicated the door he'd just closed. 'This passage behind leads down to a boot room next to the kitchen and there's a hatch in the floor. That drops down to a subterranean passage that was once the main drain from the Palazzo. It comes out a short way down the slope beneath our rock. I'll show you in detail after lunch. Now, turn out your pockets.'

She stiffened defensively. 'Why?'

'Imagine I'm a German soldier. Or an exquisitely uniformed Abwehr officer with a gun and a nasty expression. Show me.'

With a mutinous huff, she laid her map sheet by sheet on the dining table. 'It's the route Sebastiano needs to take to link up with the partisans.'

Her father glanced over her work. 'You have drawn it out very nicely and the roads you've chosen show good judgement. Some of those tracks… only a bullock cart can pass once the rain comes.' Carmela felt absurdly pleased by the praise, until her father added, 'It will make just as much sense to German intelligence as it will to Sebastiano.'

'German intelligence won't get to see it.' Did he take her for an imbecile? 'I and Sebastiano will memorise it, then I'll burn it.'

'Burn it now.' Don Gonzago beckoned her into the drawing room where he paused in front of the fireplace. Smoky debris in the grate showed that something had been set alight very recently. He said, 'You have one minute to memorise your handiwork.'

She did her best while her father relit the charred paper in the grate. 'Your minute is up.' He pressed her map into the embers until it caught light. 'How is Sebastiano?' he asked conversationally.

'He can hardly use his hands, though he won't admit it. It's why I have to help him.'

'By consulting my father's topographical maps? A good thought. Very good.'

He was being consciously pleasant while failing utterly to grasp her resolve. She left him in no doubt, explaining that she meant to conduct Sebastiano to Nola and beyond. 'Have you ever heard of a place called Tarzia?'

Don Gonzago gave a thoughtful frown and his comment, when it came, threw her completely. 'You never got to meet my mother. I'll show you something.' Taking her back into the dining room, he opened the piano stool. Rifling beneath sheet music, he produced a photograph album, which he opened at a portrait photograph of a woman with patrician features. Refined lips and dark, delicately kohled eyes. 'Maria Carmela del Bosco.'

It was the grandmother she'd been named for. She said, 'We don't look very like.'

'No, no,' her father agreed. 'Mamma had a true delicacy, whereas you are every inch Rosaria. You resemble my mother in character, however, and there's something of this lady in you too.' While Carmela struggled with freshly bruised feelings, he showed her another photo, this time of a woman with pale hair piled into a cushion-like bun. Her high silk collar was pinned with a cameo brooch. A fashion of the turn of the century. 'Now, she was formidable.'

'Who is she?'

'My father's mother, your paternal great-grandmother. Born Hannah Sonnentag, she was Austrian and…' Don Gonzago paused, as if expecting Carmela to finish his words.

'And?'

'She was Jewish, Carmela.'

'I had no idea.' Carmela gazed at the picture, seeing a strong resemblance to her father. And to Danielo. Not only in Hannah's colouring, but in the shape of her nose and chin. 'Wait a minute… the story of Hugh de Boscoët the Norman knight and tracing your line back to the Normans, that was made up? Your golden hair and green eyes were inherited from Hannah?'

'The Seigneur de Boscoët serves a purpose and will do so until the world is a different place. Jewishness is passed through the female line, so we are not Jews ourselves, but that kind of detail is often lost when the SS comes calling. You do realise that since the surrender, the number of Jews being deported from Italy has increased dramatically. A good reason to keep your head down. Travelling to Nola with Sebastiano… hmm.' Don Gonzago replaced the album and sighed. 'Any idea what time it is? I wish I still had my bronze clock. It is so very tedious to have no possessions.'

'Papà… I've been noticing all the furniture's gone. Well, lots of it. Why? And what happened to the lodgers?'

'The lodgers had to go. They were noisy and unruly. The furniture isn't sold, just temporarily removed.'

'By Adriano Vincenzo?' Violetta had referred to a job her husband had carried out for 'the Palazzo'.

Her father confirmed it. 'He needed the work and is the most incurious soul I've ever met, which is a virtue in a tradesman. I stripped the place as a precaution.'

'Against the Germans wanting to take it over?'

'Exactly. Remember the Grand Hotel Parker's, which served a "gateau moka" that was utterly sublime?'

She shook her head.

'Did I never take you there?'

He'd taken her nowhere. He'd sent her away.

He sighed. What a shame. 'Too late, as it is now called the Hotel Parco and is the Germans' Naples HQ. A couple of weeks ago, a staff officer came from there to call on me. A Major Klimt.'

'He wanted Palazzo del Bosco.' She already knew as much from Danielo. The spectre of a German takeover of this house was the reason Sebastiano had ended up in her care. 'Danielo and Gio actually arrived while this Major Thingummy was here, didn't they?'

'Yes. Such impeccable timing.' Her father's voice hit a rueful note. 'We were having a pleasant conversation, Klimt and I. He was flattered to find me a fluent German speaker, no need for the Italian phrase book one of his underlings had brought along. He was explaining that as this building was underused, I would have no objection to his moving his staff in. Hotel Parco being close by, it made perfect sense. To him.'

'And then the bell rang in the kitchen,' she guessed.

'They say "My heart stood still" and I assure you, it's no exaggeration. Fortunately, Tomaso was downstairs and was able to warn Gio to drive on. It was then about five in the evening, still light, and of course they were desperate to deposit Sebastiano here but it was impossible. They drove out into the hills until it was fully dark, then returned. Klimt had gone by then, but we felt it was still too risky to admit Sebastiano. We bathed his wounds, put him into borrowed clothes. Tomaso dosed him with morphine syrup and we dug out that camp bed for a stretcher as he was hardly conscious. Off they went again, to where we hoped would be the last place the Germans would look.'

'La Casale. To me.'

Don Gonzago patted her shoulder. 'I never doubted you, *figlia mia*.'

It explained how she had been drawn into this cat-and-mouse game. 'Danielo said nothing about your involvement, Papà.'

'No, but none of us say more than we need to. I'm only telling you now because you are involved, and ignorance is dangerous when one is in this deep.'

'I see. Thank you for finally trusting me.' It didn't however clarify why there was no sofa to sit on, and no table in the reading room.

That, her father told her, was because he'd received a tip-off about Klimt's visit in advance. 'Enough time for Tomaso and me to make the place look thoroughly uninviting. We boxed up everything valuable and summoned Adriano Vincenzo and his truck. He shipped away at least twenty loads, virtually everything but the piano, which, he said, would break his axle. I wish he'd realised that before he moved the Bechstein into its current obstructive position. When Major Klimt arrived,' her father went on, 'I was able to conduct his cohort from room to room, boots clomping, voices echoing. I could see him wondering if this would be such a comfortable billet after all.'

'Are soldiers really so choosy?'

'No, but I thought of that too. Come see.' Back to the drawing room they went, going via the corridor as the connecting doors between the two rooms were, in Don Gonzago's phrase, awkwardly obstructed by the piano. He led her to the French windows, which opened onto a balcony. Carmela stood beside him as he pointed out at the vista. 'What do you see?'

'The roofs of the city. Piazza Plebiscito, Castel Nuovo. The docks, the Riviera di Chiaia. The islands.'

'And from the lower city, you can see us.'

'On a very clear day.'

'We have those occasionally. What do you see further out?'

'Erm… the sea.'

'Precisely. I suggested to the major that once it was known that his section, which is Signals, occupied this building he would be a sitting target for a missile fired from a warship. A good shot could come straight through the drawing room window.'

'He believed that?'

'He went absolutely pale.' Don Gonzago leaned over the stone balcony. There was another such balcony to their right, off the dining room, whose supports were beginning to crumble. The building was in a sad state, Carmela reflected. No money.

She asked, 'Will you get the furniture back?'

'When the Germans are gone.' Her father pointed over the tops of the holm oaks, the stately evergreens that lined Viale Bellavista. 'You can just see the Castel dell'Ovo at Santa Lucia. The weapons it held were raided by a band of deserters and feral youths a few days ago.'

'You told me.'

'The Germans trapped the raiders inside the castle. There was shooting and the Germans, fearing they couldn't keep the weapons out of rebel hands, hurled them into the sea.'

'Where Danielo is now diving.' Carmela shook her head. 'My brother's in the thick of all this, isn't he, Papà?'

'Yes, and I suspect you are blaming yourself for his capture on the journey back from la Casale, though in reality, you may have unwittingly saved his life. But for his spell in the boys' jail, we might be speaking of Danielo in the past tense.'

'As we now speak of poor Gio.'

'But you didn't kill Gio Troisi or make his choices for him. Don't carry the burdens of the world, Carmela. Let me advise you as your father and friend.' Don Gonzago put his arm around her, and must have felt her stiffen because he sighed. 'You came back from England so very sad and angry with me.'

'Not angry. In grief.'

'It will pass, in time.'

It won't, she answered silently, *because it's still an open wound.* She thought of the snippet of hair under her pillow. Needing to get away from these thoughts, she asked if Major Klimt was likely to come back.

'Possibly. Quite possibly. The man is opaque to me. He was polite but with that edge of contempt all Germans feel for us now.'

'Then Sebastiano is not safe here,' she said, with a glance up at the ceiling. 'Shouldn't he at least be sleeping near one of the escape routes?'

Her father agreed that Sebastiano needed fast access out of the building in the event of an emergency. 'Because the Germans, when they come, arrive fast and in number. But enough talk of them. Would you go down and enquire about lunch? I will summon Sebbe to join us.'

Carmela left, only to meet Tomaso coming up the stairs, laden with crockery to set the table. She took the tray from him and put out four places. In the event, Sebastiano did not come, though they delayed until they were all so ravenous for their potato soup they started without him. Sebbe had looked more in need of sleep than food, Don Gonzago reported, and had probably drifted off again. 'We'll save his share.'

When Tomaso re-loaded the tray with the intention of going down to the kitchen, Carmela rose too, saying she'd lend a hand with the dishes. Once again, her father stopped her from shutting the dining room door.

'In my childhood you were forever ordering me to close the door behind me.'

Don Gonzago acknowledged the contradiction. 'The answer is no, of course.'

'No to what?'

'To your going to Nola with Sebastiano. I take it that is your plan?'

'It is, and I'm learning to live with danger. I will be fine.'

'That wasn't what I meant. My unmarried daughter cannot travel unchaperoned with a man, even one I happen to like.'

'What do you imagine we'd get up to?'

Don Gonzago gave a thin smile. 'Remember, you have a reformed rake for a father.'

'Papà, honestly!' She coloured as she thought of Sebastiano opening his door naked to the waist. He'd known she was on the other side of it, and could have reached for a shirt. Perhaps he was a flirt, as Gio had been, but with a different style.

Her blush didn't escape her father's notice. 'Imagine the gossip in Santa Maria della Vedetta if it got out that you had travelled with a man who was neither a close relation nor your *fidanzato*.'

'There's a war on. Those things don't matter any more.'

'Want to bet?'

'There are women in the resistance and among the partisans.' She had no idea if that was true, but she said it with conviction. 'Besides, you had no problem with us travelling together by cart yesterday.'

Her father cleared his throat. 'Exceptional circumstances. Besides, if there are women in the resistance, they will not be putting themselves in harm's way. If any have joined the partisans, they will be mothers and sisters cooking for their menfolk. *Figlia mia*, the answer remains no.'

She left him. As the mainstay of la Casale, she'd made vital decisions every day and was wholly unused to being told what she could and could not do. Perhaps her mistake had been to confide in him. People could only deny you permission if you asked for it.

As she approached the kitchen, the bell gave a couple of sharp rings. Her thoughts instantly flew to Danielo. Marcella must have passed on her message. Tomaso had deposited the dirty crocks by the sink and was prodding the wood stove, getting a flame going for his bread. The bell jingled again. 'Tomaso? Someone needs to be let in.'

'I can hear.' The old man continued riddling the embers. 'It's why I've bolted the door.'

'You carry on, I'll get the gate.'

'No.' Still in a crouch, Tomaso looked around, grimacing. 'We're not expecting anybody. We don't answer.'

'It could be Danielo,' she said.

'How do you know?'

'I told his sister – in case he needed sanctuary.'

Tomaso rose slowly. 'You told his sister our security protocol? Danielo already knows how to get in here.'

'I didn't know that then. I won't let him end up like Gio Troisi. He's been retrieving weapons and could be on the run.' The bell now began to jammer violently. 'I'm going to open the gate.'

'No – Signorina, no!'

But she'd thrust back the bolts on the door and was out before Tomaso could take two strides. 'Danielo, I'm coming!' she shouted.

She'd got the gate partly open when it was smashed in, knocking her backwards. She fell hard. From the ground, she saw a surge of booted feet. Men in field-grey uniform and coal-scuttle helmets. Within ten breaths, the butt of a machine gun was ramming against the kitchen door, voices bawling in German for it to be opened.

Chapter Nineteen

In a series of splintering cracks, the kitchen door gave way. Carmela got up slowly. The gate had rammed her knee but pain took second place to horror. Shouts echoed along Vicoletto del Bosco as well as from the Palazzo. They were surrounded.

Sebastiano's contempt echoed through her. Running after the Germans was as dangerous as it was futile. For all that, she limped to the kitchen door and with her hands raised, stepped over the threshold.

A single German soldier was in the room, staring into a corner.

Staring at Renzo.

Don't bark, don't show your teeth, darling boy. There was no sign of Tomaso. Had the soldiers dragged him upstairs? Booted feet rampaged overhead along with sounds of doors being kicked open. Pray to God, her father had got out. He'd been well positioned to do so. But Sebastiano was hemmed into an attic from which there was no escape… could she warn him? Still with her hands up, she took a sideways step. The soldier was pointing his machine gun at the dog. Renzo, with his head on his paws, was gazing upwards with a resignation agonising to see. She couldn't help herself. 'Don't, please don't.' She spoke German, and when the soldier swivelled round, his gun jabbing the air, he replied in the same.

'*Wer bist du?*'

'I'm…' Sending silent apologies towards Santa Maria della Vedetta, she said, 'Cristina Gennaro.'

The German soldier had taken off his helmet, showing cropped, fair hair and he looked to be only a year or two older than Danielo. His eyes were pale blue. Saxon colouring, like Cedric's. Perhaps this lad was a farmer's son too. 'I only work here,' she stammered. 'In the kitchen. I cook, make bread.' A nervous gesture indicated the covered bowl of dough. 'The dog won't hurt you.' Renzo had started whining at the sound of her voice. It was a mercy he was too weak to growl.

'He's yours, the dog?' The young soldier kept his machine gun pointed towards her.

'He's mine, yes.'

'Then why do you starve him? He deserves more respect. You Italians treat your dogs shamefully.'

She denied it. 'That's not how it is. He was a stray.'

'He's a hunting dog, girl, not a street mongrel. A Spinone is a valuable dog.'

'Yes, but they get turned off if they're not fast enough or too noisy at the hunt. I saved him.'

Renzo gave a well-timed whimper.

'You want to sell him?'

'No!'

'I mean to take a Spinone back with me to Rendsburg. That's where I'm from.'

'Yes, but…' *Not my dog.* Carmela warned herself to choose the right words. The German's casual manner was disorientating in light of the violent noises coming from above. But she strove to match his tone. 'Why not get a wire-haired pointer when you're home? They're more intelligent.'

'Yes, German pointers are the most intelligent dogs, alongside our shepherd dogs. I wanted to be a military dog-handler, but I was taken into the Waffen SS because I am also highly intelligent.' Was that a twitch of humour? Carmela wasn't sure. In his sharp green-grey tunic, a death's head skull embroidered on the collar front, he seemed a different stamp to the blood-spattered ghouls who had committed the atrocity at San Romualdo. His collar tab displayed a single star. Lieutenant or captain? An officer, at any rate. He wore a skull and crossbones ring on his finger. She pulled her eyes from it. 'Why are you here?'

'To lead my squad in the arrest of an enemy of the Reich. I was informed that there are secret ways into this house, so it follows illegal activities are going on. Is there a wireless here?'

'No.'

'But somebody is hiding… it will spare a great deal of trouble if you show us where.'

'Nobody is hiding.' The crump of boots was diminishing, suggest-ing the search was moving to the further end of the house. They'd find the attic stairs any moment. A crash made them both look up and the soldier's manner shifted.

'Only a fool would lie.' His voice was harsher now. 'Who owns this house?'

'A man. An aristocrat. Del Bosco.' She added, 'I never see him. I'm only here two days a week.'

'State your name again.'

'Cristina Gennaro.' Please let him not demand her identity card, which would instantly prove her lie. As her initial shock diminished, a depressing reality settled on her. This raid had come within hours of meeting Marcella. Horrible to think Danielo's sweet-faced sister had betrayed them. *So don't think it.*

'Is there a cellar here, a wine vault?'

'Yes, but the door is always locked.'

'Where is the key? Is there wine? Food?'

'I don't know.' She assumed a vacuous look. 'I don't go down there. Only my master has…' Her voice faded as the soldier took a pack of cigarettes from his breast pocket. He continued to stare unblinkingly at her until she wondered if the crossover dress she'd put on that morning was too nice for a kitchen maid. 'I'd take you down,' she stammered, 'but it's pitch black since the electricity went off and full of cobwebs.' Officers hated getting their uniforms dirty, didn't they?

The German offered the cigarette packet. 'You smoke?'

'Not very often.' She'd tried it during her teacher-training because the college common room had been so full of smokers, joining in made the air taste better. The officer's pale gaze propelled her into unnecessary explanation. 'I find Italian tobacco too strong.'

'What kind do you smoke?'

Dio, she'd jumped into a trap. 'Nothing – none really.'

'These are Turkish.' The officer flicked the base of the packet. A cigarette jumped up and he caught it between his lips, then took a lighter from his breeches pocket. 'Turkish tobacco is better than Italian. The Waffen SS is entitled to the best.'

'I expect so.' She swallowed, the next words sticking in her throat. 'Thank you for offering.'

He shrugged. 'So, is it good drinking in the cellar?'

She supposed he considered relieving them of their wine to be part of his job. 'There is no good wine any more. But I've no idea what's down there, if anything.'

'Let's see.' The gun's barrel made a sweep and, with a helpless glance at Renzo, Carmela went to fetch the key. It usually hung from a hook by the cellar door, but today it was poking from the lock, which suggested that Tomaso had escaped that way. She opened the door a crack, then shut it hard, in case he was below, hunkering in a dark corner.

'Lock the door,' the German instructed. Surprised, she did as she was told.

'Give me the key.'

She handed it over.

'If anyone is hiding down there,' the officer said, 'he is now trapped. If he tries to escape through the grating into the alley, he will find the barrel of a gun. I left two men on guard.' He walked back into the kitchen.

I could shoot him between the shoulder blades, Carmela thought, *if I had a gun and the nerve to do it.* Clearly, he thought her no threat. The blue smoke of his cigarette wreathed his fair head.

'We will find the man we are looking for.' He spoke as if they were still engaged in pleasant conversation. 'Or the woman. What is this?' He pointed to the bowl of bloody water, with Sebastiano's bandages floating in it. She hadn't had time to dispose of them. 'Somebody here is bleeding. You've taken in an injured fugitive.'

'No, it's my master. He's getting on a bit and…' She racked her brains, and remembered Zia Cristina's neighbour, Signor Esposito, who had never recovered from his experiences in the Great War. 'He has an old shrapnel injury. It gets ulcerated.'

'And you tend him.'

She nearly said 'yes', then remembered that she'd already claimed that she rarely met the master of the house. 'He tends to himself. He's very private.'

'Uh.' The officer took a leisurely drag on his cigarette and walked up to Carmela. Taking stock of her: her frightened eyes, the strained forehead. Her hair had tumbled from its grips when she'd been knocked over by the gate. She felt his gaze snake over her figure. 'Take me to him, Cristina, and save yourself a deal of pain.'

All the time in the world in which to break you with torture.

The next sound out of her mouth was a scream as the officer drove the glowing tip of his cigarette into her hairline. Pain flashed in a fizzle of scorched hair. She clamped her hand to the burn. 'Nobody here has done anything' – she flinched as he put the cigarette back between his lips – 'against your Reich. Nothing. Oh, Renzo, be quiet!' Her scream had set the dog barking.

The soldier turned and rapped out, '*Sei doch still!*' A shout of '*Scharfuehrer!*' from the stairs completed the change in his demeanour. He picked up the helmet he'd left on the table, jammed it on his head and made a stab with his gun. 'Go ahead of me.'

She led the way up the curving staircase, stumbling because fear had got into her legs. Upstairs, on the *piano nobile*, doors stood wide open and ebony floorboards, a glory of the Palazzo, had been levered up. Two SS soldiers were on their knees in the drawing room, shining torches into the underfloor cavity.

'Anything?' their officer asked.

'*Nein, Scharfuehrer.*' A soldier got to his feet and sized Carmela up in a single look. 'Who's the girl?'

'The maid. So she says.' They spoke well-articulated German, easy to follow.

'Does she know anything?'

'Oh, I should think so.'

'Give me a minute with her, then.'

'Calm down, Falk, she'll talk when she feels like it. Have you searched the attics?'

The soldier, Falk, nodded.

'Did you search both ends? These houses are like honeycombs.'

'We've done that side.' Falk pointed towards the wing of the Palazzo that had once been the male servants' dormitory. Sebastiano was sleeping on the opposite side of the house, in the maids' former quarters. The blond officer threw down his cigarette butt and ground it into the floor. He looked at Carmela.

'How many attics here?'

She shook her head. 'I don't know.'

He turned to Falk and said, 'Go downstairs and shoot the dog you will find there.'

'No!' Carmela pushed in front of Falk. 'No, don't. Don't do it.'

'Then you will show us?'

'I don't know where the attics are. I never come up here.'

'They keep you in the kitchen, a poor slave? A slave who speaks excellent German. Show us the other attic and if we fetch no prisoner down, Falk will put your dog out of his misery. It will be a kindness. Lead the way... Cristina.'

It felt like a walk of doom. Five soldiers of the Waffen SS watched her precede their commandant from the drawing room. Three were ordered to follow, two to stay behind to continue searching.

She could have sacrificed Renzo, but after that, they would have inflicted pain on her until she broke. All she could do was give Sebastiano a warning. Stumbling on the attic stairs, perhaps. If he was still trapped up there, he'd have to break the sealed window and get out onto the roof. Glass on the floor would give him away, of course, and there was no way off the roof, other than to fall or jump.

She glanced into the dining room as they passed. The piano lid was up, sheet music strewn around. The photo album had been pulled to pieces. She couldn't see if the hidden service door was open or shut because a machine gun prodded her on. On the floor above, she saw the bedrooms had been searched. Her bed was pulled about, coverlets and sheets on the floor. The sprig of baby hair… and Sebastiano's watch, buckled around the lamp! She stopped dead. Nobody would find the watch, unless they took it into their heads to steal the light bulb. Which they might… everything was worth stealing these days.

'Move!'

A side glance into her father's suite showed her the dressing table gaping open. Where was her father? Sauntering along the avenues of Vomero, she hoped. As she opened the door to the attic stairs, just breathing became an effort. Her lungs felt ironed flat. The men's breathing was different. 'Avid' would describe it. They knew there was prey here. Would Sebastiano surrender or fight back?

'After you, Cristina.' The officer's breath touched the back of her neck and it dawned on her that she was his shield if there was to be shooting. There was no need for her to stamp on the stairs. All those boots on bare treads, it must sound like a circus on its way up. She wondered if Sebastiano had locked himself in.

He hadn't, and she lurched over the threshold. The room was completely bare. Sebastiano, his bedroll, blankets, clothes, the kitbag – all vanished. Carmela stepped aside to avoid being knocked down as the soldiers vented their frustration on the vacant air. Machine gun butts were rammed against the walls, breaking through the plaster.

'Rip the floor up,' their officer roared. Soldiers set about yanking out nails with claw hammers they must have brought for the purpose. Carmela was pushed up to the window.

'How does this open? And don't say "I don't know".'

'It doesn't. Open, I mean.' The window was intact and a spurt of hysterical laughter escaped her. How had Sebastiano got out? The officer rammed her against the wall, and she wondered why she had ever thought him pleasant. His eyes were flat as coins.

'Open the window.'

'I told you, it doesn't open.'

'You have thirty seconds to open it. Or…' He called his men and they stopped what they were doing. 'Or I hand you over to my men. Do as I tell you!'

Carmela put her hands to her temples. 'It doesn't open!'

The officer tried for himself, pushing against the base, then the top of the circular frame. He failed to make it budge so he broke the glass with the butt of his gun. 'Get all the boards up,' he told his men. 'Knock down the walls. There's someone in here. They cannot be anywhere else.' A subordinate was ordered to lean through the broken window and shoot anyone on the roof.

The man looked at the spikes of glass on the floor. 'Nobody has been through this window, Scharfuehrer.'

'Are you disobeying my order?'

The soldier swiftly poked his machine gun through the jagged circle and angled himself to look up. 'There's nobody there,' he grunted.

'Then kill a pigeon.'

A burst of machine-gun fire made Carmela jam her hands over her ears. The soldier's body juddered with the force of the firing. Bullets ricocheted off the chimney stacks. There was no answering fire, no shouts or cries. Urged on by their captain, the men ransacked the attic in a fruitless attempt to locate secret rooms or escape routes. Carmela was coughing from dust – they were all coughing – when a voice shouted up the stairs, 'Scharfuehrer – come down, we've found something.'

Chapter Twenty

In the dining room, the concealed door stood open.

'For kitchen staff, to bring food in,' Carmela explained, sweat inching down her back. Asked why she hadn't mentioned this secret exit earlier, she explained, 'It's to keep food hot. Instead of the main stairs.' It was hard to think straight as the sole focus of the fury of thwarted men. 'It's just a door,' she finished weakly.

'Which you forgot about, though you are the kitchen maid.'

'It's not used.'

'You bring up the food by the main stairs.'

'Y-yes.'

'You told me you never come up here. You stay only in the kitchen.'

'I meant, I work in the kitchen. Obviously, I serve my employer his meals. He doesn't fetch his food himself.'

'But you come up the main staircase.'

She gave a slow nod of the head. She was beginning to understand what Sebastiano had been saying about interrogation. What it took to stay calm.

'Where does this passage lead?'

'A nothing sort of room, off the kitchen.'

A soldier emerged from the passage and displayed a folded newspaper. 'I found it in the room the passage leads into. It's dated yesterday.'

The officer took the newspaper. It was the one her father had been reading the previous day. 'How can it be in a room nobody ever uses? Mm, Cristina?'

Her father must have dropped it. She wasn't the only one who blundered. 'I – I dropped it when I was cleaning.' She couldn't quite get the words out. Her mouth was as dry as lizard skin. At least the soldier hadn't noticed the hatch into the drain culvert, her father's likely escape route. The officer was addressing her again, asking her where she'd learned her German.

She could hardly tell him, 'In a highly regarded girls' academy in Cambridge where Miss Leibnitz from Hanover drilled us in standard pronunciation.' She muttered, 'At school.'

'What is your real name?'

'I told you. I'm Cristina—' She reeled as he slapped her across the face. Lights danced behind her eyes and she only just heard what was said next.

'Uschaf Falk, go and deal with the dog.'

'No, please.' Forgetting caution, Carmela caught the officer's sleeve. 'If you want the dog, *mein Herr*, take him. He's called Renzo. He'll make a loyal— ah!' She cried out as the captain slapped her again with the same force against the same cheek. Bones in her neck locked and the room began to tilt.

'We are looking for a fugitive. Maybe a spy, but spies are not always men. Is it you, Cristina?'

'I'm a maid, that's all.'

'They plant fluent Italian speakers among the population, who can move about unsuspected because they were born here, or their parents were from here. Is that your story?'

'I don't know who "they" are. I've never left Italy.' She cringed, but the anticipated blow didn't land. He was speaking again. Gently. She'd misheard. He couldn't be…

He repeated, 'Take off your clothes.'

'My… no! No. You can't ask me that. I won't. Colonel Scholl has guaranteed us civilised treatment.'

'For those who obey. With someone like you, I can do what I like. Take your clothes off or I'll have one of the men do it.'

'You don't mean it. Don't you have a mother, a sister?' She searched for something human in the pale eyes. He was too young to be so casually cruel. Her hands felt leaden; she couldn't summon the will to undo the tie of her dress. A tirade of gunfire from the lower reaches of the house made her cry out like a wounded bear. Carmela hit out at the captain, whose answer was to ram his machine gun butt into her stomach. The firing went on and on, dragging her back to the slaughter at San Romualdo. 'You're monsters, animals, all of you,' she choked, doubled over. Warm air touched the nape of her neck as the French doors onto the dining room balcony were opened. Sounds flowed in with the breeze. The flutter of pigeons, a chatter of small birds in the holm oaks. The gunshots from the rear garden had stopped.

'Stand up straight.'

She did her best, though in severe pain. Her dress was being pulled off. 'All right – stop, I'll do it.' Scratching for crumbs of dignity, she tugged the side bow that secured the front of her dress and when it dropped at her feet she stood, hunched, in her underwear and stockings. It was English underwear, artificial silk in a shade called tea rose. A brassiere, step-in pants and a girdle fixed modestly over the top. She shut her eyes to disassociate herself from the coarse comments.

'You are very beautiful, Cristina. A pity you are treacherous liar.'

'I'm not.'

'Not a liar?'

'Not... beautiful.'

'But you are. A true Italian Venus, and I am going to give you a last chance to keep your beauty. Take off your underwear.'

Somehow she did it. It was like pulling off her skin, possible only because she kept her eyes closed and imagined herself at la Casale, in springtime when the peach blossom was out, she and Renzo making dual tracks in the morning dew. Renzo. Poor, darling boy.

She was frogmarched onto the balcony, her wrists lashed to the iron railing with her own stockings. Tied so tight, her hands flooded with pins and needles. The ornate railing was cold against her thighs, but it offered some modesty, at least from anyone looking up from the street. On the avenue, an armour-plated vehicle waited. It had a swastika on its roof.

The soldiers guarding the front door stepped back into the road to get a better view. They could have a full gawp of her naked stomach, her breasts and shoulders but they would not see her cry, or hear her beg. Carmela kept her eyes shut, willing this mortification to be over. Her comfort was that her father, Tomaso and Sebastiano had got out in time. Sebastiano must have packed his bag in seconds, careered down the attic stairs and left alongside her father. She was the only one left. A hideous, lonely feeling.

The French doors were pinned open and the soldiers were offering lewd observations about her figure, the shape of her backside, what they'd like to do. It took everything she had not to crumple or beg. It would be over, one way or another, at some point. She let her thoughts fly back to la Casale, to the hazelnut groves abandoned by her grandmother because, without her husband's constant attention, they'd become unprofitable. Her mind moved along the green alleys, under the shading canopies. She paused where an aged tree had been uprooted by the wind. Above her, a thrush warbled.

A bullet zinged past her shoulder, and she jerked. The stocking tourniquet around her wrists tightened.

'Good shot, ten points, Scharfuehrer!'

She twisted round and saw three men, including the commandant, sitting on the dining table, holding their machine guns one-handed. The barrels pointed through the open window. 'Don't move, Cristina,' the officer laughed.

A rank-and-file man chuckled. 'My turn.'

Another shot burned past her head. She heard, 'Nice one, Horst, ten points.'

Another single shot, another ten points awarded. A bullet ricocheting off the balcony rail brought derisory whistles.

'You lose five points, Rudi.'

The soldiers in the street below were laughing along, though they'd moved to the side out of caution. Two more bullets flew past, one so close to her head, it ruffled her hair. She was on the brink of losing control, of begging to be released. But something made her pull her stomach in. If these men killed her, would Sebastiano realise she'd held firm? Would her father acknowledge the sacrifice? Bullets smashed into the balcony rail and paint flecks peppered her thigh.

'Ten-point penalty, you lost control of your finger, Rudi. You've been using your right hand too much for the wrong reason!'

That was the game, then, single shots requiring precise trigger pulls. Once they tired, or grew bored, they'd start taking notches out of her. Her hands were swelling, the veins of her wrists struggling to pump blood past the constriction.

'Have you decided to speak, Cristina?'

She opened then closed her mouth. Planting her feet on the cold stone, she intoned in silent lip movements, 'I am Carmela del Bosco and I do not betray those I love.' Her nonna's voice rang inside her head: 'You think it is Del Bosco dignity keeping you on your feet, Meluccia? No, it is Cortazzi bloody-mindedness. Show them and shame them.'

Bullets danced along the guard rail. Carmela forgot her resolve and pulled on her bindings. The railing swayed and grated against the stone piers, and she saw the bolts fixing it were rusted through. For two terrified seconds she waited for it to plummet, with her lashed to it. The bolts snagged against the stone and held. She leaned back, dragging the rail back into place, sobbing in relief.

One of the guards shouted from below. She thought at first he had seen the balcony about to give way, and was alerting his captain but then she realised his gaze was moving to a point higher up the avenue. Through the pulsing in her ears, Carmela heard the crack of gunfire coming from the undeveloped side of the road, from behind the holm oaks. The soldiers who had been using her for target practice were suddenly alongside her, exchanging shouted information with the men below. Rudi and Horst immediately ran back into the house, doubtless intending to go down to join their comrades. Her tormenter, the blond officer, demanded of her, 'Who is shooting?'

'Somebody in the trees.'

'Obviously. But *who?* And don't say "I don't know."'

'I don't.'

'You don't seem to know any damn thing, Cristina.' He slapped her on the backside and said, 'If it's street scum or students, you'll have a front-row view of how we Germans deal with rebels. They will have a front-row view of you, tied up like a cow in the crossfire. Tell us where your fugitive is hiding, Cristina, and you can get dressed and live another day. Maybe we can get to know each other. You are good-looking. *Bella*.'

It felt like a chance for freedom. 'All right, untie me. I can't feel my hands.'

It seemed he might do it but before he could loosen the knots, they both heard a scraping sound above their heads. The Scharfuehrer straightened up and stared, as she did, at the parapet that ran around the roof. There was nothing there.

'Pigeons,' Carmela said shakily. 'The guns must have disturbed them.'

The gunfire that had been some distance away was now closing in on the Palazzo and she saw human shapes darting between the trunks of the oaks. With a harsh oath, the German officer retreated. The French doors slammed behind her; a key was turned. She was alone, with an unhindered view of the avenue. This attack had obviously caught the Germans unprepared. Outnumbered. As Carmela twisted her wrists in a hopeless bid to free herself, the well-camouflaged attackers claimed their first victim. One of the soldiers who had been guarding the front of the Palazzo tumbled backwards. He lay twitching, his comrades gathering round him while firing ferociously into the trees. A second German soldier went down, clutching his groin.

Something struck her shoulder. It was a piece of moss. She looked up.

Sebastiano was almost above her, and his expression was grim. A short gun barrel poked over the parapet. 'What are you doing there? Where the hell are your clothes?'

At least, she thought that's what he was asking. He'd spoken in a muffled whisper. 'I'm tied.' She angled her body to display her wrists.

Sebastiano gestured for her to get down on the floor. 'Give me a minute.'

It felt like permission finally to succumb to fear and she crouched, stretching the stocking ties as far as they would give. Seeing Sebastiano alive allowed her to think of Renzo and tears slid down her cheeks. Through the balcony ironwork, she watched eight remaining members of the Waffen SS spend their bullets on an elusive enemy. Their Scharfuehrer was with them, oblivious of her as he battled for his life. She was shocked to discover in herself a visceral desire to see him fall.

At this end of the avenue the holm oaks formed a thick grove that fell away down a steep incline. The attackers were now directly opposite the Palazzo and she saw them for what they were, a mob of street boys, acting with a discipline the Germans had clearly not anticipated. They came forward in line, knelt and fired. As one line retreated, another took its place. The bigger boys fired, while younger ones kept them supplied with cartridges. And they kept moving, using the trees as cover. She strained her eyes to see if she could pick out Danielo among them. She couldn't, but every gut instinct said he was there. A wholly new pride swelled within her as, shouting and whooping, boys ran forward to offer themselves as momentary targets before dashing back into cover. Carmela could hear the Germans cursing above the rattle of tit-for-tat fire. The Waffen SS was outgunned, frightened and – she guessed as she saw them take cover behind their vehicle – out of ammunition. Three of their own lay dead in the road.

Carmela could have told them that these lads knew their terrain. As if at a signal, the motley army began to retreat but the battle wasn't over. From the steps that terminated the avenue came a stealthy advance of boys, some as young as eight or nine by the look of them. They carried bottles, which glinted in the afternoon sun and which, after mounting the last few stairs, they hurled in unison. Shattering glass was followed by the *whup* of an explosion. The German truck parked in front of the Palazzo burst into flame. Searing smoke belched over the balcony rail and Carmela began to struggle frantically. She succeeded only in tightening the knots.

'Help me!' she shouted, but nobody was listening. The Germans were now stranded in the road with no cover. Ragged fire from the oaks picked off two more. The boys who had thrown the missiles melted back towards the no man's land below the Palazzo's walls. Forgetting everything but the need to survive, she yelled, 'Sebastiano – Sebbe, help me!'

The surviving German soldiers took to their heels, all except Falk, the one sent to kill Renzo. Losing faith in Sebastiano and not caring now who came to save her, Carmela screamed at him for help. Falk came as close to the Palazzo as the heat of the blazing truck allowed and shouted, '*Du Schlampe!*'

She didn't know the word but it hardly mattered because he was lining up a shot. She'd invited her own death, she realised. Every atom of her went rigid but before he could pull his trigger, Falk's concentration wavered. Military vehicles were roaring down the avenue. Reinforcements, no doubt, from Hotel Parco or from the royal villa the Germans had also taken over and whose gardens were visible from the Palazzo. Through streaming eyes, she saw five or six vehicles form a barricade. A fresh detachment of German soldiers leapt out, aiming a blizzard of gunfire into the oaks.

Falk chose that moment to take another shot at her. His bullet smashed an iron curl of the railing and left a gap wide enough for a good marksman to do better next time. He duly took aim again. She fought against her wrist ties, willing to tear off her hands if necessary.

Vaguely, she heard a key turn behind her, the French doors flung open. Sebastiano propelled himself across the balcony on his bare stomach, holding his machine gun in hands from which he'd stripped the bandages. As he'd been that morning, he was shirtless. 'Get down, right down,' he hissed. She hardly had time to obey when he pushed his gun barrel through a break in the railings and fired. Once. Falk dropped, the precision shot ending his life.

Sebastiano cut her loose with a penknife. 'Don't stand up,' he said before he too began to cough. 'Slither to safety. Imagine you're swimming.'

'You first,' she gasped. She couldn't crawl, naked, in front of him. Her Catholic upbringing, inbred modesty, made it impossible.

'I won't look, I promise. Go.' He inched back, took hold of his gun and once more nudged it through the railings. 'I'm covering you.'

From the haven of the dining room, she struggled into her underclothes and attempted to retie her dress.

Sebastiano hauled himself back over the threshold. German soldiers were attacking the burning truck with fire extinguishers, he told her. 'They've taken a toll and the mood down there is not lovely.'

He shut the French doors to keep out the smoke and drew the curtains. Their folds released a number of spent cartridges, which skittered across the floorboards.

'I counted six German bodies on the road,' he said. 'There could be more.'

Carmela didn't answer. She was trying to push a foot into a shoe and something was stopping her. She felt her emotions spiralling towards panic. 'What is it?' she begged, gazing helplessly at her foot. 'I don't understand.'

'Here, give it to me.' Sebastiano shook the shoe and a cartridge fell between the prised-up floorboards. He said, 'I'm wondering if any of them saw me take that last shot. It was going to be you or him.'

'Falk. His name was Falk.'

'Hm. Not sure I needed to know that. Can you gather yourself, Carmela? Because we must move. If they work out that one of their number was shot from this balcony, they won't hold back.' His attic would be the safest place to make a plan, he said. 'And I have to get my things off the roof.'

What he said made no sense. There was no way out of the attic, so how could his things be on the roof? Except *he* had been on the roof. Unable to puzzle it out, she told him she was going down, not up. 'I have to—' She couldn't finish. *Find Renzo.* Instead, she said helplessly, 'What about the boys out there, our boys?'

'The rebel army? They'll be back on home turf, melting into their *bassi*, or crouching in church crypts where not even their distraught mammas will find them until they're ready. Get the rest of your clothes on.' He waited, his head politely averted until it was obvious she could not finish dressing herself. 'Would you like help?'

'The boys had grenades.'

'They had soda bottles filled with petrol and motor oil. A rag of burning cotton in the neck, it explodes on impact. They call it "hot Fanta". Very *scugnizzo*, since Fanta is what the Germans drink.'

'Where did they come from?'

'The *scugnizzi* or the Germans?'

'The boys.' She already knew what had fetched the Waffen SS to the door. 'They arrived just as I needed them.'

'Then give thanks.'

Shaking from shock, and because the blood was pumping painfully back into her extremities, she failed again to tie the side bow of her dress. Her underwear was twisted because she'd dragged it on. Grinning ruffians, men and boys, had seen her naked. Sebastiano had seen her, crouched like an animal. Shame had a taste, she discovered. Fear and diesel smoke. If her father should ever find out… 'Sebastiano, nobody must know what you saw. Don't tell Papà.'

'What did I see, Carmela?' He laid his injured hands on her arms. 'I saw somebody abused and frightened. Tied up.'

'You saw me as… as you never should.'

'I saw but I didn't look. Come on, just make a knot in it.' He meant the dress tie. 'You aren't going to church.' In the end, he did it for her.

'They killed Renzo. The German, Falk, he went down—' She couldn't go on, but laid her forehead against Sebastiano's collarbone and sobbed.

'I heard it from the roof. It went on so long, I thought there must be a massacre in the Palazzo garden.' He put his arms around her. 'It would have been quick. Poor dog, but you can't give in now, Carmela. There's your father and Tomaso to think of.'

'I swore I'd never cry again. My head is spinning.'

'Course it is. You had a horrible experience and inhaled smoke, too.' He stroked her hair, which had tumbled around her shoulders. It woke a long-suppressed memory in Carmela. Her mother, brushing her hair before plaiting it, cooing because it was so thick and soft. She lifted her head. Sebastiano's face was grimed with smoke and mossy streaks. She imagined him on the roof, slithering down the clay tiles. How long had he been there, and how had he acquired the machine gun he'd used to eliminate Falk?

'What's this?' He noticed the burn mark on her brow and when she haltingly described the cigarette attack, he asked, 'Was it the bastard I killed? I hope it was.'

'No. The man in charge… the Scharfuehrer… I never heard his name, though he said he came from Rendsburg. At first, he seemed nice. We talked about Spinones and pointers.'

'He got you to lower your guard. Never do that.' He kissed her lightly where she'd been burned.

She said the first thing that came into her mind. 'Thank you.'

'For kissing you?'

'No. For being a good shot and untying me in time. You've seen battle, haven't you? You're trained.'

'I was in the army for a year before SOE recruited me. Desert infantry. Come on.' A simple touch got her moving. 'Shall we bury that poor dog?' He shouldered his machine gun, having loaded a fresh magazine. 'I'll go ahead.'

A moment later he stumbled into a void, cursing at the desecration of the ebony floor. Batting white plaster dust from his leg, he added a contemptuous whistle. 'I heard them stampeding around, shouting for foreigners to come down with their hands up. They knew I was there and I'd dearly love to know who told the bastards where to find me. Careful where you put your feet.'

Stepping between floor joists gave her the excuse to look down and not at him.

'How did they get in here so fast?' He was asking himself the question.

'They kicked the kitchen door in.' He wouldn't have heard the furore from his attic hideout. To her relief, no more was said as they made their way down the stairs.

Sebastiano turned in the hall and said, 'I can do this. You don't have to see.'

He meant Renzo, of course. 'I do have to,' she said. 'It's all my fault.'

'It isn't. But all right.' Giving her an odd look, he went ahead, pointing his gun into corners, reacting to every flicker of light. She went straight to Renzo's corner, eyes half closed, preparing herself. The bed was empty. No dog, no body, no blood. The water can she'd filled yesterday lay on its side, empty.

Falk must have slaked his thirst before taking Renzo outside. The thought of her boy suffering even a few seconds of bewilderment deepened her anguish. The kitchen door lolled on its hinges and outside, a gloriously blue sky was stained by smoke from the burned-out vehicle. Sebastiano walked ahead of her. 'Have you found him?' she asked miserably, as she joined him at the edge of the vegetable garden.

'I'm not sure what I've found.'

Her mouth dropped. Every zucchini, runner bean and tomato plant had been ripped to shreds. Every pumpkin and squash was blown open, seeds sprayed wide, their innards congealing on the fine soil. Spent cartridges littered the grass. *Dio. Santa Maria.* There were no other words for the ruination of Tomaso's precious garden.

'I was right,' Sebastiano muttered. 'I did hear a massacre from the roof.'

'Renzo? I can't look, Sebbe. Tell me. Just tell me.'

'I can't see him. Give me a minute.'

A minute passed, Carmela keeping her hands over her eyes.

'He's not here, Carmela. I'll search the rest of the garden in case.'

In case what? 'It's my fault. I did this.'

She let him go, and waited until she heard a shout from behind a shrubbery of viburnum and pink-flowered oleander. When she pushed through the untrimmed branches, she was greeted by the sight of Sebastiano with his gun raised to the sky, and a bare-legged boy pointing a handgun at his undefended chest. On the ground lay Renzo. A bandana in the colours of the Italian flag was tied around his muzzle. Too tightly. Renzo was alive, but in grave distress.

She then recognised the baby-faced boy. In a voice flayed with emotion, she told the child to put his gun down. 'We're allies. On the same side.'

'How do I know that?' the child demanded.

'Because you came to my farm, la Casale, with Danielo and Gio. You were the lad that carried the kitbag. This man' – she jerked her head at Sebastiano – 'was on the stretcher. He's a fighter like Danielo and he's spent the last hour on the Palazzo roof.'

The boy glanced in the direction of the Palazzo del Bosco's chimneys. 'Shooting Germans?'

'Ask him, but put your gun down. My dog can't breathe.'

The child was still unconvinced. 'You killed Germans, Signor?'

Sebastiano said nothing.

'What is your name?' the child demanded of Carmela, who replied, 'Signorina del Bosco. What's yours?'

'Zeffiro, like the wind. I'm the one Mamma says came out of the womb in a gust and never stopped moving.'

Zeffiro. Danielo's little brother. His shadow. 'So we all know who we are.'

'Maybe.' Small, crooked teeth showed in a half-smile, half-snarl. 'You're the lady from the tower who made Danielo wait so long, he got caught and Gio nearly did too.'

She'd already accused herself in the same way, but from a child's mouth, it hit hard. Sebastiano clearly felt her dismay, because he called the child a brat and told him, 'When you've grown some brains, you can have an opinion. Put your gun down.'

'Not until you tell me how many Germans you killed,' the child came back.

Unable to bear Renzo's suffering a moment longer, Carmela lurched past the boy. Flopping down onto her knees, she unknotted the bandana. Renzo's mouth gaped and he began to pant. He needed water.

'You should thank me,' Zeffiro told her loftily. 'I saved your dog from the *crucco*.'

Crucco, she supposed, was street slang for a German. 'You have my thanks, but you can stop threatening Sebastiano now. And you should never, ever tie a dog's muzzle.'

'He wouldn't shut up. I was with the other boys with our petrol bombs, but Danielo told me to come here instead, in case you were in the house and needed a way out.'

'Danielo was one of the rebels?' Gut instinct had already told her so.

'Course. He's their leader.'

'And you came into a building that was full of Germans? That's brave, Zeffiro.' Carmela caught Sebastiano's eye. She sensed he was planning his next move.

Zeffiro had no quarrel with her compliment. 'I *am* brave. I saw the dog and knew he was yours because Danielo told me about him. He is called Renzo.'

'Yes.'

'My brother tells me everything.' The boy puffed out his skinny chest. 'I am his trusted lieutenant. Today I saved him.'

'Saved Danielo?'

'No!' Zeffiro clearly thought her stupid. 'My brother does not need saving. The dog. I carried Renzo out, just in time before the mad *crucco* came outside and started shooting the vegetable patch. Your dog was barking, so I had no choice, but not all the time.'

'Not all the time?'

'I only tied his muzzle when someone was in the garden.'

'Any idea who sent the Germans here in the first place, lad?' Sebastiano asked. He had moved closer without the child noticing.

Unsurprisingly, Zeffiro had an opinion on that too. 'It is probably a girl who did it, because girls talk, which is why nobody ever tells them anything. Maybe I made the bandana too tight this time,' he acknowledged, watching Carmela massaging Renzo's jaws. 'I like dogs. I will have a hunting dog one day, when we are rich.' In Neapolitan style, Zeffiro communicated as much with his hands as with his mouth, and his gun followed every twist of his story. When it inadvertently pointed at Carmela's head, Sebastiano sprang, disarmed him and emptied the magazine. With a cry of indignation, Zeffiro gathered up the cartridges, thrusting them into the pocket of his tattered shorts.

'Give me my gun back. I stole it myself, from a crate Danielo brought up from the sea. It's mine.'

Putting on the safety catch, Sebastiano chucked the weapon back to him. 'Try not to blow your feet off. Go to the house and get a bowl of water for the dog.'

'There's no fresh water left,' Carmela choked. The world around her felt weirdly insubstantial, a fizzy cocktail of shock, shame and relief at finding Renzo alive. It was too much.

'Go to the house, Zeffiro,' Sebastiano amended, 'fetch a bowl then pick up some of those macerated pumpkins. Now,' he said sternly as the boy opened his mouth to argue. 'I give orders to your brother, and Danielo obeys.' When Zeffiro had gone, Sebastiano crouched down next to Carmela and stroked Renzo's head. 'What are pumpkins, but water in a fancy wrapper?'

'We have to leave, don't we?' Her tears fell onto the dog's shoulder.

Sebastiano nodded. 'The Palazzo is blown as a safe house, no question. What do you make about Zeffiro's comment, that a girl betrayed us? A woman.' His eyes were as troubled as his voice. 'That's just Neapolitan male prejudice, isn't it?' He waited. 'Carmela?'

Chapter Twenty-One

She delayed the moment of confession by suggesting they carry Renzo indoors. She had watched the dog lap up a bowl of orange pumpkin water while Sebastiano scouted around the side of the Palazzo. He returned with the news that the avenue was deserted. The Germans had gone, taking their dead with them.

'I've a hunch we haven't seen the last of them,' he told her.

In response, Carmela thrust the red, green and white bandana deep into an oleander bush. Zeffiro shouldn't wear the colours of the Italian flag. It would make him a target for Fascists.

As they carried Renzo towards the house, a diminutive figure on the roof hurled a chunk of loose render down onto the slabs. Zeffiro followed up with a cry of '*Ehilà!*' Hey there! A moment later, Sebastiano's kitbag slithered down the roof tiles and lodged behind the parapet. Zeffiro followed, using the parapet as his brakes as Carmela's heart lurched. How had the child got up there?

'Don't throw the bag down,' Sebastiano ordered him. 'It'll split. Stay there, I'll come up.'

She gripped his arm. 'That child has learned too many lessons from his big brother. Oh, I can't look.' Zeffiro was now strolling along the parapet, soaking in the view from the rear of the building.

'Don't fuss,' Sebastiano snapped. 'He has no fear of heights, so don't teach him.'

'He'll develop a fear if he falls off!'

When they were in the kitchen and had laid Renzo down, she asked how Zeffiro had accessed the roof.

'Same way I did, through the window.'

'That's impossible. The Germans had to break it because it doesn't open.'

'It does, when you know how.'

Another Palazzo secret nobody had thought to pass on to her. Forcing her mind into focus, Carmela found some scraps of food for Renzo, and hand-fed him. Where would she take him when she left here? 'I wish the Allies would hurry up and liberate us,' she said as she accompanied Sebastiano up the stairs.

'They're fighting day and night, an inch at a time through murderous terrain.'

'Of course. I understand.' It seemed a lifetime since she'd burned her map of the road to Nola in front of her father, though it was a mere two hours. Thank God he'd made her do it.

Up in the attic, she saw that the circular window was indeed open, its frame pivoted to create a gap top and bottom just wide enough for a man to squeeze through. Had Sebastiano struggled back through it to save her from the balcony? Meanwhile, Sebastiano surveyed the destruction.

'I'll give them credit for a thorough job. I thought they'd found me when one of them fired out of the window. I was stretched out alongside the dining room chimney.'

'Did you hear them breaking down the kitchen door?' she asked.

'Something woke me. Your father must have heard, because he tugged on a wire that clangs a bell in the room below this one. I was like a weasel out of a sack, bedding rolled up, kitbag out of the window and me too, fastening it behind me, in less than forty seconds.' He showed her a groove in the window's metal frame. 'See? It's in two parts, the frame and an inner circle. Pull this hidden catch, it releases the inner part, which swings forward. They had to be able to open the windows to clean the glass, and let workmen onto the roof. I have to say, your palazzo needs some repairs.' The hanging glass in the window frame had been picked out and thrown to the side, she noticed.

Zeffiro appeared just then, bringing the kitbag. Sebastiano handed his machine gun over, having put on the safety, and said, 'Alongside the first chimney you'll find a section of drainpipe, laid flat. It goes in there.'

'The gun was already out there?' Carmela asked.

'Uh-huh.'

Zeffiro did as he was asked, then returned and dived neatly through the open window. Sebastiano caught him and told him to go down to the kitchen. 'Talk to the dog. We'll join you shortly.' He waited till the child was out of hearing range, then said to Carmela, 'You need to leave, and our paths diverge from here on. I have to track Danielo down, and you…' He gave an uncomfortable shrug. 'Maybe it's safe to go back to your village.'

'You're deserting me?' Not even as an unmarried, pregnant twenty-two-year-old had she felt so afraid, so alone.

He grimaced. 'I'm unhappy about leaving you, all of you, if there's a traitor in the woodwork but I've no choice. One thing troubles me.'

This was the moment. Literally, the moment of truth.

Sebastiano went on, 'The Germans rang the kitchen bell instead of kicking their way in through the front, which would have given us all a few seconds' extra warning. It implies they knew the protocol for gaining entry. Who told them?'

'I did,' she burst out. 'I brought the Germans here.'

For the first time in their acquaintance, Sebastiano's control faltered. 'How so?'

She told him about meeting Marcella that morning. 'She came after me as I left Danielo's house. I felt she wanted to talk… not that I know her. I might have seen her in the past as a tiny girl but she's a young woman now.'

'Get to the point.'

'She seemed sweet and I was sorry for her.' Carmela described Marcella running out to return her basket to her. 'We talked about Danielo. She fears for him, as I do.'

'And that brought the Waffen SS through the door?'

'I explained to her how Danielo might get in here, if he needed to. How to ring the bell and keep walking along the *vicoletto*.'

Slowly he said, 'In the space of a two-minute conversation, you told a girl you know nothing about how to gain emergency access to a safe house?'

Even to her, her actions now seemed incomprehensible. 'You can't say anything of me that I haven't already said about myself.'

'No? I honestly can,' he came back. 'You call yourself a fool, but "informant" fits better. Marcella must have gone straight to the Germans. Unless you have contact with them.'

She stared, at first doubting his meaning, but his next comment left her in no doubt.

'I haven't forgotten how you jumped in to prevent me killing your cousin Tino while he was doing his best to skewer me.'

'I was trying to save you!'

'You threw my only weapon out of the door to stop me finishing him off.'

'Tino's a relation. My blood. I hate him but—'

'He's a Fascist and you saved his life. When you helped him home, did you mention that I'm British?'

'No, but he guessed you were something out of the ordinary.'

'Because you came into the tower brightly announcing in English, "Coffee is served!" I assumed you'd done it inadvertently.'

'I did!' She clutched Sebastiano's arm but he shook her off. 'I kept telling him that you were a deserter, a Del Bosco kinsman. You heard me.'

'I heard you invent an implausible story.' His stony look condemned her. 'You speak fluent German.'

'Oh, don't!' Now he was twisting something innocent. After the way he had held her. *Kissed* her. After the care she'd given him. 'You speak it fluently too! So does Papà. It doesn't make us Nazi sympathisers. I made one error, Sebastiano—'

'Not an error, a betrayal. Shall I tell you how my comrade Mio died?'

'No, don't.' The glittering fury in his eyes scared her.

'Then I'll tell you how my second in command died.' Sebastiano described how he'd shot Nico, his explosives expert, through the back of the skull when he realised the man had turned him and Mio over to the Germans. Mio, his wireless operator, had bitten on a cyanide pill rather than submit to capture. 'Nobody takes a suicide pill for an easy way out. Mio suffered a miserable, twitching death that gave me my chance to escape because it created a sideshow for the bastards Nico brought to our door.' He added savagely, 'If there's anyone I loathe more than a German, it's the vermin that collaborate.'

'Enough.' She was shaking at his injustice. 'It never crossed my mind that Marcella would repeat what I told her. Danielo needed a place to come, if he ever had to run.' Seeing Sebastiano roll his eyes, she burst out, 'Nobody told me that you're all working together. I'm doing my best to help those I love.'

'You've blundered, Carmela. I won't trust you again. I don't even want to look at you.' He proved it by turning away and taking a shirt from the kitbag. His hands, raw and red, caught in the sleeves and he swore.

Clambering about on the roof had opened up the blisters. 'May I help you dress, as you did me?' she asked.

'No. Don't touch me.'

This rejection, the dripping disdain, cut through her anger and left her feeling desperately sad. 'If you go out with your shirt on any old how, someone will notice and might report you.'

'Just do up the buttons then,' he muttered.

Her hands were unsteady and he flinched whenever she touched him. One of his buttons was coming loose. A few hours ago, she'd have offered to sew it back on for him; now she didn't dare.

Being this close to him reminded her of holding Cedric days before his death. He'd borrowed his mother's van, the one used for egg-delivery rounds, and had driven Carmela to a quaint old pub for lunch. Afterwards, they'd strolled by the River Cam. Sunshine and blue sky. They'd found a nook behind a bank of willows. Until then, they'd been very careful, waiting for marriage. For some reason, that day had been different. She had kissed his mouth, his jaw, his throat and then lower down until her lips had brushed across his chest, tasting the warm saltiness of his skin. *Mella*. That had been his name for her. *Oh, Mella*. Cedric's chest hair had been the colour of hopsack, not the dark whorls of Sebastiano's.

He pushed her away, slung the kitbag over his shoulder. 'Tell your father I've gone.'

'Wait. Where are you going?'

His look was withering. Clearly, she was the last person he'd tell. If this was the parting of the ways, there was something she needed to give him. She rushed down to her bedroom, which had been thoroughly turned over. Boot marks on her bed sheets, the frosted glass ceiling light smashed, doubtless with a gun stock. Miraculously, the lamp had survived and she removed Sebastiano's watch.

Why hadn't she given it to him before? *Admit it.* Because she'd wanted to make an occasion of handing it over, a magician manifesting a golden guinea from the air. *You wanted him to be pleased. To be grateful because you'd stitched the strap back on.* It was pathetic, and the greatest irony was that in her need to be important, she had reduced herself in his eyes to vermin.

She found Sebastiano in the downstairs hall, a slim blade jutting in his hand. Someone was attempting to open the forbidden front door. A moment later, Don Gonzago walked in, letting in a stench of burned rubber and metal. He jumped like a fish as Sebastiano closed the front door hard and locked it.

Don Gonzago put his hand to his heart. 'I know,' he said to Carmela. '"Never use the front", but honestly, Viale Bellavista looks like a war zone. A melted troop truck, blood on the cobbles, and the poor trees! The state of their trunks takes me back to the forests of Slovenia in the last war. I hoped to slip into my own house unseen.' He was glad to see Carmela and Sebastiano in one piece, he added.

'Where have you been, Papà?'

'Paying a social call.'

She shook her head. 'Please don't fob me off, the last hours have been terrible.'

'No, really. I took myself to the Hotel Parco, to speak with Major Klimt.'

'You are joking.'

'I haven't joked since 1926. Gloomy stoicism serves me far better.'

'Why would you visit German HQ?'

'Why wouldn't he?' Sebastiano had pocketed his blade. 'His house has been assaulted, his daughter too.'

'You, *figlia mia*?' Don Gonzago looked at her in distress. 'In what way?'

'Nothing much.' She flashed a look at Sebastiano. *Say nothing.*

'I visited Hotel Parco,' Don Gonzago continued, 'as not to make an immediate complaint would imply I have something to hide. I'm glad you are unscathed, Sebbe, Carmela. Comparatively unscathed,' he amended, taking in the state of Sebastiano's hands.

Sebastiano said, 'I'm leaving and I suggest you do the same. The Germans will be conducting a frenzied post-mortem of the last hours, and when they've stopped blaming each other, they'll come back.'

Don Gonzago nodded resignedly, having noted the kitbag abandoned on the marble tiles. 'You're off to join the partisans, Sebbe? Carmela planned your route very carefully. Has she had time to tell you?'

'Planned my route? God help me.'

Don Gonzago followed Sebastiano's glance to Carmela. 'What am I hearing?'

'It's my fault this house is compromised.' Carmela messily outlined her conversation with Marcella. 'I did a stupid thing, but it was for Danielo.'

'Danielo knows how to get in here,' her father said. 'He comes and goes at will.'

'I wish you'd told me, Papà.'

'Is my wine collection intact?'

She blinked at the heartless question. Did her father have no feelings?

'He's asking if Tomaso got out in time,' Sebastiano said impatiently.

Then why not ask that? She told her father that Tomaso had been in the kitchen, lighting the stove, when the Germans stormed in. 'The cellar door was unlocked, the key this side of it.'

'Then I'm sure he'll roll in at some point.' Don Gonzago inspected her more intently. 'One side of your face is swollen. I hope no violence was offered to you?'

His concern was a drip of salve on an open wound. 'It was, and yes, I'm hurt and there was worse. A German officer asked me over and over where the spy was hiding, and I said nothing.' She couldn't stop herself glancing quickly at Sebastiano. Once his anger had subsided, he would surely recall how he'd found her, tied up and naked, and at least absolve her of intentional betrayal. 'They threatened me in the worst way possible, but still I said nothing.' She waited for another kind word from her father, a token of admiration.

'I would expect nothing less of my daughter, but I have to ask, did you get dressed with the help of a pitchfork?'

She turned on her heel and went to the kitchen.

Renzo was fast asleep and Zeffiro was nowhere to be seen. Gone home, probably, by a furtive route known only to himself. She assumed he had the wits to avoid German patrols. She lit the little gas stove, then remembered there was no water. She'd warm up some red wine, add cinnamon from Tomaso's store. Honey too, if there was any. The sensible thing would be to get out now, but her legs wouldn't carry her far. Shock, she supposed.

The cellar key was next to the bowl of rising dough where the Scharfuehrer had left it, probably in expectation of looting the wine on his way out. He had not imagined how his day would end. Lighting a candle in the gas flame, she made her way down to the cellar and let its light play over the wine rack. The wall behind was thick with cobwebs. A bad decision to have blocked the passage behind. She chose an Aglianico, a wine from black grapes grown in the soils below Vesuvius. Its label identified it as a 1938 vintage. They'd been treading the grapes during her last, enchanted days with Cedric. She'd promised him a trip to Italy someday, enticing him with descriptions of wine, cheese, peaches and Neapolitan pizza. She'd described pizza lovingly, only to hear him say, 'I can have bread, cheese and tomato at home any time.'

Her face jerked in a smile and it took her a moment to realise that the cobweb-strewn wall behind the rack was sliding sideways. She jumped back as the wine rack moved towards her. Somebody was aiming a torch at her eyes.

'Signorina Carmela, *ciao*,' came a cheerful voice.

'Tomaso! What on earth?' The sliding wall revealed the passageway that led to the caves beneath the Palazzo.

Tomaso pointed his torch away from her. Leaves clung to his jacket, suggesting he'd been hiding out on the hillside.

Interpreting her stare, he patted bulging pockets. 'Gathering hazelnuts.' He sounded so ordinary, as if a German raid was an everyday inconvenience. 'And you?' he asked. 'All well? You smell smoky.'

They were all safe, she assured him. The smoke had come from a vehicle being set alight outside the main entrance. 'It was a near thing, and my fault.'

'Giving away secrets? They'd have got in one way or another.'

'I wish you'd tell Sebastiano that. He thinks I'm in league with the Nazis.'

'No surprise, having been betrayed by a man he trained with. Don't take it too much to heart. All fires burn out in the end.' Tomaso looked at the bottle in her hand. 'Secret drinking?'

'I'm desperate for something hot and sweet and we've run out of water.'

Don Gonzago and Sebastiano were in the kitchen, and Carmela was touched by the tender greeting between her father and Tomaso. She poured the red wine into a pan and put it on the flame, then went to the larder where she found a bottle of *olio santo* – 'holy oil' – olive oil in which chillies had been macerated. Light ruby in colour, it was good for softening stale bread. She sliced cheese and cut apples, saving half her portion for Renzo.

Tomaso grated nutmeg over the pan of heating wine and splashed in a tot of grappa. 'Good for the nerves.' As they ate and drank, ears pricked for every sound, Tomaso and Don Gonzago discussed where they might find a safe haven. 'I don't know about you, Tomaso, but I'm of the age where I need a decent mattress,' Don Gonzago said.

'You're not too old to be arrested and shot.' That came from Sebastiano. He would leave when he'd drunk his hot wine.

Tomaso was tending towards staying put. 'We have our escape routes, after all.'

'All compromised,' Sebastiano said, looking at Carmela.

'Not the cellar,' she hit back. 'I had no notion the tunnel was still usable until I saw Tomaso come out of it.'

'We could sleep down there,' Tomaso suggested.

Don Gonzago nodded. 'Keeping the door locked, something heavy in front of it. We could drag our mattresses down.'

'Days on end, with mice scampering over you? No. You need to switch location,' Sebastiano said.

Don Gonzago sighed in Carmela's direction, from which she knew that Sebastiano had given him chapter and verse of her stupidity. Betrayal, as he saw it. Hopefully her father would view her mistake more charitably. If only she could think of a way to make amends... As she wished it, sunlight shone through the window and the *olio santo* glowed translucently.

'I know who might take you in.' Eyes turned to her. 'The monastery of San Romualdo,' she said. 'The brothers rescued stragglers from the village after it was attacked.'

Her father looked unconvinced. 'They must have refugees knocking on their door every day.'

'And even holy monks need payment,' Tomaso said, though he looked more taken with the idea than Don Gonzago. 'We are rather low on funds.'

'I brought some currency with me, the savings I used to keep under my mattress. And you have wine,' Carmela said. 'Leave it, and it's likely to be taken anyway by the Germans.'

'Wine in return for sanctuary.' Her father nodded, the idea taking shape. 'Mm. A retreat from the world. It's not beyond the Nazis to storm a monastery, having said that.'

'It's a steep climb. You'd hear them coming.'

'How will you get there, loaded with bottles?' Sebastiano was putting on his jacket. His movements had the jerkiness of someone wanting to be away.

'Why did we make you jettison your donkey and cart, Signorina Carmela?' Tomaso closed an eye thoughtfully. 'There is always Adriano Vincenzo's removals truck.'

'I don't trust him,' Carmela said.

Sebastiano laughed drily. 'I am saying goodbye now, and thank you, Tomaso, Don Gonzago. Good luck.'

Knowing the omission of her name to be deliberate, Carmela took his watch from her pocket and passed it over, saying stiffly, 'Yours, before you go.'

Sebastiano stared at it, his face clouded with questions. 'You've had it all this time?'

'I… I forgot I kept it.'

'Even after I told you how much I needed it? You are quite a creature, Signorina del Bosco. Those two gentlemen' – he spoke in a low voice – 'deserve their life. Don't let them down.'

'How can you even say that?'

They held each other's gaze.

It was Don Gonzago who created a final delay. 'Sebbe, before you go, allow my daughter to put fresh dressings on your hands. I've seen cleaner bears' paws.'

'We've no water, Papà, remember?' she said.

'Then do as the Good Samaritan did for the man left beaten by the side of the road. Bathe his wounds in wine and honey. But don't use any of the whites from Benevento, and I wouldn't recommend the Asprinio. You'll find a bottle or two of everyday Falanghina.'

Sebastiano allowed her to tend to him. As she cleaned the raw wounds, she felt the pulse beating through the underside of his wrist. After applying the biblical remedy, she used up the last of the clean bandage, leaving his fingers free. 'Shall I help you put on your gloves?'

He let her, and afterwards she risked another direct look into his eyes. 'I wish you the best of luck, Sebbe. Where will you stay tonight?'

His reply was, 'Burn those horrible bandages and stay not a minute longer than you need. Don Gonzago, I'm serious. Tomaso, don't let them linger.' He nodded a final goodbye. He was leaving by the rear gate and Tomaso went to see him off. Carmela was left alone with her father.

Don Gonzago let out a wistful breath. 'One thing I hold hard to is that one day, I will meet that young man again and have a conversation with him in his mother tongue. Your brother recruited me as a safe-house provider and told me that Sebastiano's masters are an organisation known as SOE. He arrived here by boat. Other than that, nothing. We don't know where he comes from, what his real name is, or what he does for a living when there isn't war on. Did you find anything out?'

Yes. There was a mermaid tattoo on his left forearm, but she couldn't really mention having seen it to her father. 'He told me he was born in Cyrenaica, in North Africa.'

'Almost certainly untrue. He fights like a soldier and strikes like an assassin. He speaks educated Italian and English, with a grasp of Neapolitan. All I really know about him is that he feels guilty that he's alive and his comrades aren't.'

Carmela nodded, saying, 'One comrade betrayed him and the wireless operator killed himself rather than be captured.'

'Killed *herself*.'

Carmela was brought up short. 'I beg your pardon?'

'Herself. The wireless operator was a woman. Italian, exiled in Mexico most of her life. Dark-haired, dark-eyed. Code name Mio, and twenty-seven when she died. Your age, am I right?' Don Gonzago got to his feet, giving a groan. 'Running is never advisable at my age. I'm going upstairs to survey the damage, pack a few precious mementoes and a change of clothes. When you've cleared up here, *tesoro*, do the same, then you must go to Vico del Vigneto and request Adriano Vincenzo's assistance. We need his services as a driver. Tomaso will never make it to the monastery on foot.'

In the event, Carmela was spared the journey. As she cleared away their cups and plates, not from an excess of tidiness but to disguise that there had been a gathering, Zeffiro appeared in the kitchen doorway. A different figure from the pocket-sized freedom fighter of a few hours past. Underneath the grime, his face carried an ashen hue.

He demanded, 'Where is the man?'

'You mean Don Gonzago?'

'No, the man on the roof. Sebbe.'

'He's gone. What's up, Zeffiro?'

'At home,' the child said in his customary shorthand. 'Papà is shouting at Marcella, my little sisters are howling and Ettore is hiding under the bed. Loreto has taken his books to the church steps, to read.'

'Is Danielo home?'

'Yes, punching the wall. Mamma is crying and more crying. They fight because my sister Marcella has a boyfriend.'

Carmela remembered the lipstick rubbed off Marcella's lips. Lovely, young, cooped up at home, the existence of a boyfriend didn't come as a total surprise.

Zeffiro elaborated. 'Danielo is angry because it is not Gio.'

'Angry because Marcella didn't love his best friend?' she asked. Following Zeffiro took a knack for translation.

'Gio liked Marcella and she liked him, but Papà wouldn't let them become *fidanzati* because Gio had no proper job. Papà said they had to wait, but Marcella didn't wait but got herself another boy. Now she's in the back room where she will stay. I would beat her if I could.'

'Hey, that's enough. You are what, nine years old?'

'I am eleven! Eleven!'

'Well, you don't look it.'

'Take care.' Tomaso had come up from the cellar, where he had been packing wine into crates. 'Let the little hothead be eleven if he chooses.'

'He is condemning his sister, a girl of seventeen. Honestly!'

'And you wish to change a thousand years of Neapolitan culture, one grubby child at a time? This isn't the moment.' Tomaso addressed the child. 'Zeffiro, we need your father's truck, and him driving it. Tell him we'll pay.' Tomaso gave her a look, which conveyed a question: *You said you had money?*

Walking briskly down Via Aniello Falcone, Sebastiano glimpsed a lithe figure slip out from a garden, then head uphill towards the Viale Bellavista steps, which he had just come down. The figure had a black bandana tied round his head, but a glint of golden hair told him it was Danielo, on his way to see Carmela probably. Just as he was hoping to track Danielo down.

He pursed his lips intending to whistle to get Danielo's attention, when booted footsteps coming uphill changed his mind and his direction. Stealthily, he checked the knife inside his jacket, lowered his head and set off slowly in Danielo's wake. In case he'd been observed he did indeed whistle; a Verdi aria, very flat. An ordinary, exhausted labourer on his way home. When a uniformed German strode past him, Sebastiano got a glimpse of an officer's collar pip, a grazed face and a frozen profile. The field-grey uniform showed signs of action and gave off an acrid, smoky smell. Sebastiano followed him. He had a strong hunch that this German and Danielo were destined to meet very soon, and that Carmela would be caught in the middle. He'd seen that the officer was carrying his service revolver in his hand, held at a vengeful tilt.

'Yes, I'll pay Adriano Vincenzo for his truck and his time,' Carmela said. 'I'll be glad to if it gets us away.'

The rattle of the kitchen door silenced her. Fear had become her second skin. Tomaso's hand, resting on the table, showed white knuckles. When Danielo walked in, their released breath was audible. Carmela ran to him. 'At last. Did you know I've been desperately trying to find you?'

'My stepfather mentioned it.' The green eyes held a shadow. Family quarrels, sorrow. Perhaps fear, even for the dauntless Danielo. Closing the door and weighting it shut with a tin filled with stones, she asked if he'd come to fetch Zeffiro home.

'He's here?' Danielo looked around, and Carmela realised the child had melted away while their backs were turned. Perhaps Zeffiro had gone exploring upstairs.

'Have the reprisals begun yet?' Tomaso asked.

Danielo nodded, taking a gun from his hip-holster and laying it on the table as if it chafed him. 'A round-up in Montecalvario. They sent soldiers into our quarter and they were hammering on doors, ordering people to give up any of their sons who took part in the assault on Bellavista. Nobody obeyed, so they chased whoever they saw on the streets.'

'At least you're safe,' Carmela said. Her brother was dressed in the darned clothes of a young workman, shirt and jumper tucked into his trousers, his hair tamed with a combing of grease. A disguise of sorts. 'Zeffiro says you led the assault on the avenue.'

'Sure. Tomaso came as I and the boys were setting out to ambush a German patrol on Piazza Plebiscito. Payback for them killing our people outside the university. But when I heard you were in danger, Meluccia…' Danielo's familiar grin appeared for an instant. 'We showed them, ha?'

Carmela looked from Danielo to Tomaso.

'We're all in league,' Tomaso confirmed, answering her unstated question. 'I, your father, Danielo and even little Zeffiro.'

'Then why am I excluded?'

Danielo waved her quiet. That wasn't important. 'I am here to tell you, I know who betrayed this house to the Germans.'

Carmela took a breath. 'Tomaso already knows, Danielo. It was me.'

Her brother's expression didn't change. 'Yes. You passed secret information to my sister Marcella. My sister is the culprit.'

Carmela shook her head. She trusted her powers of judgement. That shy girl was not the type. 'She would have to be evil, and she isn't.'

'Not evil, but sly. *Grazie*.' Tomaso had poured the last of the red-wine punch into a cup and given it to Danielo who swallowed it in one. 'Today, I discovered my sister is a whore.'

Carmela flinched. 'Don't use that word.'

'What am I to think? After the battle, I went home and found her dressed to go out. Lipstick, scent. Her Sunday dress.'

'She's seventeen, have some imagination, Danielo!'

'I thought she loved Gio. I thought… she must be heartbroken, like me. But no. She doesn't care.'

'She's devastated at what happened to Gio.'

Danielo rammed his cup down on the tabletop. 'So devastated she was going out to meet another man, one she's been seeing nearly a year.

I made her turn out her pockets and there was a chocolate wrapper inside. Cigarettes, too, and a lighter.'

'Well, all right but—'

'Not all right! She slips out while Mamma is working, taking my little sisters with her. While Mamma cleans for a pittance, she and this lover meet. He's free to see her because he has a vehicle and pockets stuffed with money.'

'So she has a wealthy lover.' It explained the lipstick, which these days cost more than diamonds.

'What she has is a German.' Danielo laughed savagely at her shock. 'Blue eyes and a star on his collar. A German officer.'

Carmela remembered then. Marcella's little sister Pina had stared up at her, asking 'Where is Hansi?' Hans... Hansi... the most German of German names, yet she, Carmela of the superior gut instinct, had blithered on about Renzo.

'German army-issue cigarettes,' Danielo said in disgust. 'The lighter wasn't one she found in the gutter either. It was silver.'

'What will happen now?'

Danielo's gaze stilled. 'If it was down to me, I would kill her. But her Papà won't have it, nor Mamma.'

'I should think not! Danielo, it's not the Middle Ages.'

'No, it's worse. It's now. She might as well have chained Gio to the church door herself.'

Tomaso's hand on her shoulder stifled her reply. He said quietly, 'Your brother lost his dear friend in terrible circumstances, and his hopes for his sister are ashes too. Let us focus on our next move. Where's that imp Zeffiro? He can run home in half the time it would take you, and prevail on his father to bring his truck. How much money do you...' Tomaso's voice tailed away as the weighted tin scraped across the floor, allowing the kitchen door to swing open. Framed in the afternoon light was a German officer in stained battle dress. His face was one Carmela would remember for the rest of her life. He carried a gun, and without thinking, she put herself between him and Renzo.

He spoke. 'I am Scharfuehrer Weber. May I come in?'

Carmela recognised the soft, polite persona that had coaxed her on their first encounter that afternoon. So, he had an ordinary name. Mellow sunshine wrapped Weber's fair head in a halo but his face was haggard. Grazes on his cheeks hinted at a painful encounter with the ground.

Tomaso looked frightened, but Danielo was staring at the German with loathing. Fearing her brother might try to retrieve his own gun from the table, Carmela seized the initiative, asking in German, 'Why are you here, Herr Weber?'

'You must hand over any criminal fugitives that are hiding here.'

'There are no fugitives, *mein Herr*,' Tomaso answered, proving a knowledge of German Carmela had not suspected. 'I fear you have had a wasted journey.'

Weber kept his eyes on Carmela. 'You are ready to speak now, Cristina? Somebody in this house fired on one of my comrades. Identify the gunman.'

Weber would not have come alone, Carmela reasoned. There would be others outside. Any moment, the front door would be kicked in. Creeping paralysis was taking over her.

Weber asked again, still with studied politeness, that she fetch the man who had fired from an upper storey and murdered Uschaf Falk.

'What is he saying?' Danielo demanded. 'Why did he call you Cristina? You know each other?'

Answering that question with a sharp 'No!', Carmela translated. Danielo told the German what he might do to himself, in frank Neapolitan dialect.

With a sigh, as if he had anticipated this intransigence, Weber pointed his gun at Danielo and ordered him to take off his head covering. 'There was a light-haired boy firing on us in the avenue. I've heard about him.' Though Weber's voice was steady, the hand holding the pistol was not. Weber was a member of the Waffen SS who must have taken many lives, but something had shredded his confidence. Shock? His world had disintegrated; he had seen comrades fall. He again ordered Danielo to remove his bandana.

Carmela repeated the instruction in Italian, and to her relief, Danielo complied. He threw the bandana down and shook Titian-gold hair from his eyes in a blatant challenge.

'You gave us a good fight today, *crucco*,' he crowed, 'and you nearly got me, coming right up to the trees. You lost your nerve, dropped your MP 40 and ran away. Bet that didn't go down well back at the barracks. Did they threaten to send you to fight the Russians?' Danielo used street slang that Weber couldn't possibly follow. But he would understand the insulting gestures that went with it. 'We got five of yours, not bad for one day. Five,' Danielo repeated. 'How d'you say it… *Eins, zwei, drei?*' He held up fingers as he counted. 'You say the rest, I can't speak your language.'

Anguish pulled Weber's face, and for a moment, to Carmela's eyes, he was just a fanatical boy. Another Danielo in a well-cut uniform. But the only one with a gun. She saw Danielo's hand go to his hip, and a look of dismay cross his face as he found an empty holster. He must have put his gun down without being conscious of doing it. Exhaustion getting the better of him? Weber had also noticed.

The German's polite veneer showed its first cracks. 'Yes, you cowards killed five. The sixth was shot from above, to save her.' Weber's gun moved to hold Carmela in its eye. 'Falk died from a shot fired from the balcony or the roof. Hand over the killer, girl, or be blamed for it yourself.'

'How could I be to blame?' Carmela objected. 'You'd tied my hands to the railings.'

'I don't think the lad cares about the facts,' Tomaso said quietly behind her shoulder. 'He wants a head on the block, to save his own. If he can produce a fitting culprit for today, he might hang on to his rank. Don't antagonise him. We need him gone.'

Carmela stated clearly that she knew nothing of the soldier, Falk's, death.

'I'll have you taken in for questioning – and him.' Weber meant Danielo. 'He can watch you being interrogated. We hang scum like you with wire nooses. You will die dangling like sides of meat in the mortuary where my comrades lie. Even then you will not have paid for what happened today.'

'That is an arguable point.' Don Gonzago's crisply modulated German cut through Weber's spiralling rant. Carmela's father's light tread had given no warning of his arrival. He carried a small, battered suitcase and several books under his arm. Neither his voice nor his face betrayed any hint of fear. 'Do not threaten my daughter in that grotesque fashion, young man, unless you wish to be reported to Major Klimt, who is – you may find this surprising – a friend and admirer of mine.'

Weber's response was a falsetto laugh. 'I don't know any Major Klimt.'

'He is in charge of Signals at the Hotel Parco.'

'Signals? They aren't soldiers. They can't even keep the telephone lines open. Nobody cares about them.'

'But you care about Colonel Scholl, to whom Major Klimt reports. I believe Scholl is not famous for his placid temperament. Did I hear correctly, that you commanded this morning's invasion?'

'It was my operation.'

'I have only just finished relaying my floorboards. A herd of bullocks would have done less damage.'

'I don't care. We will burn this place and you in it!'

Don Gonzago lifted a sardonic eyebrow. 'As a lawyer who has seen much of this world, let me tell you that such violence will only provoke more of the uprisings that caught you out this morning. You Germans have only a few hundred men left in Naples.'

'You don't know that.'

'Three hundred, I heard. One might call it "a Spartan number". If Naples turns as one upon you, you will be in a desperate position. You might find yourself answering to he to whom Scholl reports. No names, but I think you understand me.'

Weber's poise wavered, but he recovered. 'Your name?'

'Gonzago del Bosco, and this is my house.'

The captain glanced at the suitcase. 'Why are you leaving?'

'Because you levered up my floorboards.'

'To find a spy. You harbour enemies of the Reich.'

'Prove it.'

'This place is riddled with secret passages.'

'Every significant building in Naples has secret passages. Our ancestors liked to tunnel, and the rock, being soft, lent itself to excavation. They say there is more of Naples below ground than above.' Don Gonzago put down his suitcase. 'You have levelled serious allegations.'

'We have a trusted informant.' Weber's smile was one Carmela recognised. It had appeared when he'd ordered her to take her clothes off.

'"Trusted informant",' Don Gonzago corrected, 'are mutually contradictory words.'

Nobody spoke. Danielo couldn't reach his own gun without a bullet getting him first but he looked ready to launch himself at Weber with his bare hands.

Tomaso broke the deadlock. 'Where are your men, Captain Weber?'

'Outside.'

'I didn't notice anyone in the street when I glanced out from my drawing room,' Don Gonzago observed. 'But why don't you call them in? We could open a bottle of wine. No?' Carmela's father took a couple of steps towards Weber. His demeanour was unthreatening. 'My dear boy, we mean you no harm. You may leave my house as you arrived. Unharmed.'

Weber's arm, which had been raised now for several minutes pointing his gun, seemed to weaken.

'Good man,' Don Gonzago said gently and held his hand out for the weapon.

Danielo seized the hesitation and lunged forward, driving his knee into Weber's groin. Weber doubled up, dropping his gun which went off. The bullet struck the flagstones, ricocheted and hit the wall opposite. Carmela scrambled to pick up the gun and slid it across the table. Her father seized it, along with Danielo's. Weber and Danielo were now locked in unarmed combat. The German was taller and more muscular, but Danielo had learned his tactics on mean streets. It was like a fight between a bull and a wolf, and the wolf went for the eyes.

Weber fell to his knees, howling as blood streamed down his face. Danielo turned and shouted, 'My gun. Papà, my gun!'

'No.' Don Gonzago moved behind the table. 'You are not going to murder him.'

'Why not?' Danielo was flushed in the face. 'How many of ours has he killed?'

'Far too many, and you will not provide his compatriots with an excuse to slaughter more. We're leaving and we'll tie him up, as an act of mercy. Let him find his own way out.' Don Gonzago applied the safety catch on both Danielo and Weber's guns, and removed their magazines. 'Rope, Tomaso, do we have such thing?'

'There is strong cord in the boot room.'

'Would you oblige?'

'You are a lot of old women!' Danielo raged at his father. 'There's a mass grave at San Romualdo. Go tell those inside it about mercy.'

'I understand—' Don Gonzago broke off as Zeffiro ran into the kitchen. It wasn't the child materialising apparently from nowhere that made Don Gonzago reel, it was the oversized machine gun Zeffiro carried in his arms. 'Santa Maria, where did that come from?'

'It's the gun Danielo supplied to me, which I keep on the roof.' Everyone's eyes swung to the door. Nobody had heard Sebastiano enter.

Weber was still on his knees, now moaning softly, his hands over his eyes.

'Give it to me, lad.' Sebastiano held out his arms, inviting Zeffiro to lay the machine gun across them.

Danielo said, 'Is it loaded, Zeffi?'

'Yes. I loaded it on the roof,' Zeffiro said proudly.

'Then give it to me.'

Ever the faithful shadow, Zeffiro handed the MP 40 to Danielo, who pushed the butt against his shoulder and aimed at the kneeling man.

'Danielo, don't!' Carmela saw her brother unlocking a disastrous gate and pulling them all through it. Weber let his hands fall, and through bloody sockets saw what was coming and muttered piteously in his own language.

Carmela pleaded with Danielo: 'He's telling you he has a mother and father.'

'So did Gio.'

Sebastiano stepped forward. 'No reason to execute him. Do it, and we'll reap the storm. I need your help, Danielo. I need you sane and calm. Give me the gun, that's an order.'

'You don't get to give me orders, Sebbe.' His golden hair flashed as Danielo raised his chin and steadied his stance.

'Oh yes I do.' Sebastiano switched to rapid dialect to stop Weber following what he was saying. 'You were recruited by my organisation and gave your allegiance. I'm your commanding officer. We'll tie him up and take him out of the city. Now give me the gun.'

'He'll come looking for us.' Danielo's tone was defiant.

'I'm not going to argue with you. Kill him, you put my mission in jeopardy. You make your family a target. Give me the gun.'

At the mention of 'family', Danielo wavered. Weber must have sensed the relaxation in tension because he bent his forward to take breath. Something fell from a pocket of his tunic. Zeffiro darted forward and then held the object up for his brother to see. 'Cigarette lighter. Look at what's on it, Danielo. Our sister Marcella has the same one.'

Danielo looked and a new, dangerous light entered his eyes. 'Show it to Carmela.'

It was a square, silver-plated lighter bearing an enamel coat of arms of a castle and the name of Weber's home town.

Danielo told her to read out the name.

'Rendsburg,' she said reluctantly. She could have lied, but Danielo could easily discover it for himself. He read excellently, as his mother had asserted.

Danielo rammed the machine gun against Weber's chest. 'So, *crucco*, did you teach my sister to smoke?' His mouth twisted with rage. 'Tell us about Marcella. Tell us how you seduced her and used her.'

'No. I never used any girl.'

'Don't believe you. What's your name, *crucco*, so I know who I'm about to kill?'

A jab with the gun barrel made Weber choke out his answer. 'Hans-Kristof.' Perhaps in a bid for compassion, he made the mistake of adding, in broken Italian, 'Or Hansi. Marcella calls me Hansi.'

It wasn't a single, controlled shot that ended the German's life, but a salvo that echoed around the room. As Renzo began to howl from his bed, Danielo shouted, 'That was for Marcella. For Gio. For San Romualdo.'

Chapter Twenty-Two

Don Gonzago suggested carrying the victim's body through the cellar tunnel, then rolling him down the slope. 'He'll lie for weeks in that ravine, and if we strip off his uniform he'll be unrecognisable when he's eventually found, God have pity on him.' He was visibly shocked. They all were, even Danielo.

In reply, Tomaso indicated the hazelnuts he had collected earlier that day. 'I saw several well-dressed ladies scrambling up that slope, ruining their shoes and stockings to gather nuts. He'd be found by morning.'

The thought of dumping Weber like rubbish also violated Carmela's instincts. She understood Danielo's implacable hatred and shared it, but Weber had parents. And he now had a name. Hans-Kristof. However, as Don Gonzago said over and over, they had to move the body and get out. They couldn't risk the Germans finding it here and immediately sending out search patrols to capture them.

'We don't have time to dig a pit outside,' Don Gonzago said, 'and as Tomaso will tell you, it's a mere three spade depths before you hit rock.'

Sebastiano spoke. In the moments before Danielo had fired at Weber, Carmela had seen him making a hard physical choice. His decision had been to run at her and force her down beside the iron stove, his body over hers. He said now, 'We must take him out of the city, and we can't wait until dark.' He had helped Carmela to her feet a moment ago. His weight as he pushed her down had jarred her shoulder but she was grateful to him for sparing her an intimate view of Weber's death. He hadn't accepted her thanks, moving away from her immediately. He hadn't forgiven her, and his fury at Danielo's defiance seemed to have intensified his distaste for her, as though she was guilty by association. He was now taking over, and he proposed they bury the body among the pine trees along the Sentiero della Croce, where Carmela had abandoned her cart. 'It's on the way to the monastery. We'll need transport.' He looked to Danielo.

In turn, Danielo looked to his little brother. 'Go tell your papà to bring his truck, waste no time and he'll be paid.'

As Zeffiro sped away, Carmela set about gathering up food to take with them. She glanced at Tomaso's unbaked dough. It would have been good to have bread for the journey. Would the monks take her in along with her father and Tomaso? And what about Renzo? Don Gonzago was confident they'd all find shelter at the monastery, but she wasn't sure that she'd be welcome among a male religious order. And if not, where would she go? Not with Sebastiano and not with Danielo either. Her brother, in an attempt to regain his standing as a reliable operative, had stated his intention of escorting Sebastiano to the Nola partisans. And so, her resolution to lead Sebastiano to his mission's end, with her memorised route map, smouldered like a cigarette butt cast in the gutter.

An hour after he'd left, Zeffiro reappeared. 'Papà's stopped on the avenue. He needs cash now; he had to borrow fuel.'

Carmela emptied her wallet, which she'd had the foresight to hide in her father's reading room, pressed between books that were too old and dull for the Germans to bother looting.

Tomaso and her father were bringing up the wine they would offer the monks in exchange for shelter, piling it in the front hall. Sebastiano told Zeffiro to have his father reverse right up to the main door. At last, he looked Carmela in the eye. 'You don't have to watch the next part, but somebody needs to scrub the blood off the kitchen floor in case this place is searched.'

Tomaso volunteered. 'Though we've no water... I'll have to use wine. I know, I know, Don Gonzago, not the Lacryma Christi.'

They wrapped the body in Renzo's curtains. Sebastiano took Weber under the arms; Danielo his feet. To Carmela's relief, it had been decided not to strip the body. If they were stopped, and the back of the truck searched, it was the end for them anyway. Weber, clothed or naked, was indisputably German. When the Palazzo's front door was opened, Danielo and Sebastiano hefted the body over the tailgate of Adriano Vincenzo's solid FIAT truck. The vehicle was far from new but clearly well cared for and with its high sides and box body, it would easily accommodate them and their minimal luggage. To Carmela's intense relief, Weber's body fitted into the storage space above the cab. Sebastiano advised stacking something in front.

'Some kind of barrier that won't rouse suspicion if we're stopped. Books, Don Gonzago? We can pretend you're taking the last of your treasures to your country home.'

'I wish I had one.' Don Gonzago sighed. 'All right. Raid my library.'

'We'll put the wine crates in front of that,' Sebastiano added. 'It will be something for the checkpoint police to steal. They won't want books.'

They were driving away within twenty minutes, Sebastiano up front with Adriano Vincenzo. In the back, Carmela, her father, Tomaso, Danielo and Zeffiro sat between the baskets Carmela had filled with their last provisions, and the suitcases into which they had flung a few clothes. Renzo lay beside Carmela, wrapped in her grandfather's coat. The last things she'd grabbed were the water canteens and the hand axe she'd brought from la Casale. If the monks wouldn't take her and she had to construct a temporary outdoor shelter, that blade would be invaluable. Tomaso's garden spades clanked against each other whenever the truck took a corner, an ominous reminder of the task awaiting them. Though it was late afternoon, inside the truck it was pitch dark. She felt Danielo give her a nudge.

'You think I did a wrong thing, Meluccia.'

'It was an execution. Weber couldn't see or fight back.'

'But he would have recovered, and there would have been no mercy for my family or yours.'

Maybe he was right. Trying to keep to the high moral ground while wading through blood was a false virtue.

Danielo said, 'I'm sorry, though.'

'For killing the man?'

'No, for everything else. But for me, you would be at la Casale, harvesting alongside your nonna.'

Yes. Busy dawn to dusk, fearing the invasion might spill into her territory, fighting Tino and Santo's tactics. But for Danielo, she would never have met Sebastiano… why did that strike a chill? He was uncommunicative and judgemental. He loathed and distrusted her.

'Are you all right?' Her father spoke from the opposite side of the vehicle.

'Me, Papà? I've been better.' The truck's gears clashed as their driver veered around a tight corner. They seemed to be weaving through side streets, perhaps to avoid the checkpoints Sebastiano had hinted at. Carmela's thoughts started racing. Herself and Sebastiano. Their moments of unity, their fallings-out. Side by side, they'd witnessed the worst of human evils. Out of the recoil that always accompanied the memory of San Romualdo's burning church, came an idea.

Evening was edging in as they pulled up on the Sentiero della Croce, close to the spring. Everyone climbed out, glad to gulp in fresh air. The donkey cart stood where she'd left it, the harness in the back. She saw fresh droppings close by and it upset her to think that Nearco might have plodded about, searching for her. It wasn't the moment for sentimentality, however. Handing the empty water cans to Zeffiro, she pointed to the glittering rock-face. Then, steeling herself for a rebuff, she confided her idea to Sebastiano.

'We need to bury Weber's body deep, and here we'll hit tree roots. There's a better place.'

A groove between Sebastiano's eyebrows told her he was listening.

'In the village,' she said.

He looked towards the track that led to San Romualdo Inferiore. 'You'd go back there?' He flexed his hands inside his gloves, as if the thought made his burns hurt unbearably.

She called her brother over. 'You said there was a mass grave dug for the victims?'

Danielo nodded warily.

'What would you say to us burying Weber there, in San Romualdo, in the grave itself?'

Danielo shuddered, but he didn't reject the idea. 'Gio's mother told me the monks had to lay everyone together, in one long pit. There was no time to do better. Are we close to the village?'

Carmela pointed towards the trees. 'About five minutes in a vehicle.'

Danielo was still sceptical. Bury the German in the same pit, the villagers' relations would find him when they raised their kinsfolk to place them in family mausoleums.

'That won't happen for a while yet,' Carmela replied. Nobody would dare carry out such a defiant act while the Germans remained, and anyway, the autumn rains would soon make the ground too wet to dig. 'Come on, we need to decide.' Ominous clouds were sliding over the ridge, their undersides dramatically lit by the sinking sun. The monastery shone like a gilded casket. 'One day, he'll be found and it will be a mystery that baffles everyone.'

'No,' Danielo said fiercely. 'I will tell them his name and say that I killed him.'

'Agreed, then?' Sebastiano's attention was on the road. He would press on tonight for Nola. Carmela sensed his impatience to be on his way.

'Danielo, tell your stepfather we've changed our plan. Shall we go to the monastery first and drop off Papà and Tomaso?' she suggested. 'I'll feel happier when I know they're safe.'

'And Renzo,' Danielo said. 'You won't rest until that dog has been received into holy sanctuary. What about you?'

'I'll walk up there later, when I've helped you dig the grave.' She was determined to share in this last task.

Adriano Vincenzo swore when told of the change of plan. He wanted only to be rid of the body, and on his way home. 'We agreed, he goes here.' He gestured into the pine trees. 'What's wrong with this place?'

'Depth,' Sebastiano said. 'Wild dogs and foxes will disturb a shallow grave, and I agree with Carmela. Putting him in San Romualdo churchyard makes sense.'

'Since when did you start listening to her?' A cigarette lodged in the corner of Vincenzo's mouth bobbed about, emphasising his agitation. 'You told me on the way here she was like all women, with a big, blabbing mouth.'

'True.' A flicker that might pass as a faint apology danced across Sebastiano's face. 'I now acknowledge that she didn't betray us to the Germans. That seems to have been your daughter, Signor, falling for a German officer. I understand your urgency. You want to get home to your family.'

'Before curfew, which is less than an hour off. The carabinieri will take a bribe if they catch me, but if I run into a German patrol, or Blackshirts – *pht*.' Adriano Vincenzo drew a line across his throat. The slothful individual she'd met that morning had become outright surly. Fear, she supposed. And distress too, over Marcella?

Sebastiano saw it too. 'Nobody wants this to be any more difficult. If all's clear in San Romualdo, we'll unload the body and you can drive on to the monastery with Don Gonzago, Tomaso and Carmela.' He shot down Carmela's objection. 'I, Signor Vincenzo and Danielo will do the nasty job, then Danielo can go back to Naples.'

Wait a minute… 'I thought Danielo was travelling to Nola with you,' Carmela said.

Danielo thought so too and he protested.

'I'm going on alone,' Sebastiano told him flatly. 'In my world, a man only gets to disobey an order once. You fight your way, Danielo, I'll fight mine. Carmela, if the monastery won't take you in, return to Naples – unless you can go back to Santa Maria della Vedetta.'

Don Gonzago had joined them, and put paid to any such idea. Santa Maria was not an option for his daughter if it still contained Tino Cortazzi.

'Understood.' Sebastiano turned to Danielo, who was glowering at the ground. 'You must take care of your sister then, if she has nowhere to go. You know the safe flat in Sanità?' Danielo didn't answer. Carmela saw the hurt in his eyes. Sebastiano, if he saw it too, didn't care. 'Yes or no?'

'I know it,' Danielo said curtly. 'You mean where—'

Sebastiano cut him off. 'If Carmela is homeless, take her there. There's a key hidden under a broken piece of the front step.'

'Wait – if it's one of your safe houses, might it be under surveillance by the Germans or the police?' Don Gonzago asked anxiously.

'Unlikely,' Sebastiano said. 'The locals don't tolerate authority. They empty their chamber pots on strangers' heads if they dislike the look of them and mob them if they don't move on. Danielo, take Carmela there if she can't get into the monastery.'

Adriano Vincenzo, who had been gnawing his lip, broke in then. 'I'll take nobody anywhere while you're chattering like housewives. And forget thinking I'll help you dig a grave. I won't stay a minute longer than I need to in that cursed place.' He strode to his truck, gesturing for Zeffiro to get in beside him.

Sebastiano followed and they heard him say, 'We need help digging. My hands are screwed.'

Vincenzo's response was terse. 'Nobody's paid me to dig.'

The rest of them piled into the back. When the truck stopped after a miserable, five-minute lurch up the unmade track, Sebastiano yanked open the rear doors. Evening light flooding into the rear of the vehicle brought with it a stench that made them gag. The good monks had given the victims of San Romualdo a Christian burial but they had not removed the slaughtered dogs, cats and livestock. The hum of flies was sickening.

Knotting a neck scarf over her mouth, Carmela passed the spades out. Removing Hans-Kristof Weber from behind the wall of bottles and books was done in silence. There was as yet no sign of rigor mortis as Sebastiano and Danielo carried him between them. 'I'm going with them,' Carmela told her father, who had climbed back into the truck with Tomaso and was expecting her to join them. She picked up the shovels and a can of water. 'Look after Renzo for me.' She had to raise her voice because Adriano Vincenzo was revving his engine impatiently.

'Sebbe doesn't want you, he's made that clear.' Don Gonzago extended his hand to help her in, then shook it wildly as flies landed on his skin. 'Ugh. Hurry up, get in. Please, Carmela. I want to keep you safe. Let me protect you.'

Carmela planted her feet more firmly. 'A little late, Papà. When I was ten, you sent me to England with an address label pinned to my cardigan. You didn't worry about my survival then.'

'That's unfair – not worry? *Porco Dio!*' Don Gonzago exploded, the uncharacteristic profanity spawned by the hideous atmosphere of the place they were in. 'Do you know why I sent you away?'

'Because you couldn't abide the sound of a little girl weeping for her dead mamma. And it worked. I learned to cope, and now I am going to help Sebastiano, with or without your permission.'

'*Figlia mia!*' The truck was pulling away and Carmela quickly shut the rear doors. She heard her father hammering on the partition, shouting at Vincenzo to stop. The plea was ignored and as she watched them go, Carmela prayed that the monks of San Romualdo would take pity on a dog and a pair of elderly refugees. The sixty or so bottles of wine they were taking with them would help, she was sure of it. As for her, she had no idea where she was going to spend the coming night, but she knew she had crossed a bridge. She had declared herself an independent woman and there was no going back.

She kept her eyes lowered as she passed the scorched church door. The church itself resembled a rotten tooth, roof and tower collapsed inside an oval of blackened, jagged walls. In a graveyard of lichen-covered mausoleums, she saw Sebastiano and Danielo standing by a rectangle of freshly turned earth that was strewn with yellow chrysanthemums. The flowers must have been brought by the monks. Sebastiano was scanning the sky. Though the village was deserted, there was always a chance a German reconnaissance plane might spot them. After a moment, Sebastian nodded, satisfied that the darkening skies were empty.

Carmela smacked at her shoulder. Flies were settling on her hair, hands and face. The quicker this was done…

Taking out his pocket knife, Sebastiano made cuts in the grass at the far end of the mass grave. 'We don't want to disturb anybody's resting place, so I suggest we extend the plot by a body's width.' He wiped sweat from his face. It was warm still, and humid, hinting at rain to come. And Weber had been heavy. 'Let's get rid of these bloody pink curtains,' he said, indicating the wrapped-up body. 'They'll definitely be visible from three thousand feet.'

Carmela couldn't stop herself taking a last look at Weber as the men rolled him out of his shroud. The breast of his field-grey uniform was blown away to reveal a shirt stained rust-brown. His eyes were clotted with dried blood where Danielo had gouged him. Mouth wide open, teeth grinning in gums that were starting to turn blue. Carmela remembered him laughing with his men as they practised their shooting skills on her naked body. He had been given a chance to show her pity, respect, and had not. How many Italian lives had

Danielo saved by killing him? For all that, she whispered a short prayer. A mother had brought him into the world, and would not know for months that she had lost him.

She rolled up the curtains and pushed them under a bush.

Sebastiano, who was breaking the fresh earth with his spade, digging through the pain in his hands, asked her to pour water into his mouth. They let her take a turn, two of them digging at a time. As the light faded and evening midges joined the flies, she looked into a pit four feet deep. Sebastiano and Danielo were inside, shovelling earth onto the substantial pile they'd made. It was Sebastiano who suggested they stop. 'Any deeper, the sides might collapse.' Making fists and with a grimace of pain, he heaved himself from the pit. He and Danielo dragged the stiffening body to the edge. 'Drop him carefully,' Sebastiano cautioned, then muttered, 'Hope we made it long enough.'

'Danielo, no!' Carmela exclaimed. Her brother was prising a ring off Weber's finger, the one with the death's head insignia.

'It's not a trophy,' Danielo said, dropping it into his pocket. 'It is for Gio's mamma, when I see her.'

The sun was spilling honey on the western hills when they patted down the last shovelful of earth on top of Hans-Kristof Weber. They walked back into the piazza, having thrown their spades into the undergrowth. They had heard Adriano returning from the monastery about a half-hour ago, but distantly. He would be waiting on the main track, to avoid coming closer.

'Risk makes him bad-tempered,' Danielo reassured her. He had covered his mouth with a scarf. 'And he loves his truck almost as much as he loves my mother, so he won't drive over potholes if he doesn't have to.'

'This is where I say goodbye.' Sebastiano jabbed his thumb in the direction of the church where the track wound eastward towards the Salerno–Caserta road, which he would cross to reach Nola. He didn't offer his hand.

'I wish you didn't have to walk,' Carmela said. 'You're limping again.'

'Two hours' digging was bound to reactivate an old injury.'

'It's not old.' He'd dropped from the balcony only two weeks ago.

'True but I have no choice, and I've delayed long enough already.'

'You have your food parcel?'

'Yes.' He patted his pocket.

In the minutes before they left the Palazzo, she had made a thick omelette from the last of la Casale's misshapen eggs, cooking it furiously over the gas stove while she ran about filling boxes with essentials. Cutting it in two, she had added cheese and the last scraps of bread, and wrapped it in napkins. She handed Sebastiano a nearly full water can, but he declined it.

'I'm sure to find a few streams on the way. God keep you.' To her surprise, Sebastiano leaned forward and kissed her lightly on the lips.

She felt pleasure, anguish. 'You don't still hate me?'

'I never did. Go. Go. This is a dreadful place.'

In the moments before they took their different directions, she described the route to Nola that she had sketched and memorised. 'Take my way and you can stay off the main roads. There'll be farmsteads too, where you can get food.'

Sebastiano thanked her brusquely. After one lingering glance at his departing back, Carmela joined Danielo and they walked together towards the place where Adriano Vincenzo would be waiting. For the first hundred steps, she felt the wrench of the parting. The next few hundred steps rang with all the things she should have said to Sebastiano. The final hundred was accompanied by a more pressing fear. There was no vehicle waiting at the junction of Sentiero della Croce. Adriano had been – proved by the presence of one of her food baskets and the second water canteen. Been and gone. Renzo lay on the deerskin coat, a length of rope looped through his red collar, the other end tied around a boulder to stop him straying. The truck was nowhere to be seen.

'The bastard,' Danielo fumed. 'The total bastard.'

She found a note written in her father's hand, tucked into the canteen's handle.

We have been granted asylum, *tesoro*, and the good monks were happy to take the wine but they cannot accept a dog. Too many hungry children to feed. I send this note with Adriano, who has promised faithfully to deliver you to the safe place mentioned earlier. Find a way to inform me of your arrival. *A presto.*

See you soon. That her father had meant Adriano to wait was clear. Abundantly clear was that Adriano had broken his promise. 'What are we going to do?' she asked Danielo. 'Renzo can't walk to Naples.'

'We could—' Danielo began but she cut him off angrily.

'Don't you dare suggest we leave him!'

'I was going to say, we could carry him between us.' Danielo beat his fists in frustration. 'Why did my mother marry that pig? He gives her babies and takes her money. Why did Sebastiano go off alone?'

'Because he told you not to shoot Weber and you did it anyway, which means he can't rely on you at critical moments. What if one of the boys in your gang did what you did today, fired on the Germans when you'd told him to hold off?'

'I'd kick his bum and send him home.' Danielo looked chastened, though not for long. 'We're not a gang, we're an armed unit. Anyway, Sebastiano isn't safer. He tries to hide it, but he's in big trouble with his hands and his ankle. He tore the ligaments when he dropped from the balcony.'

'Yes, I know.' She shivered. 'I don't like the look of the sky.' Thick clouds rolling down from the hills were hastening the onset of night. Moments later, the first drops of rain fell. At least she had her coat. Her prospects were better than Sebastiano's, walking through the night while stoically ignoring his injuries.

I wish I had a car. She indulged in a fantasy of driving up alongside him, beeping the horn.

She got Renzo to his feet, and, handing the basket to Danielo, encouraged the dog to plod alongside her. He was shaking with effort when they came level with the spring. She and Danielo lifted him into the back of the cart and she covered him with her coat. They decided to rest under the branches, see if the rain would abate. As Danielo fed Renzo with strips of omelette, Carmela heard twigs cracking within the trees. It could only come from advancing feet. Her nerves flared like a striking match and Danielo pulled a revolver from his belt. It was his own weapon, which he'd reloaded before they left. Sebastiano had taken Weber's gun.

'Stop right there, hands up!' Danielo ordered, making his voice deep and gruff. A moment later, he was laughing.

Nearco stood a few paces away, chewing a large hazel twig and regarding them with morose patience. His head collar was hanging off one ear and his flanks were filthy, suggesting he'd found a patch of bog to roll in. Hysterical laughter burst from Carmela too.

Unconsciously, she had made a choice when her father had said Sebastiano did not want her. Perhaps he didn't, but he needed her. Danielo had confirmed it. *He's in big trouble.* 'I think – I think we've just found our transport,' she choked. She wasn't referring to transport to Naples, either. Catching her brother's eye, she realised he was thinking the same thing.

Chapter Twenty-Three

Nearco stood passively while she put on his harness though he flinched as the cart started moving and the axle shrieked like fingernails on glass. With some coaxing, he eventually stepped out, only balking as they reached the nightmare of San Romualdo's village square. There, she handed Danielo the reins and led Nearco on foot. Stopping at the burial ground, she retrieved the velvet curtains from their hiding place. Renzo needed a bed; she needed her coat. The dog was so deeply asleep, he hardly noticed her making the exchange.

As night fell, they left San Romualdo behind. The countryside was silent, but for the steady thud of rain. Sebastiano had said the Germans were pulling back from their defensive positions above the Sorrento Peninsula to the mountains southeast of Naples. That was a good distance off and made it unlikely they'd run into any armed units on this side of the bay, but it wasn't impossible that German patrols might push forward to reconnoitre. She and Danielo agreed that if they were challenged, they would pretend to be peasants, brother and sister, on their way home. The biggest risk was Danielo overreacting at the sight of the hated uniforms.

She now completely understood Sebastiano's desire to press on alone. She and Danielo must seem like a pair of prize liabilities. For all that, she had one thing he didn't: wheels. Vesuvius was their guide that night, its smoke plume a silver haze in the darkness. She knew to keep the Pole Star to her left and point her course at the curved smile of Andromeda. Cedric had taught her how to navigate by the stars. She looked up at the heavens where she always imagined him to be and, to her horror, Sebastiano's stern features came into her mind.

She was tired, she told herself. Exhausted, and her nerves were mincemeat. It would never have happened otherwise.

At dawn, after a couple of hours' sleep from which they were awakened by a powerful downpour, Danielo spotted a familiar kitbag at the side of the road. Boot prints in the wet dirt suggested Sebastiano wasn't far ahead.

They found him having breakfast in the shelter of a cart lodge by a ramshackle cottage, looking rough-jawed and drained. Seeing them, he scowled furiously.

'What the hell?'

Carmela explained that Adriano Vincenzo had left them stranded.

'So, what stopped you going back to Naples?'

'Curfew,' Danielo improvised with an apologetic grimace. Sebastiano said nothing, but when Carmela asked the toothless couple who were hovering around offering bread and olives if there was any to spare, he didn't object. Paper currency in the old man's hand suggested he'd been well compensated for the food. After she'd gulped down the most welcome mug of coffee of her life, she told Sebastiano they were now his travelling companions. 'Admit it, you dumped your kitbag because you're done in.'

'It was getting wet, weighing me down.' She could see he was torn, his instinct to reject their company battling hard reality. When Danielo began to say something, she dug him in the ribs to shush him. They waited, silently.

Sebastiano finally gave ground. 'To Nola, then, but not as far as Tarzia.'

Tarzia was the place he'd spoken of to the monk at San Romualdo, which she'd failed to find on the map. 'Is it in the forest?'

'Tarzia's not a place,' Danielo said. 'He's a person.'

'He was Gio's partisan contact,' Sebastiano said curtly. 'At Nola, you'll go back. Both of you. That's an order.'

Danielo nodded. 'I can't be too long away from my boys anyway.'

Carmela pretended she hadn't heard. If she'd learned anything, it was that plans and promises often went awry in wartime.

Chapter Twenty-Four

When Carmela had measured the theoretical distance between Naples and Nola, it had seemed a mere thirty kilometres across the fertile, wine-growing Vesuvius plain. Her eye hadn't made allowance for the twists and turns, nor the rain. Teeming onto dry earth, the downpour enriched the colour of the ripening vines, the bean fields and orchards they passed, but the going was glutinous. To lessen the load on the donkey, they took turns sitting on the cart; Sebastiano refused special treatment.

On the night of 23 September, they parked in a stand of firs. From somewhere in the distance there came the sustained hum of vehicles. Danielo daubed mud on his cheeks and crept ahead in the darkness. He returned with the news that the main road they must soon cross was packed with German convoys. 'It's a full retreat,' he told Sebastiano and Carmela. 'And you know what? They've been looting like the end of the world is coming.' The trucks had been piled high with food and household goods. One of them, with an open back, had been crammed with paintings. 'Gold frames shining in the headlamps of the truck behind.' Some had whole beds in them, and another had been spilling horseshoes on the road.

'Plundering all the way to the Volturno River,' Sebastiano said grimly. 'Let's hope they've left something for people to eat.'

They started off on the following morning, their clothes wet through. Nobody had much to say. Danielo occasionally speculated what weaponry Tarzia's partisans might own. Sebastiano had refused to let him leave the Palazzo carrying the MP 40 machine gun. Too big, too obvious, and Danielo had reluctantly concealed it beneath a loose floorboard in the Palazzo's larder. 'The partisans will be using Bren guns, d'you think, Sebbe?'

'Light Sten guns more likely, dropped by SOE.' Sebastiano was more concerned whether the partisans' wireless operator had a working set and a generator to charge it from. He satisfied Carmela's curiosity, however, when she asked how a wireless operator who'd never seen or met him before would know he wasn't a Nazi infiltrator, spying on the partisans, or out to sabotage SOE.

'Good question, and the answer is that he won't know, but Tarzia will.' He explained that the partisan leader had led the welcoming party that had met him and his colleagues when they came ashore on a beach south of Naples, back in April. 'Tarzia is a northerner originally, but he worked with SOE to set up the Naples operation, recruiting those like Gio.' Sebastiano jerked a satirical thumb at Danielo, implying, *and him too*.

'And my father and Tomaso?' Carmela asked.

'Gio made the first approach there, but Tarzia was a lawyer,' Sebastiano said, confirming it without actually saying 'yes'. 'He never practised in Naples but he's politically well-connected and would have known about your father.'

'Papà said nothing when I mentioned the name,' Carmela said. She was remorseful at the bitter words she'd flung at her father at their parting, blaming the vile ambience of San Romualdo for her outburst.

Sebastiano shrugged as if to say, *He wouldn't, would he?*

'This wireless operator, he'll send your message to SOE? He or she, I mean.' The look Sebastiano pitched at her warned she was trespassing on forbidden ground, but she ploughed on, determined to force some admission of feeling from him. 'They'll pass on intelligence about the Germans using our towers to shoot down your planes and ambush your troops?'

'That's the idea.' Sebastiano took his revenge, saying, 'All the towers. Without exception.'

Carmela fell silent then, her thoughts circling to the rhythm of the squeaking axle as they pressed on. But as the hours passed, she found it impossible to maintain a distant air. Sebastiano's condition was really starting to cause her concern. When they splashed through a stream, he took off his boots and socks to bathe his feet in the cold water and she saw the ankle he had wrenched dropping from the balcony was painfully swollen. More alarming, the flush of fever was spreading to his eyes. Danielo saw it too and muttered, 'How much further?'

'To Nola? I hope we'll reach it today,' she replied. Looming Vesuvius on their right flank, emerald and slate-grey in the rain, created the impression that they were making no progress. But as a glowering midday sun broke through cloud, Nola's outlines came into sight. Sebastiano muttered, 'I can see them,' when she pointed out the hazy Apennine mountains on the horizon. Nothing was said of her or Danielo turning for home.

They skirted Nola and at last left open ground for the foothills. It was a relief to be among trees, out of the rain, though the going was no easier.

After taking directions from a man with a straw-laden mule, they arrived at a village that Danielo identified from Gio's reports as being sympathetic. La Rocca was where the partisans came for supplies.

Hungry-looking dogs were the first to cluster around the cart, snarling at Renzo and scaring Nearco. Men came out of their homes and work lodges, mistrust in their eyes. There were no women. Sebastiano introduced himself as Sebbe Alonso, a merchant seaman who had jumped ship and wanted to join Tarzia.

Danielo said to the men, 'You knew my friend, Gio Troisi.' They did, and also knew he was dead. Betrayed. Dark eyes narrowed threateningly. 'I'm a fighter too,' Danielo assured them, 'and I want to avenge him.'

One of the men said suddenly, 'You're the green-eyed kid from Naples, no? We've heard about you, and we hear about nobody so you must be famous.'

Nobody spoke to Carmela, though one man looked from her to Sebastiano and asked, 'Your wife?'

After a pause, Sebastiano said, 'My *fidanzata*.' His fiancée. 'This is her donkey.' He patted Nearco's neck. 'I wrecked my ankle escaping the Germans and she's our transport, but I'm sending her home now.'

Oh, really? Resentment flared in Carmela's soul, not remotely dampened when the village men nodded, as if sending a fiancée home like a bag of dirty washing was completely within their frame of understanding.

'Where's her engagement ring?' the same man asked.

'She sold it, to feed me.' Sebastiano put an arm around her. 'Try to look a little bit in love,' he muttered. 'We'd better seem like an engaged couple, otherwise they'll question your… your…'

'Reputation' she presumed was the word he was searching for. He was losing clarity, the unhealthy brightness in his eyes more marked now. 'I'm not leaving,' she told him. 'I'm travelling on with you.'

'Impossible. Tarzia's location is highly sensitive.'

'And I'm not trustworthy, even now?'

'I'm just not sure, Carmela. I'm sorry, I'm not sure. Best I go on alone.'

'You'll take my brother, even though he disobeyed an order.'

His answer was a hard sigh as though the question was too complex for him. It wasn't only his thinking that was affected. When a guide was offered to them, to lead the way to the partisans' camp, Sebastiano was limping so badly it was painful to watch.

'Ride the donkey,' Danielo suggested. 'Carmela can stay here, and the man can bring it back.'

Grudgingly, Carmela unharnessed Nearco from the cart. Sebastiano got on the donkey's back and muttered, 'Come on, get up.' Nearco didn't budge.

Danielo took the bridle. 'Move, you dope.'

Nearco refused, even when his rump was smacked. When other men got behind him with sticks, he went backwards at a speed Carmela had never witnessed from him before. They tried to drive him forward, shouting, '*Arri, arri!*'

When he began to kick out with both hind legs, Carmela intervened. She looked up at Sebastiano, who, in spite of the indignity and his evident pain, had managed to hang on. 'You should know by now, Nearco only goes for me.'

Danielo walked up. 'The men we're going to meet won't want a woman in their midst.'

'There are women in the resistance.' She'd said that to her father.

'Not in fighting units.'

Carmela looked straight at Sebastiano. 'What about Mio?'

Sebastiano had slithered off the donkey's back, and perhaps it jarred his ankle as he asked through gritted teeth, 'Who told you my wireless operator was a woman?'

'Papà. I assumed your WTO was a man, which was unimaginative. Would the men we're looking for have rejected her?'

He shook his head. 'She was different. She had a rank, she wasn't a civilian and she was trained in combat.'

And you loved her. The truth glittered in his eyes, and though she would never think ill of a brave woman, jealousy licked at her. Wordlessly, she put the donkey back between the traces and waited. After a brief stand-off, Sebastiano got into the back with Renzo, and they set off. Danielo and the guide walked ahead.

Their path took them through uncharted hills covered with dense chestnut forest. Danielo kept ahead, using Carmela's hand axe to clear a way. Their guide explained that the paths were left deliberately concealed. Men would crawl through on hands and knees if necessary, or if they rode mules, they'd get off and lead them, doubled down.

The forest echoed with the patter of intense rain, from which they were sheltered. As they went, they picked whiskery nuts that hung on the branches. The shells were too hard to crack, so they stored them in their pockets. The trees turned the daylight green, and when dusk came, it fell fast. There was something hypnotic about this final stretch of the journey. So much so that the whiplash crack of gunfire jolted them from a semi-trance. Shots whistled past, scorching tree trunks.

Their guide shouted, '*Amici!*' Friends!

Men wearing rough brown and khaki clothes filtered through the trees. Cartridge belts were slung across their chests, and under military berets, faces were daubed with dirt. All carried basic-looking machine guns. Everyone in Carmela's party put their hands up.

'Identify yourselves!'

Sebastiano gave his name to the one who seemed to be the leader, adding, 'You surely recognise me? I'm Sebastiano Alonso. You were waiting on the shore at Paestum when I and my friends landed.'

The man peered back at him, then gave a 'maybe' shrug. 'It was dark, you might be the same Sebbe... but... show me your left forearm.'

Sebastiano shrugged out of his jacket and thrust out his arm. The partisan leader rolled up the shirt and scrutinised the shapely blonde mermaid. 'The Sebbe I met had one the same,' he acknowledged, 'but anyone can copy a vulgar tattoo. There's a way to be sure, isn't there?'

'Look at her necklace,' Carmela heard Sebastiano mutter.

The leader called another man over. This second man peered hard at a detail in the tattoo, then nodded. 'Morse code in the mermaid's necklace. "Dot-dot-dot-dash", V for victory repeated three times, as the British BBC plays before all its transmissions.'

The leader grinned up at Sebbe, who was struggling to rebutton his shirt cuff. 'Our signals expert says you pass, *amico*. Good to see you again.'

Sebastiano's expression sharpened at the mention of 'signals', but there were other introductions to make. With a nod towards Danielo, he said, 'This is Gio Troisi's friend from Naples.'

It was Danielo's turn to be inspected. The leader looked right into his eyes. He grunted, satisfied. 'Green as a cat's. Who's the lady?'

Sebastiano said, 'My fiancée,' at the same time that Danielo said, 'My sister.'

There was laughter, but Carmela still sensed a caution. It would take more than good humour to fully win these men's trust.

They were told to show their papers, which Carmela had kept under her grandfather's coat, safe from the rain. When it came to hers, the leader's demeanour changed. 'Del Bosco?' He scanned her face. 'Don Gonzago's daughter?'

'Yes. Danielo and I are half-siblings. Are you Signor Tarzia?'

'I am Donatello Tarzia and these men and boys have acknowledged me as their leader in our fight against German occupation, Fascism and Nazi oppression.' Her hand was taken and kissed.

Had Carmela speculated what a partisan leader might look like, she might have conjured up Donatello Tarzia. He was older than the men around him, with cropped grey hair, intelligent brown eyes that looked out from chiselled features, and a nose that must, at some point, have suffered frostbite. He spoke with an accent Carmela couldn't place but she'd stake money he'd been in the army. A man not to be messed with, but all smiles for her. 'Welcome, Signorina. You are one of us.'

She asked, 'How do you know my father?'

'How could I not know the man who ruined himself trying to save Joshua di Lentini from unjust persecution?'

Joshua di Lentini was the Jewish intellectual her father had unsuccessfully defended, ruining his professional career in the process. 'Papà has never come to terms with it,' she said sadly. 'The man died in custody.'

'Failure does not lessen your father's greatness. A man who stands up for what he believes, despite the price, is a hero to us.'

Exhausted as she was, wet and bedraggled, Carmela stood a little taller. Her resentment of her father's neglect receded a little, allowing in pride and poignant regret. Papà rarely praised her, but had she ever praised him?

Sebastiano crowned the moment by adding, 'She saved my life at Santa Maria della Vedetta.'

Tarzia threw his arms wide. 'What could you do after that but marry her? A priest visits us twice a week if you want a wedding among the trees.' He clambered into the back of the cart next to Sebastiano, exclaiming in surprise as Renzo pushed his nose between them. 'You brought the whole family? Let's go.' He smacked the side of the cart. 'You could all do with a meal and some coffee. We had supplies dropped off a week ago. A night flight from the British base on Malta.'

Carmela heard Sebastiano ask, 'Along with a wireless and an operator?' She held her breath for the answer.

'Yes, yes, dropped in with the supplies. "Frightfully polite, terribly thrilled to be here",' Tarzia said in outrageously bad English. 'Is this why you have come?'

Sebastiano made no answer. Carmela suspected he was too emotional to speak, a feeling she shared with him.

Her first sight of the partisan encampment recalled childhood tales of outlaws and brigands. A settlement constructed from branches and canvas clustered around a set of stone ruins. Smoke rose from a fire pit, curling up through the autumnal foliage.

Sebastiano got down from the cart and limped up to her. 'I'm going to meet the WTO now. Want to be there for the moment of truth?'

Danielo hurried past them, saying he was on the way to find some boys Gio knew.

Sebastiano watched him go. 'A month under Tarzia's tutelage would do Danielo a world of good. He wouldn't disobey orders here.'

'I'm not sure,' she said.

'I'm damn sure. He knows what he can get away with around me, because you're his sister.'

What was Sebastiano saying? 'I don't see what difference that makes.'

He stared at her, raised an eyebrow. 'I didn't punish Danielo for the simple reason, I care about you.'

From anyone else, that oblique statement would have sounded like a declaration of interest. Flirtation, even. From Sebastiano it could be anything. 'I'll find Renzo something to eat,' she muttered. How could Sebastiano care about her when he didn't trust her and had physically thrust her away from him? Perhaps he was still acting the part of an engaged man so those around them would accept her as spoken-for, and out of bounds.

An alternative possibility crept in. Had her following him in the donkey cart made him change his mind about her dependability? At the Palazzo, as bullets flew, he had proved himself willing to protect her. So she would protect him in turn, and that would be the sum of their relationship. It felt right. Even Cedric, if he was looking down on them, would approve. Her lover had been a compassionate man, respectful and kind to all. He'd have been such a wonderful father. Tears sprang to Carmela's eyes, which she blamed on her exhaustion.

She turned away to lift Renzo down. It pleased her that she had recently had to loosen the red collar by one notch. Her boy was slowly gaining weight. One of the older partisans, who was a doctor in civilian life, had advised her that the dog must be encouraged to walk if he was ever to build back his muscles. 'I'll join you in a while,' she told Sebastiano gruffly. 'Go find your "terribly polite" wireless operator.'

Sebastiano didn't smile. 'The intelligence I need to send will make a long, dense message that needs careful coding. I'll also have to reveal my security check to the man so those receiving the message can verify it comes from me.'

'You don't trust him?'

'I caught a glimpse of him. He goes by the name of Mauro and he looks about sixteen.' His tone turned bitter. 'SOE recruit dreamers eager to serve their countries but they don't train them thoroughly enough to survive. In my opinion.' He misread the sudden blank fear that paralysed her. She'd assumed he was talking about himself, an eager recruit, doomed to die. 'You're worried about your father and Tomaso, I should think,' he said. 'I'm sure they're fine. Can you smell chicken cooking, I'm not fantasising?'

'I can smell it.'

'Dare I suggest you fill a couple of plates?

'Course.' She watched him go, walking unsteadily towards a shelter of branches and canvas that she presumed was WTO headquarters, and felt part of her heart dragging along with him. Infuriating, unreadable man! 'Come on, Renzo.' She and the dog followed the beckoning aromas coming from the campfire, and as she waited in line, she recalled her father's assessment that any women joining the resistance would likely be 'mothers and sisters cooking for their menfolk'.

Sebastiano isn't my man, she told herself fiercely. *He never will be but that doesn't mean I can't look out for him.*

Chapter Twenty-Five

The WTO was attaching leads to his wireless set when Carmela entered the makeshift shelter. She had shared a bowl of chicken stew and pasta with Renzo and now brought one for Sebastiano. He waved it away. He was sitting on a tree stump at a table made of rough-sawn planks. The partisan leader, Tarzia, lounged beside him but, seeing her come in, he rose and offered his tree stump to her for a seat.

'Please, Signorina. We've been waiting for you.'

Why? she wondered. 'I'll stand and watch, if that's all right.'

'No, no, please take my place, you are needed.'

So she sat down at the makeshift table. Sebastiano pushed a notepad towards her and laid a pencil on top.

'I'm having trouble.' He showed her his hands. The bandages she'd put on the day before were again bloodstained. 'Can't hold the pencil.' He sounded short of breath and, without thinking, she laid her knuckles against his forehead.

'You're burning up!'

'I don't feel… Let's get this done. Will you write what I say?' He held her eyes without blinking and she felt he was both asking and warning. *I need you. Don't let me down.*

'I'm ready.' She lifted the pencil.

'Print clearly. Say if you don't understand.' He began with a series of numbers she assumed was the identification code he'd mentioned earlier. Then came a brief explanation, in English, of why he was transmitting his message through WTO Mauro. 'Mio dead by her own hand. Nico turned double agent, betrayed mission. Nico executed.'

She hesitated over that last word. 'Executed like Weber?'

'Not like Weber. Less drama.'

'But you—?'

He shut her down. He needed to concentrate.

The next part of the message listed danger spots for advancing Allied troops. Sebastiano described concrete plinths on the heights of Capodimonte, which he had seen with his own eyes while working with his road gang. 'Bases for guns capable of firing heavy shells into the centre of Naples, reaching as far as the waterfront.' He then referred to a rumour that the Germans intended to clear the entire seafront area 'to a depth of 300 metres' and occupy buildings, creating an armed front against a seaborne landing.

'Wait,' she said. 'Three hundred metres… how many families would that displace, and do they know what's coming?'

'Nothing you hear from me can be repeated.'

'Where did you get the information?'

'Carmela… tell me you understand.' He was deadly serious.

'I understand. I don't want to be next on the list to be executed!'

His eyes flashed. Jokes were not welcome. He listed locations where German artillery would be positioned: caves, hilltops and plateaus in the uplands behind Naples. And *vedettas*. Her pencil stilled.

He met her gaze, his unwavering.

She nodded. 'All right.'

He went on, 'Stone towers commanding unobstructed views of the coast and the road approaches to Naples. These provide armed vantage points.' He stated their locations in towns and villages, ending with, 'Santa Maria della Vedetta, a village north-north-east of Naples centre.'

She wrote what he said, but his next words confirmed her cold premonition:

'Early targeted bombing advised.'

'You're telling them to bomb my home. My village. My neighbours... Nonna. My nonna might die in a burning house.' A vision of the church of San Romualdo flashed before her, and she dropped her pencil, on the verge of retching. 'No. I can't do it.'

'Fine, but I have to.' Sebastiano took the pad, tore off the page and carried it over to the wireless operator.

'Stop right there!' She followed him, knowing how her outburst must look to Tarzia and the young WTO. Unable to stop herself, she grabbed Sebastiano's jacket. 'I've just realised why you've been pretending to give a damn about me. Rescuing me, protecting me...' She sneered. 'It was to win my compliance.' In her passion and misery, she pushed Sebastiano and, because he wasn't expecting it, he almost fell.

'What is this, Signorina?' Tarzia leapt to his feet and prised her away. 'Our friend must do his job and as his *fidanzata*, yours is to help him.'

She rounded on the partisan leader. 'We're not engaged, that's another pretence. He doesn't care,' she railed, too far gone to rein in her emotions. 'You don't, do you, Sebbe? To you, war is about men like yourself. Women, children, people like me, don't matter.'

'That's not true,' Sebastiano said quietly.

'Oh, it is. You made me want you. Kissed me, confided in me, pushed me away and pulled me back. You played your games, all to draw me in. You're no better than Hans-Kristof Weber seducing Marcella!'

Sebastiano's expression fractured momentarily, but he gave the page from the notepad to the wireless operator, who was gawping at them in fascinated horror. Suddenly, the fight went out of Carmela. She sat down and began to cry. A hand was laid on her shoulder. Tarzia's.

'War engulfs us all, Signorina del Bosco. We are all called to make sacrifice. If Sebbe had to send British bombers to attack his own home, I believe he would if he thought it would bring a faster end to the conflict.' Tarzia's voice was gentle but the hand on her shoulder was resolute. There would be no more attempts to stop Sebastiano carrying out his task.

Before this moment, Carmela had been curious to watch a clandestine radio transmission in progress. Now she felt like a handmaiden to the possible destruction of her home. Wiping her eyes on her sleeve, she hugged herself in a bid to stop shaking.

The wireless operator's station was a shade more sophisticated than the table she'd sat at, being an old door on trestles and a foldable chair to sit on. Mauro had finished setting up his equipment, which was an array of toggles, switches and dials encased in a battered metal box. An aerial slung over one of the shelter's roof supports poked out into the night. He was attaching wires to a heavy-looking battery but, aware suddenly of Carmela's scrutiny, he glanced up and a blush spread to the tips of his ears.

'I'm sorry this upsets you, S-signorina,' he said, in stilted Italian. She understood then what had troubled Sebastiano. *Insufficient training.* Mauro's Italian had the stamp of an English schoolroom and his stutter would finish him in seconds if he ever found himself stared down by the likes of Scharfuehrer Weber. It crossed her mind that he might also struggle to turn Sebastiano's complex message into secret code. She felt a treacherous hope, torn between her desire to help Sebastiano and loyalty to everything else she held dear. To test if her emotions were under control, she asked Mauro if he'd parachuted in with the wireless strapped to his back.

'No, it was dropped separately, packed in an empty oil drum.' Mauro sat down because Sebastiano had tapped his finger against the written message. *Get on with it.* He took up a pencil and a sheet of squared paper and began to write out Sebastiano's words, letter by letter, under a stream of seemingly random numbers. When he'd finished, he transcribed the long sequence onto a second set of numbers. This, Carmela presumed, rendered the message into unbreakable code. As he put on spectacles and prepared to transmit, Carmela saw Mauro's hands were unsteady. Nervous at the prospect of sending a difficult message in the presence of a seasoned agent and a partisan leader?

Mauro looked her way again and politely cleared his throat. 'Pardon me, Signorina.' He indicated the oil lamp hanging over the table. 'You're blocking the light.'

Carmela backed off and that's when she realised Sebastiano was rocking on his feet. Abandoning her resentment and rage, she leapt forward to catch him. Tarzia moved at the same time, and they shared his weight as he fell.

The wireless operator stopped what he was doing. 'What's up with him?

'Get on with your job,' Tarzia said sharply. 'Your scheduled transmission time is at ten tonight, and it is now a quarter to. No?'

'It is but I'm starting to wonder if I should be sending another agent's message without authority from London. It's rather unorthodox.' Mauro cast a troubled glance Carmela's way. 'What if the information is wrong, and people die when they shouldn't?'

'You weren't sent here to preach,' Tarzia said in a menacingly soft voice, 'but to act.'

Mauro swallowed and lowered his eyes to his page of code.

Carmela and Tarzia helped Sebastiano to sit with his back against a tree trunk. He had come out of his faint and was blinking fast. Sweat gleamed on his temple.

Tarzia tutted. 'You're hot as a stove, my friend. Is it malaria?'

Sebastiano shook his head, which forced a groan of pain from him. He was burning up while shivering violently. He pushed his bandaged hand against his temples and Carmela saw signs of suppuration through the fabric.

'It's his burns,' she said and sketched the awful history.

Tarzia expressed a breath through his teeth. 'Fever could be a sign of blood poisoning. We have sulpha. Sulphonamide. I'll have our doctor see him and give an opinion.'

He went out and Carmela heard him give a shrill whistle. She took up a more comfortable position on the floor so she could support Sebastiano.

'The message,' he muttered.

'Mauro's turned it into numbers. He's going to send it at ten o'clock, which is apparently his scheduled time.'

'Don't trust him.'

'He's on your side, Sebbe. He's young and anxious, that's all.'

'Mio.'

'What about her?'

'She was slow. I told her to leave, go, go. She didn't move and later I thought, if Nico betrayed us both, the Germans would have known to look for a woman. I'd have sent her straight into their arms.'

'Why didn't she jump with you?'

'Shutters.'

'The shutters were closed?'

'We should have jumped at once.' From his muddled answers, Carmela guessed he had reviewed his choices many times. 'She couldn't. Had a dress on, wrong shoes. Mio was vain. Wrong shoes.'

'The wrong shoes for jumping?' Carmela imagined a dark-haired woman in a summer dress and sandals with a heel. Because she hadn't expected betrayal. Poor thing.

'They told us cyanide was a fast death.' Sebastiano clenched his fists and would have beaten them together had she not stopped him. 'Not fast enough. Miserable death. She knew… scared of torture. Terrified. She chose. Killed herself.'

'Signorina?' Mauro spoke loudly over Sebastiano's ramblings. 'I think I might have mis-transcribed something earlier… I'm looking at it again. Where it says "Watchtower at Santa Maria…" Is it "della *Ven*detta" or "del Lavanda"? The writing's awful. Sorry.'

Carmela wrestled with her conscience. It was her writing Mauro couldn't read, and it felt like a choice between Nonna, her home and friends versus the implacable progress of war. Sebastiano hadn't heard the question, so she could easily lie. She pictured the tower on its ridge, a clear and solitary target, and the village a kilometre away with no obvious connection to it. Nonna would be safe with Zia Cristina. But la Casale, now occupied by Santo and Brigitta and their children, could be in the bombers' path. Tarzia had spoken of sacrifice, as though it were a sacred calling. She had no right to sacrifice Santo's children, but nor could she stand in the way of the Allied advance.

In a voice little higher than a whisper, she said, 'It's Santa Maria della Vedetta. Send the message, Mauro.'

*

Tarzia returned and was clearly furious. He apologised to Carmela. 'Our medic's bag got left behind on our last operation. All he's got are a couple of tins of sulpha powder, US army issue.'

The doctor himself came in, the same fighter who had advised Carmela about Renzo. He brought warm water and efficiently cleaned Sebastiano's wounded hands, then sprinkled bright yellow powder over the infected burns. Finally, he put on clean dressings. 'I'm keeping the other tin of sulpha, in case one of our boys needs it.' He advised Carmela, 'Get him to a doctor who can continue the treatment.'

'Where's the nearest one?' Carmela asked.

'In Nola. Where's the nearest one we trust?' Tarzia raised an eyebrow cynically. 'My father, back home in Venice. No use to our friend here. Have you a doctor in Naples you can turn to?'

'No.' There was nobody in Naples she would dare approach. 'But there's one in my home village.' Dr Baccolini, her childhood friend. 'Only, we have enemies there.'

'The more dangerous choice for Sebastiano is to stay here. This isn't a fever he'll sweat out, Signorina. You need to leave tonight.' Tarzia looked at his watch. 'It's ten o'clock.'

On cue, Mauro began tapping out a sequence using the Morse key on his wireless. He had put on his headphones and was bathed in lamplight and fierce concentration. As he translated his number coding into *dot-dash-dot*, the air filled with a staccato singing. Sebastiano's message was being relayed. He had completed his mission.

Now Carmela needed to save his life.

Chapter Twenty-Six

It was only as the cart veered onto a bumpy verge and Carmela felt her chin strike her chest that she realised she'd fallen asleep with the reins in her hand. Nearco had taken advantage of her lapse, and found some juicy greenery to tear at. She had no idea what time it was as it was pitch dark, the stars and moon hidden behind cloud. Where on earth were they?

She stared around, wide-eyed, searching for a landmark.

They had left Tarzia's camp the previous night. As Mauro, the wireless operator, completed his transmission, she'd harnessed the donkey. Tarzia and two of his men had put Renzo and Sebastiano in the back, on a bed of dry ferns. There'd been no time to find Danielo, who'd gone off with the young recruits on a training exercise in the forest. Tarzia had given her food and water. He'd also offered her a gun, which she'd declined. She had the hand axe, weapon enough for her, in the deep pocket of her deerskin coat.

She remembered stopping for a brief rest at La Rocca but virtually nothing of driving back across the Vesuvius plain. Her last clear memory was of holding her breath as the cart creaked through San Romualdo Inferiore. She hoped she'd steered the donkey in the right direction for the uphill pull to Santa Maria della Vedetta.

Gradually, her eyes adjusted and she made out a familiar snake-like turn in the road ahead. It was a road she'd climbed countless times in her life. There was the apple tree where she'd tethered Nearco a few days ago as she paid her last visit to her grandfather's hazelnut grove. The donkey had brought her home.

A terrible smell of burning got her out of the cart. Surely the bombers couldn't have struck already? She checked Sebastiano, resting her hand on his forehead. At her touch, he stirred and murmured incoherently. Renzo needed to stretch his legs and she helped him off the back of the cart. Together, they crossed the dry ditch onto la Casale's terrain. A waning moon gave just enough light to make sense of the shapes around her. In her short absence, somebody had pruned the hazelnut trees. Pruned them severely. Branches were heaped at intervals. Had a bonfire been made and did that explain the burned smell?

It was too dark to make out the *vedetta* on the ridge. Instead, she looked towards the far end of the grove, tempted to run to the place she'd hidden her letters and books. To unearth them and expose her deepest secret to the moon. But there wasn't time. Sebastiano was her priority.

She returned to the cart, lifted Renzo in and led the donkey on foot. Pure guesswork, but she felt it was around three in the morning. The village ought to be fast asleep. She hoped old Signor Esposito was having a better night than usual and wouldn't need to use the latrine for the next half-hour. Her keenest wish was to find Dr Baccolini at home and for her arrival to be witnessed by him alone.

On this occasion, fortune smiled. Not daring to knock on his door in case Tino was awake in the house opposite, she hurled stones up at a window, which, after a few attempts, opened.

'Who's there?'

She hissed her name. Evidently wrenched from deep slumber, the doctor stared down at her, as she had done the night Danielo had called on her at la Casale. 'Carmela?'

'Yes.'

'Go to the side gate,' he whispered. 'Is that your cart? Bring it round the back.'

Between them, they got Sebastiano into the house – no easy feat as he could hardly walk. Then they had to get him upstairs. Signora Baccolini, pale-faced in her dressing gown, anxious to help while clearly disapproving of Carmela arriving at such an hour in company with a man, guided them into a back bedroom. They laid Sebastiano on a divan. Only then did they light a lantern so Emilio could assess the patient.

He sucked air between his teeth, but said nothing other than to ask his mother to prepare 'the usual' while he fetched his medical bag. With his mother's help, he rewashed Sebastiano's wounds and applied petroleum jelly and more yellow sulpha powder. When he asked for fresh dressings, his mother advised letting the air get to the skin.

'I was a nurse during the last war,' she told Carmela, 'when all we had was carbolic and fresh air.'

They brought cushions for Carmela to lie on the floor beside Sebastiano. 'Don't ever mention these arrangements to Padre Pasquale,' Signora Baccolini advised gravely.

'You can be sure of that.'

The doctor brought Renzo to sleep beside her, worried the dog might bark if he was left alone, and alert the neighbours. Carmela was touched by the Baccolinis' readiness to help, knowing she and Sebastiano were putting them at great risk. She tried to thank them.

Emilio Baccolini patted her shoulder. 'Let's all get some more sleep.'

She thought she heard mother and son exchange whispered words as they left her, closing the door behind them.

'I wonder if she knows what's happened at la Casale.'

'Say nothing for now, Mamma. She obviously has enough on her plate.'

She woke to discover Renzo licking her neck. Sitting up, she saw sunlight through the shutters throwing blades across Sebastiano's bed. Whispering, 'How are you?' she expected no reply, and was astonished when he rolled over to face her and said, 'I'm good.' A cautious smile spread across his unshaven face. 'You look as though you might have forgiven me.'

For making her spell out the name of the *vedetta* for the bombers? It's what she supposed he meant. 'I will never forget it, Sebbe. How can I?'

'I don't expect you to, but do you at least absolve me from criticising you and finding fault? I was often harsh, but I always admired you.'

Disturbing pleasure shot through her.

'I'm glad you're alive, Mio.' He closed his eyes and sank back into whatever fevered delusion gripped him. There was a tap on the door.

'It's Emilio. May I come in?'

Stiffly, she got up from her cushions. Wrapping a blanket around her shoulders, she went to let him in. Watching him lay the back of his hand against Sebastiano's forehead, she said, 'Has his temperature dropped?'

'A degree or so,' Dr Baccolini allowed, 'and he's certainly less clammy. I'll fetch cold water, and you can sponge his face to bring it down even further.'

'Perhaps you should do it. You have the touch.'

He gave her a close look. 'The touch, perhaps, but not the time.' He inspected Sebastiano's hands. 'Looking better already. *Dio grazie*, sulphonamides are a miracle. Before them, I'd have been preparing to amputate.'

'His hands?' That shook her. 'He thought I was someone else a moment ago.'

'Don't fret about a spot of delirium. He's sustained severe wounds and won't have slept properly since it happened. This man is important to you?'

She didn't know how to answer. 'Yes' threatened Cedric's place in her soul. 'No' would be a downright lie. It was so complicated. She sidestepped, saying, 'Neither of us has slept much for several nights.'

'I won't ask the details, best I don't know.'

'There's nothing – I mean, we're not, you know…'

'I understand. Catch up on sleep.'

She stopped him leaving. 'I want to see la Casale, but first I must call on Nonna. She's still here?'

Dr Baccolini snatched her hand, as if she'd already attempted to leave. 'No. No. You can't. A donkey in my backyard I can explain, but you… there are eyes everywhere. Don't leave this house. Understand?'

She nodded. 'Tino?'

'He's often at his window, watching my patients come and go. He'd love to catch me out in some transgression. And la Casale is Santo's home now. I can't remember, did you know that?'

She nodded. 'I suppose he and his wife have made themselves comfortable there?'

He raised her hand to his lips and kissed it, which made her jump. That drew a wan smile from him. 'All we can say for sure of this life, is that it changes. Could you find room for some breakfast?'

'Yes please, and Sebastiano needs something. So does Renzo.'

Dr Baccolini gave the dog a professional once-over. Renzo rolled on his back, presenting his stomach. 'He's doing all right, isn't he?'

'Thanks to your help,' Carmela told him.

'Mine?'

'Decoying Tino with talk of neurotic tissue.'

'Necrotic.' He smiled. 'Funny, isn't it, how a man who metes out punishments with such blind ease is scared in the face of his own suffering? I admire you, Carmela, for defying him.'

'Emilio, is everything all right at the farm?' She'd persuaded herself she'd dreamed the exchange between the doctor and his mother in the early hours. Her friend's hesitation made her anxious.

His next words terrified her.

'It's not all right, I'm sorry. Two nights ago, a plane was shot down by gunners firing from the top of your *vedetta*.'

'What kind of plane?'

'Large. A transporter, I think.'

So, the *vedetta* had claimed its first certain victim. This is what Emilio had wanted to spare her. 'When you say "transporter", d'you mean there would have been troops on board?'

He couldn't tell her anything about casualty numbers, but there almost certainly would have been a death toll. The plane had come down in flames two or three valleys distant. 'We saw the explosion from here. I drove out see if there was anything I could do, but the site was impossible to reach. A deep valley with no roads.'

She glanced at Sebastiano, her throat tight. 'Don't tell him anything about it yet.' She would break it to him when he was stronger. 'I need to see my home, Emilio. What's happened to my cattle, the goats? Did Santo and his wife round them up?'

'I've no idea.' The doctor had paled at her words. 'Nobody goes near la Casale, Carmela, not these days. Santo is like a warlord, guarding his stolen prize. The place has been teeming with Blackshirts. But like I said, things change. Driving home after the plane was shot down, I saw trucks leaving the farm at speed.'

'So the Blackshirts have gone?' Carmela felt a cheer burst inside her.

'There may be some left, I didn't count them. Santo is still there and Tino goes every day. But Carmela… they are grubbing up your grandfather's hazel grove.'

'Destroying it.' She nodded. 'My grandfather loved that grove. His grandfather planted the trees, tiny saplings grown from nuts. Nonna will be so upset.'

'But there is nothing you can do, so put it from your mind and let time bring peace.'

What word was the opposite of peace? Turmoil had burrowed into her bones. After a breakfast of fruit and bread, and with nothing else to do, Carmela lay back down on her cushions. Her muscles twitched with frustration. Renzo, having been fed and walked around the yard by the doctor, was sleeping. So was Sebastiano, even more deeply. She had bathed him as best she could, and persuaded him to take some chicken broth. With nothing to do but wait, her mind crept the short distance to la Casale. A transport plane brought down. With how many Allied troops on board – ten, twenty, more? Now she understood the burning smell on the air.

Sebastiano had been doing his job, pinpointing the *vedetta*'s location to his bosses at SOE. She could no longer argue against the tower's destruction.

But what if the bombers that came to destroy it failed to distinguish between ruined tower and farmhouse? Or hit the barns, which might have her goats and cows inside? Through her anxiety pealed the sonorous bell for morning Mass. When the front door bumped shut, she pictured the doctor's mother, darkly veiled and carrying her rosary and missal, scuttling to church. Nonna would be in the congregation and Tino too. He considered regular attendance to be part of his role as unelected village headman.

When the tolling bell stopped, silence fell. Birdsong filtered up from the yard outside. She heard the sough of the wind as it funnelled around the sharp bend at the end of the main street. Renzo woke and pushed his nose against her side. He whimpered.

'You want to go out.'

She looked at her boots, cracked and muddy. Nobody would see her if she slipped away for half an hour. Padre Pasquale's services always dragged, since he saw transgression in every face in front of him and always picked out some miscreant to lecture publicly. A quick trip down the road would reassure her that la Casale was intact. She could take her leave of her grandfather's beloved grove and be back before the church doors opened. She could also—

Sebastiano chose that moment to stir. She watched him in trepidation until he sighed something unintelligible and settled back again. She put on her boots and looped the rope leash around Renzo's neck.

It wasn't only the grove and the farm that was pulling her. She needed to stand one last time on a sacred spot and call Cedric's image close. Tell him what had happened and beg his forgiveness.

Chapter Twenty-Seven

Daylight made sense of what the doctor had told her. The hazel trees had been cleared, with the worst destruction at the furthest end, where the most weather-beaten old trees had stood.

Up on the ridge, the *vedetta* stood stark against a chilly sky. The outline of a long-barrelled gun interrupted its silhouette. The gun was pointing up at an angle as if waiting for its next victim. What kind of stupendous effort had it taken to hoist the thing up to the top? They must have built some kind of platform to take its weight, too.

Tearing her eyes away and walking slowly for Renzo's sake, she headed to the far end of the hazel grove. Twice on the way, the dog stopped, turned and growled but she couldn't see anyone following. She had made it this far unseen. Santo and his family must be at church as no sounds came from the farm that suggested human occupation. No sign of Blackshirts either. Nothing but the twittering of wild birds.

Where the largest, knottiest tree had stood, she stopped and briefly closed her eyes.

The pit where she had buried her letters from Cedric had formed when this old tree had been torn up in a ferociously high wind. It had happened the same year her grandfather had died and the depression left by its roots was there still, but now filled with dirty rainwater.

Throwing off her coat and her cardigan, Carmela knelt beside the hole and plunged her hands in.

It wasn't her books and love letters she was searching for. Four-and-a-half years ago, she and Nonna had buried something far more precious here. Her breath caught as she dug and dug. She found the letters, reduced to pulp, and the sodden remains of her English pocket novels. She then searched a different place in the pit. Then another, until eventually she had to accept there was nothing else there. The object she wanted had vanished.

She stood up, her breathing ragged, and looked down into the water her hands had stirred into a brown soup. Her dress was filthy, ruined. When a voice came from a few paces away, she almost vomited from shock.

'You fancied a swim, cousin Meluccia, or were you looking for something?'

Tino Cortazzi stood five paces away, and from the smile on his face, she knew he had been here before her. He knew her secret. She felt the ground shift under her feet.

Tino had changed since she'd last seen him. His hair had lost its oiled discipline and though he was still dressed in his paramilitary style, his shirt was unlaundered and had buttons missing. The wound Sebastiano had inflicted shone in the hollow of his cheek, plum-coloured and puckered.

Shaking muddy water off her hands, she said, 'I thought you'd be in church.'

'Santo and Brigitta are there, representing me.'

Spoken like the King of Italy, she thought. 'What are you doing to this grove?' she demanded.

Tino glanced around at the devastation. 'Preparing it for planting tobacco. That'll be a cash crop if the *americani* get a foothold here.' He spat in disgust at the thought, then shrugged and moved his eyes from her soaked sleeves to the pit behind her. 'I already found what you are looking for. Want to tell me about it, Meluccia?'

'No. I want you to go to hell.' She made to leave but he blocked her way.

'I may go to hell, but so will you.' Tino pointed at the pit. 'Zia Rosaria confessed.'

'My grandmother? When?' In her distress, Carmela inadvertently jerked Renzo's leash and he barked.

'Not long ago. Poor thing is getting frail. You shouldn't have left her, cousin.'

She bit down on her tongue. Had he forgotten why she'd left? But of course he hadn't. He was playing games with her. A sadist, her father had called him. The word expanded in meaning as Tino looked down at Renzo and lifted his lip, mocking the dog's growl. He bent and murmured, 'You're nothing but a cowering mutt. A one-bite dog. If you had any courage, you wouldn't have ended up locked in my wash house.' He straightened up. 'He bit me, but it was a like a girl slapping your face. I made him sorry, didn't I?' When she didn't answer, he left a short silence then indicated the flooded pit. 'Tell me the story. I want to hear it. Burning the rest of these trees can wait.'

'Where is the box, what have you done with it?'

'You mean your grandfather Mario's mandolin case? Imagine my astonishment when I was digging out roots and unearthed it.' He imitated the anxious excuse Carmela had thrown out at dinner when he'd put her on the spot. '"We burned it, it got weevils in it." Confess, you lied, cousin.'

'*Figlio di troia*, you'll get no apologies from me.' She reached for her coat and pulled out the hand axe.

Tino threw back his head and laughed. 'Death by pruning? You're too feeble! And Nina's daughter dares call me the son of a whore?' Savagely, he mocked her again: '"I gave myself in England, but I'm still untouchable!" Beg my pardon, now. Beg on your knees, Meluccia, and I'll tell you where the mandolin case is. Then we can discuss the contents.'

'You don't have to tell this man a damn thing, Carmela.' Sebastiano stepped across the dry ditch. He was hobbling badly, swinging his arms to compensate.

Tino was thrown off guard by the appearance of a wild-looking man and it was clear he didn't immediately recognise Sebastiano, who hadn't shaved in several days, his dark stubble thickening into a decided beard.

'Stop gawping and get behind me, Carmela.' Remnants of fever shone in his eyes but Sebastiano clearly knew who she was now. Thank God. There was no wavering of the hand that held the black-bodied pistol Carmela recognised as the one Hans-Kristof Weber had pointed at them in the Palazzo kitchen.

Sebastiano ordered Tino to put his hands up.

Slowly, Tino obeyed. 'I know you. You're the Englishman from the *vedetta*. Meluccia's lover. Well, well.'

'Never her lover, to my regret.' Without looking at her, Sebastiano finally let his anger out on Carmela. 'What the hell got into you? I heard the doctor telling you under no circumstances to venture out of the room.'

'You heard? You didn't say anything.'

'I didn't want to. Sometimes I prefer to listen. What about the mandolin case this swine's going on about?'

Carmela shook her head. 'It's not important.'

'It sounded important.' Sebastiano took in the mud on her arms, her skirt. Drying on her skin.

'I will tell you,' Tino offered. 'If you lower the gun.'

Sebastiano declined.

'Then let me tell you, man to man, something you should know about my cousin Carmela.'

'Tino, don't.' Carmela's knuckles whitened. She still clasped the hand axe in her right hand. 'Please. It's not your story, it's not Sebastiano's. It's nobody's but mine.' Hers and Cedric's. She hadn't made her peace with Cedric yet.

The brief nod Tino made in reply gave her a moment's relief. Until he turned to Sebastiano and, with his mouth stretched in a smile, said, 'She came to la Casale with a bastard child in her belly. She gave birth in secret, then buried the baby without baptism, without holy rites. They thought to cover up their crime, and buried the little mite in an old mandolin case. Not even a coffin. True, Meluccia?'

He knew it all. Heaven knew what tactics Tino had used to drag the story out of poor Nonna. And yet he knew nothing.

'Tell us who the father was, Meluccia.'

No. Tino Cortazzi would not break a window into her soul. She faced Sebastiano, discovering that she could not bear that he should doubt her, even for a moment. 'My baby Carlotta was born too early. Stillborn.' The word was so hard to say. 'She came at a little under seven months, and never took a breath. I nearly died giving birth. Tino is right in one thing. We'd hidden my pregnancy because Nonna couldn't bear the shame. So rather than call in the doctor, I laboured in the bedroom of la Casale. Something was wrong... but I was so scared and in so much pain, I wouldn't let Nonna leave me to fetch help. It was my fault she died. When Carlotta was wrapped in a cloth, we agreed not to call for the priest. Padre Pasquale has so little compassion. As soon as I was able to get up from my bed, we buried her here and you' – she rounded on Tino, spitting in her anguish and rage – 'you have disturbed her grave. Now tell me where she is or I will bury you.'

'I could tell you… What's it worth, Meluccia?'

Something broke inside her. Carmela hurled the hand axe at Tino but she misjudged her aim and it clumped harmlessly in the grass beside him. He laughed, picked it up and tossed it back to her. 'The mandolin case is in the *vedetta*. Come, I'll show you.' He glanced at Sebastiano, who nodded and waved him on with the gun.

Carmela sought Sebastiano's eye, but his gaze was fixed on Tino's back. She knew how disgraceful her behaviour must sound, when delivered so bluntly. In the years since she and Nonna had placed Carlotta's body in the ground, she had been haunted by the decision. It was dishonourable, craven and an insult to her baby and to Cedric. No excuses. But once done, impossible to put right.

They hadn't made it out of the hazel grove when disaster struck. Sebastiano was finding the un-scythed grass strewn with cut branches hard going and he fell. The pistol flew out of his hand, landing just out of his reach. Tino spun around at his shout of pain and ran to seize the gun but Carmela got there first. She picked it up, lurching back a few paces, and aimed it at Tino.

'I will pull the trigger. I will, Tino.'

'You haven't the guts.' He came towards her, daring her.

Did she? Sebastiano was getting to his feet, and she knew without looking that he'd be reaching into his pocket for his knife. If Tino took the gun from her, he'd turn it on Sebastiano. Closing her eyes, she pulled the trigger.

The gun made a faint snapping sound. Tino was laughing at her.

'The safety hammer flipped up when he dropped it,' he crowed. 'Throw it on the ground, there's a good girl.'

A movement crossed the corner of Carmela's eye and before she could react, Tino was on his back on the ground and Renzo's jaws were against his throat. From somewhere, her boy had found the will to pounce. Never had she seen her dog behave like this, snarling with an almost diabolic intensity, his teeth snapping a hair's breadth from Tino's jugular.

'Call him off, call him off,' Tino screamed. When she had given the gun back to Sebastiano and he had cocked it, she cautiously approached Renzo and took hold of his leash. As she pulled him away, his snarling subsided. He was shaking, his strength spent.

They left him tied up in the grove while Tino, once again at gunpoint, led the way to the *vedetta*.

Inside the tower was almost pitch black as the open roof had been filled with a sturdy platform to support the gun. 'Where is this thing we're looking for?' Sebastiano demanded, flicking on a torch he'd taken from his pocket.

Tino pointed up the stairs.

'Go on then, we'll wait.'

'It's too dark.'

'Too bad. Get climbing.'

Carmela heard rather than watched Tino go up the steps, asking herself why she'd been so ready to be brought here. Not only was there a risk in coming deeper into Blackshirt territory, but if Tino had been telling the truth, she was moments from being presented with the mortal remains of her baby. Her skin tightened and her heart lost its rhythm. *Her baby*. Her secret, wrenched open and exposed. Half opening her eyes, she saw that Tino was reaching into the same niche where she had concealed her letters and Sebastiano's kitbag. She heard scuffling, some agitated swearing and it was suddenly too much.

'I can't do this.'

Sebastiano stepped behind her, stopping her from making a break for the daylight. 'He's going to torment you about this as long as he breathes,' he said tersely. 'My advice, get it over with.'

'I don't know—'

'Why you're doing it? To put the past to rest. To find peace.' He spoke directly against the back of her head and his words seemed to vibrate inside her skull. She nodded.

'For Cedric. My – *our* baby must find her proper resting place. I owe it to them both. I won't break down.'

'No, because you're tough and you won't let your cousin see what it means to you.' Sebastiano called up scornfully, 'Get a move on, cousin Tino, and bring Carmela her property.'

Within a minute, a black shellac case was in her arms. Holding it to her chest, Carmela stumbled from the *vedetta*. Her grandfather's mandolin case smelled of the same dirty water that caked her arms. She was aware of the men behind her, Tino probably looking for his chance to jump should Sebastiano stumble again. She prayed for him to be sure-footed. Overhead, thunder rumbled, suggesting a storm rolling in from the mountains.

The rumbling intensified as she walked through the tomato terraces. And then she realised: it wasn't thunder.

She looked up as Tino pelted down the slope, passing her without looking her way, blank fear on his face.

'Planes!' Sebastiano shouted as he came towards her. 'Bombers. Get down, Carmela.'

No. She wasn't going to lay her face on the earth. She gripped the case tighter and ran, her thoughts racing ahead to the grove where Renzo was tied. She wouldn't lose her boy again.

He was straining against his leash, barking frantically. Laying the case on the grass, Carmela untied him and hunkered down, pulling him against her.

The air above and the ground beneath became a vibrating ocean of noise that swelled to a thunderous roar, pierced by hellish screams that she realised were falling bombs. She held Renzo for dear life as he struggled to escape her grip. As the first detonations erupted, someone dropped down beside her.

Another pair of arms wrapped around the dog. '*Gesù-Maria*, I didn't predict this,' Sebastiano muttered.

When it was finally over and the planes a distant drone, the air was acrid. Dust particles caught in their throats.

'How did they come so fast?' What she said next was unfair but her nerves were grated to shreds. 'Your SOE sent them. You brought them.'

'I did not.' Sebastiano got to his feet, staggered, but kept his balance. They could hear the shouts of people running down from the village. 'I did not bring them. Those weren't British bombers. Nor American. Carmela? Listen to me! They were German.'

The last time Carmela had left Santa Maria, she'd had an hour to get out. This time was even faster. Sebastiano stayed with Renzo as Carmela returned for the donkey cart. Former neighbours ran past her to gauge the bomb damage. Some half recognised her but were clearly confused in the shock of the moment. Perhaps one or two would sit down later and ask themselves, 'Did I really see Carmela del Bosco, streaked with mud, stumping up the road carrying a mandolin case?'

She found Emilio Baccolini at home, packing a medical bag in case there were casualties. She was able to put his mind at rest. 'Nobody's hurt unless my cousin Tino fell down a well or something in his haste to escape.'

The doctor looked at her reproachfully. 'You promised to stay here. And I believe you lured my patient with you.'

She admitted that she had, as Sebastiano had pursued her when he woke to find her gone. 'I'm sorry. I didn't mean…' She fell silent. That excuse was well and truly stale. 'He's back to himself. Your sulpha miracle worked.'

'I would personally have allowed a few days before making that decision.'

'When you get a chance will you tell my nonna that I love her and that I'll see her soon? I can't stay here.'

Her old friend knew better than to try and detain her. 'What's that you're clutching?' Emilio frowned at the grubby mandolin case. Carmela told him, in the simplest terms.

For once, the doctor made no effort to temper his voice. 'A baby – you… you were pregnant?' He thumped the air. 'I knew it! I *knew* when you came here you were being reclusive for a reason. More reason than a bad case of nerves, anyway. Why didn't you tell me, Carmela? Didn't you trust me? We were such good pals.'

'One word. Nonna.' Tears tumbled. 'You don't know how deeply I regret hiding away. If I'd asked for your help, my baby Carlotta would have lived.'

'*Might* have lived. Or might not. You cannot know and neither can I. Every mother who loses a child at some point blames herself. And so, this is her little body? What will you do with it?'

Carmela had no idea. Tears splashed onto the black lid.

Emilio held out his hands. 'Leave her with me until you come home.'

'Your mother—'

'Need not know. But Mamma is kinder than she sometimes lets on. I will take this to the church. No, really,' he said as she tried to prevent him taking the case from her. 'I won't tell the Padre. I'll place it in the crypt, to which I have a key, and I'll do it early in the morning when nobody is about. You can decide later what to do with it. Oh, Carmela. What a world.' He used his own handkerchief to wipe away her tears. 'Where now, *amica mia*? Where do your restless footsteps take you?'

'Naples,' she said. 'Sebastiano has to go back and I want—'

'To be alongside him. You have met your future.'

She denied it hotly. 'But he needs me a while longer, and I want to be there when my father comes home.'

A short time later, as the cart rolled past la Casale, Nearco tossed his head at the pall of smoke and dust that hung over the road. She and Sebastiano craned through the trees, towards the ridge. Where the watchtower had stood for almost a millennium was now a swathe of burning firethorn, a heap of blackened stone at its centre.

While he waited for her to bring the cart, Sebastiano had spoken with a man who had a cousin in the Blackshirts and therefore a claim to know the sequence of events that had led to the attack. Sebastiano passed on what he'd learned. 'The Blackshirts brought down a plane a couple of days ago, from the *vedetta*.'

So Dr Baccolini had told her. 'It crashed in a valley some way off,' she said. 'I would have told you, when you were stronger.'

'It wasn't an Allied plane they shot down, Carmela, it was a Junkers 52. Those Blackshirts were trained to shoot aircraft but not to use their brains. They downed a friendly German transport plane with fifty men inside.'

That explained why they'd piled into trucks and left so suddenly. Why the Germans had taken their revenge in flattening the *vedetta*, doing the Allies' job for them. It also explained why Santo was nowhere to be seen, and why Tino looked so haggard.

'He may be up for a court martial,' Sebastiano agreed. 'Or summary execution. There's probably a moral to be drawn that begins and ends with Renzo, but I'm not sure I have the mental capacity to say what it is.'

Chapter Twenty-Eight

Monday, 27 September

They returned to Palazzo del Bosco. They could have gone to the flat in Sanità where Carmela should have been driven by Danielo's stepfather, but Sebastiano was reluctant. When she pressed him, he explained it was pretty comfortless. She didn't believe that. Something in his expression told her his reason for staying away went far deeper than personal convenience.

'Isn't it risky to be seen near Viale Bellavista?' She meant, where Hans-Kristof Weber had terrorised her and died.

'Everywhere has risk, Carmela.'

What settled the question was an outbreak of firing coming from the Toledo, Naples' central thoroughfare. When they stopped at a viewpoint and gazed down on the city, they spotted military vehicles moving slowly towards Piazza Plebiscito. Flares burst between buildings as though incendiaries were being hurled. The pitiless game of Naples versus the Germans seemed to be reaching a climax and it would be just as dangerous for them to drive into it as to go to the Palazzo.

They reached Viale Bellavista as the sun sank into the sea, taking the day with it. They would eat well tonight, Carmela thought, if their fancy turned to the hazelnuts Tomaso had picked on the day they'd last been here. Nearco could have the run of the garden, but Sebastiano and Renzo needed something more substantial. At least they had fresh water, as she'd filled the cans at the rock-face spring as they passed.

The gate at the end of the garden was still hanging off its hinges. Sebastiano tied it up while she went inside and stood, absorbing the disturbing atmosphere. When Sebastiano joined her, she pushed the kitchen table against the door to hide the rusty smears of Weber's blood. She checked the front entrance was bolted. Nothing would stop a determined assault, but she trusted the Germans were now too preoccupied fighting curfew-breaking rebels to bother coming here.

Carmela saw Sebastiano lift a cloth off a bowl and put his nose close to the contents.

'Edible, see what you think,' he said. It was Tomaso's bread dough, left behind in their hurry to be gone. Carmela pressed it into thin cakes on an iron griddle and cooked it over a gas flame. It was surprisingly delicious drizzled with *olio santo*. Renzo had his with the last drops from a can of olive oil. She found a bottle of red wine by the cellar steps, and they took it up to the dining room. There, they sat at the table with a candle stub sending starry flickers across the room and ate Tomaso's hazelnuts.

'Welcome home, Carmela,' Sebastiano said.

'It won't feel like home until Papà and Tomaso are back.'

'And the furniture. I want to see this place in all its glory.' Sebastiano raised his wine glass. '*Alla nostra.*'

'Yes. To us.'

'To a period of peace and rest.'

They clinked glasses. They'd both managed to get a wash, a rare luxury, using rainwater Carmela had strained through several layers of muslin and then boiled. In an act of defiance against the constant prick of fear, she had put on one of her London outfits, a green silk dress with a matching bolero jacket, and a dab of perfume she'd found in her mother's room. Probably a gift from her father to her mother, and hardly touched. It was lucky the Waffen SS hadn't spotted it – one of them would have pocketed it for his girlfriend. Having washed her hair, she'd put it up in a plaited bun. Checking her reflection before she came down, a vestige of 'chic Miss del Bosco' had stared quizzically back at her. She'd almost pulled off the dress, fearful that Sebastiano might think she was bidding for his attention. After all, he'd only ever seen her in frumpy work clothes. But in the end, she'd risked it because it felt so good to be groomed and elegant, if only for an hour or two. If he commented, she'd say she was marking the fact that his mission was accomplished.

It had thrown her to discover that Sebastiano had spruced himself up too, wearing a shirt and trousers that must have been ones Danielo, or Gio, had acquired for him. He'd trimmed his beard to stubble using scissors, and she was thinking how attractive he was when he caught her.

'I – I was just telling myself, you look less of a vagrant than when we arrived,' she blurted out.

'Whereas you look like a duchess.' He tugged his forelock. 'Honoured to be dining with you, *mia graziosa signora.*'

He was lightly mocking her, she realised. Certainly not overpowered by her beauty, so she needn't have worried. And now she had to say something. 'This will be our first and last dinner together, as just the two of us.'

'Why so?'

'Because I've come back to Naples so I'm here when my father returns. He deserves to know I'm safe. You're tied to SOE.' He would keep gathering intelligence to aid the Allies' seizure of Naples. It could mean more journeys to Tarzia's partisans. He'd confided to Carmela that he also hoped to find out where Mio's body or ashes had been buried, so that he could eventually inform her family. It troubled him to think she might have been thrown into the same pit as Nico, who had betrayed her. But that in turn troubled her, because it would take him to the margins of safety. He would have to talk to policemen. Undertakers. Informants, even. It made his toast to 'peace and rest' feel ironic.

Her eyes must have signalled her feelings because Sebastiano raised an eyebrow.

'I know something's bothering you.'

'Show me your hands,' she said in her nurse-voice, concern disguising emotion.

He obediently held them out. Under a yellow sheen of sulpha that Dr Baccolini had given her, they were still raw in places but scabbing over. A precursor to healing.

'Promise me you won't do anything to open those sores again.'

'I want them to heal too,' he said, his voice changing. 'I want the use of my hands, Carmela.' A gleam in his eyes made her look down abruptly and reach for the board and the little hammer she was using to smash the hazelnuts open. She'd been unable to find the nutcracker. Three or four solid whacks broke the intimate atmosphere. Sebastiano sat back in his chair, with a thoughtful half-smile on his lips.

'Do you object to me finding you beautiful?' he asked. 'Say, and I'll sublimate my instincts. It shouldn't be difficult. I went to an all-boys' school, and a male-only university college. It's easy to do. You just hum inside your head or conjugate irregular Latin verbs and if you do both at once, Venus herself could sit on your lap and you wouldn't notice.'

She shook her head, disturbed to learn that he did like what he saw. 'I threw this dress on because… well, it was in my wardrobe looking lonely.' She handed him a few cracked nuts and said, 'It would be lovely to have goat's cheese with this.'

'Carmela?'

She met his eyes.

'Can we get something out of the way? Those things Tino spewed out at la Casale. Your past is none of my business, you don't have to say a thing but if you want to… I can't know the pain of losing a child, but I know what it's like to lose someone.'

Was this the right time to speak of Carlotta, to explain again how her baby had come into being? The patience in Sebastiano's eyes, his easy posture, helped. She didn't plan what to say. Words burst out.

'When I first met Cedric, we were very careful. He wanted to wait until we were married, because he was respectful and old-fashioned. But after he joined the Reserve, something changed. Being with other men, fellow pilots, affected him. I'm not saying he wasn't just as respectful, but he became more…' She paused for the right word. It wasn't 'demanding'. 'He was more direct and it confused me. I'd been told by all my friends, "get the ring on your finger first". We all knew girls who had jumped the gun and had to leave college suddenly. Something changed again when he finished his training and started flying. We saw a lot of each other as he was still living at home. He'd take the train to Southampton, pick up a Spitfire, fly it back to Duxford. He'd achieved his dream, but one night he came back very glum. Wouldn't say what it was.'

She'd eventually teased out the truth. Two of his pilot colleagues had suffered fatal crashes within the space of three days. A rumour was gathering pace that the new Spitfires were either unreliable or being sabotaged.

'I heard something of that. They stalled mid-flight,' Sebastiano said. 'He was scared, I guess?'

'More "grit-toothed". The joy went out of flying, and it just became something he had to do. I was the scared one and it changed my outlook. Why hold off, why deny ourselves what we wanted when anything might happen?' She picked up her wine glass and took a deep swallow. 'By the River Cam, behind a screen of willows. Not only once, either. It was wonderful and I'm so glad I did it.'

'And then he died.'

'Yes. I struggled on through a term of teaching, but it was so hard. His parents were devastated, of course. They wanted me to stay and I would have done, except that it was getting difficult being an Italian in England. Mussolini had aligned himself with Germany and, for the first time, I started getting cold looks in shops. A man spat at me when I tried to buy a newspaper, and some boys let Mr Folgate's cows out of the field and painted "Fascist" on the gate. Only, they spelled it F.A.S.H-ist.'

'Mr Folgate was Cedric's father?'

She nodded. 'He was a lovely man and didn't deserve that. It made up my mind up. I gave in my notice and bought a ticket home. I had no idea I was pregnant until I was on the ship. *Dio*, I was sick. Nothing unusual in that but the ship's doctor looked into my face on deck one day and said, "Are you travelling alone?" When I said, "Yes," he looked down at my stomach and said, "Are you sure?" I almost fainted and was so desperately ashamed but when I got used the idea, I was secretly glad.' She met Sebastiano's gaze, doubting that a woman had ever spoken so openly to him before. 'I had something of Cedric's to keep. Except it wasn't to be.' Reaching inside the bodice of her dress, she took out a little muslin bag, opened the drawstring and put a circle of the finest hair on a napkin, then pushed it over to him. 'That's hers. She would have grown up to have chestnut curls and dark eyes. I like to think so, anyway.'

'You should have it put into a ring,' he said. 'And wear it.'

'Perhaps. When Nonna's passed on, not before.'

'Did you hide your pregnancy to spare her feelings?'

She nodded. 'And Papà's.'

'He never knew?'

'Not a thing! Nor did he guess. I came straight here when my ship docked at Naples, and I twice fainted in front of him and once, when peppered mackerel was served, I ran from the table.' She sighed. 'He had Tomaso mix me a Marsala *all'uovo* to repair my nerves.'

She was referring to a popular Italian pick-me-up – Marsala wine with an egg beaten in. Sebastiano agreed, it was an acquired taste.

'I think Tomaso suspected but he's so discreet and knows not to rock the boat. There would have been scenes worthy of a tragic opera if he had. "My daughter, a fallen woman!"'

'I think you misjudge your father, Carmela.'

She got up without a word and began to collect up the glasses and plates.

Sebastiano picked up the candle and followed her down to the kitchen where they washed and dried everything, putting it all away to conceal signs of their occupation. The empty wine bottle went into a cupboard along with the tea towel.

Then he said, 'I think we should go to bed.'

Something in his tone tightened a knot in her stomach. 'Where will you sleep, Sebbe?' Not the wrecked attic room. 'The bed's made up in my father's room.'

'I wasn't thinking of sleeping there.' He fastened dark eyes on her and the air became electric.

She swallowed. Her pulse was jamming her throat.

He went to the larder where she heard the crack of a floorboard being lifted. When he returned, he was carrying the MP 40 he'd made Danielo leave behind. He took Weber's short-nosed pistol from a body holster under his clothes and gave it to her. 'If the Germans come, we can die together in a hail of bullets. I would like us to be together tonight. Meluccia?'

Shivering at the intimate use of that name, the first time on his lips, she reached out her hand. 'This is a hard thing for an unmarried woman to say, but yes, I would like to go to bed.'

'With me?'

She half cringed, half laughed, because his eyes were consuming her. 'Sebbe, stop it.'

'I want you to say it.'

'All right, but you're bad. Very bad. Yes, I want to go to bed with you.'

Morning light squeezing through the shutters found two changed people. If Sebastiano had imagined he was taking a timid, inexperienced girl to bed, he had been mistaken. Carmela had given him a lesson in southern Italian passion. Having admitted her desire, she'd discarded modesty and made love to him with an intensity that left him breathless. Because of his injuries, her knocks and bruises, they had been considerate with each other in a way that concentrated the intimacy. He took her over the edge of pleasure, withdrawing before climax. She stroked him, kissing him as he came with groans of pleasure.

They lay in each other's arms. Carmela felt she was in a gently rocking boat on the river. They slept, and were woken at dawn by the avenue's pigeons.

'The Germans didn't come,' she said drowsily.

'This is the first time I've slept past dawn in months. Years maybe.' He sat up, and reached behind his neck. 'What's this?' He showed her an object decorated with cheap rhinestones, which caught the morning light. It was the twin to the hair slide she'd found in the bed the first night she'd slept in it.

She took it and threw it across the room.

'You say I misjudge my father, but how would you feel if your father brought women into the house and rutted with them on his true wife's bed?'

'I would say…' Sebastiano replied thoughtfully, 'God help the woman if my mother caught them, and God help him too. Vesuvius has nothing on my mamma if she ever sees another female eyeing up her man.'

'She's Italian?'

'Every inch.'

'Will you tell me about yourself, your life? Who you are, really?'

'It may still be too soon for that.'

She asked if he trusted her. 'You must have forgiven my errors by now, or you wouldn't be here with me.'

He agreed, it did look as though he'd forgiven her. Rolling towards her, he took her in his arms. 'I've learned to trust you with my life, Meluccia, but there's one thing I need to mention…'

She braced herself for a harsh home truth.

'When the bombers were closing in on the *vedetta*, you left me and ran to save your dog. What does that say?'

'It says you know how to look after yourself, Sebbe.'

He grunted. 'I grant you, it's always easier to run downhill than up. Or jump off a balcony rather than take the stairs.'

She realised then that she'd said the wrong thing and that poor, lost Mio had slid under the sheets between them.

Sitting up, she punched the pillows into a back support. 'I told you something last night that no other creature has ever been allowed to know. Your turn now.'

He'd folded his arms behind his head, staring moodily up at the ceiling. 'My turn?'

'Did you love Mio?'

His face turned towards her and the answer was simple. 'Yes.'

She brooded on that in the garden as she picked apples. Six veteran trees with a wizened crop could hardly be called an orchard, but Nearco wouldn't object. He deserved a treat, having pulled more than his weight over the last weeks. Actually, he deserved a sack of oats but that was a distant dream.

She'd got up moments after Sebastiano's single-word answer. It shouldn't matter that he had loved a comrade, any more than it should matter to him that she still loved Cedric. Why was she making a fuss? She would fix breakfast, and make peace at the same time. Last night had been wonderful. Her stomach turned over at the memory. To be held and loved, to know that she still had the power to make a man lose his senses was reward enough for a long abstinence. She had lost her senses too and had better not succumb again or it would be unbearable when they parted, which they must. And soon.

After she'd given Nearco his apples, she fetched her coat and checked there was money in the pocket. She picked up a basket and tied a scarf around her hair. There was a baker's on Via Aniello Falcone, and though she had little hope of decent bread, it was worth a try.

To her immense surprise, fewer than a dozen women were queuing. She realised why when gunfire sputtered from somewhere in lower Naples. A woman behind her muttered, 'Those boys are still at it, showing the Germans what-for again!' Two mothers rushed away, scared for their children. Carmela stuck it out and got a disc of rye bread for her pains. It looked more like a cowpat than the crusty loaves of her childhood, but it would fill them up.

As she hurried back towards the Palazzo, a German armoured car parked at the kerb made her check her pace. The vehicle was full of recognisable uniforms. Knowing the worst thing would be to turn and run, she pressed on, keeping her eyes down. In a shapeless dress, an over-washed cardigan and her headscarf, she'd look like any careworn matron on her way home with breakfast. A German soldier shouted something facetious, but they didn't stir from their vehicle. It was parked pointing uphill, towards the stone stairs that led up to Viale Bellavista and the Palazzo. As she began to climb, a man she didn't know passed her on his way down. He muttered, 'Watch out, lady. Blackshirts ahead.'

She moved to the edge of the steps where untrimmed shrubs offered some camouflage and continued stealthily. A few steps from the top, she saw what the stranger had meant.

Two men in Blackshirt uniform stood directly outside the Palazzo. They were staring at the fire-blackened frontage and the burned-out shell of the Waffen SS troop truck that Zeffiro and his friends had set alight, and which had yet to be towed away. The men's thickset bodies and near-identical profiles were unmistakeable. It was Tino and his brother Santo.

She froze. They hadn't seen her but if she turned and went back down, the Germans in the armoured car would wonder what she was doing and their suspicions might be alerted. In fact – was their presence a coincidence? Because if not, she was trapped between two enemies. There was only one escape, and that was to take the mule path that served the Palazzo's caves. In her childhood, this path had been a means of bringing supplies into the Palazzo. It opened off the top of these steps, but years of neglect meant it was lost in a forest of bramble and overgrown shrubs. She might get scratched to pieces. Or break her neck, because it ran along the lip of a steep ravine. One of the soldiers in the parked vehicle shouting up at her forced a decision on her. She parted the branches of an oleander bush at the same moment Santo Cortazzi turned to see who was shouting. Their eyes met.

He called, 'Carmela. Stay there. Don't move.'

Dropping her bread and her basket, she dipped her head to avoid gouging her face on a thick bramble stem and pushed through. Ouch. She heard Tino and Santo thundering down the steps, heard them shouting to the Germans. 'It's her!'

She had the advantage of knowing there was a way through, which they could not see, and her need to reach Sebastiano added a fierce impetus. There was a chance the Palazzo was surrounded, that this was an organised stake-out. Tino's revenge?

She found the path. It was slippery from recent rain and treacherous with roots, but a clear way had been cut through, probably by Tomaso. Reaching the first of the caves with her clothes torn and blood dripping from a badly scratched ear lobe, she found the metal security grille was pulled across. It was locked. She could hear men cursing in German: soldiers battling with brambles. A burst of machine-gun fire confirmed it. The grille at the entrance to the next cave slid easily, suggesting it had been recently greased. The cave itself was empty, and the entrance to the passage behind clearly visible. It would be just as visible to the men coming after her. She plunged into the darkness, praying that when she reached the end, she would be able to open the door into the cellar.

If not, she was a fox caught in a trap.

It was so dark she hit the end of the passage head on. Recovering, she scrabbled for some kind of handle. She couldn't find it, and in her panic, she hammered with both fists. 'Sebbe, help me!'

Germans were in the cave now. She could hear the echo of their feet. 'Sebbe, it's me! Help!'

He wouldn't hear her. It was over. 'Sebbe, please, for the love of God!'

A grating noise answered her prayer, and when the door in front of her moved sideways, she almost collapsed through it, dazzled by the light of a lantern. She was hauled unceremoniously from the passage and left to pick herself up while Sebastiano shut the door and pushed the wine rack back into position. His breath was labouring almost as loudly as hers.

'Come on, no time.' He pushed her, a hand in the small of her back, to the cellar stairs, and once they were through the door, he turned the key in the lock. In the kitchen, he threw his jacket to her and passed her the lantern. 'Don't drop it.' In one swoop, he picked up Renzo and balanced him over a shoulder. She could hear the thud of heavy feet in the depths of the cellar. The front door was also under siege as though a stump of wood was being driven against it. Gunfire rattled. They were shooting at the lock!

Sebastiano led them into the boot room. 'Close it, lock it.' He meant the door.

She fastened the boot room door with fingers that felt thick and useless. Sebastiano had kicked aside a rug to reveal a hatch. As his arms were full, she opened it. Peering down, she saw a wooden ladder disappearing into the darkness.

'I'll go first with the dog and you close the hatch behind us,' Sebastiano muttered. Heavy-booted feet were passing the door. The Germans were inside. After a moment's frozen dismay, Sebastiano mouthed, 'Lantern.'

She'd put it down. Once he was part-way down the ladder, she followed and, one-handed, pulled down the hatch behind her. The click of its catch was a gift from heaven. Her fear diluted a fraction.

'Unhook the ladder and lay it on the ground.' In the lantern light, Sebastiano seemed twice his normal bulk. Renzo's eyes were two mirror-discs.

Carmela did as he asked, and felt a little more secure.

'Keep close.' Sebastiano set off. Her father had told her this hatch led to a drain, but it was nothing of the sort. They were in a passage hewn from the volcanic tufa rock, which opened into a low-roofed cavern. From the chisel marks and the numerical symbols on the walls, she knew she was in an ancient space, long predating the Palazzo. Hunching, she followed Sebastiano and soon discovered exactly what kind of underground world they had entered. Recesses cut into the stone contained skulls. Scores of them. They were in a catacomb crypt.

'Why have I never seen this before?'

Sebastiano stopped and said, 'Because your father thought it would frighten you, I suppose. What child wants to know she's sleeping above hundreds of ancient heads? This catacomb is early Christian, though it was used later, for plague victims.' As he spoke, he took a skull from a recess and held it in the lamplight.

'Don't,' Carmela said with a shudder.

'Its owner is long past caring.' But he put the skull back. 'That's enough rest. Let's go.'

A child's red hair ribbon lay on the floor, an incongruous object in this macabre place. Carmela stepped over it. Who would bring a child this way? That question dissolved as the lantern illuminated another cavern, this one piled high with furniture. As Sebastiano stopped to open an ancient-looking door, she recognised the top of the inlaid ebony table that was missing from the library. There were mirrors too, pictures, side tables. A velvet chaise longue… Her father had got rid of everything so the Germans wouldn't see the Palazzo as a desirable billet. Here was all their furniture, but how had it been brought here?

The riddle was answered when Sebastiano led her from the cavern into a vaulted space of coloured windows and smooth masonry. Musty and marble-cold, a flight of carved angels at roof level struck an instant chord. 'It's the Del Bosco chapel!' In the glory days of the family, Mass had been preached here by a private chaplain. The chapel been closed up a century ago. The furniture would have been brought in through the front entrance. Carmela remembered then, Violetta Vincenzo commenting on her husband's lack of work, saying 'the job at the Palazzo' was his only one in three months. Adriano Vincenzo had not repaid the favour, stranding her and Danielo at San Romualdo.

'This way,' Sebastiano said. 'The main doors are barricaded. We use this one.'

'You've obviously been here before.'

'I learned all the escape routes.' He led them to a plain side door. The key to unlock it was lying by the threshold. They emerged into a walled enclosure, and Sebastiano had her relock the door and push the key underneath. Ready for the next person.

'Once we're on the street, we'll separate,' he said. 'They'll be looking for a pair. I'll take Renzo but he'll have to walk. A man carrying a dog will quickly be a talking point.'

'Where can we go?'

'To the place we should probably have gone yesterday. Head for the two-arched bridge on Via Sanità. There's a church right behind it, with a huge, coloured dome. Take refuge there and I'll find you.'

Before they separated, she alerted Sebastiano to the presence of Tino and Santo Cortazzi, which she hadn't had the breath to mention until now.

'I saw two Blackshirts lurking on the avenue.' Sebastiano made a face. 'So your cousin has teamed up with the Germans to dig us out. Santo is… remind me.'

'Tino's brother.'

'Did they see you?'

'Yes.' Something niggled her. 'How did you come down to the cellar in the nick of time? I was trapped in the passage.'

'I spotted your cousins when I went upstairs to fetch the MP 40. I searched for you in the house and the garden.' His look was reproachful. 'The cellar was the last place I thought to look, thankfully. So – that's the way out.' He pointed to an iron gate within the chapel's perimeter wall. 'You go first. *A dopo.*'

'*A dopo.*' She kissed his rough cheek. 'And thank you.'

'Oh, you know, any time.' As she went, he called after her, 'I did love Mio, but not in the way you imagine.'

*

She reached the domed church by the Sanità Bridge by early evening. A five-hour walk because every time she heard a vehicle or footsteps, she'd darted into a side alley, or somebody's garden. She hoped Sebastiano wasn't far behind, and regretted they'd had to leave the donkey cart at the Palazzo.

She hated the thought of Tino or Santo finding Nearco in the garden. They were capable of letting him go, to spite her. And what new destruction had those soldiers wreaked on the Palazzo?

Don't think about it. They'd got out alive.

She was so hungry she was starting to hallucinate the loaf she'd thrown away. It was on the road in front of her, dancing above balconies, replacing hats on men's heads. She bought food from a street vendor, pieces of fried potato wrapped in a brown paper cone, and forced herself to eat slowly. Though it was hard to do, she left half to give to Sebastiano and Renzo.

A fountain was trickling near the Toledo, whose cobbles were littered with broken glass and scarred with tyre and scorch marks. The gun battles that had peppered the morning had fallen silent. The city sat tense. Waiting. When she finally got to the front of the queue of people lining up to drink and fill water jugs, she put her mouth under the flow, swallowing thirstily until a woman behind her shoved her aside. As she turned away, an urchin dug his hand into her coat pocket and stole the package of fried potato. He'd disappeared up a side-street before she'd finished screaming her fury at him.

She had to ask the way to Sanità, and the woman who gave her directions told her, without any shred of humour, to watch her pockets. 'Don't stop, don't make eye contact. Try not to look like a visitor.' It reminded her of Sebastiano's comment, how the Sanità locals hated authority. The place sounded lawless.

As she approached the bridge that Sebastiano had named as their meeting place, she felt she must resemble a nervous bird, her head twitching side to side, obsessively looking behind her. Feral boys were roaming. Waiting for nightfall, to break curfew and lure the Germans out into the labyrinthine alleys. Her footsteps echoed as she passed beneath one of the bridge's two massive arches. She knew she was in the right place when she saw a church whose dome shone like patterned eggshell in the fading light. And there was Sebastiano, seated on the shallow steps, Renzo at his feet. She waved in relief. As she went to flop down next to him, her foot struck something metallic.

'That's my begging bowl. Help a poor indigent, Signora.'

She hunkered close to him and stroked his face. 'There's nothing in it.'

'No. Not even the priest threw a coin.'

She told him about the fried potatoes, how they'd been filched. 'We must be down to our last life.'

'I'm on credit, and have been for a long time.'

'Can we go to the safe house?' She was longing take off her boots and lie down.

'Not for a few hours, not till I'm sure there's no chance of us being seen going in. Huddle up.'

She shared her coat with him and they leaned against each other as darkness fell. As the hours dragged by, they talked sparsely until they were too cold and hungry for chatter. Renzo whimpered for food, which was hard to bear. Carmela dozed, then jerked awake with angry thoughts on her mind. 'Tino brought the Germans to our door because Renzo bested him at la Casale. It's his revenge.'

'Very probably,' Sebastiano agreed in the gravelly voice of fatigue. 'Or he might be trying to buy favour. Delivering up an English spy and an enemy sympathiser to offset his lethal blunder in shooting down a German plane.'

'I don't suppose he shot it down himself.'

'It was on his patch. It was his plan.'

'It puts Marcella Vincenzo's betrayal into perspective,' she said. There was little doubt that Danielo's sister had repeated what Carmela had told her in confidence. 'But I don't believe she deliberately sent her boyfriend to smash down the doors, though it was catastrophic for us.'

'Even more catastrophic for the boyfriend. I wonder if she waits in hope for her Hans-Kristof.'

'Poor girl. She wanted only to please the man she loved.'

After what felt like a reluctant pause, Sebastiano agreed. 'That is mildly in her favour. It's a good trait in a— Shh!'

Feet were approaching along Via Sanità at a brisk pace. 'Could be curfew wardens,' Sebastiano whispered. 'Or police. Pretend to be asleep.'

Carmela pulled Renzo closer then crumpled as if in a cold, stiff slumber. Sebastiano sat back against the church wall, his head lolling. Through partly open eyes, Carmela saw two men walking side by side. They wore belted coats, hats pulled low and they carried torches. A shaft of light hit Carmela and Sebastiano, but the footsteps didn't falter. Clearly, she and her companion had passed inspection as a destitute couple and their dog, waiting for the church doors to open. The two figures disappeared under the bridge.

'Surveillance, German,' Sebastiano said. 'Armed and nervous, and looking out for gangs of *scugnizzi*.'

'Or scouting out your safe place?'

'No. I checked. This is the second time they've been past and last time they didn't so much as glance towards the building we're going into.' When the men's footsteps had faded away entirely, he got to his feet. 'Ooh.' He arched his back. 'It feels to me like four in the morning. This is our moment.'

They weren't completely alone, as they discovered as they walked under the bridge and caught the low hum of voices from the parapet. Going slowly so Sebastiano's dragging foot wouldn't give away their presence, they distinctly heard a whispered exchange taking place above their heads. The voices were not Neapolitan. Carmela and Sebastiano looked at each other, a flash of a glance in the dark.

As they emerged from the bridge, he whispered, 'Other side of the road, the flat above the shoe mender's. Our home for however long, and there's something I need to tell you about it, but let's get in first.'

He checked the street before they crossed, left to right. A cat, all bones, slunk past them carrying a kitten in her mouth. Renzo strained to follow it, but Carmela quelled him. Tottering from exhaustion and cold, she waited as Sebastiano crouched in front of a scruffy door and lifted a broken chunk from the stone sill.

She heard him swear under his breath. '*Porco Dio*, it's not here!'

The key? Surely not! She tapped his arm as her ears picked up a new footfall. Someone was approaching from under the bridge. Dressed all in black, some kind of scarf wound around his head and throat. He stopped right behind them and said in a low voice, '*Mi scusi*, I need to get in.'

'Danielo?'

'Meluccia?' Danielo peered into her face. 'What are you doing here?'

She shushed him, pointing towards the bridge. 'Germans up there. Sh! We're finding sanctuary. What are you doing back here? It's not safe.'

'It's not exactly safe in the hills either,' Danielo muttered. 'After I found you'd gone, I sort of signed up with Tarzia but even then I knew my life was here, with my boys and my family.'

'You didn't run away, then?'

'No!' The partisan leader had let him go, sensing Danielo would be more use on home turf.

Sebastiano, who had given up searching for the key, growled, 'So why aren't you at home in Quartieri Spagnoli?'

'Because I'm staying here.'

'Really? At what point did you presume to let yourself into Mio's flat, Danielo?'

'Mio's flat?' Carmela glanced up into the shadows to a stone balcony. 'This is where she… where you escaped from?' Where Nico had been eliminated? Now she understood why Sebastiano had been cagey about coming here. He'd waited until they were on the doorstep to tell her why. 'I don't want to go inside,' she said.

'I don't want to either but it's here or the church steps.' Sebastiano had not finished with Danielo. 'If you've been bunkering down here, fair enough, but give me the key and go home. Go see your family. This isn't your place.'

'It is.' Danielo removed a segment of render from the front of the house, and took keys from the gap behind. He let them all in and once the door was shut behind them, turned on a torch. Continuing to whisper, he said, 'Mamma and the others had to leave Vico del Vigneto, because after Gio died, the police wouldn't leave the neighbourhood alone. Mamma was frightened, so I sent her here.'

'Your family is upstairs? You put them in the last safe house?' Sebastiano's rigid shoulders suggested he was on the brink of exploding.

'Understand, Sebbe' – Danielo laid his hand on Sebastiano's arm – 'they're my people and Mamma would have looked after Carmela if she'd been brought here.'

'If your stepfather hadn't abandoned us,' Carmela reminded him. She sympathised with Sebastiano. Working undercover in Naples, where there were few secrets and family ties trumped everything, must have been a trial.

Danielo started up the stairs. 'I'll go up and tell Mamma I'm alive, then see if I can find out what Germans are doing on the bridge. Come on, bring the dog. Mamma will make you coffee and I stole a tin of crackers from a German sidecar that was parked outside a knocking shop.' He tapped his jacket front, and something gave a metallic sound.

The prospect of food was a powerful incentive. Carrying Renzo between them, Carmela and Sebastiano followed Danielo up the stairs. Before they had reached the second floor, a door burst open and a short figure flung himself at Danielo.

''Nielo, 'Nielo, I knew you were coming! I dreamed you.'

'Quiet, let me breathe.' Danielo lifted his little brother Zeffiro up into the air, his torch sweeping a ceiling festooned with cobwebs. 'What's been going on? Done anything wicked?'

'Plenty, and I want to tell you.'

Within moments, a small crowd had gathered in the apartment doorway. Adriano Vincenzo, in long underpants and a shirt, scowled resentfully. Next to him stood Loreto in pyjama bottoms and a singlet. Ettore was shivering in only a vest that must have been his father's. Danielo's baby sisters, quite naked, crawled through the legs, demanding attention. No sign of Marcella. Violetta pushed through.

'*Figlio mio!* My Danielo!' She pulled her son into her arms. Sebastiano went ahead into the flat. Carmela went after him with Renzo, who flumped down on a pile of discarded clothes next to the fireplace where embers burned. The room contained a double bed, a collection of odd chairs and smelled of fish and wood ash. The subdued glow from the fireplace was the only light. It was a long room, running front to back, but split into two by the same sheet that had provided privacy in the Vincenzos's previous accommodation.

So this was where Mio had suffered her agonising end. Carmela gazed reluctantly around, thinking that if anything would exorcise a violent suicide, it would be the Vincenzo family's noise and clutter. Her eyes went to the doors that opened onto the balcony. They were boarded over and seemed to be lashed shut with string.

That's when she saw Marcella. The girl was seated in the corner, in front of the balcony doors. Staring at her hands in a posture that exuded defeat.

Loreto came in and took a seat close to his sister; the angle of his chair suggested he was guarding Marcella. If she got up, he was there to push her back again.

Sebastiano, meanwhile, was rebuking Adriano Vincenzo for abandoning Carmela in the hills. 'It was cowardly. Unforgiveable.'

'I'd done my part, everything I was paid for,' the man answered sullenly but when his wife gasped, 'Adriano, no! How could you?' he seemed to shrink and couldn't look in Carmela's direction.

Danielo came in, shutting the door. Violetta carried her little naked daughters through the curtain, presumably to return them to bed. Ettore left with them. Zeffiro, who had glued himself to Danielo, left the apartment at a word from his big brother.

Carmela willed Danielo to speak to Marcella. To offer some kindness or comfort. When he did not so much as glance into the window corner, Carmela squeezed past Loreto's chair, determined that somebody should at least greet the poor girl. There was an open school-book on a desk next to Loreto's chair, a reference manual containing tables of the chemical elements. Loreto was a dedicated scholar, no doubt about it. Too clever perhaps to understand his sister's pain but Danielo had less excuse. She was about to appeal to her half-brother's conscience when she realised that Marcella was speaking. Repeating something to herself in whispers.

'I trusted him. I trusted him.'

'Are you speaking of Hansi?' Carmela touched Marcella's elbow. 'Hans-Kristof?'

Marcella shrank into herself. 'I trusted him. He promised.'

Loreto told his sister to shut up.

'What did he promise, Marcella?' Carmela asked.

The girl's eyes swam. 'That we would be married.'

'German officers don't marry stupid Italian girls,' Loreto jeered.

'He promised.'

Carmela gestured at Loreto to hold his peace. 'Marcella, you passed on what I confided, about ringing the bell to gain entry to the Palazzo. You told a German! It nearly cost four people their lives, mine included.'

'No!' Marcella's gaze jumped up. Tears massed in her eyes. 'You told me to tell nobody but Danielo. I did not tell Hansi about the Palazzo.'

'What about Gio?' Danielo abandoned cold disdain and stepped forward, his face savage. 'You told that German pig about Gio being in the resistance.'

'I did not. The only thing I told Hansi was about a boy in Monte-calvario who...' Marcella forced the next words out. 'Who pimps the girls in his house. He offers them to German soldiers though he knows they have, you know…' She shot her brother an anguished look and lowered her voice to a scratch. 'The *disease*.'

'You mean, a sexual disease? That's all the information you passed on?' Carmela repeated it so Marcella's parents and Sebastiano could also hear.

'You told your German about a brothel?' Adriano Vincenzo sounded bemused. 'Why?'

Marcella looked equally bewildered. 'I don't know. I think I wanted Hansi to be pleased.'

'Please a German when you've seen what they do?' Danielo spat. 'You are wrong in the head, *sorella mia*.'

'Because you loved him,' Carmela suggested. 'You feared you might lose him, so you gave him a snippet of information about a place of ill repute.'

Marcella nodded, and tears bounced down her cheeks. 'I still love him. He said he would have the house closed down, and he did. I know it was wrong. The girls lost their home because of me.'

'If not you, then who told Weber – Hansi – about the Palazzo?' Carmela wanted to believe what she was hearing but it strained credibility. It had been Marcella's boyfriend who had kicked down the Palazzo's door, after all. 'Tell me who because I need to know.'

Marcella whispered something. Carmela leaned close. 'Say that name again.'

Another whisper and Carmela stood up, a sour taste in her mouth. So, there was the answer. Simple and so humiliating.

'There's no point mooning over your German, Marcella,' Loreto crowed. 'He's dead, dead as a door nail, because Danielo shot him.'

Marcella got to her feet with a cry. 'No! Loreto, you're lying.'

With a furious roar, Danielo strode across the room and yanked Loreto off his chair, then hurled him to the ground. 'You'd tell the world I killed a German? Go on, then. Shout it out in the street, then run before I cut your stupid tongue out.'

'That's enough, leave the boy alone.' Adriano Vincenzo got between Danielo and the squirming Loreto. He dragged his stepson off by the collar. 'This is all your fault, Danielo. Yours and Marcella's. Now she's crying again.' Vincenzo told his daughter sharply to stop her whimpering. 'It's over. Understand that. Over. Traitors have no right to tears, *figlia mia*.'

Unable to bear the sound of Marcella's sobs, Carmela shouted, 'She's not a traitor. I did it. All right? It was my fault.' She sought Sebastiano's eyes, then Danielo's. 'I told Marcella how to get into the Palazzo in an emergency and you can all believe her when she says she kept the secret. I told her in front of her baby sisters, and one of them prattled it to Hans-Kristof Weber.' *Pina not like dogs. Pina like Hansi.* 'The rest was inevitable but I set it in motion.' Marcella's boyfriend had proved he was a German officer before he was a lover. And he'd acted with a speed nobody could have expected. 'It was my fault,' Carmela repeated and addressed Adriano. 'Stop tormenting your daughter. Danielo, stop judging your sister. Nobody in this room has the right.' Her eye landed on Violetta, who had returned from putting the infants to bed, drawn by the noise. When Violetta declared in a hard voice that Marcella had brought shame on the family, fresh fury welled up in Carmela. A pair of cheap hair slides left in her mother's room was proof of sickening hypocrisy. Carmela aimed her next words with feeling. 'It's time to stop casting stones, Signora Vincenzo, unless we want the same stones hurled back in our faces.'

Zeffiro ran in just then. He grabbed Danielo's sleeve and his voice came out in a high-pitched jabber. 'I went into the church, and got out onto the edge of the dome. There are Germans on our bridge, for sure. I saw and heard them and my friends did too.'

'What friends?' his mother demanded. 'Who's outside at this hour?'

'My *scugnizzi* friends,' Zeffiro replied in a tone that suggested *who else?*

'Did you actually hear them, or see what the Germans were doing?' Sebastiano asked. He'd untied the balcony doors and the shutters behind to let in the chill night breeze. Something told Carmela that his murdered comrade Mio was in the room. It felt to her that the mutilated ghost of Gio Troisi stood with them too.

'They're fixing little packets to the parapet and to the legs of the bridge,' Zeffiro said. 'The packets are joined up with string like decorations at Christmas.'

Sebastiano absorbed this detail, then said, 'Fuse wire. They're laying out dynamite.'

'Why would they do that?' Violetta's demand ended a horrified pause. To Sebastiano, however, it made perfect sense.

'Via Santa Teresa runs over the top of the bridge and it's one of the main routes into Naples from the north. Bringing down the bridge will stop the Allied advance into the city. The Germans can then concentrate their troops and fire on the Allies when they get bottlenecked.'

'Destroying the bridge will crush the homes underneath,' Violetta moaned.

'That's why they're creeping and whispering,' Sebastiano said bleakly. 'Hoping to cause mass carnage, which will teach the rebellious citizens a lesson.'

'We must get out.' Violetta looked wildly around her. 'We must wake up the street.'

'No.' Sebastiano and Danielo spoke in unison.

'Do that, Mamma, everyone will run out of their houses screaming and the Germans on the bridge will pick them off like rabbits,'
Danielo said.

Sebastiano agreed. 'We need to deal with the Germans before they
finish setting their explosives. Rather them than a hundred Neapolitan
lives. Anyone want to join me?'

Danielo hardly needed an invitation. In what must have been
a glance of truce, offered and received, he and his stepfather began
to quickly pile furniture onto the bed. They rolled up the carpet.
Up came the floorboards and, as his mother gasped and pleaded,
Danielo reached in and handed rifles to Sebastiano, Adriano and to
the cowering Loreto.

'Take it,' Danielo ordered his younger brother harshly. 'Come out
and fight unless you're all mouth.'

'He's a scholar, Danielo,' Violetta said in anguish. 'Not a street
fighter.'

'He can be both.'

'No!'

Danielo curled his lip. 'Let him stay at home with you women,
then. Zeffiro is worth ten of him.'

A voice cut through, for being soft and clear. 'I will take the gun,
Danielo. I will fight.' Marcella walked to her brother and held out her
hands. Danielo wavered, but shook his head.

'No, stay here and look after the family.' A pause and then he
added, '*Sorella mia.*'

'Give me the gun,' Carmela said. She knew they wouldn't accept
her in their ranks but somebody should stay and defend the family if
the plan to ambush the Germans went sour. Danielo again hesitated,
so she took the rifle from him.

She thought Sebastiano was going to confiscate it but what he did was turn her so she was facing the open balcony doors. 'Hold it like this.' He showed her how to nestle the gun's stock into her shoulder. 'The recoil can cause a dislocation, so shove it hard into your muscle. Your coat will absorb some of the shock.' He loaded the magazine, showed her how to engage and disengage the safety. 'Don't go out onto the balcony and don't come outside. Keep the family calm.' He kissed her brow. 'I want to come back here and find you alive.'

She kissed him briskly on the lips. 'The same goes for you. I won't lose you, Sebastiano. There's so much for us to say to each other.'

'There's still something I have to tell you—' He broke off, because Zeffiro's friends, the *scugnizzi* who had no beds to sleep in, had swarmed up the stairs. Armed with a medley of rifles and handguns, they were ready to attack the Germans and they wanted Danielo. They were going to fire on the Germans from the church dome, which ran level with the top of the bridge.

'Form into a band. Silently!' Danielo ordered them.

Adriano and Sebastiano left. Danielo kissed his weeping mother and led his troop away, pushing Loreto out in front of him. As they clattered down the stairs, Violetta made a desperate headcount of her remaining children and wailed as she realised Zeffiro was gone too.

Carmela pulled Loreto's desk to a better vantage point in front of the open window and rested her rifle on it. The night had flown. Dawn was creeping in, bathing the bridge in pastel light. It must have been built later than the houses, because the front windows of several dwellings stared straight out at the massive stone piers that supported it. Those homes would be engulfed if the bridge came down. She had a good view of the parapet too. Her legs were beginning to tremble from lack of nourishment and she asked Violetta if there was any chance of coffee. The men had taken handfuls of the biscuits from the tin Danielo had stolen but there were a few left.

'Certainly, Signorina del Bosco. Marcella?' Violetta's tone as she asked her daughter to heat water was softer than it had been before. When the girl was out of hearing distance, filling an aluminium *cuccumella* with water from a clay jug, Violetta came close to Carmela.

'I know what you meant a moment ago, about hurling stones.'

'Mm?' The last few minutes had erased all recent conversation. 'Oh, you mean when I said we shouldn't judge Marcella?'

'I understood the look on your face. I want you to know, Signorina del Bosco, that I have never… *never* sinned with your father since I married Adriano. Not once.'

'But you see him. You visit.'

Violetta nodded guardedly. 'Sometimes, to discuss business matters. You father helps me.'

'With money? He doesn't have any.'

'Not money. Well, not often. He writes letters if I need them. For Adriano's work, you know? And he got Loreto his scholarship. Look.' Violetta picked up the chemistry book that lay on Loreto's desk. Opening the flyleaf, she showed Carmela an inscription: 'From the library of Don Gonzago del Bosco'. 'If my son gets a good job, becomes an engineer, then my younger children have a chance. I don't like to be dependent, Signorina, but if you are poor in Naples the only ladder up is an influential friend. And I do love your father. I can't help it.'

'Neither could my mother.'

'You love a man too, so you understand.'

'What? You're talking nonsense!'

But Violetta had stepped out onto the balcony, drawn by the sounds of feet in the street below. Carmela went to see. Boys and men were slipping from their homes to join Danielo's rebels, summoned by incomprehensible, invisible means.

Violetta gripped the rail. '*O, Dio santo*, let them all come back. My man, my boys.'

Carmela gave a sidelong glance at the woman who had been her mother's rival, her mother's replacement, and saw someone torn apart by fear. She couldn't hold back a swell of compassion. Tomaso had said that Violetta was trying to make amends for her past conduct. Perhaps 'paying a price' was closer to the mark. *What if it was my child, heading to the church with a gun? I'd run out after him. Violetta can't because she has little ones here to look out for.*

Marcella put a tin mug of black coffee in front of her. 'Is it really true that Danielo killed my Hans-Kristof?' she asked quietly.

'Yes. In a way, he was defending your honour.'

'He didn't need to. All we did was kiss. Hansi really did want to marry me, whatever they think.'

Carmela doubted it, but this wasn't the moment. There never would be a moment. She sat down and gulped her coffee. She had just experienced a chilling vision, of a body laid out on the bed. Another death in this room.

Chapter Twenty-Nine

The crack of rifles soon came from the direction of the church. It was answered by the stutter of automatic weapons fired by German soldiers, caught out in an act of sabotage they must have hoped would literally catch the neighbourhood asleep.

In the strengthening light, Carmela could make out a wire strung with small bundles running along the parapet and down the piers of the bridge. The Germans had used darkness to lay enough dynamite to pulverise the structure, without any care as to who might be trapped and killed beneath. Now trapped themselves, they were fighting back. With firing coming from the church on one side, and a house overlooking the bridge on the other, they couldn't escape. Nor, thankfully, could they detonate the dynamite – unless they wanted to go up with it.

For the next twenty minutes, there was no break in the tit-for-tat fire. Carmela pictured Sebastiano, Adriano and Danielo edging around the lip of the dome of Santa Maria della Sanità, keeping the Germans pinned down. And not falling, please God.

The population of Via Sanità was awake, and every window now had its own gunman. Or boy. By the time the sun had fully risen, shots were flying from every house within fifty metres of the bridge. Women shouted from their balconies, banging pans.

Marcella put a plate of cold pizza crust beside Carmela. Apart from Renzo, who had got up on the bed to escape the noise, they were the only ones left in the room. The rest had taken shelter behind the sheet-partition. Marcella asked if a bullet could accidentally set off dynamite, and bring down the bridge. 'If it does, I hope I am underneath.'

'Don't say that.' Carmela had no idea how dynamite worked. 'Your family will change now they know you're innocent.'

Marcella shook her head. 'But I'm not. I found a boyfriend, a German, so I am shamed forever.' Her voice was bruised, like a flower stem pressed between heavy books. 'He was so gentle, my Hansi.'

Not to me, Carmela answered silently.

'How quickly did he die?'

'That is for Danielo to tell you.' Carmela hoped her brother would spare Marcella too much knowledge.

'One of Mamma's old cousins told me that occupation makes for love affairs, not marriage.'

'I think your cousin is right, Marcella.' She might have to drink the same medicine. Sebastiano would leave Naples and she, Carmela, might be just a one-night adventure for him. A memory to take away then forget. Should it matter? They had been careful; there would be no human consequence to give birth to in nine months. But she couldn't delude herself. It *did* matter, very much, and Violetta Vincenzo had noticed something Carmela feared to admit to herself. *Love.* If the payment was Sebastiano's life, she knew all too well the pain that would follow. She was given no chance to meditate; Marcella went out onto the balcony only to call in alarm, 'Come, quick, see this.'

Once again abandoning her promise to stay in the room, Carmela joined her. A fleet of armoured cars was pulling up in the street. Hardly were the tyres at rest than German troopers had disgorged and begun firing at houses on both sides of the road. A return volley from the defenders brought two of them down. Their comrades ducked behind the vehicles. Gun barrels fanned out, aiming at every window. Carmela dragged Marcella back inside.

'Did you see the Blackshirts?' the girl asked her.

'Those were Germans, Waffen SS.'

'There were Blackshirts breaking into the house on the other side of the street. A bunch of them.'

Carmela hadn't seen them. 'Maybe they've been called in as reinforcements,' she said grimly. 'They see the Germans as the rightful overlords and our boys as criminals.' Moving Loreto's desk so her rifle would not be seen and attract revenge fire, she told Marcella to sit out of range of stray bullets. The girl didn't move.

'What's that noise?' Marcella asked.

It was the grind of something huge chewing its way past. Getting down on her stomach, Carmela shimmied onto the balcony. Through the railings, she saw a tank rolling past. It continued on under the bridge. *Don't let it be making for the church.* A second tank followed, but stopped short of the bridge. Its arrival created a pause in the shooting on both sides. The few seconds' tranquillity gave Carmela time to understand what Marcella had been saying. Every balcony of the house opposite contained black-shirted *squadristi*. They knelt behind the door piers, machine guns pointing left, right and forward through the balcony rails. All at once, they opened fire and bullets raked homes either side of her. She scrabbled back inside as screams poured from neighbouring windows.

'Italians firing on Italians,' she said, still face down on the floor, catching her breath. 'Fascists killing women and children.'

'If women and children shelter subversives and rebels, they must take the consequences.'

Carmela felt spiders crawling up her spine. The words had not come from Marcella.

Chapter Thirty

Her cousin Tino stood with his back to the wall. His forearm was clamped to Marcella's throat and a handgun pointed at her head. 'On your feet, Meluccia, with hands raised.'

There was a drowsy throb to Tino's voice. Had he been up all night, trying to find her and Sebastiano, or firing on his fellow citizens? He had new injuries to his face but there was no mistaking the resolute malice that poured from his eyes. He ordered her to pick up the rifle that lay on the desk. 'Turn to face the window. Get down on your knees... slowly. Now slide it across the balcony and over the edge. Do it.'

She did so and heard the rifle crash on the road below.

'Now face me.'

Before he'd finished speaking, the house shook as a fireball burst above the parapet of the Sanità Bridge. The first tank had fired into homes on the other side of the bridge. Like a wobbly drunk, Carmela staggered to her feet. Tino was inspecting the floor, where the boards had been inexpertly replaced. The carpet was still rolled aside.

He made a sound of disparagement. 'Boy soldiers. Babies with guns. Then they cry and pray to San Gennaro when it all goes wrong for them.' He looked contemptuously at a gaudy picture of Naples' beloved saint above the fireplace. In a brutal move, he shoved Marcella towards the bed. The furniture piled on it tumbled on top of her and Renzo, who began to bark.

From the room next door, a distressed voice called, 'What's happening?'

Carmela shouted back, 'It's all right. Stay where you are.'

'Who's in there?'

'Violetta – stay where you are.' Carmela made it a warning.

'The family, cowering and praying?' asked Tino.

'A mother, little boys and girls. Not worth your rage.'

'Where is your brother Danielo?'

'Where do you suppose? At the church, defending the bridge.'

'And your lover?'

'Ditto.' It was not lost on Carmela that she had answered the question without even pausing.

Firing broke out again, the shelling of their neighbours rousing the resisters to new anger. A blinding glare hit Carmela's eye and a mirror on the wall shimmered with reflected flame. Tino pushed her out onto the balcony where she flinched at the hot breath of a fire consuming the roof of a house behind the bridge. Tino pressed up against her, his gun resting alongside her temple. She smelled the stale sweat from his shirt.

'What a beautiful sight,' he said into her ear.

'The Germans in retreat? They must be losing hope if they've called you in to help.'

'Those.' He pointed towards the bridge which was gauzy with smoke. 'Fresh targets.'

Diminutive figures were massed along the parapet. The German saboteurs must either have been killed or have fled. Not even the presence of tanks had defended them from relentless sniper fire from the church roof. Those on the bridge were boys, who surged and retreated in line, throwing bottle bombs, which exploded around the troop vehicles on the street below. The troops who had arrived first had no choice but to leap into their vehicles and reverse, their wheels aflame, abandoning the bodies of their comrades. Still holding her, Tino fired at the boys clustered along the parapet, as did his comrades in the house on the other side of the road. Their efforts were greeted with howls of disdain.

The battle was about to turn again, however. The tank this side of the bridge reversed a short distance. Its huge gun rose. Bottle bombs bounced off it, exploding harmlessly. *Dio santo*, it was going to fire at the boys. But no. With a sluggishness that stretched time unnaturally, its turret swivelled until its great gun was levelled at the second and third floors of a house just before the bridge. Carmela saw civilian men withdraw fast from the windows. A woman came out onto the balcony, a small child in her arms. She was screaming down at the tank, waving a white cloth. A baby's nappy. Waving, pleading. Carmela could see her lips moving in panic.

An ear-splitting detonation was followed by piercing screams. When the first of the smoke cleared, Carmela saw that the house had a hole in its façade, from which flames billowed. Two bodies fell, burning, to the road. Tino punched his fist in the air.

'Musso! Musso!' he chanted. Carmela stepped back into the room and her eyes met Marcella's. The girl held a rifle. One of the floorboards had been moved. Carmela silently held out her hands for it, but Marcella advanced towards the window aperture, towards Tino, who, with his back turned, was still maniacally punching the air. Carmela's premonition flashed again. A body laid out on the bed.

Two steps away from the window, Marcella fumbled at the rifle's safety bolt and the movement made Tino spin around. He fired his pistol. Marcella fell.

Her body was the first thing Sebastiano saw as he burst through the door, a child in his arms. He stopped so abruptly, the child's arm swung. Carmela recognised the ragged shirtsleeve, the undeveloped bones. Zeffiro.

'*Ciao, amico,*' Tino said in a gleeful growl.

His eyes on Tino, Sebastiano slowly laid the child on the floor. Zeffiro moaned. A rosette of blood spread outwards from his sternum.

'So here we are again, the three of us.' Tino kept his back to the window, apparently oblivious to danger. Outside, the shooting had stopped. The tank's gun had spoken. '*Inglese*, get down on your knees with your hands raised.'

Sebastiano obeyed. It felt to Carmela like a re-enactment of his and Tino's first encounter, when Sebastiano had lain helpless on his camp bed.

'I am going to make Carmela watch you die, but first tell me your real name.'

'Philip Clarendon.'

'Age?'

'Thirty.'

'Occupation?'

'Killing Fascists.'

'Did you know Meluccia came home from England pregnant?'

Sebastiano's calm response made Carmela's heart fold over in gratitude. 'You've already told me that. It makes no difference to my feelings for her.' He didn't look her way.

Tino soaked in the words, then said, 'It's why she is so attached to her farm, because she buried the child there. I will take her home, and she will have other babies and forget you. Turn your palms to the light.'

Sebastiano did so, revealing his healing burns. His expression was blank.

'Did those hands ever do a day's work?'

'They never shot a girl, if that's what you're asking.' Sebastiano gave Marcella's still body a heavy look. 'Are you intending to let another child die?' Zeffiro's body twisted with pain. The child had wet himself and he whimpered for his mamma. 'At least let Carmela tend to him.'

'No.' Tino turned his eyes to her. She wrapped her arms around herself. Marcella's staring eyes, Zeffiro's agony numbed her. Tino's voice reached her as through water. 'We will talk to the priest. We will visit Padre Pasquale. Your grandmother may return and live with us, if you wish. See, how I can forgive you. What do you say?'

'Yes,' she said, to borrow time. She wished she had counted how often Tino had fired his pistol. There might be more bullets in the chamber or he might be holding an empty weapon.

'You cannot love this man, or else you would have told him about your baby.'

She had told Sebastiano eventually but what did Tino want to hear? She needed to think, and so she looked at Sebastiano as she might a stranger. 'You're right. I didn't trust him enough to tell him that I conceived a child with my late fiancé.'

'So you won't mind too much when I kill him.'

'That's right, Tino. He's a liar. He pretended to care for me, but I think he loves someone else.'

'It happens, Meluccia.' Tino smiled and she detected a smidgeon of pride. 'We men are rogues. It's how we are.'

'True. Tino, can I please put my coat over the boy? Seeing blood makes me feel unwell.'

'All right. But move slowly.'

Carmela began to unbutton her grandfather's coat.

'I thought I had come to Naples to die,' Tino said, 'but I'm thinking that I might be spared. My life and yours, together forever, in exchange for the death of an English spy.'

'That seems fair.' She slipped the coat off her shoulders and laid it over Zeffiro's lower body. She dug her hand inside the pocket and felt a worn leather hilt. Tino's gun was pointing at Sebastiano's head, and from his concentration, he must be calibrating the angle for a shot. Now or never.

Carmela withdrew the hand axe that she'd thrown in the nut grove at la Casale. Then, she'd missed Tino. As she raised it behind her head, her grandfather's voice sped through her mind. 'Look, aim, don't grip too tight.' She hurled it and the fat little blade struck Tino in his side, above his hip. Sebastiano threw himself face down as the pistol in Tino's hand went off. He seized the gun as it fell to the floor, and with what he later told Carmela was the last bullet, put a single shot behind Tino Cortazzi's ear.

There were dozens of dead to count that day at Sanità Bridge but Danielo and his stepfather returned. With the help of friends, Danielo raced Zeffiro to the nearest hospital on a door pulled off its hinges to make a stretcher.

Loreto crept home hours later, having hidden in the church crypt of Santa Maria della Sanità. He found his family weeping for his sister who was laid out on the bed.

Chapter Thirty-One

4 October 1943

Tomaso came up to the dining room, interrupting another of the Palazzo's scaled-down lunches shared between Carmela and her father.

The Naples uprising had lasted two more days, leading to a full German withdrawal from the city. As they retreated, German artillery fired indiscriminately into the city's heart, killing and maiming hundreds of men, women and children. On 1 October, a British regiment, the King's Dragoon Guards, entered Naples to the cheers of an exhausted population.

'A visitor, Don Gonzago. Shall I bring another plate?'

'That depends who the visitor is.'

'Sebbe. He brings gifts.'

'In that case, bring a large plate.'

Carmela's heart bumped. A week since she'd seen him. A week jammed with anxiety and confusion. He hadn't sought her out. Did it mean any feelings he'd had for her had perished in the mayhem of battle?

Sebastiano came in. He'd brought Carmela a bar of American 'D ration' chocolate and, for Don Gonzago, a small bottle of Scotch whisky, which he claimed to have won at cards from a British sergeant.

He had news, good news. The bullet that had struck Zeffiro had not punctured a lung or hit his spine. He had shattered ribs but would live.

Don Gonzago expressed his pleasure at the news. 'I would send something, if I had anything. Carmela, what about some of your chocolate?'

'Yes, of course.' She would visit the hospital later and, on her way, call at the main post office where it was still possible – some of the time anyway – to use a public telephone. She would call Emilio Baccolini so he could let her grandmother know that she was alive and well. If there were a few seconds left in the call, she would pass on the news of Tino Cortazzi's death. Though not the details of course. There was always a queue for the telephone and people listened shamelessly.

Her father urged Sebastiano to sit. 'I don't feel so awkward now asking Adriano to bring our furniture back, now Zeffiro's out of danger. There is so much looting with the Germans gone and I'm worried someone will break into the chapel. And there is the matter of my books.'

'Adriano Vincenzo has a lot on his mind, Don Gonzago. They buried their daughter yesterday.' Sebastiano turned to Carmela. 'Danielo sends his love. He is very low. He blames himself for Marcella.'

'I'll go and see him too.' Unable to sustain the intensity in Sebastiano's eyes, she looked away. After the battle for Sanità Bridge had ended, she'd stayed on with the Vincenzos while a volunteer fire crew battled to extinguish the flames in the shelled house opposite. Female neighbours had poured in to hold and comfort Violetta. Marcella, laid out in her white confirmation dress, was the most desolate sight Carmela had ever seen. The girl's only crime had been to fall in love with a handsome, manipulative German. If the family had shown more compassion, Marcella would not have felt the need to prove her worth by picking up a gun.

Carmela took a share of the guilt. Who had brought her killer, Tino Cortazzi, into their house?

Tomaso fetched an extra breakfast. Sebastiano thanked him but after Tomaso had left, he offered the food to Don Gonzago and Carmela. 'Sorry to sound smug, but I'm now receiving army rations.'

'Have they put you up somewhere nicer than here?' Don Gonzago laughed when Sebastiano answered that he was billeted in a waterfront hotel, only two-thirds bombed out. 'You're welcome to move back. Tomaso and I came home yesterday and thought we might find you, but it was only my daughter, her dog and a donkey. Not that it wasn't a pleasure to meet them all again,' Don Gonzago added hastily, seeing the pinch in Carmela's face. 'After days living among monks, I was delighted to encounter creatures that enjoy making a noise.'

Sebastiano answered that he was working with British military intelligence. 'They're rooting out Fascist resistance and I'm giving them what help I can.' In his night shifts as part of a road gang, he had made contacts in Naples' underclass, men who were now only too glad to name and expose collaborators. 'There's a blacklist of German sympathisers to arrest.' He gave Carmela a significant glance. 'Santo Cortazzi's name is on it. I made sure.'

'Oh, happy reversal of events!' Don Gonzago clapped his hands and refilled their coffee cups.

Sebastiano cleared his throat. 'Don Gonzago, would you object to having a road mender as a son-in-law?'

Silence fell. Don Gonzago looked enquiringly at Carmela, who began to collect up the breakfast plates. She was out of the door so fast, knives and forks fell as she went. Renzo, lying on her coat in the corridor, stretched out his tongue to lick them clean.

Sebastiano found her out in the garden, picking out Nearco's hooves. Rain had come down overnight and the little paddock she had created for the donkey was churned up. Her hands were muddy and slippery.

'Can we talk?' Sebastiano asked.

'One more back hoof to do.' She wiped her palms on a cloth.

Sebastiano waited until she'd washed her hands in rainwater. 'Carmela? You're avoiding my eye. Can we sit and talk?'

'It's a bit wet to sit out.'

He took her arm and led her to an open shelter where the cart was parked. They sat in the back, side by side, but she kept her face averted. 'Are you angry? Should I not have spoken to your father?'

Scared, was the truth. 'You stayed away so long, I thought I'd never see you again. Now you're back talking about marriage. It's too sudden, Sebastiano.'

'I couldn't come until now because I'm no longer my own man. I'm under military orders. Secondly – Carmela, please look at me.'

She did so, reluctantly. 'I'm not sure who I'm looking at. Sebastiano Alonso or Philip Clarendon.'

'Philip Clarendon, though to be honest we're not much different except that Philip gets more chances to shave.'

He smiled but she resisted the pull of humour, saying crossly, 'I still don't know anything about you. Where you come from. Nothing.'

'Then let me tell you.' He reeled it off in a rush. He'd been born in a village outside London, to an Italian mother and an English father who was a teacher at a boys' school. The same school Sebastiano had attended. 'That place dominated the first eighteen years of my life. It's not always easy being a master's son. There were compensations, though.' He was pretty good at cricket and classics, but chose to study modern languages at university, 'Because I thought it was more use. On graduation, I feared becoming a replica of my father, pressed into a lifetime of teaching, so I escaped to Italy.'

Back to his mother's region, to Campania, where he'd spent two of the happiest years of his life, 'Shifting grit at the excavations at Pompeii. After that, I worked for a while at the archaeological museum here in Naples. I already spoke good Italian but I became fluent. I learned Neapolitan dialect too.'

'Weren't you afraid you'd be recognised when you came back as an agent?'

It had been a concern, he admitted, but SOE had been struggling to recruit fluent Italian speakers to be infiltrated into the country so they sent him anyway. 'I looked very different when I first came here to dig at Pompeii. Oiled hair, thin moustache. Linen suits, can you imagine? But to go back to my life story, in 1935 I went home.' Back to Oxford University to begin an MA in ancient languages. He wasn't there long before he was recruited by SIS, Secret Intelligence. 'They wanted a translator for the British consulate in Cairo. This was before SOE was even thought of but I'd begun my slide into espionage.'

'So you were a spy even then, not a translator?'

'Both. I had some work pushed my way but after hours, I was encouraged to slouch about in Cairo. I learned market Arabic and wandered around the old town, drinking strong coffee, chatting with working men. My evenings were spent in bars, encouraging German and Italian travellers to drink with me. They drank gin. I paid the bartender to fill my glass with ice and water. I was the eager ears into which Fascist businessmen poured their secrets. When the war started, I joined an infantry regiment and would probably have lived and died in the western desert, except that my previous work had made me a sitting duck for SOE when they needed a fluent Italian-speaker to head Operation Naples. That's me, potted.'

No it wasn't. It didn't even touch the surface. 'Your parents?'

'I mentioned them, didn't I?'

'You're being obtuse again.'

'Sorry. My mother's originally from Battipaglia. That's why I chose it for Sebastiano Alonso's home town. Her parents emigrated to London when she was eleven. My father is from Oxshott in Surrey, which is as Home Counties as you can get. He's now head of languages at the school he's taught at for thirty-three years, minus a stint fighting in the last war. They live on the school campus; my mother doesn't work.'

She continued with questions, as though conducting an interview. 'Brothers and sisters?'

'Two sisters, one married to an army officer, the other in the Women's Royal Navy, the Wrens, somewhere in the north of Scotland. I haven't been in touch with any of them for months. I have no idea how they're doing and they probably think I'm dead.'

'Do you love them?'

He blinked at the question. 'Of course I do.'

'There's no "of course" about it. I don't always love my father.'

'I wish you would talk more to Don Gonzago. But listen, my dad is as uncomplicated as meat and potatoes. Ernest by name, earnest by nature. He's scrupulously fair. Says what he means and tells ponderous jokes, which he then explains. My married sister takes after him. My mother, by contrast, is short, plump, dark. An exploding teapot when anybody misuses her family. My Wren sister favours her.'

'And you? Who do you take after?'

'Who do you think?'

She thought about it. 'You're a bit of both.'

'All right. Can I ask you something? Why haven't you told your father that you gave birth?'

She batted away the question. 'He doesn't need to know, but I can't pretend that my decision helped mend things between us. He thought I was choosing my Cortazzi family over him, but I couldn't bear… couldn't bear him looking at me with pity and disappointment. The shamed daughter. You know how that story goes.'

'You misjudge him. He massively underrates you, but he wouldn't have rejected you.'

'Perhaps.' She gave a sharp laugh. 'Nonna wasn't much better! The prospect of an illegitimate grandchild was the worst gift I could bring. *Dio!* It was history repeating itself. For all that, she let me stay. Cared for me, protected me.'

'What was the plan, had your baby lived?'

Carmela wished she'd worn her coat. She was shivering. 'To keep her, of course. Nonna kept mentioning convents in Naples that take the babies of unmarried mothers, for adoption. She didn't understand' – emotion burst out – 'that as far as I was concerned, Cedric and I *were* married. We hadn't had the ceremony but we were man and wife. I loved him with all my soul, and my body.' Sebastiano was looking away from her, but she had to say it. 'You must have known when we went to bed it wasn't my first time. Nor my second.'

'I did know. You told me. Carmela, I've never been in doubt since the day your father brought up the subject of your engagement that you loved Cedric. Part of me wishes you'd stayed in England and given those poor parents of his a grandchild. You must wonder how your life would have been.'

'I try not to, it's too painful. The "what ifs".'

Sebastiano picked up her hand and pressed it into his ribs. 'Lives veer in strange directions. What if I had chosen medicine instead of languages? Did you ever tell his parents about the child?'

'No. I started a letter to Cedric's mother when I arrived back in Naples. That was just after Christmas 1938. Europe was still at peace, so I could have sent it but I thought, what if they despise me for sleeping with their son out of wedlock? And then, what if, instead of being overjoyed, they write back saying they don't want a bastard grandchild?'

'From what you've said of them, that doesn't sound likely.'

'Pregnant women who have lost the love of their lives aren't think-ing clearly.' From the pressure of his fingers, he'd heard her declare there was no room for another man in her life. That wasn't true. She ploughed on. 'When my daughter was stillborn, Nonna didn't want me to name her – "Name them and they break your heart." But I called her Carlotta because it's a little bit like Cedric, and he had a grandmother called Charlotte. By then it was too late to tell his mother. We buried Carlotta between the roots of a tree, Nonna and I. But why couldn't my baby lie with others of my family on sacred ground? I accused Nonna of being glad she'd died because it solved a problem.' Carmela dipped her head, fearful of falling back into that vortex. 'It was a horrible thing to say. It was a dreadful time. I love her, and Tino was right in one thing. I can never abandon Nonna.'

Sebastiano's arm had gone around her, and though she was aching to lean into him, she stayed poker-stiff. Having implied that she could never love again, she had just now signalled that she would never leave Italy.

'Is Cedric the love of *all* your life?'

'I don't know what life I have left.' That was skirting the question, but now it was his turn. 'What about Mio – can you ever get over her?'

'Not really, but it's different. Her name was Silvestra Damiano, and she fled to Mexico with her family when she was a child. They were anti-Fascists and SOE recruited her because, as I said a moment ago, there was a desperate shortage of trustable, fluent Italian-speakers in Britain, so they cast the net wide. She shouldn't have been drawn in.'

'Why not?' The warmth in his voice was not lost on Carmela.

'She was too nervous, and to drop her into enemy territory was unforgiveable. Did you know, wireless operators have a life expectancy of about three weeks? SOE might as well have thrown her to the wolves. Her Morse skills were adequate, but slow, and she would forget things and panic. I felt sorry for her, but exasperated because she was the weak link in the three of us. Or so I thought.' He pulled in a breath and let it out. 'She had to stay in her room most of the time and be looked after by our couriers because she spoke Italian with an accent. We couldn't get her a job. I was not kind to her, Carmela. I was impatient.'

'You feared she'd betray you?'

'Yes. I was on the rack every day but it was Nico who broke. He seemed tough as bull hide, nerves of steel, until one day he saw German secret police in the street outside his flat and had to run. He got a message to me and I found him different lodgings. Told him to change his appearance and lie low. But he was rattled and I can only assume he went over to the Germans rather than be caught. He bought his survival with Mio's life and very nearly mine. I felt nothing when I killed him.'

At this he paused, for what seemed a long time. 'You asked me once if I loved her.'

'Mio? And you said "yes".'

'Which was true if caring deeply about someone is love. Her death is scored on my soul. It haunts me that I didn't trust her. The last thing she did before she died was do her best to destroy the cipher codes she was working from. She packed up her wireless. She didn't go to pieces, didn't try to run. She went through practised procedures in the expectation that I would get us both out. That I failed her is hard to live with.'

He put his lips to her hairline and fell into English. 'I cannot let you go because loving you is my redemption.' He opened his hands, which showed signs again of blistering and bruising. Clearly, he wasn't swanning around the city only in the role of adviser. 'These hands will grip and never let go. If you can't leave your nonna, then we will stay with her.'

She had to ask: he really wanted to marry her? It wasn't an infatuation fuelled by being so far from home?

'No. I think I fell in love with you when you first took my hand, when I was doped and lying on a stretcher. When I came back off a night shift and found you having breakfast with your father, I knew it and it frightened me. Who wants to care passionately for someone who is in so much peril? Still, it's the best aphrodisiac – don't ever let anyone fob you off with oysters.' He waited for her response and grew impatient. 'Come on. I know you love me a bit or you wouldn't have stuck by me when most women would have been glad to see the back of me.'

'I do love you,' she admitted. 'When did it start…?' It had crept up on her. 'But the way I felt when you told me I'd lost your trust proved it, not that I was ready to admit it. Your words cut me to the bone. And then there was your watch.'

'My watch – which you hung on to for a week?'

She wavered. It seemed so childish. *Be honest.* 'I kept it from you because it was the only part of you I could touch and get close to.' The hardest thing, she said, was allowing herself to feel passion again. 'I persuaded myself that I was betraying Cedric. It was my shield. My excuse for pushing you away because I know – I knew even then – that Cedric would not want me to be alone.'

They kissed and held each other until it was too cold to stay outside. As Sebastiano helped her down from the cart, she said sadly, 'We can't marry before you go. There's no time.'

'No, and it's against the rules anyway. No marriage permitted between British military personnel and Italian civilians. Will you wait?'

'Mm. Maybe.' She couldn't sustain the teasing. 'Not long ago, you wanted me to marry a good man and have babies.'

'And my wish hasn't changed, except I hope you will accept a good-ish man.'

'I will, on one condition.'

'Conditions already?'

'That you accept what I said about Cedric. I still love him, I always will.'

He digested her words. 'I consider myself lucky to be the one you choose for a second go.' He brought a small box from his pocket. 'Your father gave me this, along with his permission.' Inside the box was a ring, a smooth pearl set inside diamonds.

'That was Mamma's!'

'I promise one day to buy you one of your own.'

'No. This one is perfect.' She let him put it on her finger and they kissed until he broke away and returned to give their news to Don Gonzago and Tomaso.

Within five days, Sebastiano was gone. To Rome, seconded to US military intelligence.

Carmela spent a week at Santa Maria della Vedetta with Nonna, who, she discovered, was rather enjoying her extended holiday with Zia Cristina now her fears for her granddaughter had lessened. Whilst there, Carmela went to the farm daily, checking on her animals and assessing the dilapidations inflicted by the Blackshirt occupation. Her goats and cows had all survived, but she would have to break it to Nonna that their black Siciliana flock was no more. Whether the chickens had ended up in the pot, or victims of a fox, nobody could say, but if they wanted eggs again they would have to begin afresh.

She and Nonna could not yet reclaim la Casale. Following Santo Cortazzi's arrest by British military police, the commune authorities had quickly installed a manager to ensure the farm stayed productive. It was an imposition Carmela intended to fight and she needed a lawyer. Her father would finally get to practise again.

A month after Sebastiano's departure, two postcards arrived at the Palazzo. One was from him, a few words that he was well and missed her. The other came from Zurich, Switzerland. Taking it up to her father, Carmela couldn't resist glancing at the message on the reverse, written in a child's hand. It went:

Dearest Don Gonzago, we are now safe and happy at our grandmother's house. Mamma sends her blessings and Papà is working for a man who makes paint for artists and he is well. Simone is not coughing so much now and we both go to school. Sometimes

I have a nightmare about the caves but not often now. We hope you are well too. Your grateful friend, Gisela.

Her father was lounging on the crimson chaise longue in the drawing room, reading a newspaper and with a cup of ersatz coffee at his elbow. He took the postcard, read it slowly and said, 'Well, well.'

'Who is Gisela?'

'She's the granddaughter of Joshua di Lentini, the man I defended long ago. My last case and the end of my career. Though he died in police custody, he had a wife and a son, Roberto. Gisela and Simone are Roberto's children.'

'What does Gisela mean about the caves? Wait a moment. Is she talking about the ancient crypt under our feet?'

The image of a child's red ribbon had stuck in her mind.

Don Gonzago sat up. Patted the sofa. 'Sit down, because I can tell you now. You know of course that Joshua di Lentini was Jewish. When Mussolini was deposed last summer, the status of Jews here became precarious. I offered help, but too late. Roberto had been forced to abandon his home and was in hiding with his family. I couldn't find them, and I didn't dare search in case it alerted the Germans. Then I received a tip-off from a trusted friend. They were hidden in a rat-infested *basso* not far from the boys' prison where Danielo was briefly a guest. I hired Adriano Vincenzo and we fetched them away in the back of his truck. They stayed here while I organised a place for them to go.'

'That was a risk, Papà. I mean, with your paternal grandmother also being Jewish.'

'Ah, what is life without risk? Mere existence.' He went on with the story. The day before the family was to be spirited to Nola, where Tarzia's partisans would take responsibility for them, there had come an insistent knock on the door. 'Tomaso opened it. On the step, in full uniform, be-hatted and even, would you believe, with a monocle in his eye socket, was one Major Klimt. While Tomaso kept Klimt waiting in the entrance hall, I spirited the Di Lentini parents and children through the secret door in the dining room and into the boot room, and then by ladder down into the crypt. There the poor things stayed for many hours. And while Klimt was striding about, measuring these rooms for barracks, who should clang the bell from the *vicoletto* but your brother Danielo. Sebastiano had found his way to Gio's home, covered in blood. Gio as you know borrowed a van, picked up Danielo and together they'd driven Sebastiano here. Of course, I had to say no, take him elsewhere, I am entertaining a German officer.'

'That's how Sebastiano ended up at la Casale.'

'And how I came the closest I've ever come to having a heart attack. I am sure rumours somehow got around that the Palazzo harboured fugitives. Another of the Vincenzo children, perhaps, overhearing a snatch of adult conversation and gabbling it innocently… it was nerve-racking, the whole time. A French farce with a large dose of horror thrown in.'

She picked up her father's hand and kissed it. 'I'm glad I have such a brave papà.'

'I'm honoured to have such a bold daughter. Shall I surprise you further and tell you who tipped me off about the Di Lentinis' whereabouts in the rat-riddled *basso*?'

'Go on.' She assumed it would be some old legal contact or perhaps a political ally, creeping out of the woodwork.

'It was Violetta. She had been cleaning the offices at the Hotel Parco, German headquarters. She worked there through the whole German occupation and it was she who tipped me off about Major

Klimt, by the way. On one particular day, she emptied a wastepaper bin where somebody had chucked a memorandum. She can't read German but she recognised the name "Di Lentini". She put the paper in her stocking and brought it to me.'

Carmela said nothing.

Don Gonzago made his point. 'The cleaners were searched every time they passed through security, on their way in and out. If she'd been caught smuggling that scrap of paper, her life would have been over.'

Still not ready to concede Violetta's courage, Carmela mentioned the hair slides she'd found in her bed. 'I assume they are that woman's.'

'*Figlia mia*,' Don Gonzago said in reproach, 'I ought to be flattered, but remember, I am sixty-three and Violetta is married. We are friends with memories, nothing more. Ah, wait. Little Gisela lost her hair slides, I remember now! She was so upset. She and her mother used that bed while they were here. When we know an address, we can post them.'

Carmela thought of a little girl in the crypt below the Palazzo, hair falling over her face because she'd lost her slides and a hair ribbon too. Her brother coughing in the close air. Terrified by the skulls but eventually making their way to freedom.

'I ought to apologise to Violetta,' she said gruffly.

'She saved a Jewish family from deportation. Perhaps you could allow that to be her legacy, *tesoro*, and not the mistakes of the past?'

She nodded. 'I'll try.'

'And another thing,' Don Gonzago said after a moment of intense throat-clearing. 'You accused me amid the desolation of San Romualdo of sending you to exile in England so I could be rid of you. "A little girl weeping for her dead mamma" was too much for me, you declared.'

'I shouldn't have. I was distressed.'

'No, you were revealing a truth, long denied. I admit, your tears, your bewilderment made my guilt over Nina unendurable, and instead of comforting you, I sent you away. I let you down.'

A lump formed in her throat and she couldn't speak.

Her father had more to say. 'I was a coward, but you know, it wasn't all that much of a mistake in the long run. I spared you a Fascist education that would have fitted you for the kitchen and nowhere else. But now you will be Sebastiano's wife, Mrs Clarendon, an English lady. He's very well connected, you know.'

'Stop it, Papà! His father is a schoolteacher, not a duke. And he has to survive for me to become his wife.'

'He will. So let's start work on retrieving your farm because you'll need a dowry to take to your husband and I can't give you one.'

The result of this conversation was that Carmela and her father grew closer. She continued to ask about her mother and Don Gonzago talked as he never had to her before. His answers were bittersweet. Her mother had loved him with a devotion he could not return, and after Carmela's birth, she had fallen into depression. He had married Nina because the woman he truly loved, an English 'honourable', had jilted him when her family had objected to his religion and his lack of wealth. 'Your mother was sweet, uncomplicated and very pretty. And when your grandfather came to see me, to say she was pregnant and to plead with me to marry her, I thought, why not? Be a man about it. But I wasn't a good husband. I shall try to be a better friend, and I hope you forgive me.'

She almost told him about Carlotta then, but held back. Later, she confided to Tomaso, who said, 'What would telling him achieve? Let him be happy, Signorina Carmela. Take your secret back to la Casale.'

Chapter Thirty-Two

Twenty months later

1 September 1945

The war in Europe ended on 8 May, the news pouring into la Casale's kitchen from the battery-powered wireless Sebastiano had given Carmela before he left. The wireless had come from the Hotel Parco, which British Field Intelligence had taken over. Sebastiano had pulled the German badge off the front. In a broadcast from the BBC, the King of England, George VI, spoke of 'a great deliverance'.

Carmela danced around the farmhouse kitchen to the British national anthem, with Nonna clapping from her chair. Don Gonzago had won the farm back for them in weeks. Ever the pragmatist, he'd bypassed the legal process and offered the commune's mayor the bronze clock he was so fond of. The mayor was a collector and the clock was a rare object.

Rosaria had returned to la Casale in triumph but the harsh winter of 1944 had weakened her. An eruption of Vesuvius in March that same year had terrified her so badly, she suffered a stroke. The eruption had never threatened la Casale – the villages destroyed by the lava flow lay on the volcano's flanks – but it made her think the war had started again. The firm-willed woman Carmela had battled with and loved was a shadow of her former self, but still determined to live to see Sebastiano come to claim her granddaughter.

Her last outing into the village was on the day her great-grand-daughter Carlotta was privately interred in the family mausoleum. Stern Padre Pasquale had moved to a new parish and his successor, a younger man less prone to judgement, had presided over the secret ceremony. With the weight of guilt lifted from her, Nonna now spent her days sitting in the kitchen, listening to the wireless, or in the sunshine with her new chickens pecking around her feet, with Renzo keeping watch and Nearco grazing nearby. She had mellowed to the point that she called the dog and donkey by name and talked to them.

'We are waiting,' she would tell Carmela. 'Your Englishman had better not leave it too long, ha? Why does he not write?'

'Because there is no postal service, Nonna, and the war goes on.'

Carmela replied similarly every time, keeping hope in her voice and her fears to herself. Fears that Sebastiano had forgotten her or that he numbered among the heavy casualties of the Italian campaign.

At last, one afternoon, news came.

It had been a fine September day with the air full of birdsong and humming insects. As the sun began its descent, Carmela left the harvest women picking tomatoes and walked to the hazel grove to finish marking out lines with stakes and string. The old trees that Tino and Santo had hacked had been cleared and she had a hundred new ones to plant. With Renzo at her heels, she walked a straight line and fixed her string to the final post. There would be five rows of male and female trees, planted not in the original holes but in new ground. Grass grew thickly over the place where Carlotta had lain. Sunlight coated the ridge to the colour of *olio santo* and put a sheen on the shattered stub of the *vedetta*. Looking at the mutilated wreck of the tower, Carmela wondered if this was her world forever. Herself, alone, questioning the hours and the stubborn routines of the farming day.

Renzo barked and began to lollop back along a marked-out row. A man was walking towards her, and for a startling instant, Carmela recalled Tino's threatening appearance in this exact spot.

The man stopped and scratched Renzo's ear. The dog ran circles around him as he continued towards her. Tall and lean, a kitbag over his shoulder.

Carmela began to walk towards him, and when there was no doubt who had come home, she gave a deep cry and started to run.

A Letter from Natalie

Dear reader,

I want to say a huge thank you for choosing to read *The Italian Girl's Secret*. If you enjoyed it and want to keep up to date with all my latest releases, just sign up at the following link. Your email address will never be shared and you can unsubscribe at any time.

www.bookouture.com/natalie-meg-evans

I hope you loved *The Italian Girl's Secret* and following Carmela's heart-stopping journey as much as I enjoyed writing it! Sometimes a character takes over your heart and I couldn't rest until I had taken 'my Meluccia' through all the trials of living in a war zone, to her reunion with the man she loved. To do so against the backdrop of glorious southern Italy was a real treat. Did you find Sebastiano as frustrating at times as Carmela did? If so, I hope you saw beneath the tough exterior to the man who yearned only for the freedom to love and live. In war, people live intensely, never sure if today is their last, but always with the hope that the clouds will clear and life can begin again. Writing about these times is a passion of mine, and I'd love to hear your thoughts. You can get in touch on my Facebook page, through Twitter, Goodreads or my website – see below.

If you are able to leave a review, please know that it makes such a difference, helping new readers to discover one of my books for the first time.

Thanks,
Natalie Meg Evans
Suffolk 2021

 NatalieMegEvans

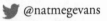 @natmegevans

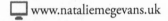 www.nataliemegevans.uk

9 781838 886073